MW01253420

Decisively Engaged

Warp Marine Corps, Book One
By C.J. Carella

Published by Fey Dreams Productions, LLC

C.J. Carella

Acknowledgements

Special thanks to the beta readers whose critiques improved this book: Wesley Harris, Duane Oldsen, Scott Palter, Kevin Rose, Joshua D. Shaw, and George Tur. If any mistakes remain, they are on me; if there are few or none, it is thanks to them.

Books by C.J. Carella

Warp Marine Corps
Decisively Engaged
No Cost Too High (Forthcoming)

New Olympus Saga:
Armageddon Girl
Doomsday Duet
Apocalypse Dance
The Ragnarok Alternative
The Many-Worlds Odyssey (Forthcoming)

New Olympus Tales:
The Armageddon Girl Companion
Face-Off: Revenge (Forthcoming)

Beyonder Wars:
Bad Vibes (Short Story)
Shadowfall: Las Vegas
Dante's Demons

C.J. Carella

"People sleep peaceably in their beds at night only because rough men stand ready to do violence on their behalf."
- George Orwell

"There is a special Providence that protects idiots, drunkards, children and the United States of America."
- Otto Von Bismarck

"In this corner of the universe, *we* are the Klingons."
- *War Amongst the Stars: A Brief History of Post-Contact America*, by Admiral Hubert De Grasso (ret.),

Prologue: First Contact

The Hrauwah cruiser *Wisdom of War* emerged from warp space somewhere between the single star in the system and its nearest planet, spewing atmosphere from several breaches in its hull.

"Go into full stealth mode," King-Captain Grace-Under-Pressure said as soon as she recovered from warp transit, her demeanor befitting her Chosen Name. Her vessel was damaged, and their warp jump had taken them to an uncharted world on the tail-end of the galaxy, but panicking would achieve nothing but the loss of dignity before one's inevitable demise.

"As you wish," her Lord Engineer said. Their wireless neural interfaces made words superfluous, but verbal commands were traditional, and tradition was one of the building blocks of the Hrauwah Naval Service.

All non-essential systems on the cruiser – everything but basic life support and its force fields – shut down, reducing its energy signature to the point that its pursuers would have to come within a light-minute to detect the vessels' presence. Doing so was risky, but at the moment the *Wisdom of War* was unable to fight or flee; hiding was the only viable option left.

For two long hours, the *Wisdom* drifted in space as its damage control teams worked desperately to restore its damaged systems. King-Captain Grace used that time to curl up in her command chair and take a nap, her tail wrapped tightly around one of its gripping bars, following instincts carried down from her species' arboreal ancestors. One slept when one could in times of war. She woke up when her neural implant hissed in her ear, alerting her that she was needed.

"Warp emergence detected," Lady of Tactics Courage-and-Discretion announced coldly. "Approximately five light-minutes away."

Passive sensors were low-ranged, but it was all they dared use at the moment. Even running silently and with force fields diffusing the ship's heat signature into something barely above the ambient temperature of outer space, the *Wisdom* was dangerously close to the enemy's emergence point. Captain Grace waited patiently while Lady Courage analyzed the data.

"Target identified as a Risshah *Three-Claw*-class battlecruiser. Same energy signatures as the vessel that engaged us at Star

System Ninety-six."

A chorus of growls greeted the news; everyone in the bridge bristled in anger and apprehension. The Risshah were hated throughout the galaxy, and their unprovoked attack on the *Wisdom* only confirmed what everyone knew: the Snakes were murderous, treacherous savages.

"Silence in the bridge," King-Captain Grace said. "We knew we were up against the bloody Snakes, didn't we? All we can do now is try to be ready for them. Unlike the last time," she added soberly.

A *Three-Claw* battlecruiser had a good ten percent more firepower and fifteen percent stronger shields than her vessel. The Snake warship had ambushed the *Wisdom* by hiding behind an asteroid and using a decoy beacon to lure the Hruawah cruiser into range. Only sheer providence had saved it from total destruction. Sheer providence and the skill of its crew, who had managed to launch its own salvo of missiles and beams before fleeing into warp-space. The ensuing stern chase had been long, with only a faint hope they might be able to evade their enemy. The *Wisdom* had sped through warp space until reaching a suitable emergence point. All Grace could hope for was that the enemy wouldn't find them until her crew could restore the *Wisdom*'s damaged systems and offer battle on slightly better terms.

Minutes passed, grew into hours. The King-Captain used the time to examine the data on the system they'd found themselves in after performing that most dangerous maneuver: an unplanned warp-jump, following a random gradient in space-time leading to the nearest major gravity well. The chances that such a jump would leave them stranded in the strange sub-universe between warp points were somewhere in the twenty percent range. Only the fact that certain death at the hands of the Snakes had been the only alternative made the maneuver advisable.

So where in the Seventeen Heavens and Hells had they arrived? Grace-Under-Pressure accessed the data her exhausted Lord Astrogator had hastily assembled. A Class Seven star with eight major planetary bodies. Including one inhabited world, the star's third closest planet. One blue world, rich in water, inhabited by a technologically-proficient species; it radiated enough energy in the electromagnetic spectrum to stand out like a bonfire in the night. Her blood ran cold. The Snakes chasing her ship would assume that they had followed the *Wisdom* to a hostile system. And the Snakes dealt with potential hostiles in only one way.

"Lord Engineer," she said, her icy tone of voice hiding her

terror and despair. "What is our status?"

"We are back to seventy percent in all essential systems. Two missile tubes remain non-operational, but the rest are ready. Lasers, plasma and graviton cannon are all online, although I fear some of them are good only for one or two volleys before..."

The King-Captain cut him off. "Thank you, Lord Engineer." She switched to the general channel. "Battle stations. We will engage the enemy shortly."

"Your Majesty, the Risshah have performed a warp jump!" It took a few minutes to detect the Snake's emergence. "Target reacquired! They are..."

"In orbit around the third planet from the sun," Grace finished for her Lady of Tactics. "And are preparing to depopulate it."

Lady Courage nodded, wide-eyd and panting from stress.

The news was over four minutes old. The enemy vessel would take five to ten minutes to start its attack run after emerging from warp-space, depending on how efficient its crew was, how well it would recover from the warp-transit process, and how much damage the *Wisdom* had inflicted on it before fleeing. The only chance the helpless primitives on that planet had to survive would require Grace-Under-Pressure to risk her ship and all aboard her.

Her Royal Court, the officer-noblemen charged with managing each aspect of her vessel, received her orders in silence. There were doubtful glances cast back and forth, but no one questioned her, and she allowed herself a moment to savor her pride in them as they rushed to do battle with a superior enemy under highly adverse circumstances.

"Prepare for warp jump," she said as her implants delivered the coordinates to her crew. "We will emerge at long range, launch an automated missile volley, and conduct a direct approach after warp recovery." Her terse orders were put into effect, years of training paying off. All the details were worked out in under a minute.

"Warp engines ready. Coordinates set."

"Engage."

Transition.

The *Wisdom of War* ceased to exist in normal space. Grace's perceptions shifted, surrounded her with hallucinations and manifested memories, fears, emotions, some of them her own, others belonging to her crew, and yet others having no relation to any reality she knew. She forced herself to ignore the distorted sense of time that made the transition process seem to last several minutes, all the while surrounded by howling, crying ghosts. Her dead parents were there – father, bearer and mother, all three of them cursing her for dishonoring her family and the Supreme Arbiter. Shame and fear became physical sensations, sending shivers down her spine.

Closing her eyes didn't help; warp perceptions had nothing to do with physical senses. The meditation techniques that all Starfarers practiced did help, a little. Only one percent of her species could enter warp-space while awake and aware. Another five percent could do so only while unconscious or in suspended animation. The remaining ninety-four percent could not endure warp transit; exposure resulted in death or incurable insanity. Even among the warp-rated, multiple jumps had a tiny but gradually-increasing chance of inflicting serious side effects. Every transition could be one's last.

Emergence.

They were back in the universe where they'd been born, the place where light had a fixed speed and space-time's curvature could be deduced and manipulated according to knowable laws, a universe that made sense. Recovering from transition took some time, however, as her mind struggled to set aside the fading but still vivid alien stimuli and grasp reality yet again.

During that time, only the automated systems on the *Wisdom* were able to act. They dumbly followed their programming and fired eighty-three missiles.

Grace's ship had emerged one light-second away from the Snakes. Her missiles would cover that distance in two minutes – plenty of time for the enemy battlecruiser's sensors to burn through their stealth systems and its point weaponry to destroy them all. The volley was a distraction, meant to buy time while her crew recovered from the warp jump and rushed into optimal firing range, under half a light second, close enough for missiles and beam weapons to overcome their target's force fields and point defenses.

They were too late, however. The Snakes had already launched on the unsuspecting planet below.

The Risshahh's genocide tactics were simple. A swarm of hundreds of missiles zeroed in on concentrations of electric light, radio waves, and graviton emissions. Down below, on the planet's night side, circles of red light started to blossom, each marking the funeral pyres of millions of sophonts. Grace recovered in time to watch half a world die. After the first swarm of missiles was exhausted, more volleys would follow, destroying every city, then every town, and finally every village, hamlet, and air, land or sea vehicle they could find, murdering everyone except for a handful of survivors in the most remote areas of the world, where they would be hunted down at leisure.

"The Snakes are turning to face us!"

"Maintain course."

"They are engaging our missile salvo, but... Their point defense systems are degraded. Attrition rates are too low. They won't stop them all!"

All eighty-three missiles should have been detected and destroyed in a minute or less. The enemy battlecruiser had indeed been damaged by the *Wisdom*'s parting shots, however, and the Snakes hadn't had enough time to effect repairs. Their sensors were having trouble locking onto the incoming missiles; their effectiveness increased as the ship-destroyers got closer, but not enough.

Seventy-six missiles were destroyed. Seven reached their target. They detonated against the battlecruiser's force fields, their graviton and plasma warheads battering the invisible barriers protecting the ship. One got through a breach in the shields and struck the battlecruiser's armored hull.

"Hit!" The visual and data display showed the effect; the Snake battlecruiser lurched in space, knocked off course, ejecting burning atmosphere at the point of impact. The damage was enough to turn a hopeless fight into one that the *Wisdom* could win.

"Fire as you bear," the King-Captain ordered, unnecessarily yet again, but the proper forms must be followed. She wanted to throw her head back and howl in triumph, as her ancestors had done in the emerald forests of her planet's prehistory, but she retained her composure.

Her first volley smashed through the enemy's remaining shields. Gravity-beams, plasma bolts and multi-spectrum lasers cut through the hull and its internal force fields, turning vital components and hissing Risshah crewmen into undistinguishable vaporized matter. The enemy struck back, but their return fire was diffuse and badly coordinated; the *Wisdom*'s force fields held under the onslaught as it continued its attack on the crippled, dying Snake ship. Inevitably, a beam or missile struck the containment field around the battlecruiser's gluon power plant, releasing massive amounts of energy. The enemy vessel vanished in a flash of light that half the planet below saw as a new sun glowing in the sky, blindingly bright.

Any joy Grace might have felt over her victory was short-lived. Over two-thirds of the planet's cities had been consumed, mostly on one hemisphere, although no land mass had been spared. A world's civilization had been crippled, possibly beyond repair.

The Hrauwah did not cry. They expressed sorrow by whimpering and howling, and the pain Grace felt watching the destruction wreaked by the Snakes could no longer be contained. She was far from the only one doing so: the crew's combined keening filled the bridge.

Her ship-domain – her entire species – owed the people of that planet a blood debt, and they would help in any way they could. The survivors of the unprovoked onslaught would have to make their own choices, however, and learn to survive in the new reality that had come crashing upon them.

"Welcome to Starfarer society, you poor sophonts," Grace said.

Down below, thousands of cities continued to burn.

Excerpts from *First Contact: A Multimedia Archive*:

"This is the President of the United States. We surrender unconditionally. We only request that you extinguish the arson weapons you have deployed against our cities. In the name of decency and compassion, I beseech you to spare the innocent lives of millions of people who never meant you any harm. Whatever our sins may be, we will repent and make amends. We... We beg for your mercy."

"This is Trish Valenzuela, reporting from the Empire State Building. The entire city and its suburbs are surrounded by a ring of fire. The flames appear to be growing in height and intensity, and rolling steadily inwards, consuming everything in their path. They..."
(She winces at an explosion in the sky)
"That was news chopper, I think. It hit some sort of invisible barrier, near where the fires started. It's... *(long pause)*. "I'm getting reports of at least a dozen major urban centers similarly affected. Thousands are already dead, and if the fires are not contained, millions will follow, including this reporter. May... May God have mercy on our souls. Back to you at the studio, Morty."

Robert Freemantle @RobAtHome67
The fires are getting closer. Most of the Valley already engulfed. Smoke is getting bad. I think we're all goners. #LABurning
101 replies 83 retweets 3 likes

"Mom, dad... If you're still in town, get out into the country as soon as you can. If you can. It's all happening in cities, they're targeting the cities. I'm... Listen, I love you both very much. I... I have to go now."
- voice mail from First Contact, courtesy of the Benson family.

"They were able to use their phones until the end. Dad was on a business trip in Chicago. He called us from his hotel, and we talked until his room caught fire. We heard him scream before the line went dead."
- Testimonial by Theresa Delacourt.

Last upload from YouTube star Gina Pebbles: The video shows the skyline outside her apartment in Atlanta. It is wreathed in flames, reaching hundreds of feet in height. Police sirens can be heard in the distance. "Radioactive" by Imagine Dragon is playing in the background, the music mixing with the sounds of disaster outside. Down below, several figures run from the conflagration; some of them are already on fire.

Gina turns her smartphone camera on herself. She is crying.

"This is it, people. I'm gonna upload this before it's too late, 'kay? Love y'all, and if there's an America after this is over, don't forget us, 'kay? Find the fuckers who did this and make them pay."

Janice Quinn @hnybny112
PPL R BURNING TO DEATH. SOMEONE DO SOMETHING HELP US
72 replies 329 retweets 0 likes

"This is Johnathan Britten, KDFW, outside Dallas-Fort Worth. The dome around the metropolitan area is completely filled by rising flames; everybody inside must be dead. The last reports we received from the other side of the dome came from a group calling from a bomb shelter, who claimed temperatures were reaching lethal levels before going off the air. I'm told the structure, the energy field apparently, is containing most of the heat inside it, somehow preventing it from spreading beyond its confines, which is the only reason my crew can film it from under a mile away. It's still very hot in here. One might say hellishly hot.

"The fires are obscuring everything at the moment, but a news chopper captured visuals of the Reunion Tower as it collapsed. The heat inside the domes is intense enough to melt concrete and steel. It's... Excuse me for a moment."

(Johnathan moves out of frame; the sound of retching can be heard even through the roar of the flames).

"New York, Los Angeles, Chicago, Washington DC, Baltimore, a dozen other cities, they have all fallen silent. Millions are dead. The rest of the world is, if anything, in worse shape." *(pause).* "Okay, fuck the teleprompter. We all saw the UFO footage from the ISS. E.T. came back, the motherfucker. He came back and killed everyone. We're fucked, you hear me? Fucked!"
- Charlotte NBC Anchorman Keith Neelan, moments before his suicide.

"Much is lost, but much remains. We will never forget this day, and we will never surrender to those who seek our destruction. We will rebuild and restore our strength. God Bless America."
- US President Albert P. Hewer, shortly after being sworn in.

Year Zero AFC (After First Contact)

"Good to see you, Mister President."

"No rank in the mess, Ty. Sit down."

Tyson Keller sat on a plush sofa facing the man who until a few days ago had been the country's Secretary of the Defense. More specifically, the about-to-be-fired Secretary of Defense. Albert P. Hewer had left the Army as a one-star general, had been the head of the CIA for six years and then been tapped for Def Sec by an administration trying to deal with the latest cluster-fuck in the Middle East. Hewer had started butting heads with everybody from the get-go, and inside sources in DC claimed he'd soon be announcing his regretful resignation in order to spend time with his family, a funny exit line for a childless widower.

Then the aliens had come.

Tyson looked around the study, in a manor-style house in an undisclosed location. The Secret Service and Marines had come to his house outside Charlotte, which was possibly the largest US city still in one piece, bundled him into a chopper, and flown him here, here being somewhere almost four hours' flight away. If he had to guess, they were somewhere in Kansas. Wherever it was, it was nowhere near the Beltway. There was no Beltway anymore.

"First of all, I'm sorry for your loss, Ty."

"Thank you."

When the balloon went up, Tyson had gotten a phone call from his oldest daughter Rebecca, who'd been a junior in Boston College. He'd listened to her as she burned to death.

The grief was there, pressing against his chest, and it almost overwhelmed him when Hewer's words stirred it up. Almost. He pushed all emotions down somewhere deep, somewhere they would not show until he was alone with Mathilda. There were tears still to be shed for Becca, but not here and now. This was business.

"It's just you and me," the President of These Very Fucked Up United States went on. "No recording devices on the premises. You can speak freely, Colonel."

"I'm just an accountant now, Al. And I was about to quit my day job, after the last book hit it big on the Kindle." Not anymore,

13

of course. Even if half the reading public in the US hadn't just gone up in smoke, Tyson figured science fiction was as dead as the dodo, now that real aliens had shown themselves and bombed the world back to the Stone Age.

"Read a couple of your novels while I waited for you," Hewer said. "Not too bad. Not my cup of tea; I'm into historical fiction, when I read fiction at all. But not too bad."

"Don't forget to leave a review at Amazon. Wish more people did."

"Heh."

Hewer grinned. It wasn't a pleasant grin, or a pleasant face for that matter. Albert would have never gotten elected to any major office. Not photogenic enough. His face could best be described as 'Nixonian,' the kind of mug cartoonists and comedians would have a field day with. He was President only because everyone else above him had gone up in smoke, along with untold numbers of Americans. Including one of Tyson's children.

"So what do you need, Al? Want me to reenlist?"

"No. I've got plenty of trigger-pullers. I need someone willing to do what needs to be done."

"Which is?"

"We've got to rebuild this nation, Colonel. This is the biggest disaster in the history of this country, of this planet. We lost, by the latest estimate, a hundred and sixty million people in CONUS alone. We're probably going to lose another million or two, maybe a lot more, by the time the winter's over. We have no economy. We've got plenty of food, but we may not have the fuel to move it where it's needed. The aliens hit the twenty largest population centers in the country. Charlotte's metropolitan area is number twenty-one, by the way."

Tyson held up his thumb and forefinger, about half an inch apart. "Missed me by this much."

"Lucky you. Lucky us."

"What do you plan to do about this, Al?" *What the hell* can *you do?* He kept that last question to himself.

"There were two bunches of aliens up there, Ty. One of them took out the ones that blasted us. If they hadn't, we would have been obliterated. We got hit by the first of what would have been successive bomb waves. As it is, we got off lightly, here in the US. The initial spread happened over Asia; we got the tail end. China and India have effectively ceased to exist. Ditto Japan, Australia, Indonesia, both Koreas. Billions are dead. Europe's got a few cities left, but their power grid's collapsed; a lot of the survivors won't make it to next year. The second wave would have finished off what's left. The friendly aliens saved our bacon."

"And what happens now? Do they figure we owe them? Or that they own us now?"

"Not exactly. They feel a measure of obligation towards us. Their ship has left, but a few technical advisors and their equipment stayed behind. Their technology is just this side of magic, and they're sharing it with us. With the US."

"Not with the whole world?"

"No. For whatever reasons, they like us the best from all the countries that survived. The Russians are still around – some Russians; a lot of their military facilities didn't get hit, and their rocket forces are relatively intact. But the good ETs don't care for the Ivans. One of the first things we got from the Puppies was an anti-ballistic missile system that makes the Russians about as dangerous as a kid with a peashooter."

"The Puppies?"

"Wait till you meet one. Kinda look like a cross between a raccoon and a light-skinned Dachshund. Cute as hell."

"Mammals?" Tyson had always figured aliens would be absolutely different, not humans in funny costumes like in the TV shows he loathed.

"Pretty much. They are a DNA- and carbon-based life form, according to my Science Advisor, who happens to be another sci-fi writer on the side. Apparently it turns out some theory about the origins of life was right: 'antiperspirant' or something like that."

"Panspermia, is that what you mean? Life originated somewhere else and came to Earth via comets and meteors?"

"Bingo. That's one of the reasons I need you, Tyson. You've thought about this kind of shit already. That puts you miles ahead of your average government pinhead."

Tyson's head was spinning from the things he'd just learned. The hopeless malaise that had infected him ever since Becca had died began to give way, replaced by something else, something several Jihadists had become acquainted with shortly before their demise.

"I never cared for alien stories," he said. "Figured if they showed up they'd be so far ahead of us we'd end up like the Aztecs and Incas at best, or like ants under a boot at worst. Guess I was only half right."

"Now you don't have to guess, and you're mentally prepared for this stuff, more than most people. The other reason I want you, of course, is that you're a hard case, an utterly cold-blooded son of a bitch. I need the Hun."

"I never cared for that handle. Huns were undisciplined barbarians."

Al had given Tyson that nickname, back when they'd gone through OCS together, a long time ago.

"You weren't afraid of getting your hands dirty, Ty. Or bloody. That's Hunnish enough."

Tyson shook his head. "Al, you really don't want me in a position of power. The country's suffered enough already."

"If we're going to come out of this alive, we need to become something else altogether. We need to clean house and prepare, or we aren't going to survive. The Puppies will help us, but sooner or later we're going to have to stand on our own two feet. Sooner rather than later. We need to become a new Sparta."

"And how do you propose to do that?"

"By any means necessary. Look, we lost a hundred and sixty million Americans, and ninety-nine percent were innocents who didn't deserve what happened to them…"

"More like ninety-five percent. At least eight million of them needed killing. In my humble opinion."

"Maybe. But the point is, most of the people who would be against the changes I'm going to institute are gone. We're going to have to rearm, implement the new technologies we just got, and gird our ever-loving loins for war. One of the first things I'm doing is reinstituting the draft. Universal and mandatory. Everyone serves. Everyone spends a couple years in uniform, getting the stupid knocked out of them. Men and women. Ladies got the vote, so they get to put on combat boots and march while some drill instructor yells at them."

"Good luck getting that passed."

"There is no Congress. There is no Supreme Court. The only effective source of law and order in the country is the military, plus a handful of state governments. And yeah, that means getting around the Posse Comitatus, but my new Attorney General's on the job. You might know him; he did some sci-fi writing himself. Luis Corazao."

"The Mountain? The NRA activist?"

"And gun dealer. And lawyer. And writer. Talented guy. Took some doing, but he's on board. Pro tem, since we don't have enough congresscritters to do confirmation hearings, or fill a short bus for that matter. And that's fine. It's pen-and-phone time, and I've got the pen and the phone. And the trigger-pullers to make it stick."

"That Portagee bastard's got my vote. You probably should start reading some SF yourself. Start with *Starship Troopers*."

"Oh, I read that one a while back. Lots of good ideas there."

"You're going to take an axe to the Constitution, aren't you?"

"The Constitution was dead before fucking E.T. came a-knocking. Between 'penumbras and emanations' and 'living Constitution' and all that other bullshit, it was on its way out. The old America was dying, and now it's dead. Before I go, I'm going to leave behind a new America. One that can survive in the universe we happen to inhabit, not the fantasy land the usual suspects kept dreaming of, all while they cheerfully dismantled our civilization, with no guarantees whatever replaced it would be one iota better."

"Don't have to convince me, Al. I'm the one who said eight million needed killing. Which is why you don't want me in charge of anything major. Most of my solutions come in 9mm Parabellum."

"I'm hoping most fuckheads will appreciate the gravity of the situation. The rest... We'll see."

"We'll see," Tyson agreed. *I've got a little list. Most of the names are crossed off already, but not all.* "Tell me more about the aliens."

"Turns out the galaxy's a nasty neighborhood, Ty. Wait till you get briefed on all the things the Puppies are telling us. It's Might Makes Right all the way down."

"So there's no Prime Directive? No congenial peace-loving aliens?"

"Heh. I hated *Star Trek* when I was a kid. No. It's nineteenth-century-style international politics. To the winner go the spoils. Primitive species are forced into trade agreements at gunpoint, or exterminated without a second thought. The lucky ones get sort of adopted by the nicer aliens, like the Puppies. In this case, we're getting a great deal of help, because the Puppies accidentally led the Snakes – the motherfuckers who wiped out half the planet – here, and they feel they owe us."

Is that so? Then, yeah, hound-dogs. You owe us.

"So there's no rules at all?" he said out loud. "That's rough. What's stopping the Snakes from dropping a dinosaur-killer asteroid to finish us off?"

"There are some rules. Can't inflict major damage to a planet's biosphere, apparently. That's why they didn't use nukes or big rocks; their city-busters are designed to exterminate the tool-users while leaving most everything intact. Things like bioweapons aren't allowed, or 'grey goo,' whatever that is."

"You don't want to know. Who enforces the law?"

"The Puppies were a little vague about it. Elders of the Universe or the fucking Q Continuum, something like that. Whoever it is, they mostly leave the Starfarers – the guys with starships – alone, as long as they stick to some very loose rules."

"Good enough." Tyson thought about it for a second, but the answer was never really in doubt. "All right, Al. You've got me, for whatever it's worth. I think I know what we need to do."

"I thought as much. We can't afford second-guessers or self-haters to get in the way."

"It's not going to be pretty. The cure might be almost as bad as the disease."

Hewer's expression hardened. "As long as we survive and we carve a place for us among the stars, I don't care. Three hundred years from now, college professors can denounce me as an evil tyrant. And that's fine, because that means our species will be around three hundred years from now."

Tyson nodded.

"Let's go to work."

One

Year 163 AFC, D Minus Ten

One step at a time.

USWMC First Lieutenant Peter Fromm's left leg wasn't working right, but he limped along, ignoring the stabbing pain that flared up with every shuffling stride. The artificial muscles in his combat suit weren't working anymore, and the combined weight of his body armor and the unconscious form of Captain Chastain was becoming unbearable. Fromm's desperate dash for cover with a body draped over his shoulders had quickly turned into a limping walk. Even hunched over, he knew he was too high off the ground, making a perfect target, but he also knew that if he went down he would just lie there.

One step at a time.

Nothing else mattered. He had to reach the entrenchments ahead of him, had to save the captain's life. The CO of Charlie Company was a casualty only because Fromm had knocked him unconscious less than an hour ago. He'd had good reasons, but he couldn't leave the man to die, even if the first thing he did upon waking up would be to order Fromm's arrest.

Friendly fire ahead of him, flashes like fireflies in the night. Hostile fire behind him, the whine of ionizing charges followed by loud explosions whenever charged particle bursts or laser beams hit something solid. His force fields were down, and the only thing between him and the storm of deadly energies raining all around was his body armor, which might stop a hit, but most likely would not.

Just a few more steps.

A stray laser pulse from a Lamprey grav tank clipped him from behind.

There was one more thing standing between him and certain death: the limp form of Captain Chastain slung on his back. The unconscious officer he'd been carrying to safety burned under the megawatt glare of the Lamprey weapon. Sublimated armor, flesh and bone erupted in an explosion that smashed Fromm to the ground.

His mouth was full of blood. He couldn't breathe.

I'm dying, was his last thought before the universe vanished.

* * *

Captain Peter Fromm, United Stars Warp Marine Corps, woke up with a start, memories of blood and breath still vivid in his mind.

He was safe. Astarte-Three was hundreds of parsecs away. The 'police action' that had decimated his company and led to the death of its commander was over, and peace reigned in the galaxy. He was safe.

"We're putting you in a quiet spot out in the galactic boondocks until we figure out what to do with you."

Colonel Macwhirter's words echoed in Fromm's mind as he watched the spectacle below the descending shuttle.

Uncontrolled fires ringed Kirosha's capital city. Some quiet spot.

Unrest and warfare were common features in primmie planets even before making contact with a Starfaring civilization, and things usually got even more lively afterwards. The technological and sociological shocks of First Contact always brought about unintended consequences.

Earth's own First Contact had been particularly harsh. Over sixty percent of the planet's population had died within hours of discovering humanity was not alone in the universe. The survivors had adapted, even thrived in the aftermath, but it'd been a rough few decades. Fromm's great-grandfather had shared lots of stories with him before passing on, shortly after his hundred and seventy-sixth birthday. Super-Gramp's depictions of First Contact had made a much greater impression than any history lesson: the blooming fire-domes that marked the deaths of most cities on the planet; the struggle to survive amidst privation and unrest; nights spent shivering in the dark. Given that, Fromm wasn't terribly sympathetic to the current socio-economic woes of Jasper-Five's natives.

A closer look revealed the fires were outside the capital city proper. Fromm's imp – the implanted cybernetic systems linked directly to his nervous system – laid a map schematic over the visual feed from the shuttle as it orbited the only spaceship-rated landing facility on the planet, waiting for clearance. The spaceport wasn't exactly bustling with traffic, but its facilities could handle only one landing at a time. A Wyrm Cargo Globe had arrived shortly before the human freighter that had brought Fromm to his new posting, which meant a wait of half an hour if not longer until the alien vessel was unloaded and the landing pad cleared. Fromm could imagine the grumbling in the shuttle's cockpit about spent fuel and wasted man-hours. Civvie freighter crews owned shares in their ships: all expenses literally came out of their pockets.

The delay gave him time to study his briefing packet and compare it to the reality he'd soon experience first hand.

Jasper-Five was almost identical to Earth, with a mostly-compatible Class Two biosphere and a dominant tool-using species. A pretty accomplished species, as a matter of fact. It had developed technologies roughly comparable to Earth's first century before First Contact, or the twentieth century in the old calendar. Most sophonts in the galaxy never advanced beyond the Iron Age (the vast majority stayed at Paleolithic levels, as a matter of fact) before a Starfarer species showed up and uplifted, enslaved or exterminated them. Earth and Jasper-Five were exceptions to the rule.

The planet had been discovered some twenty years ago by an American survey ship, and First Contact had been established shortly after. The United Stars had placed the system and its inhabited fifth planet under its protection and largely ignored it, until a follow-up survey had discovered large deposits of rare earths, among the most valuable commodities in the galaxy. While asteroid mining provided most of America's rare earth needs, new sources were always in demand. Jasper-Five's lanthanide deposits were concentrated in one of the planet's continents, dominated by the Kingdom of Kirosha.

While some Starfaring civilizations would have just seized the kingdom's mineral wealth by force, the USA found it easier to negotiate with the locals for mining rights, providing them with hard currency they could use to improve their technology and living standards far beyond what they had before First Contact. It was cheaper than outright conquest, and in the future might provide the US with a client species that might serve as an eventual ally. The US could always use more friends in a largely hostile galaxy.

Over the ensuing two decades, Kirosha had changed a great deal; the formerly insular, relatively backward kingdom had become the most powerful nation on the planet. Its newfound wealth had allowed it to purchase the best military equipment available from its neighbors (no Starfarer was willing to sell them high-tech weaponry for the time being) and modernize their kingdom.

From the smoke dotting the edges of the city, it looked like the changes had brought their share of problems as well.

The fires were mostly concentrated on a ring of shantytowns

that had accrued around the city proper like crystals in a supersaturated solution. The briefings didn't provide any reasons as to why the locals seemed intent on arson as a form of protest. Fromm would have to figure that out by himself after he made landfall. He couldn't even query his own command or the Embassy beforehand, not with two rival Starfarer delegations in place, quite capable of eavesdropping on any but the most heavily-encrypted communications.

"Ladies and gentlemen," the shuttle's pilot announced. "We've been authorized to land, and will be arriving in under five minutes. Be advised; there are reports of civil unrest throughout the capital. Transport to the Foreigner Enclave has been provided for everyone, courtesy of Caterpillar, Inc and Star Mining Enterprises. Venturing outside the Enclave is not recommended. If you must go into the city proper, make sure you do so in groups. Things are a bit rough out there. Hope you had a good trip. God Bless America."

"God Bless America," the passengers chorused back. A couple of remfie suits sitting near the captain did so while rolling their eyes in jaded cynicism, but the miners, technicians and machinery operators who comprised the majority of the passengers said the words with the mildly bored sincerity of people raised to love God, Flag and Country from earliest childhood. Fromm's own response was heartfelt, but tempered with the knowledge of the price involved in upholding those words. God might wish America His best, but He left most of the heavy lifting in the hands of mere mortals like Fromm and his beloved Corps.

There was the usual rapid shift in pressure as the shuttle dropped the last several hundred feet towards the ground, throwing itself on the mercy of the gravity grapples dirtside. The abrupt motion slowed down during the last few seconds, and the hundred-ton vehicle came down in a gentle, almost imperceptible motion. Fromm grabbed his personal satchel from the overhead compartment. His orders had come so abruptly that he'd left most of his meager possessions behind; they would follow him here eventually, which given the remoteness of his new posting meant weeks, if not months. On the other hand, a few weeks ago he'd fully expected to spend the rest of his life behind bars, which given the capital nature of his crimes was likely to be a very short time. A hasty posting to a planet in the ass-end of nowhere was a much better alternative.

The Marine took a deep breath as he stepped onto Jasper-Five's soil for the first time. It was a bit of a ritual he had, marking his first impression of each new world he visited. Every planet was slightly different, even Full Goldie worlds like this one, where conditions were nearly identical to Earth's. 'Nearly' always turned out to be a rather elastic term. In this case, there was a hint of spice in the air, likely coming from the cultivated fields beyond the spaceport, vast expanses of some kind of yellow-capped plant, broken by scattered copses of leafy trees. Mixed in with the fragrance of the local flora was a faint smell of burning things, coming from the capital city thirty klicks away.

He looked up. A huge moon was clearly visible in the mid-morning sky, easily four, five times larger than Earth's. His briefing classified it as a planet, actually, but it looked like Earth's Moon: a white, pockmarked disk, bereft of an atmosphere and life. The sky surrounding it was a blue so light it faded to white in places. Out in the distance, a line of snow-capped mountains filled the horizon. The temperature felt cool to his skin; his imp helpfully reported it was fifty-nine degrees Fahrenheit at the moment, with a high of sixty-three and a low nighttime temp of fifty-two degrees. Not too bad.

The landing pad was a flat concrete circle a quarter of a mile wide and sixty feet tall, surrounded by the squat shapes of the port's landing grapples. Loading cranes and trucks moved towards the shuttle's cargo hold as the passengers disembarked. A fenced pedestrian path led to a flight of stairs and a lower level where ground transport was located. About a dozen humans and twice as many locals were waiting there.

His imp highlighted one of them: a woman in her mid-thirties, her light brown hair covered under a colorful shawl thrown over a utilitarian civvie outfit, a jacket over pants tucked into leather boots with sensible rubber soles, dressy but perfectly good for walking and running. The imp ran an overlay onto his field of vision, containing all her basic data: Heather Tamsin McClintock, Department of State, Deputy Charge D'affaires of the US Embassy on Jasper-Five. Her Facettergram profile was set to private; so was her curriculum vitae. *Spook*, he decided as she walked up towards him, a pro forma smile on her face.

Normally, he would have expected to be met by his platoon sergeant and a driver, maybe with a squad's worth of grunts if an escort was deemed necessary. Nothing about this situation was normal.

"Captain Fromm," she said, shaking his hand. Her nails were short, her grip strong, indicating someone who worked with her hands at least some of the time, if only for physical fitness purposes.

"Pleased to meet you, Ms. McClintock." Imps made personal introductions largely superfluous, except for politeness' sake, which remained rather important.

"Ambassador Llewellyn wanted to keep all military forces at the embassy, due to security concerns," McClintock said, answering Fromm's unspoken question. "Given the current situation, he deemed them necessary for the protection of the Foreigners' Enclave."

"I see," Fromm said. *What the hell's going on in here?*

"I'll brief you in the car." She looked at his satchel. "Is that all your luggage?"

He nodded, noting with some envy that most of his fellow passengers were dragging hundreds of pounds of baggage on their mag-lev carriers. It was nice to have stuff.

"You carrying?" she asked.

"Colt PPW." The 3mm pistol was standard Marine issue. Fromm could not imagine being out and about without a gun. It'd be like forgetting to wear pants in public.

Her smile became harsher and sincerer at the same time. "Good. You probably won't need it for the trip to the Enclave, but you know how it goes."

Fromm nodded. Better to have a weapon you didn't need, than need a weapon you didn't have.

When you needed a weapon, you needed it very badly.

Two

Year 163 AFC, D Minus Ten

Heather McClintock led the newly-minted Marine captain to the embassy car. The locally-produced four-wheeler was overbuilt and massive, a civvie version of a Kiroshan military vehicle with off-road capability. It was painted a light sky blue, a color that indicated high-caste ownership. Her staff driver was leaning against the car. He was of the same species as the denizens of the Kingdom, but from a different nationality and ethnicity. The locals called themselves Kirosha, a term that covered the capital city, the greater nation-state, and its citizens, not unlike Earth's Rome. Her driver's name was Locquar, and he was the most trusted member of her staff. Among other reasons, because he wasn't Kirosha, but a foreigner, as loathed and hated by the locals as any other aliens.

Like most sophonts from Class Two biospheres, the natives of Jasper-Five were humanoid in shape and general biology. They were bipeds with opposable thumbs on their four-fingered hands, with body size and mass well within human ranges. Their skin had a reddish tint, ranging from a deep scarlet to a light flamingo pink, the lighter varieties being most common among the Kirosha; they had very little body hair, concentrated mainly on a ridge beginning at the top of their heads and running down to the small of their backs. Their large eyes and smooth heart-shaped faces gave them a cartoonish appearance to human sensibilities.

Locquar's skin was a deep scarlet, which clearly marked him as an outsider. He also shaved his ridge-hair, as was the custom of his tribal group but was considered barbaric by the locals. His small mouth was set in what Kirosha would consider a grim expression and humans would perceive as a comical moue.

"Captain Fromm, this is Locquar Asthan, Embassy Staff."

To her surprise, Fromm squatted down, hands upraised in a standard Kirosha greeting, instead of trying to shake hands American fashion, as both she and Locquar had expected. The jarhead had done his homework, which put him well ahead of many Americans, who mostly assumed it was the locals' job to learn their customs and language. The squat was awkward – human leg joints couldn't quite reproduce the Kirosha motion – and he showed more deference than appropriate to the driver, who was technically three social rungs beneath him. The gesture was still miles better than what most State Department employees usually managed, let alone the other two thousand-plus humans currently dwelling on the planet. Cultural sensibility was not high on the list of US priorities. Understandable, given that humans were viewed largely as barbaric parvenus in Starfarer society and treated with contempt, but often regrettable. The only other human polity, the Greater Asia Co-Prosperity Sphere, was even worse; being largely Earth-bound, its behavior wasn't readily apparent across the stars, however.

Locquar returned the squat – the greeting wasn't what his people used, but he was well-versed in Kirosha mores – and batted his eyelashes at the Marine, the equivalent of a warm smile.

"It is a fine day, is it not?" Fromm said in Kiroshan, or tried to.

"It is, and also a pleasure to meet you, Captain," Locquar said in English, which he could manage better than humans could speak the local languages; the natives' audible range was a little past what human vocal chords could manage without mechanical aid. Heather's throat implants, courtesy of the US Embassy, allowed her to talk like a native.

"We'll leave as soon as everybody's ready," she said. The colorfully-painted bus Caterpillar Inc. had provided for its employees was filling up fast; a van hired by Star Mining Enterprises was collecting its own share of the shuttle's passengers. They all had agreed to leave together. Safety in numbers. Things had gotten bad enough that no Starfarer dared leave the Enclave alone; two AmCits had been injured in separate incidents during the past week, and the Kirosha authorities didn't seem to be in a hurry to round up any suspects. The arriving human passengers would travel in a convoy comprising the bus, van, and Heather's embassy vehicle, sandwiched between two escort cars manned by armed private contractors.

Fromm spotted the lead and chase cars just before they drove off. "I guess it's time for that briefing."

"I'm sending chapter-and-verse to your imp," she said. Analyzing that information would take time, however, so she went on. "The gist of it is, a peasant rebellion has been simmering for several months. At first it was limited to the outlying provinces, especially southwest from here, but the discontent has spread to the capital."

"I see," Fromm said, looking out the car windows. He nodded towards the smoke cresting over the horizon. "When did that start?"

"They set the first fires two days ago. You'd have been in warp-transit then."

"Yes. A twenty-hour warp jump, New Parris to Lahiri, a day in-system, and then caught an inbound freighter here for an extra eight hours."

New Parris was a harsh, barely inhabitable planet the Warp Marine Corps had adopted as its training and staging center. The Lahiri star system had no planets at all, but its neutron star was a major warp nexus, with space-time 'valleys' that led to dozens of other systems, including Jasper. A total of twenty-eight hours' warp travel over three days was no picnic, but the Marine seemed to have handled the trip well.

"What's the rebels' beef with the government?" he asked.

"The Crown has been raising taxes to modernize its armed forces for some time, which wouldn't have been so bad if a drought hadn't hit half the continent a year ago. And there's been the usual problems with rapid modernization: peasants being displaced by farm machinery and discovering factory work is not to their taste, that sort of thing. The main issue is that a faction within the Kirosha ruling class is manipulating the rebels into blaming foreigners for all their problems."

"Not a big leap, since Kirosha hate just about everyone who doesn't look like them, right? The info files I got made that clear."

Heather nodded. "Pretty much. Their words for 'foreign' and 'wrong' are closely related. 'Foreigner' also translates as 'evil.' If you aren't Kirosha, you're a demon, basically. Humans and any other Starfarer species are known as Star Devils."

"They sound like a great bunch of guys."

"They're kind to their children, and love their pets. But if you're an outsider, watch out. The Preserver faction hates the influence Star Devils have over the Kingdom's affairs. Everything from the new mines to missionaries opening hospitals, schools and orphanages. And it's using the rebels against us."

"This is a fucking mess," Fromm said. "Why are we letting this happen?"

"Money and politics. We don't want to handle the expenses necessary to assume direct control of the country, for one; it'd likely cost more than what we're getting from the mines. And the Kirosha might turn to the Wyrashat or Vehelians for protection, which could lead to tensions between us. Which means we're treading softly, for now."

"Sounds awesome."

"And you're the senior military officer on site. Congratulations," Heather said.

The Marine probably wasn't the right man for the job at hand.

Then again, no recently-promoted captain was meant to handle something with the makings of an interstellar incident. Unfortunately, Ambassador Llewellyn wasn't up to the task, either, in Heather's opinion. The developing situation was above everyone's pay grade and, worse, their competency level.

They fell silent while Fromm mulled things over and accessed the raw data she'd uploaded into his computer implant. He started outlining some key data out loud, seeking confirmation and elaboration form her.

"All right. There are over two thousand Americans on Jasper-Five: about two hundred Embassy personnel and dependents, the rest either corporate employees or missionaries of assorted denominations, plus about two hundred military contractors."

She nodded. "Plus a few odds and sorts, raising the total human presence on Jasper-Five to twenty-five hundred or so. About three hundred are working in the main mining operation on the Neesha Valley, about five hundred clicks inland. They should be safe enough there; the mines are isolated and far away from population centers. About half the military contractors on the planet are out there, providing security."

"Got it. If things go wrong, the US military presence consists of my Marine contingent: a platoon plus a number of attached units, including the original Marine Security Detachment: seventy-eight personnel total."

"There is also a hundred or so military contractors in the capital, an Enclave constabulary force with fifty-two peace officers, and a hundred and eighty-two Navy personnel, including thirty master-at-arms ratings, mostly stationed at the spaceport."

"I guess that's better than nothing," Fromm said. Technically, his command's sole mission was to protect the embassy. In practice, he and his men might be called upon to help any Americans in need.

"At least almost everybody is in one place. A lot of people were working on assorted projects outside the capital, but after the first riot they've been advised to confine themselves to the Enclave. Which has caused no end of trouble; housing is scarce, and the area is packed with idle miners and machinery operators, not exactly the most placid folk. The constabulary force is having trouble keeping order."

"I hope nobody thinks my Marines can help with that."

"Not as far as I know. In fact, nobody at the embassy really knows what to do with your unit. The ambassador isn't happy about the quote-unquote 'needless expense.' We got the reinforced platoon nine months ago; before that, our Marine Security Detachment consisted of nine men. The assignment happened over the ambassador's protests, mostly because it's put a big crimp on the budget even after additional funds were assigned for the platoon's upkeep. He'd much rather spend the money on social functions."

"Remfie," Fromm muttered. Not the smartest thing to say, calling an accredited ambassador a Rear-Echelon Motherfucker, but Heather appreciated the gesture. She understood; he was placing her in a position of trust, because he needed somebody to trust among the Embassy's weenies, or what was likely to be a nearly impossible mission could cross out the 'nearly' part.

"He is," she admitted with a rueful grin. "Still doesn't explain why we got reinforcements nobody asked for, unless someone in higher has figured out a way to foresee the future and anticipated we'd be having problems."

"No, it had nothing to do with local conditions," Fromm said.

"Budgetary?"

"You got it. The Corps had to disband five Marine Expeditionary Units after Congress overrode President Hewer's veto and initiated cutbacks. A lot of their personnel got discharged, but a few units ended up distributed in penny-packets around the galaxy, with their upkeep paid for by the Marine Security Detachment budget. The Corp didn't want to lose the trained cadre those troops represented, and this way the State Department pays for most of their upkeep. The Congress-Rats love the State Department, so they didn't cut its budget."

"Ah." Heather had suspected something along those lines, but delving in Marine Corps' politics wasn't her job. Her professional curiosity was largely focused on the affairs of non-humans. "Sneaky," she added appreciatively.

"We're going to need those units," Fromm said. "The Lampreys got slapped down hard on Astarte-Three, but they aren't done playing games. I was there. I…"

The Marine froze for a second, his eyes focused on something only he could see.

"True enough," Heather said, breaking the awkward silence. Fromm snapped out of it and turned his attention back on her.

Her own info on interstellar affairs was more detailed than a Marine captain was cleared for, and she agreed with his estimate. Of course, Fromm's knowledge was of a far more personal nature; he'd lost most of his platoon during the skirmish on Astarte-Three. Said 'skirmish' had decimated a Marine Expeditionary Unit and almost sparked a full-fledged war with the Lhan Arkh – better known as the Lampreys – and their client races, which included the few Snakes left in the galaxy.

"Of course, none of that matters here. We're nowhere near the Lhan Arkh's sphere of influence," she concluded.

"Yeah. Higher thought this would be a nice quiet spot to stash me away for the time being."

The events at Astarte-Three were on the public record, as were Captain Fromm's promotion and commendations resulting from the incident. Something else, something unofficial, had led to his transfer to the ass-end of nowhere, not to mention a command below his new pay grade: a reinforced platoon did not a company make. She'd have to do a little digging to find out more.

The captain took a moment to check out the countryside as they drove on. The bucolic scenery was pleasant enough: Kirosha children in colorful knee-length tunics ran through orderly rows of gold-tinged Jusha; their antics were both work and play, serving to scare an assortment of flying critters away from the food-bearing plants. Jusha's nut-like seeds were the principal staple of the continent, being used for everything from bread and noodles to a variety of alcoholic beverages, some of which were quite pleasant to human tastes, even the ones who also were violent emetics to human metabolisms. New visitors to Jasper-Five were warned not to consume any drinks before using their implants to run chem tests on them. A few practical jokers loved to offer newcomers the bad stuff. That didn't apply to Marines, though: their digestive nanites would strip anything even remotely organic of any toxins and allow its nutrients to be absorbed. Marines could almost literally make a meal out of mud and cardboard.

"It looks peaceful enough around here," Fromm said.

"It normally is. But there's signs of trouble even in the country. Coming up in a couple minutes, as a matter of fact. The village to the left of the road."

A makeshift camp had been erected near the village, haphazardly arranged canvas tents contrasting with the neat rows of wooden houses that served as the peasants' permanent dwellings. A group of about twenty Kirosha, mostly males, were gathered on a fallow field nearby, practicing with spears, swords, throwing axes and weaponized farm implements. They all wore black tunics emblazoned with a distinctive sigil: a hand clenching a set of spiked brass-knuckles.

"Meet the Final Blow Society. Or the Order of the Coup-de-Grace, if you will," Heather said as they drove by. A few of the black-clad warriors stopped their drill to look at the passing vehicles. Her hand instinctively reached for the shoulder holster under her jacket before she stopped herself. They hadn't attacked her car on its way to the spaceport, and they probably wouldn't attack them now, either. The armed peasants' glares were definitely unfriendly, though.

"One of the rebel groups?"

"The largest one. They've been flocking to the capital over the last few days, allegedly to present their grievances to the Crown. They are suspected in participating in the arsons plaguing the shantytowns around the capital, but either their sponsors are protecting them or the authorities are choosing not to suppress them."

"And all they've got is spears and swords?"

"Yes, for the most part. There's been a few snipers at work in the slums, shooting at firemen, that sort of thing. The Crown has very strict laws on firearm ownership, so those weapons must have been stolen from the police or military."

"When I see a bunch of people wearing the same colors, it says 'military' to me."

"The Kingdom is willing to look the other way as long as they pretend to be a martial arts club."

"Who's paying for all of this?" Fromm asked. "The uniforms, the weapons, the food they eat? Can't be cheap, having a bunch of peons running around playing with sticks instead of raising crops or digging ditches."

"The food's easy: they ask for 'voluntary' contributions from nearby villages, which come out of whatever is left after the royal tax men get their cut. The rest comes from whoever is sponsoring them. The Preserver faction is the likely culprit. It is composed mainly of high-ranking bureaucrats, the Magistrate class, along with a smattering of aristocrats."

"Rats will be rats," Fromm said.

The motorcade left the village and the gang of martial artists behind. The smoke pillars up ahead grew larger. Heather saw Fromm was leaning forward, his eyes narrowing.

"The fires are nowhere near our designate route," she said.

The slums and the fires beneath the rising smoke were hidden from sight by a series of hills, each topped by a small fort and a watchtower. Fromm switched his attention to the fortifications as they drove past them. The ones nearest the road were relatively modern, their squatting, sloped walls designed to deflect cannonballs. Soldiers in colorful blue and pink uniforms and peaked caps milled atop the forts' battlements; their gates were closed, and cannon and machinegun barrels poked behind the crenellations above, further protected by metal gun shields.

"Sixty-millimeter rifled artillery," Fromm said, mouthing the specs his imp gave him. "Antiquated even by local standards, but almost as good as French seventy-fives from the second century BFC. And eleven millimeter heavy machineguns. Enough to penetrate standard infantry force fields after ten, fifteen direct hits. The locals really got far on their own, technologically speaking."

"Good thing you won't have to fight them, then," she said.

"My job is to assess capabilities. Intent I leave to the politicians."

"Fair enough. And although we aren't formally allied with the Kingdom, we do have a trade agreement and full diplomatic ties."

"You know who had all kinds of trade agreements and full diplomatic ties? France and Germany, just before they went to war with each other."

"Sure, but neither France nor Germany could blast every enemy city to cinders."

"Neither can we, not right this second. That would take at least a corvette in orbit," Fromm said as the car passed the line of fortifications and drove past the suburbs, white-washed houses with green triangular roofs and black-and-red trimming, surrounded by similarly-decorated walls. Road traffic was strangely sparse for this time of day, Heather noticed. "We have no Fleet assets in-system, last I checked."

"There is the squadron at Lahiri. That's eight hours' warp-transit away. None of the nations on Jasper-Five have any space assets beyond the weather and communication satellites we sold Kirosha, none of which are armed. The local tech is below even what Earth had during First Contact. They are completely helpless against us."

"How about the other Starfarers in the area? Our good friends, the Wyrms and the Ovals?"

"The Wyrashat and the Vehelians have trade concessions and an embassy and a consulate, respectively," she said, pointedly using the two species' proper names rather than the borderline-insulting slang terms. "They have no military vessels anywhere near us."

"They've got about five hundred people apiece in the Enclave, though," Fromm said after checking with his imp. "And a short company's worth of soldiers each."

"A Velehian security detachment, and a Wyrashat Honor

Guard. Hardly a threat. Hold on," she said as her imp chimed in with a call from the Ambassador. She answered it.

Javier Llewellyn's disembodied head appeared in front of her, the image inputted directly into her visual cortex by her imp.

"I just received a request from Envoy Lisst," the Ambassador said, not bothering with any pleasantries before getting to the point, as was his wont when dealing with underlings and other inconsequential people. "He's returning from the Royal Palace following a meeting with Her Supreme Majesty and would like to join your convoy on the way back to the Enclave. Security concerns."

"We can rendezvous with him in a few minutes, as long as the roads are clear," Heather said.

"Do so. Convey my regards to the Envoy."

Llewellyn's projection disappeared.

Heather turned to Fromm. "Speaking of the Vehelians, their Envoy wants to join our little parade."

"Guess he's worried," Fromm said.

"With good reason. Something is wrong."

Heather contacted all the vehicles in the convoy; the contractors in the escort cars weren't happy about the detour, but a call to the Caterpillar top exec took care of their complaints.

The street they were on was wide and straight, but the rest of the city was a maze of narrow, twisting little paths weaving between wood and brick buildings, mostly three and four-story structures with peaked roofs that were clearly attempts to ape the more prosperous houses in the suburbs. Things didn't look normal, though.

When she'd left for the spaceport, the city of Kirosha had been teeming with people, mostly on foot or on bicycles and tricycles, along with a few internal combustion cars reserved for the well-to-do. The streets were curiously empty now; the few Kirosha she could see – men in their traditional wide trousers, flowerpot or pointy hats and colorful tunics, women similarly clad except for shawls covering their heads and shoulders instead of hats – were clearly in a hurry to be somewhere else. A few of them were even running, something the dignity-conscious Kirosha only did when in fear of their lives.

"Are we going too far out of our way to pick up the ETs?" Fromm asked.

"A few minutes. At least traffic won't be an issue."

The street they were on – Triumphal Thoroughfare One – led straight to the Palace Complex, series of buildings and monuments that had started out as a fortress on top of a hill and had grown in leaps and bounds as successive rulers put their own stamp on it. Its principal building was the Royal Ziggurat, a flat-topped four-hundred-foot tall pyramid off to the side of the original hill, painted a bright canary yellow the Kirosha considered beautiful and Heather found painful to look at. The complex was surrounded by its own fortifications, an old-fashioned curtain wall with towers placed every hundred feet and watchful Royal Guardsmen standing on its battlements. Far more guardsmen than normal, Heather noticed.

The main gates to the palace were still open, however, and two black-painted cars emerged from them, each vehicle flying a little banner festooned with the colorful dark-blue and gold sigils of the O-Vehel Commonwealth. Heather's imp chimed again.

"Greetings and good health, Ms. McClintock," Envoy Lisst's projection said in perfect English, or rather, his implant did. Vehelian imps were more sophisticated than anything humans could manufacture themselves: their implanted nano-chips could access the Envoy's thoughts and translate them into any of the seventeen Prime Languages of the known galaxy. Just as well; to human ears, Vehelian speech sounded like an unintelligible collection of growls and hisses.

Vehelian heads looked like large eggs, their noses and mouths so flat they appeared to be drawn on their surface; their only other facial features were rows of little bumps that the human eye could barely discern but which were the primary way for the species to recognize each other and to express emotions. Heather was a trained exo-diplomat; she could read the slight discoloration in the upper row of bumps over the Envoy's eyes as clear signs of worry.

"And good health to you," she said. "We welcome the chance to render assistance. Please follow my car, and we will hopefully reach the Enclave without incident."

"May hope become fact, and bless you for your kindness."

"You honor me," Heather said. Most VIPs wouldn't have personally addressed a mid-level flunky like herself, but the Vehelians were rather informal in such matters, which made them a rarity in Starfarer society.

Her imp talked to their imps, and the two limos put themselves in the center of the formation, between Heather's car and the bus, driving single file as they turned from Triumphant Thoroughfare One to the Road of Good Fortune, which would lead them straight to the Enclave. Problem was, there were a few questionable neighborhoods along the way.

Decisively Engaged

As the motorcade left the palace grounds, it travelled through more built-up areas, residential buildings with shops on their lower levels, tightly packed except for the occasional park or plaza opening little clearings in the warren-like mass. One such plaza was empty; gone were the usual bunch of peddlers, laborers and beggars. Drums and gongs started playing as they drove by, however, and she spotted men in black tunics and brass-knuckle symbols coming out of nearby buildings. Coming out at a run.

"Trouble," she said, moments before a rocket-propelled grenade struck the lead car.

Three

Year 163 AFC, D Minus Ten

The new skipper showed up just in time to ruin Lance Corporal Russell 'Russet' Edison's card game. The death and mayhem that followed were just par for the course.

In Russell's experience, all officers had lousy timing. The former CO of Third Platoon had been an okay guy for a First Lieutenant, but he'd managed to walk right in front of a speeding Ruddy motorcar. Sad way to buy the farm, run down like a dog on the street, but those were the breaks.

"Shuffle up and deal already," Russell told fellow Lance Corporal Conroy, who was wrinkling his nose and casting glances out the window of the break room. Russell understood Conroy's worries. He could smell the not-so-distant fires, too. The Ruddies were aliens, but their atmo and chemistry were Class Two, just like humans, even though they looked more like animated red-skinned dolls than people. Their food was even edible, not that was an issue for Marines. The fires that were burning outside the big city smelled just like they would in a human world.

And just like in a human world, the smell of arson was the smell of war. Things were getting hairy on Jasper-Five.

Until recently, their current deployment hadn't been too bad. Russell didn't like having his platoon out by itself, but life away from a regular base had its benefits if you weren't married or otherwise encumbered. The food was damn better, for one; the Marines didn't have a mess hall, so they ate at the Embassy's cafeteria, where the chow was miles better than any tray-rats he'd ever had on base. And there were no MPs to worry about, just a bunch of 'constables' who treated the Marines with kid gloves. The platoon sergeant ran a tight ship, granted, but he couldn't be everywhere at once, and that meant the more creative grunts like Russell and his gang had plenty of opportunities for extracurricular activities.

Conroy shook his head and finished shuffling the cards. Russell had checked the deck himself, making sure there were no marks on them. Using your imps to cheat was a tradition as old as the Warp Marine Corps itself. The same micro-implants that let the soldiers do all kind of nifty things to the enemy also made them hell to supervise in peacetime. Even the fact that imps could record every second of your life wasn't enough to stop them; there

36

were ways around that, if you had a creative mind.

"Smells like the Ruddies are having a party," said the one private at the table. PFC Raymond Gonzaga was a little rat-faced guy who'd been busted down the ranks a good dozen times. Good guy when the chips were down, but a complete disaster during peacetime.

Russell was like that, too. He'd made it all the way to E-5 before he'd been caught trying to catch a ride back to base while naked, drunk as a skunk and in the company of a couple of bug-eyed tentacle-waving aliens – he never found out what species – who were also drunk. The details of the escapade remained hazy (he'd disabled his imp's recorder at some point and whatever he'd taken had done a number on his short-term memory), but it'd earned him several Ninja Punches, including a demotion back to Private First Class.

Overall, the gun club had been good for him, though, non-judicial punishments and all. He'd put in twenty years already, starting at age sixteen, when he'd left his former life as a gangsta in the Zoo and used his Obligatory Service Term as a springboard into the fleet. Once he figured his way around the bullshit and discovered that the Corps valued his talent for killing people and breaking things, he realized he had found his calling.

His plan was to put fifty years in, which guaranteed him a twenty-five-year pension. That and a few shady dealings on the side would allow him to buy a bar and spend a couple or more decades having fun. Unless things got boring enough to make him want to go back to the Corps. Or the twenty-five-year pension ran out and he needed another source of income. Nobody was sure how long humans could last, now that they'd worked out most of the kinks on life-extension meds. One of the first casualties of life-ex had been lifetime pensions. Now you got back half the time you put in. Maybe he'd end up serving another fifty years in the Corps after taking two decades off.

Or maybe he'd switch outfits. Some people ended up serving in every branch of the service, from the shit ones like the Army or Coast Guard all the way to the Navy. Russell didn't know how well he might do as a bubblehead – he hadn't met many bubblies he liked – but you never knew till you tried.

"They're burning down the slums," Russell said, setting aside his plans for the future. "Not our problem. Enclave's the safest place to be in the damn planet, other than the Ruddy Queen's bedroom."

He didn't mind that the guys were worried about what was

going on outside the Enclave. Worried grunts made stupid bets, which meant he might be able to get out of the hole he'd dug for himself. A hundred bucks in the red so far, which was a good half a week's pay for a lowly Lance. Sure, a dollar went pretty far Ruddy-land, a.k.a. Jasper-Five, but if you ended up with zero dollars in your pocket you were screwed until the next payday. Twenty years in, and he had less than two hundred bucks in his savings account. Booze, smokes and hookers; all his money always ended up split three-ways between them. Russell had a big score in the works, selling some combat-lossed high-tech equipment to a notorious smuggler passing through Jasper-Five, but it'd be a while before he collected his cut, and hookers and booze couldn't be bought on promises, even if his word was good enough to cadge a few smokes.

"Guess you're right, Russet," Corporal Harold 'Rocky' Petrossian said after he ponied up the small blind; when the dealing was done, he looked at his hand, and clearly saw something he didn't like. Rocky was good people but if he looked unhappy, that was because he'd gotten a lousy hand. Rocky couldn't bluff for shit.

"I know I'm right," Russell replied absently, glancing at his hand: pocket sixes. Good enough to stay in the game.

"You shoulda been in New Lancaster when the Lizards torched their own town before we could get to it," Gonzo told Conroy. "It spread out all over the forests around it. Flames all over the horizon, far as the eye could see. They had these trees, they were full of this gummy paste, and man, did that shit stink when it caught fire. Suit filters couldn't cope with the fucking stench."

"Yeah, that was nasty," Rocky said. "We kicked ass, though."

"Kill bodies," Gonzo agreed.

Flop came out. An ace, a six, and the other six. Russell's expression didn't change an iota as his mind started figuring out the best course of action.

He never got a chance to work out the angles, though. His imp chimed in his ear – everybody's imp did. Priority call.

"Stop whatever the fuck you're doing, fuck-socks," Gunnery Sergeant Miguel Obregon said through the command channel. "The new CO is on his way from orbit, should arrive in about an hour. I want y'all out on the yard, field unis and gear, looking sharp, in forty-five minutes, or y'all gonna be on police call all over the embassy grounds. Acknowledge and get moving."

Russell dutifully sent an 'Acknowledged' signal from his imp, which would show in the platoon display as a green light. A yellow light meant the Marine in question had failed to acknowledge, and Obregon would track the miscreant down and made him sorry he'd ever been born. With an imp right inside your skull, your only excuses not to acknowledge a command were death or a situation where taking a second to answer a call was worth your life.

The skipper had already screwed Russell over and he hadn't even shown up yet. Fucking officers.

The card game broke up as everyone's imps transferred their wins or deducted their losses from their accounts. Russell tried not to think about his depleted savings as he took a quick shower and put on his field 'long johns' back on. They wore the skin-tight gray-green bodysuits most of the time; the material was self-repairing, self-cleaning, breathed better than most civvie clothing, local or American, and was tough enough to resist knife slashes, something that Russell could attest to from personal experience. He clamped his back-and-breast clamshell armor over the long johns, followed by the articulated knee, elbow and wrist pads that, along with his helmet and the force field projectors built into them, made each infantryman invulnerable to explosive fragments and most civvie and primmie small arms, and highly resistant to modern weapons. Russell had been on the receiving end of arrows, spears, blunderbusses, bucketloads of plasma, grav beams and Lamprey lasers rifles, spread over seven different engagements in two wars and three minor conflicts, which had earned him a three-star Combat Action Ribbon and a Purple Heart with three oak leaf clusters. Considering he'd also bled like a stuck pig, shit and pissed himself, and endured more pain than he'd thought possible, he would have happily declined the honors, not that the fucking ETs trying to kill him had given him a choice in the matter. His armor was one of the reasons he was still around to bitch about it. Dumb luck and being a sneaky sumbitch were the other two.

The helmet closed around his head with a hiss as it pressurized its interior. The thin eye-slit provided fuck-all peripheral vision and little enough frontal vision, but his imp made up for it, projecting the take from his helmet sensors right into his brain. As far as his peepers were concerned, it was like he wasn't wearing a helmet at all. Nanowire filaments sneaked out from the clamshell breastplate until they connected to the armor pads and his boots, creating a network of artificial muscle that allowed him to carry a hundred and fifty pounds of weapons and equipment with almost zero strain and fatigue, although it took training to overcome the momentum you generated while running under a full load.

A quick check showed that the two power packs mounted on the back of the clamshell armor were fully charged. One was dedicated to the force fields; the other kept the suit's systems running for up to twenty-four hours, give or take, depending on how active those hours were. You could divert power from one pack to the other at a pinch, at the risk of running out of juice for the shields or the suit. It almost never came to that, but there'd been exceptions, and then it became a race between the force fields going down or having to move under a hundred and fifty pounds of weight while trying to see out of the little slit in your helmet without the benefit of your sensors. If both packs ran out, you ditched the armor and prepared to have a really bad day.

He and the other Marines emerged from their barracks – a converted warehouse behind the American legation buildings – and headed for the armory, a makeshift structure made out of three starship cargo containers welded together into a 'U' shape. Gunny Obregon was there, overseeing the weapons issue personally, probably to make sure nobody tried to walk away with more than their allotted stuff.

As the leader of a fire team, Russell's issue weapon was a triple-barreled IW-3a – his Iwo, as all Infantry Weapons were affectionately called in the Corps. He checked the gun – his gun, there were many like it, but this one was his – to make sure it was the one he'd lovingly maintained and cleaned as if his life depended on it, because it did.

The IW-3a fired 4mm explosive bullets from a 50-round magazine, 15mm grenades from a 10-round tube, and a single-shot 20mm self-propelled projectile that came in a variety of flavors. Ordinary grunts made do with an IW-3 that only fired the 4- and 15mm stuff. Gonzaga was the fire team gunner; he got a ALS-43 burp-gun with more firepower than the rest of the team combined. Russell was happy enough with his Iwo, though. He went over the gun as if greeting an old friend.

Ever since they'd arrived to Jasper-Five, Marines not on guard or maintenance duty had been ordered to leave all their weapons – even their personal ones – at the armory. The order had come from the ambassador himself, relayed through the Regional Security Officer; Lieutenant Murdock had no choice but to go along. After Murdock got run over by a car, Gunny Obregon had done the same, even when things started heating up during the last few days. Russell had availed himself of a new set of personal hardware – a switchblade, a revolver and a holdout two-shot derringer, both .41 caliber, all of Ruddy manufacture – soon enough, but he'd much rather have some good American gear at hand instead. He was worried he might need it.

There was a lot to worry about. Third Platoon shouldn't be here, out of contact with Charlie Company and the rest of the battalion some fucking Rat had broken up to save a buck or two. A weapons platoon wasn't mean to operate by itself. The pogues in charge had stuck them in an embassy, enough grunts to cause trouble but not enough to defend shit, and if anything happened he and the rest of the unit would be expected to do the impossible. The platoon wasn't in bad shape – even the boots that had come along for the trip had gotten a clue, thanks to the Gunny's constant training – but if it was expected to protect the Enclave by itself, they were fucked.

He'd been in the shit often enough to tell when he was about to take another dip in the brown stuff.

Of course, he didn't expect it to happen quite so soon.

His first hint that something was going on was a distant *crump* sound he recognized immediately. That was an explosion: either one of the fires had lit up something volatile, or someone had detonated some military-grade ordnance. A second one followed mere seconds later. Ordnance it was; you rarely got explosions that closely together unless someone was making them happen.

Obregon stepped away from the armory and started talking into his imp. Russell couldn't overhear the conversation – the NCO had engaged his privacy filter – but his furious arm gestures made it clear he was having a violent argument with someone. Probably some Embassy puke.

The Gunny was getting the take from the swarm of micro-drones flying over the city, so he knew exactly what was going on out there. Obregon didn't get excited easily, so whatever was happening wasn't good.

"What's the deal, Russet?" Gonzaga asked him; the short private had his ALS-43 Automatic Launch System slung over his shoulder; the big gun was almost as tall as he was, which made him look slightly ridiculous, but Russell knew some very lethal things came in stupid-looking packages.

"We'll find out soon enough, Gonzo," he said. "But don't stray too far from the armory, because I think…"

"Gun Squads One and Two!" Gunny Obregon shouted on the priority channel. "Grab a combat load! We've got to extricate civilian and military personnel under attack. We're rolling hot in five! Martin, you're in charge till I get back. Organize a perimeter defense and break out the mortars, on my authority. The Ruddies have gone wild."

"I knew it," Russell muttered as he and the rest the Guns Section squads followed Obregon's orders and geared themselves up for the real thing. For combat.

Fifteen of them, without proper vehicles, out in the big city, which last time he'd checked held some two million ETs.

He didn't need another oak leaf cluster, but life sure as fuck was doing its damnedest to get him one.

* * *

The initial flash was warning enough. Fromm slunk down on the passenger seat before the lead car's gas tank exploded. The shockwave from the ensuing conflagration washed over the embassy's vehicle. The oversized four-wheeler shook but wasn't flipped over; no hot air – or flames – filled the inside of the car, so its windshield had held.

"They are coming," Locquar said from the driver's seat.

The ambush had hit the convoy at an intersection, where a small road cut across the main street they'd been using. The rocketeer must have fired from the rooftop of one of the three- and four-story buildings lining both sides of the street.

Dozens of armed Ruddies were coming at them from both sides of the smaller street and from a plaza next to the tail end of the motorcade. Fromm saw them all clearly, thanks to the micro-drones following the convoy from a hundred feet up, recording everything with their artificial eyes. The crowd had erupted from several houses where they'd been hiding until just now. They were armed mostly with spears and swords, but a couple of the black-tunic wearers had rifles with straight box magazines in front of their triggers. Standard-issue Kirosha Army assault weapons, firing .29-caliber chemically-propelled slugs from a twenty-round magazine, capable of selective fire.

The last car in the convoy had eaten another rocket; its smoldering remains blocked most of the right lane of the road.

"Go!" he yelled at Locquar. Standing still meant death. Moving might not save them, depending on how fast the rocket team could reload and fire, but it provided their only chance.

The Ruddy driver reacted well enough. Tires squealed on the pavement as he accelerated; they spun in place for a brief instant before regaining traction and propelling the car forward even as one of the lead attackers brought his rifle to bear.

Fromm fired first, holding his weapon in a two-handed Weaver

42

grip.

The Colt Plasma Projectile Weapon spat a 3mm steel-sheathed bullet that left a neat hole in the side windshield on its way out. It hit the Ruddy rifleman a little high and to the left from his center of mass. On impact – the hit on the windshield had occurred before its warhead was armed – the tiny round detonated, unleashing a jet of pure plasma, half an inch wide and eight inches long. Designed to defeat body armor or damage light military vehicles, the explosive bullet's effects on mere flesh and bone were devastating. The unfired rifle went spinning off into the air, its wielder's torn-up arm and a piece of shoulder still holding on to it. The explosion that dismembered the rifleman consisted mostly of steam from his own vaporized bodily fluids. ETs on each side of the target recoiled as bits of bone shrapnel and burning steam hit them, along with an overpressure wave powerful enough to rock them on their feet.

Fromm fired six more times, squeezing the trigger as soon as the targeting dot slid over another target. He missed twice – firing from a moving platform wasn't easy even with neural implant targeting – but blew four more Ruddies to Kingdom come, turning them into miniature bombs that wounded several others. The car kept going. It shuddered but did not stop when Locquar hit a couple of attackers and sent their bodies caroming over the vehicle. On the other side of the passenger's seat, McClintock was shooting as well; the screech of her beamer was noticeable even alongside the supersonic cracks of Fromm's weapon.

Their car sped past the burning wreck of the lead vehicle and ran clear of the charging mob. Fromm twisted in the back seat to see what was going on behind them. The two Vehelian limos were following closely, knocking down Ruddies and running them over even as swords and spears glanced off their sides. The bus followed in their wake. A couple of firearm-wielding Eets raked the vehicles as they went by, but they were firing from the hip, spray-and-pray style, and Fromm didn't think they hit anybody. He couldn't see the van anywhere. Nothing he could do about that, except hope they all made it through the ambush point before the rocket launcher teams…

A puff of smoke erupted from the top of the second limo's roof.

… reloaded.

The explosion didn't look like much, but Fromm knew what it meant even before the limo swerved off course and drifted lazily to a stop. The missile had crashed through the top of the vehicle and shredded everyone inside. Only someone in sealed combat armor could have survived, and he doubted armor was part of Vehelian diplomatic dress code. The bus behind the doomed Oval car didn't slow down, clipping the stopped vehicle and sending it off on a spin. The horde of Ruddies giving chase fell upon the stopped limo like lions tackling the slowest member of a fleeing herd.

McClintock looked at him, a question in her eyes. He shook his head. There was nothing they could do for the passengers of the doomed vehicle. The only consolation was that the mob tearing into the vehicle would only find corpses to desecrate. She bit her lip and checked the charge levels on her beamer. The energy weapons were as lethal as the plasma rounds his gun fired, but their effective range was measured in feet rather than yards, and their batteries only held enough power for five to seven shots, depending on the model. The Embassy spook changed battery packs. Fromm replaced his gun's magazine with a fresh one. He'd only brought a spare magazine, never thinking he'd need more than forty rounds. Now he was down to thirty-three.

"Are we there yet?" he said, deadpan.

McClintock chuckled. "I will turn this car right around." She went on in a sober tone: "Half a mile as the crow flies. A bit more on the road, but it's a fairly straight shot there, unless…"

The road they were on had taken them over a slight rise on the ground. When they reached the top of the shallow hill, they saw the massed crowd it had hidden.

Several local vehicles, powered and animal-drawn, had been dragged across the street, blocking it.

"Quiet spot my ass," Fromm grumbled.

The roar of the Ruddy mob drowned out his words.

* * *

"Where the fuck did they come from?" Gunnery Sergeant Miguel Obregon said as his imp fed him data from the overhead micro-drones. There was plenty of news, and all of it was bad.

One thing was clear: the Ruddies knew the Americans had them under aerial observation. They had come into the city in small groups and gathered indoors, out of sight until they'd used gongs and drums to let everyone know it was time to come out and play. A proper Intelligence section would probably have noticed the Ruddies' movement patterns and figured out they were massing for an attack, but Third Platoon didn't have an

Intelligence section, just a pack of attached Navy bubbleheads, each trying to do the job of three or four people. Neither did it have organic vehicles, aerial support other than their micro-drones, or much of anything else. They'd been tossed into this miserable shithole with a whole lot of fuck-all.

It didn't matter. One of their own, and a bunch of civvies, were out there, surrounded by an estimated five thousand bloodthirsty Ruddies, and it was Obregon's job to go out there and extricate them by any means necessary.

Improvising while being ass-deep in alligators was part of the job. Obregon knew that the Dark God Murphy was always waiting in the wings, ready to strike. He'd taken precautions against that possibility, aided and abetted by Lieutenant Murdock, God rest his soul. Even so, the only reason this sortie into hostile territory wasn't a forlorn hope was the fact that his unit had been Charlie Company's weapons platoon, and that the same whimsical Rats who had sent them to this God-forsaken mudball had also sent all their equipment along. As soon as Obregon got his feet under him and realized they needed a mobile element in case the shit hit the fan, he and the other NCOs had gone to work, acquiring several native vehicles by means fair and foul and spending their own time and money to turn them into improvised infantry fighting vehicles.

The traditional term for such makeshifts was 'technicals.' Obregon had been raised in a dirt-poor colony world where you had to build most of the stuff you wanted, simply because the hard currency you'd need to buy it wasn't available, and the few fabbers on site had more important things to produce than consumer goods. Between his hard-earned skills, the info the imps helpfully provided, and a lot of sweat and the liberal application of super-duct tape, he and his volunteers had assembled something better than a typical fleet of technicals.

A mental command opened the rolling door to their improvised vehicle depot as he and Sergeant Muller approached it. Inside awaited the fruit of their labors. The three monstrosities had started their lives as a cargo van, a ten-ton truck and a demilitarized Ruddy version of the venerable Humvee. Form followed function, and the native-designed vehicles had been roughly similar in appearance and capabilities to their equivalents from Earth's 20th century. Had been.

Force field generators had been cannibalized from the platoon's area defense gear and welded onto every possible surface on the three vehicles. The devices used Starfarer Tech to bend space-time itself, generating invisible planes of force capable of deflecting all kinds of energies from one direction while allowing their users to shoot from the opposite side. Never mind how – according to Woogle, human brains couldn't understand the physics behind the force fields; most Eets didn't, either. Their coverage wasn't perfect – the vehicles' tires and parts of their undercarriages were still hideously vulnerable to mines and IEDs – but they would stop a direct hit from the 93mm Ruddy artillery pieces that did triple-duty as general bombardment, anti-aircraft and anti-tank weapons. At least, they would do so as long as their improvised batteries could supply energy to the fields. His imp's best guess was that three or four hits of that magnitude would deplete the force fields' power packs, at which point the technicals would turn back into pumpkins, and just as easy to smash. Until then, though, they'd be proof against most things.

They hadn't just added defenses to the truck, of course. Obregon and his team of volunteer mechanics had taken a sizable fraction of the heavy weapons in the platoon's Table of Organization and Equipment and attached them to diverse parts of their vehicles. ALS-43s were the bastard plasma-spitting children of the pre-Contact M240 machinegun and the Mk 19 automatic grenade launcher; he'd gotten at least one of them mounted on every vehicle. His command van had a ALS-43 and two 20mm self-propelled missile launchers, which gave the unit – they'd named it Rover Force – more firepower than a local tank company. He had no desire to get into a running battle with the local ETs, but if he was forced into one he intended to win it.

Obregon all but leaped into the driver's compartment of Rover Two. He turned the primitive ignition system's switch, and the vehicle roared into life. He did a status check: most everything was green, and the systems highlighted with blinking yellow lights would do, for a while.

"Y'all fucked with the wrong people," the Marine growled as he gunned the engine.

Four

Year 163 AFC, D Minus Ten

They were probably screwed, but it wouldn't be because they hadn't tried everything they could think of.

"There," Heather said, her imp marking the building she'd selected as Locquar swerved to a stop, less than a hundred yards from the barricade. Nobody had shot at them yet, but that was bound to change.

The structure she'd led them to was an auto garage situated at the top of the hill. The locals' propensity to steal anything that wasn't nailed down meant the lot was surrounded by a sturdy wall, concrete blocks with razor wire strung on top, its main entrance sealed off by a sliding metal gate.

"We can make our stand inside until the authorities drive off the rioters," she said.

"Fine," Fromm said. He didn't sound terribly convinced, but time was short and he clearly knew that a bad plan of action executed now was better than a perfect plan contrived after it was too late. "Get everyone inside. I'll cover you."

"Locquar, help him," she said as they left the car. The Vehelian limo began to go around it, then stopped when its driver saw the barricade and mob waiting down the road. Behind them, the bus also came to a stop. A glance told her the mob giving chase behind them wasn't very far away, and it'd been reinforced by more militant society warriors and regular civilians. Her imp could have given her a good estimate of the number of aliens rushing towards them, but she didn't really want to know. More than enough, she was sure.

"We're going to fort up over there," she announced through the imp, which overlay a virtual arrow all humans and Vehelians would see through their own implants.

Heather headed towards the garage's entrance. There was an intercom by the metal gate but she was sure the people inside weren't going to be hospitable. Instead of trying to communicate with them, she placed a hand over the gate. Its lock was electronic, a new model using imported Starfarer tech, the kind of cheap trinket any fabber could produce for pennies' worth of raw materials and then sell at a nice profit to primitive worlds. Her imp's special apps took over the lock's crude systems, and the gate started rolling open. Off to her right, the captain's blaster coughed once, followed by a burst from the submachinegun Locquar kept under the driver's seat. Things were getting lively already, and there was no time to lose.

She rushed inside as soon as enough of a gap opened up. There were two Kirosha on the courtyard, a man in grease-stained coveralls who'd been working on a sporty-looking two-door car, and an older male in the informal tunic, pointy hat and pantaloons of one of Kirosha's small but growing entrepreneurial middle class. They were both unarmed, which was unsurprising, since city ordinances made possession of firearms of any kind a crime punishable by mutilation, torture or death, sometimes all of the above.

"You are not welcome here!" the shop owner shouted at her, his head shaking up and down in the Kirosha negative gesture.

"Sodomizing foreign devils!" the mechanic said, rummaging through his toolbox.

He was probably looking for something hefty enough to batter someone's brains out. Heather didn't give him a chance to try; a warning shot aimed at the ground between the mechanic's feet sent him scrambling away as dirt flew from the point of impact, some of it hot enough to sting wherever it touched his skin.

"Now you sodomizing listen to me!" she told them in flawless Kirosha with enough of a high-class accent to command respect. The sight of the Star-Devil-filled bus and limo rolling through the gate added to the intimidation factor. "Stay out of the way, and you won't be hurt. We need to remain here until the authorities disperse the riot. You will be compensated for any damages, and receive a fitting reward for your hospitality. Do you understand?"

Both Kirosha squatted down in submission.

"Yes, Blessed Star Devil," the owner said. "The Final Blow Society will kill us all, but perhaps my family will be compensated for my sacrifice, yes?"

Outside, a flurry of blaster and slug-thrower fire seemed to confirm the Kirosha's pessimism.

* * *

At first, the Ruddies at the barricade just stood there and watched them. Fromm accepted the momentary truce with gratitude. If the ETs charged before they could get behind cover, he and every human and Oval in the convoy were dead.

The quiet only lasted a few seconds. One of the leaders, a big Ruddy with a fluttering banner strapped to his back, stepped in front of the barricade and started haranguing the troops, who cheered him on.

Fromm turned to Locquar. "Will shooting him help or hurt?"

"Can't hurt," the friendly said with a shrug.

"Okay."

The plasma discharge set the banner on fire as it burned a hole big enough to fit a grapefruit into the leader's torso and sent his head flying up like a popped cork. The crowd fell silent at the sudden and gruesome death, and Locquar added a three-round burst into the mix, riddling another banner-man. The driver shouted something at the rioters. Fromm hoped it was something meant to scare them into withdrawing.

The mob swarmed over the barricade, screeching like a gaggle of angry human schoolgirls.

Well, that didn't work, Fromm thought as he fired the remaining nineteen rounds in his Colt, pivoting to the right to spread the joy over a wide front. The rioters were packed so tightly together that each round injured or killed at least two or three extra targets. Locquar followed suit with his submachinegun, and between the two of them they filled the street with limp and writhing bodies. Fromm ducked behind cover and switched the empty magazine with the partially-full one that was all he had left. Fourteen rounds and a target-rich environment added up to a really bad day.

The Embassy Rat had gotten the compound's gate open and the bus and limo were already inside. Good. There would be no time to move their car, though. He and Locquar scrambled towards the gate as the Ruddy mob made its way past the bodies they'd dropped. The sliding metal door was already closing; he made it through with a couple seconds to spare.

Now that he was behind cover he had time to answer the phone.

One of the problems of modern communications was that people kept trying to talk to you while you were too busy staying alive to talk back. Imps helped by answering some calls themselves. The faux-AI systems learned a number of preset responses by watching their owners over time. Some things required a personal touch, however.

The imp downloaded several voice messages directly into Fromm's memory, a highly-uncomfortable process used only for emergencies. Suddenly remembering things you hadn't known a moment before could induce several forms of mental trauma.

Suddenly remembering some very bad news was no fun,

trauma or no trauma.

Gunnery Sergeant Obregon was mounting an impromptu rescue and the Embassy was trying to contact the Kirosha authorities to lend a hand. Problem was, the locals weren't answering the phone and the Embassy remfies were dithering instead of authorizing the rescue mission. That kind of SNAFU wouldn't be solved before the mob outside stormed the compound and slaughtered everyone inside.

"Gunny, I authorize the rescue operation," he sent out; his imp added all the requisite legalese that would turn the sentence into a formal command and would place all responsibility and blame squarely on Fromm's shoulders. It wouldn't be the first time he'd pissed off assorted officers and gentlemen. The last time, he'd ended up assigned to Jasper-Five, and it clearly couldn't get much worse than that.

The Embassy woman was busy organizing the passengers as they disembarked from the bus. The Ovals from the surviving limo included three civvies in colorful robes of office, good only for catching rounds that might hit somebody useful, and a driver/bodyguard armed with a short-barreled combat laser, the kind of weapon the US still couldn't afford to manufacture in quantity. The Oval and his ray-gun would come in handy.

About two-thirds of the human passengers had some kind of weapon. Only about half the Rats, of course – *corp-o-RAT, bureau-cRAT, city-RAT*; the immortal song's lyrics flashed through his mind – but most of the passengers were miners or machinery operators, the kind of men and women who felt naked without something that could cut, bludgeon or shoot. McClintock directed the ones with handguns to take cover behind the vehicles scattered around the garage, where they could pick off anyone trying to climb over the razor-wire on top of the walls. For a Rat or even a spook, she was turning out to have the makings of a damn good sergeant.

He looked around, studying the battleground at hand. The walled enclosure was a rough square, some sixty feet on each side. A cinderblock wall surrounded the perimeter, topped with the Ruddy version of concertina wire. Good enough to stop bullets and keep the rabble out, for a little while at least, although it wouldn't prevent the mob from tossing things over it, anything from spears to hand grenades or Molotov cocktails. There were two buildings inside the perimeter, the larger one in the center; the other was a supply shack near one of the walls. The bigger structure was two stories tall, a box with a peaked roof. The upper level had a window overlooking the street.

Fromm had his imp contact the Vehelian bodyguard, who promptly walked over to him. Ovals looked like what you'd get if you shaved a bear, replaced its head with an ostrich egg, and painted a face on its surface. The bodyguard was a particularly large specimen, a good seven feet tall and almost as wide; hopefully he'd be able to fit inside the building.

"Follow me!" he sent out; the implant translated the order a couple of seconds later.

"I will comply, Marine Captain," the ET said in English.

Fromm turned to the Ruddy driver. "Locquar, assist your boss. We're seizing the high ground."

The Kirosha tilted his head sideways, his version of nodding yes. Fromm left him to it and headed for the main building, gun ready. The front door was open; Fromm took a quick peek inside. He felt horribly exposed – fucking naked – doing a building entry evolution without backup other than an ET he hadn't worked with before, and without grenades to clear the way. He went in, fully expecting to get shot.

Nobody shot at him. The room had a glass counter with several auto parts on display, a couple of armchairs in a reception area, and a statue of a naked fat Ruddy riding some sort of dragon. There were no signs of life. He had to kick open a couple of doors before he found one leading to a set of stairs going up. The Oval behind him had to squeeze past a couple of tight spots, but was able to keep up with him.

Meanwhile, the enemy had arrived. He could hear them screaming all around the compound. Someone was beating on the metal gate. They'd better get a move on or they'd be overrun.

A dash up the stairs led them to a narrow corridor and two closed doors. Fromm heard a fusillade of gunshots and beamer discharges, which increased his sense of urgency. He kicked down another door and found the window he'd seen from outside.

Two cowering Ruddies were inside the room, hiding behind a desk. He watched them over the barrel of his Colt, his imp painting targeting carats over their centers of mass. An old male and a young female, looking absurdly cute with their oversized eyes and narrow chins. Seemingly unarmed.

"Go!" he shouted at them in American, gesturing with his head for them to get out. They got the idea and scrammed. Leaving two potential hostiles loose behind him was not a great idea, but there was no time to do anything other than shoot them dead or let them go, and he needed to save his last fourteen rounds for confirmed hostiles. At least, that was what he told himself as he and the Oval headed for the window.

The view was terrible.

The street outside was jammed with ETs. At the moment, most of them were beating ineffectually at the walls and gates. One body was draped over the razor wire on top of a wall, leaking blood and pureed tissues from a through-and-through wound. That death wouldn't deter them for long, however.

The Oval knew what to do. "Do I kill them now?" he asked.

"Yeah."

The laser weapon usually fired micro-second pulses, each packing about half as much energy as a blaster round, with a cyclic rate of six hundred pulses a minute. Against the massed crowd, the ET switched to a continuous beam setting, and swung the long line of coherent light like a giant industrial cutter, tilting the weapon so the energy stream cleared the wall and slashed into the rioters at a shallow angle.

The Ruddies protected by their proximity to the wall were unharmed as the beam passed over their heads. Those further back were sliced in two by the one-millimeter coherent-light weapon. The laser went through a hundred feet of cloth, flesh and bone like piano wire driven into a block of soft cheese. The beam wasn't hot enough to cauterize the wounds, so Ruddy blood spurted freely from severed limbs and torsos as dozens bodies fell in two pieces; variations in biochemistry gave the fluids that spattered everywhere an orange coloration and a greasy quality. The ones closest to the laser had the tops of their heads loped off; the ones further out, their necks or faces. Dozens of rioters were bisected at the chest or waist, some of them still alive as their upper torsos slid off the convulsing lower halves of their bodies. As the beam angled down, it severed hips, thighs, knees.

Three seconds. A hundred dead. Another hundred maimed and dying.

Fromm watched the massacre without reacting; he might or might not feel something later, but at the moment all he cared about was the tactical situation. The untouched members of the mob – eight-tenths of them or more – recoiled from the horror show the laser had created. A few leaders tried to rally them, noticeable by the wood and paper banners propped up behind their backs.

Fromm picked them off one by one.

The little rounds of his pistol had an effective range of a hundred and fifty yards, and his imp made aiming ridiculously easy, estimating range, windage and bullet trajectory in the time it took Fromm to level his weapon, and painting a red dot on the estimated landing point of his shot. *Crack*, and a sword-wielding warrior's head vanished in a cloud of plasma and vaporized brain matter, his audience screaming as pieces of his skull tore into them. *Crack*, and a woman who'd clambered over the abandoned car bent sideways as her hip bone exploded. *Crack. Crack. Crack.* Five shots, five dead leaders.

"Do it again?" the Oval asked Fromm. He'd inserted a fresh power pack into the magazine well in the pistol grip of his laser, and was ready to cut down another two hundred Ruddies.

"Wait a bit," Fromm said. Maybe the stupid bastards would decide to run and live to fight another day. Maybe...

He didn't hear the rocket's detonation as it hit the second-story wall, but he sure as hell felt it.

* * *

The weight of all the extra equipment strained the van's suspension something fierce, making Obregon's seat bounce uncomfortably, but that didn't bother him. It kind of reminded him of life in Jazmin-Two, of driving to the town's general store in his Pappy's barely-functional jalopy, a hydrogen-burner made of equal parts rust and baling wire.

What bothered him was seeing the gate leading out of the embassy's compound was still closed. And that the assholes manning said gate – the *Marine* assholes manning said gate – were waving at him to stop.

"Open up!" he sent through his imp.

"We've got orders to keep all combat forces inside the compound," replied Staff Sergeant Amherst, the former commander of the Embassy Security Group. Amherst was an officious asshole who'd long forgotten what it meant to in the Corps, but Obregon couldn't believe he was pulling this shit. "You need to deploy to protect the Embassy, Gunny."

Obregon's three-vehicle formation – Rovers One through Three – was coming up to the gate and he had to make a decision. The take from the micro-drones was streaming on his field of vision's right quadrant, and he could see that the walled property the Americans had holed up in was being hit with rocket and small arms fire, not to mention a couple thousand ETs with swords trying to get over the fence. The skipper was too busy fighting for his life to deal with this bullshit.

"Move it or lose it," he said.

"Say again, Gunnery Sergeant?"

"Open the gate or we're busting it open. Last chance."

"You don't have the balls," the asshole said, just about the worst thing he could have uttered.

"Light it up," Obregon told Corporal Hendrickson. The gunner was on the improvised cupola they'd put on the van's roof, manning the ALS-43 auto-launcher.

"Copy that," Hendrickson said without hesitation. The ALS-43 could fire a variety of 15mm projectiles at a rate of three hundred rounds a minute. To blow the gate open, Hendrickson fired a three-round burst of anti-armor plasma rounds. The shaped-charge explosions tore the gate apart without doing much damage to the guardhouse on its left side.

'Much damage' is a relative term, though. The structure wasn't destroyed outright, but it did catch fire. Amherst and the other sorry bastard inside got a little bit scorched, given that they were wearing dress blues and no armor. They'd live, though, and the gate could be fixed in under an hour, given all the fabbers the Embassy had. No harm done.

There would be consequences, of course, but he didn't give a shit. He had a job to do.

* * *

"We're gonna get in trouble, aren't we?" Private First Class Hiram 'Nacle' Hamblin asked as their car drove past what was left of the guardhouse.

"Fuck 'em if they can't take a joke," Russell said. "Gotta save the new skipper, don't we? Those assholes were acting against orders."

"But the ambassador...?"

"Fuck the ambassador. He ain't in the chain of command. He gotta tell the RSO and the RSO gotta tell the skipper, and then he tells the NCOs, and they tell us what the fuck to do."

Nacle – short for Tabernacle – shrugged, still clearly uncomfortable. He was good people, but also a Mormon, and they mostly didn't like coloring outside the lines, although Russell had met several wild and woolly exceptions. He'd calm down when they got to the hostiles. Nacle didn't have any problems shooting ETs. None of them did. Travel the galaxy, meet colorful aliens, and blow the shit out of them. That was the name of the game.

Rover One was on the ass end of the formation as it drove

through the streets of the Foreigners' Enclave, heading for the curtain wall surrounding the area and yet another gate, a much bigger one, manned by Ruddy Royal Guardsmen. Ruddies who were probably going to object to their going out there and killing a bunch of their friends and neighbors. Things might get hairy in a minute.

The walls around the Enclave were manned by a battalion of Guardsmen. They wore light blue and pink uniforms – no accounting for ET tastes – but although their equipment was all local-made and out of date, it included artillery and even a tank platoon. Ruddy tanks were no great shakes, about as good as an up-gunned Sherman from two hundred-plus years ago on Earth, but their 79mm main guns were no joke. Russell wasn't sure the shields they'd mounted on their technicals would take more than a few HEAT rounds from one of those. Even if they did, his Hummer-like car would probably end up flipping end over end just from the shockwave. Which would suck, since the fucking thing was open-topped and body armor wasn't going to help for shit if you landed on your head with five thousand pounds on top of you.

What the fuck you gonna do, he told himself.

They drove past the Wyrm Embassy, which the ETs had built for themselves rather than rent out some Ruddy houses like the Americans had, and which looked like someone had melted a bunch of different kinds of scrap metal and poured them over a giant sea shell. The Wyrms were on lockdown; Russell could see the tell-tale soap-bubble shimmer that meant their shields were up. Russell didn't care for the scaly bastards; they were biologically related to the Snakes, the assholes who bombed the shit out of Earth during First Contact. Still, the Wyrms had always respected the US and were sort of friendly. If the Royal Ruddies got shitty, the Wyrms would lend the Americans a hand instead of piling on. So would the Ovals, especially since they had people out there too.

The main gate to the Foreigners' Enclave stood dead ahead, surrounded by sixty-foot walls and four towers with the pointy-hat roofs Ruddies loved to put on everything they built. The Enclave had once been a fortress before cannon made their walls obsolete. Russell had gone through the gate almost a hundred times during his deployment on Jasper-Five, mostly on his way to and from one of the discreet whorehouses they had downtown. Ruddy women weren't exactly built like Americans, but all the important parts fit well enough to get the job done, although you had to watch out for their bristle-backs if you were into doggie-style. It had been a while since he'd gotten his dick wet. If he didn't get killed, and if the fucking curfew was lifted, he'd have to do something about that.

"Rover One, Rover Three, hang back," Gunny Obregon said. "I'm gonna try to talk us through the gate. Get ready to start blasting on my command, or if the Ruddies get frisky."

"Fuck," Russell said, driving off to one side, some hundred feet away from the gate. Traffic was light – only complete morons would choose to venture into a riot in progress – so he had a nice view of about a hundred Ruddies in Royal Guard uniforms milling around the gate, and a couple hundred more on the battlements atop the walls. No heavy weapons he could see, but he knew the Guard had plenty of portable rocket launchers, and those mothers packed a hefty punch. More than enough to overload his personal force fields with a direct hit; enough of them would do for the slapped-on shields on their Rovers, too. It would suck if they had to fight their way through.

They had people out there, though. You didn't abandon your own. That shit had been true when Marines had deployed out of wooden ships, or when breaking out of Frozen Chosin, long before they'd added the word Warp to the Corps' name. Russell had forgotten most of the useless crap they'd tried to teach him at boot camp, but the history lessons had sunk in.

The two massive iron-bound doors at the gate were wide open, which was about the only piece of good news so far. Rover Two headed towards it and the troops standing guard in front of it. None of the Ruddies leveled their assault rifles in its direction, but they were holding them at port arms, so that could change in a hurry. If the shit hit the fan, Gonzaga and his ALS-43 would unleash hell on the Ruddies on the ground floor while Rocky on Rover Three raked the battlements above and Nacle and Conroy dropped 15 and 20mm death on them. That should suppress them well enough for the three technicals to roll out without taking too much fire. Should. If Russell had a buck for every time things didn't turn out the way they should, he'd be sitting pretty.

That left the small problem of what would be waiting for them when they got back. The Ruddies would have plenty of time to warm up their tanks and assemble their arty by then, and they might be pissed off enough to use them.

The whole situation was weird. Whatever happened today, the fleet would show up sooner or later, and every ET involved in shooting Americans would end up dead. The city might even eat a bloomie if things got bad enough. Americans frowned on using city-busters but were willing to make exceptions, as the Snakes had found out. The Ruddies would have to be crazy to get in the way of a rescue. Problem was, people didn't have to make sense, be they alien or American.

Russell decided to let leave the big questions to the assholes in charge and concentrated on marking targets for his IW-3a with his imp; he could drive with one hand and fire his Iwo's missile launcher with the other. There was a Ruddy officer off to one side riding a fucking horse – the Ruddy version looked more like a skinned deer than a horse – who was begging for a 20mm frag round, and Russell would be happy to oblige him.

Obregon's voice came on again. "Rovers, we're clear. Proceed."

The Rovers got moving. Russell's fire team kept an eye out in case the Ruddies were playing games, but they rolled without incident past the guards, through the thick walls surrounding the gate, and out into the open. Other than the fires still burning out in the distance, the only sign of trouble was a much nearer mess of smoke less than a klick away.

"Here we go," Russell muttered as Rover One drove towards their date with the Ruddies.

Five

Year 163 AFC, D Minus Ten

Heather McClintock hated violence. Shots fired meant she'd failed at her job, which was to get things done without the enemy's knowledge. And she had a dim view of war, which she considered a mostly irrational activity. Both sides in a conflict entered it with the expectation they would win, and at least one of them was dead wrong; often everyone involved was.

Case in point: the Kirosha mob outside had to know the most they could accomplish today would be to commit a few dozen murders, and that the consequences would be dire. The implants inside their victims' skulls would record the identities of their attackers, and the US government would demand no less than death for anyone involved. Given the Kirosha penchant for judicial torture, a quick death would be the best outcome for the rioters.

The hundreds of screaming aliens outside didn't seem to care for the facts, though.

Half a dozen of them had managed to make it to the top of the walls and tried to throw rugs or other heavy chunks of fabric over the razor wire barrier on top. Heather had shot two of them herself: one head shot, one center of mass hit. Each beamer shot sent a stream of charged particles towards the target that packed about as much punch as a twelve-gauge shotgun; a kinetic baffle made it effectively recoilless. The weapon had shitty range but was very effective against unarmored opponents, provided you could shoot straight, which she did.

She loathed violence, but she'd discovered she was distressingly good at it.

The others had died at the hands of her fellow humans, several of whom had been armed with an assortment of weapons ranging from beamers like her own to an ancient Colt 1911 slug-thrower. All the US citizens had gone through their four-year Obligatory Service Term, which included going through Basic and learning how to shoot. A dozen handguns were not going to stop the mob outside for long, but they would help.

The Vehelian bodyguard on the second floor helped a lot more. His laser slaughtered dozens of rioters, and the survivors were too stunned at the massacre to do anything for several seconds. Heather used the lull in the action to download a status report straight into her brain, a definitely unhealthy way to access information, but needs must when the devil drives.

She shuddered at the sudden influx of knowledge.

As soon as news of the attack broke – a matter of seconds, given the small swarm of micro-drones watching the city – the Embassy had contacted the Kirosha City Prefect to ask for help. The official had refused to accept the call; a secretary claimed he was indisposed. Heather was sure he'd get well soon, but by then the Americans and Vehelians trapped in their makeshift fort would be beyond help. Calls to other ministers had also been met with lies and avoidance; so had an attempt to reach the Queen herself. The Kirosha authorities were leaving them out in the cold.

There would be consequences for this. At least six people were already dead, not to mention the seven or eight passengers in the missing van. And the O-Vehel Envoy had been in the destroyed limo. You didn't kill an emissary of the Commonwealth without risking massive retaliation. If the US did not avenge the Envoy's death, the O-Vehel might risk war and send a fleet to Jasper-Five to settle the score themselves.

Heather barely had time to assimilate the info dump when something flashed above her, leaving a contrail behind; an instant later, an explosion shook the main building of the auto garage. A piece of glass flew less than an inch past her head and struck the ground. Other debris pelted her and everyone else in the courtyard.

The rocketeers were back in action, and they had taken out the Marine and the Vehelian.

She needed to get to the laser, if it was still operable, and try to take out the rocket launcher team, or the next hit might knock down the gate and let the murderous hordes pour into the compound. The screams outside turned into triumphant roars when the rocket hit, and rioters started trying to get over the wall yet again.

"Hold them off!" she shouted unnecessarily and rushed to the building.

The lights were out, and smoke filled ground floor. She found the stairs in the dark, and ran up. Someone was screaming, the high-pitched sounds almost certainly coming from a Kirosha. One of the garage's employees or its owner, probably, and either way irrelevant to the situation at hand.

He found the bleeding forms of her travel companions on the second floor. The rocket-propelled warhead had blasted a hole in one wall and filled the room with shrapnel. The Vehelian had been closest to the blast, and his body had shielded Fromm; the alien was dying, his injuries too severe for even Starfarer tech to save him.

Fromm was breathing, and his wounds appeared to be superficial, not that she had time to do anything about them if they weren't. She desperately searched through the wreckage, praying the Vehelian's weapon hadn't been destroyed.

There! The explosion had flung the laser against the other side of the room, but a quick look showed her it had only sustained a few scratches. The weapon was ID-locked, though; it would only work for authorized users with the proper biometric signatures, which a human State Department employee certainly didn't have.

Fortunately, Heather wasn't just a State Department employee, and her imp wasn't an ordinary implant. She used it to hack into the weapon's security system. By the time Heather made it to the window, the laser's sights were slaved to her implants and she could use them to track the rocket team. Or teams, she mused, expecting a second rocket to blow her into bloody rags at any second.

The rocket team was on the roof of the building across the street. One man wore the black tunic of the Final Blow Society, but the other was in the khaki uniform of a Kirosha Army regular. Both were busily reloading the launcher. The specs on the Kirosha RPG Mk III claimed a trained team could reload it in fifteen seconds. This team was still struggling with the warhead, some thirty seconds later. They clearly hadn't been properly trained.

They were never going to get any better, either.

She'd only used lasers during a weapon familiarization course back at the Farm – lasers were too expensive to see much use in the USA – but the weapons were idiot proof. Instead of a continuous beam, she fired a pulse burst, ten micro-second discharges, each powerful enough to penetrate several inches of hardened steel plate.

The rocketeer had finally reloaded and was trying to sight the weapon when the laser burst exploded his mid-section. Dying reflex squeezed the RPG's trigger as the man toppled backwards, sending the missile flying towards the sky as the launcher's back blast incinerated him and his partner. Heather shifted aim to the still screaming, burning figure of the loader and put him out of his misery.

Bullets hit the building as gunshots cracked outside. Lots of shots. Heather ducked under the window. The initial group of ambushers only had a handful of rifles; the volume of fire hitting the compound was several times greater.

Heather lifted the laser over the window, using its sights to see what was going on without exposing herself. Sure enough, a formation of Kirosha soldiers had joined the fray – in support of the rioters. They weren't Royal Guardsmen; their khaki uniforms, identical to the one worn by the now-dead rocketeer on the roof, marked them as Army men; several units were on station near the capital. Some of them – about a company's worth, she guessed at a glance – had decided to join the rioters, in a complete reversal of everything she'd known about the political situation. The Army – or at least most of its officers – had been under the control of the Modernist faction. The crowd parted before the soldiers as they took the second floor of the garage under fire.

She fired the laser one-handed, held over her head so she could remain behind the wall. Even though the weapon was recoilless and she was using her imp to aim it, the position wasn't ideal for shooting. She still managed to pot a couple of soldiers as they sent a storm of hot lead in her direction. Most shots hit the exterior wall. A couple of them penetrated the cinderblock structure. More rounds went through the window and the hole the rocket had made. Ricochets bounced all around her.

This was not her idea of a good time.

* * *

Fromm woke up to the staccato sound of rapid gunfire.

His first attempt to move from his prone position sent a jolt of agony through his skull. He touched his head and felt wetness running down his right temple and cheek. His medical nanites had clotted the spot where a piece of shrapnel had lacerated his scalp, but not before a few ounces of blood had spurted out. His imp answered his unspoken query, displaying a stick-figure diagram of his body, red highlights marking all the injuries he had sustained in the explosion. Mostly bruises and scratches, except for the scalp wound, a minor concussion, and a piece of masonry that was embedded into his right biceps; the nanites had stopped the bleeding, numbed the area and surrounded the fragment with antiseptic gel, but it would take a corpsman to remove it from his flesh. For the time being, he could use the arm, and that was all that mattered.

He blinked through the pain and took a look around. Heather McClintock was hunched down behind a wall, firing the dead Oval's laser without exposing herself. The Ruddies were returning fire, and they had a lot more rifles in play than before.

Another mental query got him an overview of the situation. A detachment from his not-yet-assumed command was on its way to the compound, but was encountering heavy resistance: more rioters, reinforced by regular army units. He thought about contacting Gunny Obregon, but dismissed the idea; no sense joggling the man's elbow while he was in the middle of a fight.

His first impulse was to try to find his Colt amidst the wreckage and return fire, but he would be more effective after he assessed the situation and figured out a way to deal with it. He flopped onto his stomach and crawled towards a wall for extra cover, ignoring the bullets flying overhead and the occasional bouncers passing even closer to him. He'd either get hit or not.

First things first. He sent a call to the Regional Security Officer at the embassy, who had been trying to reach him since shortly before the Ruddy RPG had knocked him out. A gray-haired man's face appeared in his field of vision. He looked pissed off.

"What's the situation, Captain?" were the RSO's first words.

"We have a bit of a situation here, sir," Fromm said as a ricochet kicked up a little cloud of dust a few inches off his face. "Thirty-three American civilians are surrounded and in imminent danger."

"We're trying to have the proper Kirosha authorities come to your aid."

"Sir, we're taking fire from what appear to be Kirosha military units."

"I see." The RSO checked the drone feeds and mulled things over for a couple of seconds. "All right, do whatever you have to do, Captain. I'll cover your ass from this end." Which was great, but wouldn't matter all that much to Fromm if said ass-covering was posthumous. Fucking Rats.

"Understood. Thank you, sir."

The RSO wasn't a complete asshole, for a fucking Rat, but that wasn't saying much. You had to serve a minimum of six years in the military to get a State Department job, let alone one dealing with security matters, but remfie ways always managed to seep into their heads after a few years of looking at the world from the comforts of an office, where nobody bled and screamed in impossible agony. No matter. Fromm had been given a green light – more or less – and he planned to make the most of it.

He had to make a plan with the assets at hand. He'd been handed a reinforced weapons platoon, with its full TOE. Which meant...

He made another call, this time to the NCO Obregon had left in charge.

Decisively Engaged

Staff Sergeant Martin's chiseled features were marred by a worried expression and funnels of sweat running down his face. "Sir! About the guard house..."

"Never mind that. I need you to deploy the hundred-mike-mikes. Immediately. On my command. Understood?"

Martin nodded, looking relieved now that he had orders to rely upon. "Aye, aye, sir. Deploying 100-millimeter mortars, roger. Soonest, roger."

"Carry on."

Soonest would probably be no less than five minutes. The heavy weapons would be inside armored containers next to the barracks. Now all they had to do was survive for the next five minutes.

Fromm rolled towards the Oval's body. *I'll say a prayer for you later, buddy,* he mentally told the dead ET as he pawed through his robes, looking for weapons and ammo. He found a weapon belt; there was a spare battery for the laser, a ceremonial dagger Oval followers of one of their religions always carried, and a featureless cylinder that he had to Woogle through his imp: it turned out to be a razzle-dazzle grenade. Shiny.

He couldn't arm the damn thing, not without ID codes he didn't have, but he was betting the spook who was firing the dead Oval's laser could. He rolled towards her.

"Trade you," he said.

She stopped firing, saw what he'd found, and smiled.

* * *

"What the fuck's going on, Russet?"

Russell assumed Gonzaga was asking about the mass of Ruddies filling the road ahead of them. Most of them were wearing black bathrobes over black pajama bottoms, nothing like the khakis Kirosha regulars wore or the light blue and pink of the Royal Guards, but when a buncha people dressed the same, that was a uniform. Throw weapons into the mix, and that made them military uniforms. And if they fucked with you, uniforms or not, that made them the enemy.

"Fucked if I know, Gonzo. Ruddies got a hard-on for us all of a sudden."

His imp ran the numbers off the corner of his eye. There were two hundred and seventy-nine ETs massing up ahead, mostly armed with spears and swords, the poor bastards. Gunny Obregon was shouting something at them via his loudspeaker implants, but despite the fact he was talking Ruddy at them, they didn't seem to care.

"Hold fire," Obregon said over the command channel. "I'm firing a warning shot. All hands, hold fire."

The Gunny leaned out of the van's window and fired a single round into the ground somewhere between the Marine vehicles and the mob of Ruddies a hundred yards away. The exploding bullet melted a hole in the asphalt-covered road and the concrete below, plasma sparkling like a Roman candle.

The crowd took it in for a moment. Then some dickhead with a flag or something attached to his back started shouting and the Ruddies surged forward, waving their swords like this was yet another remake of *Braveheart vs Henry V*.

"Fuck it," Obregon said, sounding disgusted. "We're going through them. Engage the hostiles."

That was all that Russell was waiting to hear. He stood up in his seat gave the ETs a three-barrel salute, firing alternate blaster and grenade rounds after dropping a 20mm anti-pers care package on their laps. Gonzo cut loose with his squad gun. One burst apiece from the heavy weapons in each vehicle, plus one from each grunt who wasn't driving. The plasma bullets were rated to go through a foot of hardened steel and they turned each Ruddy they hit into a bomb. The anti-personnel grenades were worse, detonating overhead and showering the ETs with fragmented ceramic shards. The dumb fucks should have known better than to bunch up; they'd had automatic weapons for a good while in this planet. But the assholes charged forward, packed together shoulder to shoulder, the stupid motherfuckers, and got massacred. Maybe they expected the Marines to use tear gas or some other non-lethal shit. Dumb fucks. Marines weren't cops.

The street had been wide enough for all three vehicles to shoot, and by the time they checked fire, the enemy counter off the corner of his eye read sixty-three. That's how many Ruddies were still lively enough to pose a threat. Not that they were, not really; the sixty Eets who weren't dead or hollering on the ground were running as if their lives depended on it. Which they did.

Ruddies sounded like little kids when they screamed. It made him feel bad.

After the shooting was over, Rover Force's biggest problem was rolling through the pile of corpses ahead of them. The van got stuck a couple times and people had to unass and move bodies from under it. The Jeep and the truck mostly drove over the crunchy bumps beneath them. A couple of times they stopped to drag living Ruddies off to one side. But mostly they just drove on and ignored the sounds the live ones made when they got crunched.

They'd lost too much time already.

* * *

Heather handed Fromm the laser and took the Vehelian area effect weapon. She'd never seen one in the flesh, but their specs had been part of her courses in Starfarer tech. Its security locks were slightly more intricate than the laser's, but she got through them easily enough, leaving her with the decision of how to use it.

The cylinder in her hand was self-propelled, able to travel for up to two miles before its batteries burned off. It had two settings, one non-lethal, the other outright deadly. Both relied on using light pulses to overload their target's nervous systems, sending anybody caught in its area of effect into convulsions, unconsciousness and, at the higher setting, a nasty death.

Heather opted for the non-lethal setting. Some victims would die nonetheless; as many as one percent of the targets, depending on the species' sensitivity to light and sheer bad luck; a simple fall from a standing position could be lethal enough. The rest would be incapacitated for half an hour or longer without lasting ill effects. The weapon glided gently out of her hand and flew to its optimal detonation height.

"Everyone turn back and close your eyes!" she shouted into the defender's imps. Some of the civilians outside might not react in time, which was the main reason she'd picked the non-lethal setting. Heather followed her own advice, hunching down against the wall.

The flash was still noticeable from her protected position; it must have been like staring into a supernova for those outside. The gunfire hitting her position stopped with abrupt suddenness, except for one long burst fired when someone's clenched hand locked onto the trigger mechanism of his weapon, emptying it in a few seconds.

She took a quick peek out the window. Every Kirosha within a block radius was down, some lying perfectly still, others writhing in galvanic convulsions, the few lucky enough to have been behind some cover staggering blindly around, functional except for their temporarily overloaded optic nerves. Everyone attacking the walled garage was unconscious, dead or blind.

Fromm stopped firing the Vehelian laser. There was no need, at least for the time being.

"Not bad for a remfie," he told her.

"Who're you calling a remfie, jarhead?" she growled back; they were both smiling.

"Ovals have the nicest toys," Fromm said, peering over the window frame. "Wish we could get them."

"It'll be another couple decades before we can," Heather said.

"Too bad. We could use them. As in right now. We've got more trouble coming."

She accessed the video feed from the micro-drones overhead.

Two more large groups were out and about. One was busily setting barricades between them and the approaching Marine relief force. The other was rushing towards the garage. Both groups were several hundred strong, and about a tenth of them were Army assault troops with full combat gear.

They weren't out of the woods yet.

* * *

"Those rat bastards."

A new bunch of Ruddies had shown up. They'd blocked the main street with a pile of overturned carts and cars, and many of them were armed with rifles and rocket launchers. They engaged Rover Two the second it turned the corner. Bullets hit the frontal force field, sparkling pinpricks of light as they flattened against the solid but invisible surface and hanged on for a second or two before sliding down like so many dead flies. Lots of dead flies. An RPG round flashed overhead and hit a storefront behind them as Rover Two frantically backed up the way it'd come.

"Gotta go around," Obregon said. "But let me say goodbye first."

He hadn't used any rockets yet, so he fired off a spread of four 20mm missiles from the box launchers on the van. The drone cameras showed him the results as the salvo detonated right above and behind the barricades, turning dozens of ETs into ground chuck. It wasn't enough, though. Rover Force might smash through the barricade and kill everyone there, but it would take time and keep them in one place long enough for more enemy forces to converge on their position. They didn't have time to spare. Or ammo. His imp politely pointed out they'd already gone through ten percent of their basic battle load.

Better to stay on the move.

"Follow me," he told the other two Rovers as he directed his van towards one of the side streets. Kirosha was an old town, built long before motor transport was even a glimmer in the eye of some engineer, and most of its streets reflected that. Come to think of it, Obregon had read that the handful of big straight avenues in the city had only been built after gunpowder was discovered; the broad streets were designed to allow muzzle-loading cannon to shoot straight into any rampaging mobs who dared disturb the High King's Peace. They certainly had helped his troops mow down the current crop of rioters.

The side streets were narrow and twisty, following even minor terrain features rather than cutting through them. The Rovers could only negotiate them single file; without the micro-drones helping navigate they would have gotten lost in short order. Luckily most Ruddies had decided staying indoors was the thing to do, so the Marines had the streets mostly to themselves. At least at first.

Smaller groups of insurgents kept trying to catch up with the three technicals. A tall Ruddy wielding something like a big can opener at the end of a stick jumped in Rover Two's path. The van was moving at a good thirty miles per hour when it hit, too slowly to trigger the force fields; the impact with the welded-on metal grill on its front sent the wannabe warrior flying, the big axe-spear thing still in his hands when he hit a wall and bounced off it.

"Someone's shooting at us," Hendrickson said. More tiny points of light appeared wherever a Ruddy bullet hit the force fields around the van. They were taking fire from above. Houses were so packed together that you could get around jumping from one rooftop to the next, and some enterprising Ruddies with guns had done just that.

"Take 'em out."

Hendrickson complied as Rover Two kept moving. The ALS-43 stuttered a long burst into the sniper's building. Armor piercers: the big plasma rounds, designed to spear through force fields and composite armor plate, sawed through the third level of a four-story structure, tearing through support beams, walls and anybody unlucky enough to be inside. Hendricks drew a line of bright explosions as he traversed the weapon on its improvised mount. The top floor staggered before neatly collapsing into the shattered ruin of the third floor; a rifleman was tossed out of the building, screeching like a crying baby before the impact with the ground shut him up. A moment later, the entire building crumbled, scattering bodies and brickwork everywhere.

The shooting stopped.

"I think that did the tr…"

A Ruddy RPG hit the front of the van. The superheated gases of the shaped-charge warhead flattened against the force field, giving Obregon a close look at the fiery core of the anti-tank weapon's detonation. It was a bit like looking at what awaited all sinners in the end. The deafening sound washed over him and made his teeth vibrate painfully even under his helmet. No damage, but the front shield's power supply was down fifteen percent. He kept driving. They all knew that if they stood still they'd just make a better target.

Hendrickson's reaction to the explosion was much livelier. "Motherfuckers!" he screamed, swiveling the ALS-43 around and laying down a storm of fire. He walked a series of bursts towards the rocket team's position around a corner. The café they were using for cover blew apart in a conflagration of hot plasma and superheated brick and mortar. The launcher and the burning upper torso of one of the rocketeers rolled out into the street. Rover Two drove over the body; Lance Corporal Edison in Rover One leaned out and destroyed the launcher with two point-blank shots from his gun.

All of which was well and good, but the micro-drones had spotted several more groups of armed men rushing out into the streets. They were going to have to fight for every inch of ground between them and the people they were trying to rescue.

"Gunny?" PFC Kowalski said from the passenger's seat.

"Yeah?"

"Hope the new skipper's worth all this trouble."

"Me too, Kowalski. Me too."

Six

Year 163 AFC, D Minus Ten

"Got 'em cocked and loaded, Captain," Sergeant Martin said.

Less than a minute. Which could only mean Obregon had ordered the weapons deployed before Fromm thought about it. Having a good NCO made all the difference when commanding a platoon; despite his promotion to O3, Fromm's instincts were still geared towards platoon command, which was good at the moment because that was all he had.

"Well done," Fromm said. "Marking targets. Load anti-personnel rounds. Fire when ready."

"Anti-pers, aye. Firing when ready, aye, aye."

Fromm focused on the take from the micro-drones and his imp's dispassionate analysis of their data. As riots went, this wasn't very large; there were about three thousand Ruddies involved, including what appeared to be two or three Army companies, which gave the rioters some three hundred rifles and a couple dozen rocket launchers. No machineguns, artillery or heavy weapons; those were held at the brigade level in their own units, and none of those had joined the rebellion. Infantrymen were recruited mainly from among the largely illiterate peasants in the hinterlands, much like the secret society members they'd decided to support; artillery and heavy weapon units came from what passed for the Ruddy middle class, the kids of merchants and artisans, and their sympathies wouldn't be with the rioters.

Fromm matched the list of targets with the assets he had to engage them. The 100mm mortars could fire fifty self-guided rounds each before their internal magazines had to be reloaded, a process that would take some thirty seconds. Three guns; a hundred and fifty bombs. That should be enough.

The mortar section opened fire, the discharges too distant to be noticed from where he crouched, especially since the newest batch of Ruddies were both shooting and screaming at the top of their lungs, their high-pitched voices adding a disturbing note to the whole thing. His imp projected the path of the self-propelled rounds as they engaged their miniature motors and headed towards their designated targets: every major enemy concentration that could threaten the civilians with him or Obregon's rescue force.

Given that they were fighting unarmored, unshielded enemies, Fromm had opted for a wide spread. The mortar rounds were spaced some twenty-five yards apart; each bomb exploded fifty feet off the ground, lashing the area below them with thousands of ceramic shards traveling at supersonic speeds. The frangible shrapnel would shatter harmlessly on walls and roofs, though God help anybody looking out a window when the shells detonated. Against cloth-clad humanoids in the open, the effect was devastating.

Ruddies stumbled and fell, bleeding from dozens of wounds. Entire groups were mowed down to the last man, charging warriors turning into lifeless corpses so suddenly the whole thing looked like a clumsily choreographed dance. A six-round stonk hit the group attacking the walled compound. Those bombs went off a mere ten feet off the ground, too low to damage the human and Oval civvies in the compound, but still perfectly able to turn hundreds of aliens into bleeding, quivering meat. The attackers' shouting was silenced by the multiple explosions; when the last echoes abated, only a handful of scattered cries could be heard.

Fromm forced himself to watch the scene. There were maybe a dozen Ruddies still on their feet, and they were on the run. The rest of the attackers in the last wave were down, along with the poor bastards who'd been unconscious or stunned when death came calling. Most of the fallen lay unmoving on the ground, with a few ghastly exceptions. He saw a Ruddy trying to stuff a coil of intestines back into his body cavity before appearing to fall asleep. A uniformed soldier, his legs gone, crawled toward a nearby canteen and died right after taking a final swig of water. There were a few similar scenes up and down the corpse-strewn street, but only a few. Most of the tangos were dead.

Americans had learned the hard way that in the game of war you played for keeps.

He raised Gunny Obregon. "Road should be clear now."

"Yes, sir. Biggest problem now is driving over all the bodies. Might damage an axle. Wish we had grav cars."

"Beggars, not choosers, Gunny. Good work with those technicals, by the way."

Obregon's face twisted in a grim smile. "Thank you, sir."

Fromm knew he'd just passed a test. Some commanding officers, even in the Marines, would have come down on the Gunnery Sergeant for militarizing civilian transport on his own initiative, and likely against the Embassy's guidelines, if not direct orders. Fromm might be an asshole, but he wasn't that kind of asshole. When out in far-foreign, or on the green hills of Earth herself for that matter, you did what you had to in order to fulfill your mission.

"ETA?"

"Two, three minutes."

"We'll be ready."

He turned to McClintock, but she was already heading down the stairs to start preparing the civvies for evacuation. She must have been eavesdropping on his subvocalized conversation. Not something he would normally approve of, but she had her own mission to carry out, and he wasn't going to second-guess her.

An asshole, sure, but not that kind of an asshole.

* * *

"Casualties first," Heather McClintock told the gathered travelers. There were no objections.

Nobody had died, thank Random Chance, but some Kirosha rebels had tossed spears and throwing axes over the wall, and several people had ended up with cutting and stabbing wounds, some of them serious enough to require first aid. Luckily, the bus had a med-kit. All the injured had gotten a shot of nano-meds, and the microscopic robots were busily repairing damaged tissue and speeding up the creation of new blood cells. The process drew a great deal of energy from the victims' metabolism, which meant they could barely stand up, let alone walk. Heather rounded up volunteers to put them in the bus.

The gate had been damaged, but a few strong backs got it open, just in time for the arriving Marines and their improvised combat vehicles. Getting out took some doing. The bus drove slowly out onto the street while some hastily-drafted volunteers dragged or kicked corpses out of its way. Fromm squeezed himself into the van, sandwiched between a Gunnery Sergeant and another soldier. Heather ended up in the rear of a four-wheeler, along with three Marines.

"Welcome to Leatherneck Taxicabs, ma'am," the Lance Corporal in charge of the car said. She brought up his official files: the image of a ratty looking man – Russell Edison; numerous commendations, and much more numerous non-judicial punishments – popped up in her field of vision.

"Thank you," she replied, making room for herself in the rear seat, which was filled with ammo boxes and other equipment. Russell sent her a friend request on Facettergram, which she summarily rejected.

"We'll have you back to the Enclave in a jiffy, ma'am," Edison went on as the three-vehicle convoy began rolling. "I think the Ruddies ain't got no fight left in 'em."

The car took the lead, the two Marines not busy driving ready for action, one standing behind a pintle-mounted heavy gun, the corporal holding his assault weapon ready. Heather herself was cradling the Vehelian laser – by rights she should have handed the weapon over to one of the survivors of the delegation, but she felt better with it at hand. The last hour had taught her to relish firepower in a way none of her previous training had.

"Mofos," the driver said, startling her out of her reverie.

"Yeah," LCPL Edison agreed.

She checked the drone feeds. Up ahead, forming up between them and the walls of the Enclave, stood several Kirosha tanks.

* * *

"Pleased to meet you, Gunny," Fromm said to his platoon sergeant.

Neither man saluted; you didn't do that in the field. Obregon led the way to the van he was using as the task force's command vehicle. Fromm could see where force field generators had been attached to the Ruddy van, and smiled when he saw the simple but effective cupola they'd welded to its roof.

"That must have cost you a pretty penny," he said as they squeezed into the driver's compartment; the rear was taken up with several civvies, people they hadn't been able to fit into the bus because of the wounded taking up extra space. Among them was McClintock's driver: Locquar was still wielding his submachinegun, and none of the Marines had given him any trouble about it, which meant they knew and trusted the local.

"Ain't that many places to spend your pay around here, sir," Obregon explained as the vehicles moved towards the Enclave. "Plus a third of the men are Mormons or Star Baptists, and they don't drink, don't gamble and don't whore around all that much. We passed the hat around and it came back full."

"You're getting a commendation for this, by the way."

"Thank you, sir. We made it here in one piece, that's the important thing, and God willing we'll make it back likewise."

Fromm nodded.

"Sorry we didn't meet you at the port ourselves, sir."

"You had your orders. Things are going to change after this, however."

"Yes, sir. Nobody expected them Ruddies to come at us like

this, or our Ruddies to let them. They usually come down hard on troublemakers around here. Thieves and murderers get tortured to death. Rebels get it even worse. Letting those assholes come after us like that, it kinda worries me."

"It worries me too, Gunny. I guess I've got to hit the ground running. How's the unit?"

"In general, it's fine, sir. Got a dozen boots just before we deployed, but they're shaping up okay. Everyone else has been round the block and know what's what. Been keeping everyone busy, mostly PE and virtual field exercises. Between that and a steady dose of field days, they've mostly stayed out of trouble."

"Guess you thought this deployment would be easier than Romulus-Four."

Obregon's Third (Weapons) Platoon, Charlie Company, Third Battalion, 53rd Marine Regiment, had seen action against the Lampreys during yet another 'police action,' something very similar to what Fromm had faced at Astarte-Three. What had begun as a raid on a pirate base had devolved into a pitched battle when the pirates turned out to have sizable contingents of Lamprey 'deserters' armed with mil-spec gear. Those two battles and a space skirmish that led to the utter destruction of a 'rogue' Lamprey squadron had made the ETs cry uncle, pay reparations and withdraw from several disputed star systems. Nobody thought that was the end of it, though, or at least nobody with a brain did.

"Romulus-Four was no picnic," Obregon said. "But we had three Marine regiments on the ground, battlecruisers orbiting overhead and plenty of support. If we hadn't been rescuing hostages we could have blasted them from orbit. Here, it's just us: a platoon plus a couple squads' worth of attached personnel, including the worthless sumbitches in the Embassy Detail. We had to blast our way out of the Embassy, sir."

"I noticed. I'll be having words with Sergeant Amherst when we get home. The RSO will give you a pass. I'll see to it. But let's try to avoid this sort of incident in the future."

"Absolutely," Obregon said; the words sounded heartfelt. He started to say something else but froze when he saw the same thing Fromm did.

While they talked, both of them had kept the visual feed from the micro-drones up on one corner of their field of vision, so they both noticed when several Ruddy tracked military vehicles exited their revetments and started moving.

Moving towards the gates of the Enclave. And they were going to get there before the convoy arrived.

"Looks like a blocking force, sir," Obregon said.

"So it seems." Fromm was thinking furiously while he spoke. That was a tank platoon rolling into position; three tanks, one mobile gun that could serve as a tank destroyer or artillery piece, and two light infantry fighting vehicles. Not the most efficient unit organization – the mobile gun was both slower and less well-protected than the tanks – but it was deadly enough. The tanks in question weren't too bad for the local tech level, with seventy millimeters of sloped armor on its front and turret and a 79mm main gun that would batter through the improvised shields protecting the Marine vehicles after three or four shots. The tank destroyer mounted a 93mm cannon on its turretless chassis, and a HEAT round from that monster would probably blow up any of the three Rovers with a couple of shots. The IFVs mounted heavy machineguns and two recoilless rifles on open-top turrets, which made them a minor danger but nothing to laugh about, either.

"A burst from an Iwo will open up those bitches, easy," Obregon said, focused on the tactical rather than strategic picture. "We can wipe them out if we hit them on the move. Or just have the hundred-mike-mikes drop some AV rounds on them."

"That's not the problem, Gunny. Problem is all the other Ruddy units in-theater. And if that isn't enough, their First Army is only a couple days away. As in *field* army."

"They can't be that crazy," Obregon said. "That'd mean war, no-shit war, and one our corvettes could turn this town into rubble, or every town, city and village on the fucking planet, even if it doesn't drop bloomies on 'em. Hell, an *assault shuttle* would eat this whole planet's lunch. They got nothing to stop an orbital attack. They're worse off than Earth was during First Contact!"

"Yeah. None of this makes sense. Which means either the Ruddies are bugfuck insane, or they know something we don't."

"So what now, sir? We're about to come into their line of fire."

"Going to call higher first. Full stop."

"Yes, sir." Obregon didn't sound happy as he issued the order to the rest of the convoy. Stopped vehicles were easy targets.

Fromm reached out to the Embassy. The RSO's face came into view once again.

"We see them, Captain," the security officer said. "We're still unable to reach anybody in the Royal Court. Nobody with the authority to do anything about this, at least."

"We've stopped. There's no immediate threat but the drones are picking up movement on the outskirts of the city. We may have more armed mobs headed our way."

"I'm going to speak with the ambassador. Don't do anything else without running it by me first." His face disappeared.

Fromm decided to do some intelligence gathering of his own while he waited.

The Ruddies had learned about modern communications only recently – most of their radio sets were human-made trade models, cheap electronics that didn't use the far more reliable grav-wave transmitters Starfarers relied on. They hadn't even developed the telegraph on their own, relying instead on long chains of semaphores and heliographs that spanned their continent. Upon making Contact, the Kirosha had fallen in love with wireless communications. Radio antennas had sprouted like so many mushrooms throughout the Kingdom, serving both civilian and military needs.

The Embassy routinely recorded all radio traffic in the continent; accessing it was just a matter of entering his security signature into the American intranet system. Deciphering and translating the last six hours took hardly any time. Massaging the data into a useful summary took a little longer, but the whole process lasted a couple of minutes. If only his other problems could be solved that easily.

Bottom line was, the Ruddies didn't know what the fuck was going on, either.

Orders and counter-orders had flown back and forth over the airwaves all day long, some properly coded and encrypted, others sent out in the clear. Units had been instructed to mobilize, then to return to barracks, then to muster out and march away from the capital. Officers had been promoted, only to be arrested hours later. Generals had been countermanded by Magistrates, Magistrates by the Prime Minister himself, the Prime Minister by the High Queen herself. The left hand didn't know what the right hand was doing, or was actively trying to sabotage it. This was a cluster-fuck of epic – no, mythological – proportions.

The tank platoon sitting bestride Fromm's escape route had been ordered there by the colonel in charge of protecting the Foreign Enclave. Its orders were to prevent anyone from leaving or entering the area. Fromm couldn't tell if the instructions were meant to protect the Starfarers in the Enclave or to get in the way of the ongoing rescue attempt. For all he knew, it was designed to do both.

On the other hand, he had someone he could talk to. Or have someone talk to him; his imp could translate English to Kirosha, but there would be a noticeable time lag and the software would likely make mistakes, since Kirosha wasn't a widely used language. His imp would eventually work out any kinks in translation, but doing so while having a life-or-death conversation probably wasn't a good idea.

Fromm contacted McClintock and briefly explained the situation.

"I know Colonel Loor," she said when he was done. "He's a political appointee. Comes from one of the bureaucrat clans in the capital; only reason he's in the military is that his family couldn't find him a better sinecure."

"Great, a Rat in uniform." Dealing with Rats always grated on Fromm. Military Rats were worse still.

"I'll talk to him," McClintock said. "Let me run it by RSO Rockwell first."

She did; Rockwell agreed to her plan. McClintock tried the Ruddy's personal phone line. She got through after a few rushed words with the officer's secretary. Fromm listened in as she exchanged greetings with Colonel Loor.

"I am speaking to you on a matter of some importance and urgency," McClintock said formally. "I and some guests of the Crown are trying to return to the Enclave. There has been some unpleasantness, and we are concerned about the military forces blocking the main gate."

"I hear Americans have used artillery against royal citizens," Colonel Loor said. "This is a violation of the Star Treaty, and a grave offense against the Queen and People of Kirosha."

And we should give a shit because? Fromm thought; he kept the comment to himself, though. At the moment the Kirosha's opinion had a lot more weight than it would when a starship arrived in system and explained the facts of life to the locals.

"Such determinations are to be left to those greater than you or I," McClintock replied levelly. "I wish to return to the Enclave. Will your men prevent us from doing so?"

There was a pause before Loor replied. "I have no orders to hinder you. You and yours may pass through the gate. I will issue direct orders to that effect."

"I hear you and accept your words."

Once the call was over, McClintock's virtual icon turned to Fromm. "I think Loor is fence-sitting. Not sure which faction to back. A Modernist would have helped us out wholeheartedly, while a Preserver might have pushed the issue. Guess his family feels the same way, or someone would have given him definite marching orders."

Fromm nodded at her and continued monitoring the Ruddies' radio chatter. Orders were radioed to the blocking force: let the Star Devils pass.

"We're clear."

Rover Force drove into the broad avenue leading towards the Enclave, presenting a nice no-deflection target for the Ruddy tank platoon.

Nobody shot at them. They drove towards the tanks and maneuvered around them.

An officer was leaning out of the nearest tank's turret hatch. He glared at the humans as they drove past. It was better than being shot at, but not all that great otherwise.

Fromm checked the time. He'd been planetside for about two hours.

Interlude:
The First Battle of Terra

Solar System, Year 29 AFC (After First Contact)

"Emergence detected, five light hours away."

"Here they come, black as hell and thick as grass," Captain Anthony Carruthers of the *USS Roosevelt* said as the first Sierras icons appeared onscreen. Everybody on the bridge loved the skipper, despite his penchant for using classical military quotes at every opportunity.

A few crewmembers chuckled; their laughter was on the edge of hysteria.

Commander Sondra Givens tried not to gulp as figures started running down the screen. Everyone could see them, but it was her job to verbalize the harsh reality of the situation. "It looks like the entire Risshah Armada, sir."

"Snakes had to stop screwing around sooner or later," Carruthers commented. The previous three incursions had consisted of single ships or small squadrons, all of which had been destroyed. "I guess they finally figured out nobody lost a fight because they brought too many ships to the event."

"Twenty *Fang*-class frigates. Thirteen *Three-Claw*-class battlecruisers," she went on, fear giving way to a burst of anger. The *Three-Claws* were the workhorses of the Snake fleet; one of them had immolated half of humanity. *Not this time, you bastards.* "Three *Dragon*-class battleships." She took a deep breath before continuing. "And a *Merciless*-class dreadnought."

The Risshah invaders would be met by the entirety of the US Space Fleet, the product of nearly twenty years of hasty, desperate efforts; some of its vessels had been commissioned less than a week ago. If the Snakes had waited another month or so, the *USS Ronald Reagan* would have joined their order of battle, but the latest *President*-class cruiser was still moored to the space docks in Low Earth Orbit, its gravitonic drive incomplete. Should the Snakes make it past the Fleet, the half-built ship would serve as an improvised space fortress, even though only one third of its armament was operational.

Of course, if the Snakes got into range of the *Reagan*'s guns it meant that the rest of the US Fleet had been obliterated and the

Earth was hosed. One half-finished cruiser wasn't going to achieve anything beyond making a futile last stand.

Sondra was terribly afraid that the operational Fleet — seven cruisers, nine 'frigates' most Starfarers would designate as corvettes, and eight assault ships — wouldn't be enough to do the job, either. Even calling the American ships of the line 'cruisers' was rather charitable. A *President*-class was four hundred meters long and had a displacement of two hundred thousand tons. A Snake *frigate* was three hundred meters long and weighed in at a hundred and twenty thousand tons. Their battlecruisers were six hundred and half a mill, respectively, and their battleships ran a thousand meters long and encompassed three million tons of drive, shields and armaments that alone out-massed all seven American ships of the line combined. The dreadnought was slightly under a mile in length and its tonnage was just ridiculous. The discrepancy in shields and armament was, if anything, proportionally greater.

The Snakes hadn't given them enough time to prepare, and the Puppies could no longer prevent the aliens from finishing the job they'd started.

Sondra Givens had been born in the year 3 After First Contact. The chief feature of those early years had been scarcity. Everything was rationed: food, fuel, clothes. The country — what was left of it — spent its first decade rebuilding infrastructure, adapting Starfarer Tech, and arming itself. She'd never starved — there had been enough food, just about — but she'd never had enough of anything. Her parents had told her repeatedly how lucky she was, how lucky America had been. Some countries, like Venezuela, had been effectively depopulated, ninety percent of their inhabitants wiped out during First Contact. China and India had lost every major urban center and the better part of a billion people each, all for the crime of being closest to the first wave of city-busting missiles. By comparison, the US had gotten lucky; they'd only lost half — half their people, half of everything they'd had.

The Hrauwah, better-known as the Puppies, had given them the means to lift themselves up from economic ruin. By the time Sondra was ten, eating until she was stuffed was no longer a special occasion, and blackouts didn't happen regularly anymore. Things were going back to normal. When she turned twenty, she chose the Navy after her four-year Obligatory Service commitment was over.

The Snakes left them alone for almost three decades. At first, they'd been too busy fighting the Puppies, who had pushed them out of the galactic region that included Earth. The peace that followed gave the US more time to prepare. Things changed, however. A year ago, the Snakes' patrons, an older and more powerful species known as the Lampreys, had intervened in their favor. Under pressure from the Lampreys, the Puppies had been forced to withdraw. Earth's only friends had abandoned them. The Snakes hadn't even bothered with ultimatums or declarations of war: weeks after the last Puppy ships departed, a Snake battlecruiser had invaded the Solar System – and been promptly obliterated. That victory had been meaningless, unfortunately. The war they'd been dreading was upon them. Nobody was coming to humanity's aid. Nobody.

"Ready warp engines."

"Ready warp engines, aye."

"I expect all of us to do our duty," the Captain said. "Let's engage the enemy more closely, shall we?"

The USS Roosevelt joined her six sister ships in the battle for Earth's survival.

* * *

A human visitor to the bridge of the dreadnought Sunspot would have found its environs murky and oppressive. Its atmosphere was dank, uncomfortably hot and full of toxic trace elements, which among other things generated a powerful stench. The lighting appeared to be weak, mainly because it heavily trended towards the ultraviolet spectrum. In other words, it was just the way the Risshah liked it.

The long warp jump had taken its toll. One of the dreadnought bridge crew was dead, most likely due to unbearable mental stress. It wasn't the only casualty; out of the sixty thousand Risshah in the Armada, three had died, and five had become deranged and been summarily put down. More importantly, all crews had been incapacitated for nearly three hours, due to their lengthy exposure to the mind-destroying environment of warp space.

After those three hours, during which the Risshah Armada had been at the mercy of automated systems, order had been restored. High Admiral Purple-93,017 turned towards Pilot Yellow-2,301,117 and issued its first command in the enemy system. "Commence the planned advance."

Its order was transmitted and the fleet made one short warp jump, placing them three light minutes away from Earth. After the five-minute warp recovery such a jump entailed, the Risshahh vessels began moving towards the fur-heads' homeworld at cruising speed, slightly below 0.001 c. They would be in position in fifty-three hours, plenty of time to prepare for battle.

The paltry fleet the humans had assembled was orbiting around the planet, and the Admiral wondered if it would sail forth to meet the Risshah halfway, or fight their futile last stand in orbit, where its demise would be visible from Earth. In either case, they were doomed. Now that the fur-faces had been forced to withdraw, this portion of the galaxy belonged to the Nest-Mothers and their brood, the People of the Egg. The local sophonts would be exterminated, the planet's biosphere modified to suit the victors' tastes, and in three centuries the blue sphere would be indistinguishable from the other seven worlds the Risshah had colonized.

"Emergence! Half a light-second away, master," the tactical officer hissed, its sibilants distorted with shock and surprise.

"Change course! Battle stations!"

The fools! A three light-minute warp jump would leave the crews of the human ships incapacitated for at least thirty seconds, during which their ships would be in range of the Risshah's main guns and missiles. Nobody made that sort of maneuver in the face of an enemy; it was tantamount to suicide. And while the Armada was unprepared for battle at such short notice, its crews could fire before the enemy recovered. At best, the humans could fire off a few automatic missile volleys, which would accomplish nothing. It was almost a pity. The Admiral had been looking forward to an actual battle, but a massacre would suit it fine.

"It's their entire fleet, in close formation!" There was a pause as the Tactical Officer struggled to accept its sensor readings. "They are maneuvering, master!"

The Admiral could not believe the images in the tactical holotank. The human vessels had come out of warp but were maneuvering under manual control. The rumors were true, then; humans could withstand warp space better than any other known species. The enemy fleet started firing within seconds of their emergence, before the Risshah were at battle readiness, and the Admiral felt cold doubt running through its circulatory system.

The largest human combatants, little more than oversized frigates, mounted eight heavy graviton cannon each. They struck the Risshah column when it was at its most vulnerable, its formations designed for ease of travel rather than protection. Their initial volleys destroyed two frigates and severely damaged three more. The Admiral hissed in impotent rage while the Armada's weapon systems were made ready and began to return fire.

Each Risshah battlecruiser had ten main guns, each more powerful than their American counterparts; the battleships had eighteen guns apiece, and the *Sunspot* twenty-four. Their initial response was sluggish, as crews rushed to their posts and brought their weapon systems online. Only fifty-three heavy graviton cannon unleashed their power, out of a possible two hundred and eight; terrible performance, but understandable, since no vessel had been at battle stations when the engagement began. Still, each human pocket cruiser was targeted by no less than seven streams of coherent gravity, designed to shatter force fields and shred anything they touched. The beams crossed the distance between the fleets almost instantly. They all scored hits.

"No effect! Master, no effect!"

The beams hit *something* in front of each human vessel and vanished without inflicting any damage.

"What happened"

"I... I'm not sure, master. We are detecting warp signatures, too small for a jump. Purpose unknown."

"Warp shields," the Admiral said. The very concept was insane. No sophont could endure being in the presence of an ongoing warp aperture for more than a few seconds without dying, going insane, or both. And yet, there they were; their presence was the only explanation for the unscathed ships in the tactical display.

"Keep firing! They cannot keep those shields up for long!"

More energy volleys were exchanged; the Americans had stopped advancing and were maneuvering to keep their warp apertures between them and the Armada's fury. They return fire kept scoring hits, and a growing number of those hits became kills. They kept targeting the Risshahh frigates, steadily whittling away the most maneuverable element of the fleet.

Missiles from both sides began to add their power to the fray. Some of the human weapons detonated while still over five thousand kilometers away; the explosions channeled the energy of their thermonuclear warheads into coherent beams of x-ray and gamma radiation. Ingenious, if one was reduced to using fissionables as a weapon, and dismayingly effective. The beams were devastating against frigates and were able to inflict some damage even on ships of the line. Three more ships fell out of formation, their breached hulls leaking gasses like the dying breaths of some great beast. Their crews were doomed, after being exposed to brief but lethal bursts of radiation.

The human vessels kept fighting in close formation, protected by shields made of defiled space-time. Follow-up volleys turned four more *Fang* frigates into burning, lifeless hulks and damaged half a dozen more. More salvos of radiation-disgorging missiles flew forth, followed by regular graviton and plasma warheads: the humans had saved their most modern weapons until they were at close range, where point defenses would have less than a minute to detect, engage and destroy them.

"Concentrate fire on enemy cruisers," the Admiral ordered with an assumed calmness it did not truly feel. The Armada disgorged more missiles and its secondary batteries – laser and plasma weapons – added their fire to the heavy graviton guns. Most of them were stopped by the American warp shields; a few managed find unprotected spots, but not in enough volume to batter down the enemy's regular force fields. "Spread out! We must maneuver to strike their sides!"

The Fleet struggled to carry out the unconventional order. Normally there was no need to target specific sectors in a ship, as they all were equally well-protected by force fields, except for the rare occasion when disabling a vessel was a desirable goal. The Armada's crews were as well-trained as any formation in the known galaxy; they did their best, even as the enemy's own missiles and beam weapons bled them dry. Twelve Risshah frigates were down already; the rest were all damaged to some degree, and a battlecruiser turned into an expanding fireball when a brace of thermonuclear missiles struck just as a graviton beam salvo temporarily shut down a force field section.

Risshah losses were already five times higher than the most pessimistic estimate had predicted, and no enemy vessel had been destroyed, or even heavily damaged.

"We will devour their young," the Admiral hissed.

The battle turned into a complex dance, humans turning to keep their impregnable front quadrants – and, in the case of their cruisers, their rear ones as well – between their hulls and the Risshah's fire, while the Armada maneuvered to attack from as many different directions as possible. The Risshah forces had to scatter to do so, which meant their ability to offer mutual support and protection was degraded. The Americans' tight formation enabled them to concentrate their fire on single targets and combine their point defense systems to wipe out entire missile barrages. After every frigate was destroyed, the battlecruisers were targeted next. They were much harder eggs to crack, but even they could not withstand the pounding of dozens of heavy graviton guns and hundreds of plasma and laser emitters fired at point-blank range.

If the humans had fielded more than a handful of cruisers, the outcome might have been in doubt. The Armada had too many ships of the line, however; it took the combined fire of at least three enemy cruisers to destroy a battlecruiser, and the dreadnought and battleship force fields could survive anything the humans threw at them for any practical length of time. Sooner or later their enemies' unprotected underbellies would be found and torn open. The Armada's losses would be dismayingly high, but the end result would be the same.

The Admiral's newfound confidence was proven right a moment later, when one of the tiny cruisers was caught between the *Sunspot* and the battleship *Death Coil*. A missile barrage struck an unprotected quadrant and tore into the inferior vessel's shields and armored hull. The ship became a glowing cloud of expanding debris.

You fought well, for prey. Better than the fur-faces ever did. But now it is time to die.

* * *

"I'm a little teapot, short and stout," Tactical Officer Johansson sang as he tried to claw his eyes out. Two security officers Tasered him into submission and carried his limp form towards the infirmary.

Commander Givens nearly giggled at the sight, but suppressed the urge at the last moment. That was fortunate, because any signs of insanity were being met with non-lethal but painful force. She blinked away ghost-images of her dead brother, looking just like the terrible night when she'd found his body, after a gang of draft-dodgers had killed him for his clothes and shoes. For some reason, she found the look on her dead brother's face utterly hilarious.

Several things helped people resist warp-induced madness. Meditation. Assorted drug cocktails. Prayer. Statistically, prayer worked best. Givens had been raised Presbyterian, but hadn't had much use for religion until joining the Fleet. Multiple exposures to warp space had turned her into a bit of a non-denominational Bible-thumping zealot.

"Even though I walk through the valley of the shadow of death, I will fear no evil," she muttered as she worked the controls of her station. A Snake frigate had managed to pepper the *Roosevelt* with a close-range graviton volley before being blown to smithereens, and the ship's force fields were down to thirty percent on one quadrant of the ship. The warp shields had worked like a charm, but the cruiser could only generate two of them at once, leaving a lot of hull protected only by standard force fields, its rather inadequate armor plating, and God's grace. "I will fear no evil, for you are with me; your rod and your staff, they comfort me."

They were kicking ass and taking names, but it wasn't going to be enough.

"The assault ships are in range, finally."

It was up to the Devil Dogs now.

* * *

USMC Lance Corporal Adam David was a reluctant patriot.

His father had been a civil rights attorney before the ETs burned down half the world, an attorney who'd made the mistake of getting in the way of the new world order that followed and ended up in a work camp for his troubles, doing hard manual labor alongside banksters, tenured professors, assorted former government officials and employees, survivalists who hadn't gotten along with the program, journalists and other undesirables. By all accounts, life in the camps had been no picnic, even in post-Contact America, where the old and the infirm had dropped dead in droves. People there had been last in line for everything, from food and medicine to toilet paper, and they'd died in droves, too. Adam's dad had been one of the lucky ones.

After his release a few years later, the former attorney had settled down in a small farm in Minnesota, raised a family – that's where Adam was born, the fifth and final child – and kept his opinions to himself. The stain of being a convicted troublemaker and traitor stuck to his children, however. Young Adam had been picked on incessantly in school, until he'd loudly and publicly denounced his father and everything he stood for, and pretended to be a true-blue all-American patriot, yee-haw and Ay-men, you betcha.

Along the way, he'd discovered a sad truth; if you pretended to be something long enough, the role became reality. He hardly ever thought about all the constitutional violations the US government committed on an almost-hourly basis. He certainly wasn't thinking about any of that shit now, as he cradled the M4 carbine/grenade launcher he would wield during this historical event. All he cared about was killing as many ETs as possible.

Everything that had happened to him and his family had been the fucking aliens' fault, after all.

C.J. Carella

Adam made sure his sealed helmet was screwed in correctly, and all the attachments on his chest armor, gloves and boots were air-tight. He was about to enter not one but two hostile environments, and a hole in his pressurized suit would kill him. The grunts in the weapons platoon had been issued personal force shields, but the rest of Alpha Company would have to make do with Kevlar, carbon nanotube field fatigues and plain dumb luck.

"I got a bad feeling about this," another Marine said behind him.

"Shut the fuck up, Carl," Adam said, concentrating on not looking down. He'd done seven drops already, and he'd hated each one a little more than the last. This would be his first combat drop.

If only they could just teleport some nukes aboard the Snake ships and be done. Neat idea, except for two things. First, warp catapults only worked on people. You needed a living, thinking being to get in and out of warp; they'd tried using animals, and even smart ones like dogs and dolphins couldn't make the trip on their own. And second, warships had internal force fields that would prevent nukes from doing too much damage. The fields wouldn't stop troopers from walking through them, though. And forget about opening a warp hole too close to a ship's grav reactor, because you couldn't. No idea why.

"Catapult ready," an impersonal voice announced through the mike in his helmet. "Launch in ten, nine, eight..."

The big disk on which the platoon was standing began to vibrate. Adam closed his mouth tightly, clenching his teeth. He'd bitten off the tip of his tongue the first time he'd dropped into warp, so now he always made sure his jaws were locked in place, even if he ended up cracking a tooth, which he'd also done. Twice.

He fucking hated warp drops.

"Six..."

"Hold on to your cocks, here it comes."

"I said shut the fuck up, Carl," Adam said through clenched teeth and hoped the fucker bit his tongue off.

"One."

It started with a fall, or at least a feeling like you were falling. The first thing they taught you during drop training was to fight the urge to flail uselessly against the false sensation. The first time, despite all the lessons and meditation techniques and all that crap, Adam had shit his pants and bit off his tongue. Now he merely closed his eyes and prayed. His father had been born Jewish but had lived life as a staunch atheist; Adam had picked up

86

his prayers from his Catholic neighbors; his other choice had been the LDS but he and the Mormons hadn't gotten along even after he'd turned into a flag-waving good ole boy.

The Lord's Prayer did the trick. He kept saying it over and over; he always tried to keep track of how many times he recited it during a jump, but he always lost count somewhere around the seventh or eighth time.

The ghosts were the worst. Dead people, live people, people he didn't know. They capered all around him, and he saw them even though his eyes were tightly shut. They whispered in his ears and made him want to flip open his helmet and let the wild energies of warp space rip his face clean off. He prayed silently instead.

Deliver us from evil, deliver us from evil, for thine is the kingdom, deliver us from evil, please, please God.

And it was over, all of a sudden, the horrors receding from his memory like fragments from a forgotten dream. They said you only remembered a little bit of what you saw in warp, and Adam was fine with that, because what he could remember sucked ass. They had landed in a dim corridor, all black shadows and sickening blue and red lights. Snakes breathed all kinds of toxic shit, so a breach in his suit would mean a Deep Regret vid-mail to the folks at home. His father would probably dance on his grave.

"You didn't have to become a Myrmidon." Those had been Dad's last words to Adam.

"Sound off," Sergeant Jimenez ordered, his harsh voice cutting through the haze in Adam's head. Everyone did. They'd all made it. So far, nobody in Adam's company had died during a drop, although you heard stories about people who had died, or worse, who hadn't made it out the other side. Nobody wanted to talk about what happened to you if you ended up stranded in warp space. Adam sure as fuck didn't. At least he was back in the physical universe, where the worst that could happen to him was death or dismemberment.

"Let's move, people."

Their arrival had torn a big hole inside the Snakes' ship – their fucking dreadnaught, that'd been their target – but it was all interior bulkheads, so it didn't matter. They followed the HUD displays on their helmets towards their target, the Engineering section. They made it through a good hundred feet before they saw their first Snake.

The Risshah had scaly skin just like their namesakes, but its body plan also included bits and pieces of octopus and spider. Its center of mass was like a boa constrictor's, a big twisting tubular shape about as wide as a basketball, ending in a prehensile tail. Sixteen tentacle limbs sprouted from the central trunk, and in turn bifurcated into thirty-two smaller tentacles, each of which could serve as a hand or a foot. Its head was bulbous, with big beady eyes and a mouth filled with fangs; it was the ugliest thing Adam had ever seen. The Snake was wearing a purple t-shirt, which made it a petty officer equivalent. It wasn't armed: Starfarers rarely engaged in boarding actions.

Sergeant Jimenez took care of him. A short burst from his M4 did the trick. The 5.56mm bullets had plasma-filled tips that blew the hideous alien into bloody chunks.

"Fucking-A," Adam said. He'd never felt as happy as he did watching the ET fuck off and die. At that moment, surrounded by his fellow Marines, he felt right at home.

"Let's roll. Things to do, ETs to kill."

They rolled on.

* * *

"Engineering is under attack. Secondary control room is under attack. Troop quarters…"

"Are under attack," the Admiral said. "Prepare to repel boarders."

The dreadnought had three cohorts of Spaceborne Infantry amongst its crew, but they'd never been meant to be deployed inside the ship. One loaded troops into shuttles and sent them out to board crippled vessels or to attack targets on planets or large space installations. One cohort was in their quarters, without their weapons; the other two had been detached to assist damage control units – also without their weapons, lest they accidentally damage the ship. To arm themselves, the troops would have to reach the central armory – which was also under attack.

Demons. We are fighting demons.

Those were its last thoughts before a warp bubble erupted into the bridge, killing it and most of the crew. The few survivors had just enough time to behold their executioners before a storm of explosive bullets wiped them out.

"Ugly motherfuckers, aren't they?" a Marine second lieutenant said after the last Risshah crewmember had stopped twitching. His voice broke into an adolescent squeak in mid-sentence, which embarrassed him to no end.

"Come on," he said gruffly. "Let's clear up the rest of this nest."

* * *

It worked. It freaking worked!

Commander Givens barely resisted the urge to jump up and down in glee as the last Snake battlecruiser blew up on the screen. Total wipeout.

A quick glance at the tactical screen quenched her elation. The *Lincoln* was gone; the *Eisenhower* and *Bush* were drifting, engines down, life support barely hanging on, most of their other systems off-line and a good one-third to half of their crews dead or wounded. The Assault Ship *Chosin* had also been destroyed, all hands lost, along with a Marine Expeditionary Unit. The casualties among the fleet's frigates were still to be tallied up. The Snakes had kept fighting even after losing their dreadnought, two battleships and seven battlecruisers to Marine boarding actions. Even with the new warp shields, it had been a close-run thing, as Captain Carruthers would no doubt say at some point.

Rescuing the thousands of Marines now stranded inside the derelict Snake ships would take some doing: warp catapults could send you out, but couldn't bring you back in; drops were one-way trips. You won or you died, and if you won you were stuck in a captured ship until someone came to get you or you ran out of consumables and died, or the ship self-destructed and you died. Not the kind of job she would have volunteered for. But those Marines had made all the difference in the end, and those captured hulls would make a major different in the fighting to come. Givens wondered if they'd try to refit the Snake ships or simply strip them of useful weapons and other systems.

Behind her, Captain Carruthers spoke. "We won this time, but we can't expect them to come on in the same old way. Now they know we're more than just a primitive tribe to be swept aside. We've proven to be a threat."

Better a threat than a victim, Givens thought.

The burning remains of the Snake fleet glowed on the screen like beacons of hope.

Seven

Year 163 AFC, D Minus Ten

"You fools nearly ruined everything."

High Magistrate Eereen Leep seethed at the rudeness displayed by the bald statement. The hooded figure facing him hadn't bothered learning even the basics of Kirosha courtesy. The Star Devil's arrogance matched his hideousness, which was so abhorrent the only way Eeren could stand his presence was for the alien to keep his features hidden from sight; having seen them once, the Magistrate had no desire to ever do so again. All Star Devils were unpleasant to look at, but this one was shaped like a nightmare made flesh, like a monster from mythology.

"Errors were made," Eereen said politely, internally wincing at the loss of face even that neutral statement signified. "Some lesser leaders among the rebels saw an opportunity to strike a blow against the Star Devils. The chance to slay one of their emissaries proved to be too tempting for them. They have paid for their mistake with their lives. Their families will suffer even more." Their deaths would also provide a convenient scapegoat, should the Queen decide to back the Modernists instead of Eereen's Preservers. Her Supreme Majesty had yet to make up her mind.

"I warned you that you would be helpless against the outsiders without my aid," the hooded Devil said, compounding his insults by belaboring the facts. "Their weapons are too advanced. Their drones spy on your every movement. Without my gifts, you are less than insects to them."

"We await your gifts with great anticipation," was Eeren's mild reply, his own rebuke tastefully implied and thus completely missed by the monster. Dealing with barbarians was exhausting. "One would wish they had been distributed already."

"The items are being assembled even as we speak," the Devil said, or rather, the machine that did his talking for him did. The monster had a revolting sucker-like mouth, surrounded by multiple rows of teeth and featuring not one but two snakelike tongues; it could not produce sounds like normal people, or even the more Kirosha-like Star Devils. "Smuggling modern devices is rather difficult. Even the notoriously lax Wyrms will check for suspicious energy signatures in their cargos. We had to hide the components among seemingly harmless consumer products, which now have to be extracted and put together, one by one. Only a trained laborer can do so, and you only provided a handful of them. Any further delays are your fault."

"Watchmakers and other skilled craftsmen are somewhat scarce and easily missed. I humbly apologize for failing to gather them in sufficient numbers to meet your needs." At this point, the Star Devil should have replied with an equally fulsome apology, restoring the balance. Instead, he took Eereen's words as his due, dealing yet another irreparable offense. Barbarian!

"At the current rate of progress, it will take two, maybe three days to have everything in place. I hope the slaughter the filthy humans inflicted on your cannon fodder will not discourage the rest of you."

"A mere three thousand dead? That is nothing, a trifle," Eereen said confidently. During the last great rebellion, over a million revolting peasants had been slaughtered. There were always more low-caste vermin than were needed, and with the proper slogans and rites you could lead them to slaughter easily enough. "When the time comes, we will command a hundred thousand secret society devotees. The Royal Guard will not stand with us, at least not until Her Supreme Majesty comes to see the wisdom of our cause, but they will not interfere. And enough of the Army will support us to give us many rifles. Augmented by your gifts, we shall slaughter every Star Devil in Kirosha in a day and a night."

Eereen's boasts seemed to mollify the demon.

"That is good. When my gifts are ready, I will send word to you."

The Magistrate watched the retreating hooded figure with a mixture of distaste and relief. The visitors from beyond the sky had brought change and chaos to the High Kingdom, upsetting a millennia-old balance that had maintained peace and harmony for its people, barring a few regrettable incidents. Some had happened recently enough to sting: barbarians had forced trade concessions from the Kingdom, and even launched humiliating invasions. Kirosha had endured, however, and Ka'at, the Way of Things, had been restored.

Until the Star Devils came.

This new breed of invaders was far more dangerous than any other, corrupting with offers of wealth and power instead of using naked force, while still retaining the option to use force should the Kingdom refuse to accept their gifts. It was an intolerable situation, one that would lead to changes that could not be undone.

The hideous Star Devil offered an alternative. His hatred for his rivals, especially the Americans, was so great he would do anything to eradicate them, both in the Kingdom and in other worlds among the stars. Eeren cared little for the universe beyond the realm, of course. Once the outsiders were gone, too busy warring against each other to bother Kirosha again, balance would return to the land.

If reaching those goals meant dealing with the rudest and least seemly of all the Devils, it was worth it.

* * *

The American Embassy in Kirosha had once been the High Monarchs' Summer Palace. The original building was a good thousand years old, and it had been more of a castle than an actual palace, with utterly functional walls around a solid fortified keep, complete with drafty walls and arrow slits rather than windows. Additions and modifications over the centuries had improved it: the walls and moat had been knocked down, although you could still see their outlines on the colorful gardens that had replaced them. The main building had had additions and entire wings added before High King Jeesha IV had built a nicer place outside the capital some two hundred years ago and turned the old palace into a rooming house for honored guests, a courtesy that had been extended to the US after making Contact.

The place was still deuced hard to heat up in the winter, however.

Heather felt a chilling draft run past her – almost through her – although some of what she felt had to be the aftereffects of her first taste of actual combat. She was shaky, cold and ravenous. And rather randy, perversely enough, not that she had anybody to help her work off such frustrations. Not what she'd expected, she considered as she leaned back on the sofa in the antechamber where she waited to be summoned by the ambassador.

She'd almost been killed, had helped butcher hundreds of sapient beings, and she felt... what? Grateful to her instructors at the Farm, back on Original Earth, for one. The paramilitary facility had put her through a refresher round of Basic training – she'd done her four years in the Army, beginning at age seventeen – before being sent to the CIA's version of Ranger School, which she'd only managed to pass thanks to a full muscle-enhancement procedure her fairly wealthy parents had bankrolled even as they decried her awful career choices. After that she'd gone through a full SERE course, combining *extremely* realistic virtual simulations – they said that after you died during a FVR Sim, the real thing was no longer a surprise – with hands-on drudgery as she learned all about Survival, Evasion, Resistance and Escape. All those hours of pain and suffering had paid off: when the real thing came along, she'd reacted instinctively instead of panicking and losing her composure and likely her life. She reminded herself to send a thank-you e-mail to her instructors.

Gratitude, yes. Some measure of pride, yes. Guilt? Not as much as she thought she would, or should feel after something like that. The Kirosha she'd killed had chosen to be there, weapons in hand. Her intellectual side could list all their many grievances, both against the High Crown and the US interlopers, but the rest of her didn't care. They'd made their choice.

Pacifism had mostly been exterminated during Earth's First Contact, along with nearly five billion other humans, mostly city-dwellers caught in a merciless honeycomb of force fields and then baked to perfection by the Snakes' city-busting 'bloomies.' The weapons were designed to turn the core of any built-up areas into a flat expanse of mineral-rich slag by the expedient of heating the area to a balmy twenty-five hundred degrees Fahrenheit for several hours and then venting the waste heat outside the atmosphere. Of all of Earth's great modern monuments, from the Eiffel Tower to the Empire State Building, very little remained; only those far away from cities had survived. The rest had been blended into the many congealed metal-and-concrete 'soup bowls' that still dotted much of the planet.

What the vengeful Americans had done to the Risshah some thirty-five years later had been equally savage – and she still couldn't find it in her heart to condemn them. She'd seen the remains of those dead cities, after all, watched the extant records from the Old Internet, watched people saying goodbye to their loved ones as they slowly burned to death. It took about an hour for the temperature inside the domes to reach lethal levels, and the force fields that contained the fires did not stop electro-magnetic communications from getting through. Millions of people had plenty of time to make a record of the holocaust as it happened. The Selfies of Doom.

She'd joined the Agency because, like many of her peers, she wasn't done extracting payback from the universe. Over the years she'd acquired some sense of nuance, and come to respect and even like some of the Starfarer polities America must learn to live with, but she never felt able to trust them wholeheartedly. There was no community of Star Empires. There were only fear and calculation, masked by largely empty platitudes. Heather hated the reality she lived in, but couldn't think of a feasible alternative that wasn't worse.

"The ambassador will see you now."

"Thank you, Molly," she said, sitting up. She hadn't had a chance to change her torn and bloodied suit; as soon as she arrived the Ambassador had demanded her personal brief and then kept her waiting for a good half an hour. The State Department seemed to attract more than its share of dickheads, and although Ambassador Llewellyn wasn't a career diplomat, he fit right in.

The office could have been located in New Washington or any city on Earth; its furniture was Old Earth wood, imported at great expense. A hologram of President Albert P. Hewer filled most of one wall, dominating the room with the man's dour but intense presence. Heather nodded towards it with instinctive reverence – President Hewer had been a constant in the lives of every American born since First Contact; he had won twenty-six elections in a row after the end of the state of emergency restored democracy, for some values of democracy – before turning to face her boss.

Ambassador Javier Llewellyn was tall and handsome, his once-red hair gone mostly silver; anti-aging drugs didn't alter time's effect on melanin production, although cosmetics could take care of that easily enough. In his case, the mane of white hair matched the man's patrician features perfectly, giving him an aura of gravitas Heather could only wish matched the reality within. His eyes were sharp, but whatever wit they displayed was of a low kind, reserved for political in-fighting and dedicated to his personal survival and prosperity. A Rat, in other words.

Even before his appointment to Kirosha, Llewellyn had been a perfect example of the dangers inherent in a hereditary aristocracy. His family were among the new USA's upper crust: well-to-do industrialists before First Contact who had been instrumental in incorporating the new technologies the Hrauwah had gifted America to make amends for leading the Snakes to Earth. The Llewellyn clan had supported Hewer's seizure of power during the chaotic years following the Snakes' attack, the state of emergency during which the country's laws and customs had been fundamentally altered, and in the process became part of the cadre that founded the United Stars of America.

As it turned out, Founding Parents could have rather troublesome children.

This particular Llewellyn was a third-generation scion of that illustrious family. In olden times, he would have gone to an Ivy

League university (none of those had survived First Contact); in the new one, that meant Brigham Young for his Bachelor's degree after completing his four years' military service, and The Citadel for his Masters in Engineering. No law degree: lawyers remained in distinct disfavor throughout the country.

Young Javier had spent most of his school years partying, even at Brigham Young, which frowned upon such things, and had managed to turn every opportunity his family extended to him into a disaster. Twenty years in the private sector had led to one failed business venture after another; a term back in uniform with the Army Corps of Engineers ended in a dishonorable discharge rather than a court-martial only because the clan had gone to bat for him; after that, he'd been exiled to a minor colony world, where he'd managed to get himself elected Governor for two terms before corruption charges led to a resignation in disgrace, barely avoiding impeachment.

Heather wasn't privy to the machinations behind the man's current appointment, but she could guess that the Llewellyn clan had exchanged its support for the President, who was facing increasing opposition from Congress, in return for a nice sinecure for their little darling, somewhere out of harm's way and out of sight. An ambassadorship in a planet of little strategic significance had probably seemed like a good place to spend a few decades. Except that the lives of over two thousand Americans might well depend on the decisions made by this ancient trouble child.

The Regional Security Officer was in the room as well. Mario Rockwell had joined the State Department after two decades' service in the Navy, where his career had plateaued at the rank of Commander when, as the executive officer of the Assault Ship *USS Lewis Puller*, he'd participated in the Battle of Risshah, where the last Snake fleet had been destroyed. Unable to advance further for reasons unknown – she suspected Navy politics – Rockwell had resigned his commission and moved into the diplomatic service.

Heather had been working with the RSO for two years now, and she still wasn't sure how she felt about the man. Rockwell often came across as an ass-kissing, time-serving political animal, the kind of Rat that gave Rats a bad name. And yet, he usually managed to do the right thing, or helped get the right thing done, typically by sweet-talking Llewellyn into it. She hoped he wouldn't throw her under the bus this time.

"Ms. McClintock," the Ambassador said as he stood up for her. The bastard had the gall to wrinkle his nose when she shook his hand.

Sorry for stinking up your office with the stench of combat, she thought as she forced a smile onto her face.

"What happened out there?" Llewellyn asked.

They already had her report and her imp data. What they wanted now was analysis, less than an hour after exchanging gunfire with murderous aliens. The only easy day was yesterday; one of her instructors had been fond of that saying.

"A group of alleged rebels, likely sponsored by the Preserver faction of the Court, launched an attack on human and Vehelian personnel, with the support of elements of the Kirosha Army," she said. "And, at the very least, did so with the tacit acquiescence of the Queen and the rest of the Court. To put it bluntly, they left us hanging in the breeze, and now they'll probably raise a stink about the way we defended ourselves."

Llewellyn's eyes widened. "That's ridiculous. What would they hope to accomplish? The whole rebellion is the work of disaffected elements in Kirosha society. Peasants, led by a religious cult." The tone he used when saying 'religious cult' would have served equally well for 'pedophile social club.' "That sort of rebellion is a common fixture here; they have one every couple decades or so. I don't see a conspiracy at work. Just incompetence. What else can you expect from primitives?"

"The lack of response from the Royal Guard suggests otherwise," Heather said. "Historically, they are charged with suppressing riots, acting as the enforcement arm of the Crown. This was a relatively small uprising; less than five thousand people were involved. A Guard regiment would have slaughtered them, and there are five such regiments in the city or its environs. The Final Blow Society shouldn't have been able to mass in numbers inside the city proper, let alone be supported by Army units."

"We also have to consider the Crown's refusal to answer our calls," Rockwell said. "We still haven't heard from anybody at the Magistrate level, let alone the Prime Minister. Something is not right."

"That does concern me," the ambassador conceded. "But that could be some internal matter that doesn't involve us directly."

It involved the dead pretty damn directly, Heather thought. Out loud: "The faction trying to co-opt the rebellion is focusing their anger on us 'Star Devils.' Whatever their goals are, we are being made into targets."

"Well, if the Ruddies get too uppity, we'll just have to call up a starship and bomb them further down the totem pole than they already are," Llewellyn said. "I'd rather things didn't get to that point. Having to be rescued by the Navy will make us all look bad."

It will make you look particularly bad, and I'm guessing this posting is your last chance before even Mommy and Daddy decide to give up on you, Heather thought. Llewellyn's inept handling of the Kirosha Court had likely made things worse.

"Hopefully the incident will discredit the Preserver faction," she said. "The Crown lost face, showing itself unable to protect their 'honored guests.' They take hospitality very seriously here."

Except when they don't,' she didn't say out loud. Kirosha history was full of incidents where one ruler or another invited his enemies to a social gathering, and then proceeded to butcher them in the middle of the festivities. It was the most dishonorable thing a host could do, but winning big covered a multitude of sins.

"Well, I'll have Deputy Norbert draft a firm note to the Queen. Demand reparations for all the dead Americans those peasants murdered," the Ambassador said. "They killed, what, seven AmCits?"

"Fourteen," Heather corrected him. "A van full of Star Mining employees got separated from the rest of the convoy. All eight passengers were massacred."

"Well, we can't have that, can we? How come the Marines weren't able to rescue them?"

"It took too long for the rescue force to reach us," she said. "By then, the van had been overwhelmed. The rest of us are lucky to have survived."

All thanks to you trying to keep the Marines at the Embassy, guarding your cowardly ass.

Something must have shown in her face. The glare Llewellyn sent her way showed how little he cared to be corrected by an underling, even indirectly. Heather knew she needed to learn how to play the game at this level, or she'd never move beyond her covert agent status. The ambassador was about to say something when he paused for several seconds; someone had called him, which meant the call had been important enough to interrupt the meeting.

Saved by the bell, Heather thought.

"You will have to excuse me," the ambassador said. "The Vehelian and Wyrashat want to hold a conference call regarding the incident. We will continue this later." He turned his chair around so its back was facing them, his way of dismissing them without having to say a word.

Heather and Rockwell left; the RSO gestured at her to follow him. They went outside, to a large balcony overlooking the Enclave and the city beyond. The fires around Kirosha were still burning, but the conflagrations the Marines had started during the rescue operation had been put out, a clear indication the royal authorities were back in control over the city proper. Assuming they'd ever lost control, that was.

Rockwell got down to business. "What did you think of the new Marine CO?"

"Competent. Takes his job seriously. Handled himself well in combat."

"As did you. Maybe the Company should move you to Operations instead of Intelligence."

Heather shrugged. "I go where they send me. Although so far Intelligence is failing miserably. I never suspected the Crown would allow insurgents to enter the city and ambush us."

"Nobody did," Rockwell said. "The Kirosha were hunting down every secret society that poked its head up, as recently as a few weeks ago. Something has changed."

"I don't see what could have changed. They know what Starfarers are capable of."

During Kirosha's First Contact, the High King – the current monarch's father, dead some five years ago – had been taken aboard an American destroyer, flown to Jasper-Four, the second component of the binary planetary system, and allowed to see what a full spread of plasma missiles impacting a mountain range looked like. The whole thing had been presented as a show meant to 'amuse' the king, but the implicit threat had been clear.

Not the nicest thing to do, but most other Starfarers would have been even less kind. The Vehelians were pretty nice, but if turned down they would have simply gone to the Kirosha's nearest neighbor, given them enough tech to overrun the Kingdom, and then made a deal with the new owners of the mineral deposits they wanted to exploit. The Wyrm would have made a demonstration of Starfarer firepower somewhere clearly visible to the entire city, probably melting down one of the nearby mountains with a plasma barrage, and never mind the panic that would have caused.

The Lampreys would have slagged the city of Kirosha, and negotiated the surrender of the whole continent with whoever came on top in the aftermath. Or depopulated the entire planet. The US didn't do that sort of thing lightly; First Contact had seen to that.

Which makes us the good guys, I suppose.

The United Stars of America preferred to colonize empty planets, but when it had to deal with primitive worlds, it behaved in a manner that might be described as 'relatively fair' if you were charitable, or 'evil capital-imperialistic' if you were not, although the latter view was not exactly safe to spouse openly. Oh, you wouldn't get sent to a gulag if you spouted it – not anymore, at least; things had been much harsher during the State of Emergency years – but your name would go on a list, and someone would be given the job of figuring out a way to legally screw you. Even if you were a hundred-percent law-abiding – a minor feat in itself, because even after the Great Law Simplification of 47 AFC, most people still committed an unwitting felony or two at some point – you would be quietly discredited; doors would be shut, career paths blocked. Dissent was fine – to a degree. Past that, your choices narrowed until the best that you could hope for was a billet in some remote part of Earth or the galaxy.

After a while, most people figured out that going along was the way to go.

"Penny for your thoughts," Rockwell said; Heather realized her mind had wandered off for a second or two.

"They aren't worth that much. Still can't think of a reason for the Crown to behave like this."

"Unless they think they can get a better deal from the Wyrms or the Ovals," the RSO said.

"They'd have to be nuts to think that. The Kirosha have been getting ripped off even in the handful of trade concessions they've negotiated with the other Starfarers. We at least try to pay our bills with something of value; the others are always looking for an angle."

"I know it. You know it. But maybe the Kirosha don't."

"If that's the case, they sure picked a strange way to curry favor with the Vehelians."

"Well, there is that. Maybe the Envoy was the target. The Ovals can rub people the wrong way."

"Hm. That might explain it, actually," Heather said. "But they could just as easily PNG the whole Vehelian delegation, and we'd back them up. We like the O-Vehel Commonwealth, as much as we like anybody, but we don't want to compete with them if we don't have to."

"Yeah. Declaring the Envoy persona non grata is a lot more sensible than blowing him to hell. Much lower chance of having your cities slagged." He shrugged. "We need more information."

"I'll check with my people," Heather promised, meaning her

agents, the small network of mid- and low-level Kirosha functionaries she'd turned into spies through a variety of means, fair and foul. The fact that none of them had given her a heads-up about the uprising concerned her a great deal. You always worried when your agents failed you; it could mean they weren't placed high enough to find out what was going on, but also that they had chosen not to share their information with you. Either way, it was bad news. Intelligence work wasn't easy.

It was still better than playing kill-or-be killed games. She'd save that for the Marines.

* * *

Fromm walked past the assembled men and women in his unit.

Mostly men; there were exactly two women in Third Platoon. Combat units were slightly over ninety percent male on average, for a variety of reasons, some of which he agreed with, others not so much. Mostly men in their mid-twenties to early thirties, except for the few boots in their early twenties. The NCOs were far older, on average; they might look like they were in their thirties, but most of them would be pushing fifty or sixty. The Warp Marine Corps valued experienced personnel, and there was no pressure to pick up rank or get out; some people found a comfortable niche and stayed put. They were less likely to be promoted beyond their level of competence, which had been a problem back before First Contact.

The troops' helmet faceplates were up, but with their short hair – about half of them had 'highs and tights,' the rest the more relaxed medium-reg haircuts – and clean-shaven faces they all looked the same, except for variations in skin and eye color. His imp highlighted each face in turn and flashed their records. Over half of them had Combat Action Ribbons: they'd been with the unit at Romulus-Four or had seen action elsewhere. A small minority were replacements, fresh off boot camp at New Parris and assigned to the platoon just before it was sent to Jasper-Five; they'd had nine months to learn how things worked in the real world. Fitness reports showed that Gunny Obregon had worked everyone mercilessly, doing his best to keep the unit in fighting shape.

Fromm worried that all that training might be put into practice sooner rather than later.

"Looks like this billet isn't going to be as peaceful as I

expected," he said out loud, getting a few chuckles in return. He wasn't wearing his helmet, and they could all see the shiny spots on his forehead where Nu-Skin had been applied to cover the shrapnel wounds he'd taken. "But as long as we all do our jobs, like you did earlier today, we'll be fine. Dismissed."

The troops relaxed and walked away, most headed back to barracks to take off their armor, others moving to replace the two squads he had up as a quick reaction force, cocked and loaded and ready to rock. Fromm headed back to his office. Less than three hours since he'd landed, and he'd already been in a firefight, had a counseling session with Sergeant Amherst, and was about to have a meeting with the ambassador. He hadn't had a chance to unpack his bag. His only other stop had been at the inaptly-named Battalion Aid Station, where a Navy corpsman had treated his concussion, removed the chunk of foreign matter from his biceps, and recommended eight full hours of rest. Fromm had chuckled at the suggestion.

The borrowed armor chest piece Obregon had brought for him chafed him. He needed to have the platoon's armorer fit it for his frame, the kind of thing you expected to have time for when you arrived to assume command of your unit. Nothing about this assignment had turned out as expected. Then again, he'd seen this billet as a second chance, although he didn't think anybody had foreseen just how challenging it would be.

The office chair molded itself to his body. A computer screen on the desk came to life, obsolete but still mandated by regulations; desktop comps were heavily shielded against disruptive attacks that might neutralize or even kill an imp, and everything important had to be routed through them. They still made you type reports on a keyboard, just to keep you from getting lazy. Generally speaking, anything that could kill your imp would most likely kill you too, and even if it didn't, the sudden loss of input would leave you too messed up to do much, including typing, but regs were regs.

He had about an hour to kill before his meeting with the remfies in charge. Fromm spent the time going over logistics. Until Fleet showed up and taught the local primmies not to attack American visitors, his troops had to be prepared for the worst. Like he'd told McClintock, his job was to evaluate capabilities, not intentions, and he needed to know what his people were capable of doing.

Things weren't as bad as he'd feared, but they weren't great, either. Third Platoon had shipped out with a standard combat package: all the weapons, ammo and consumables needed for three weeks of sustained combat operations. Fromm had learned first-hand that the three-week estimates were wildly optimistic. In combat, you always ended up using more than you expected; more of everything, from ammo to asswipes to human beings.

His unit also had two dedicated fabbers at their disposal, not counting the Embassy's own fabricator facilities and several private ones in the Enclave. Fabricators were the most ubiquitous piece of Starfarer tech in the galaxy: 3-D printers that could be programmed to produce anything from ordinary nuts and bolts to the components of a plasma missile. Ammo and spare parts would be little trouble to replace. The ordnance they'd spent in the brief skirmish in the city would be fully replaced in a few hours, as long as the fabbers had access to the raw feedstock necessary. The platoon had enough of the mixed-material powder to produce another two weeks' worth of combat materiel, maybe more if they could use local raw materials to eke out the feedstock reserves. Five weeks' ammo and spares. Given that a relief fleet could show up in as little as eight hours, they should be okay.

Fromm checked the figures one last time before getting ready for his meeting, replacing the armor and field uniform with his dress blues after a much-needed shower. He pitied McClintock, who'd been ushered to the Ambassador's presence with blood on her clothing. The thought led to his wondering if she was single. The sudden brush with death had gotten him revved up; she wasn't in his chain of command, and she'd looked damn good before, during and after the fight, bloody clothes or not. Something to think about.

A short walk to the Embassy complex gave him a better feel for the place. There were plenty of good fields of fire, the walls of the main building would be proof against small arms fire, and the gardens surrounding the property consisted of low-height flowerbeds that would offer little cover to an advancing enemy force; the gentle slopes leading towards the compound could be improved with entrenchments that would allow a small number of well-equipped troops to hold off an army. All in all, there were worse places to defend.

Assuming the remfies let them, of course.

He was led to the office by an unsmiling secretary. There was no hand-shaking, no offers to sit down. They kept him standing while the Ambassador spoke.

"I find it deplorable that you allowed your troops to act against my standing orders," the Rat-in-Chief said. "While I appreciate the desire to safeguard human lives, we have a chain of command for a reason. My main concern was the safety of the Embassy, which would have been left unprotected if all your Marines had gone gallivanting into the city. If your men had waited a few minutes, or if you had bothered consulting with me beforehand, I would have approved the rescue mission. I suppose that, since things turned out all right in the end, we can overlook some of the breaches in protocol. I will have to write a report about this, however."

Fromm didn't say anything; he'd be filing his own report soon enough, and Llewellyn wasn't going to come off well from this situation. That kind of egregious remfie bullshit didn't get you very far in the USA. Llewellyn had spent all his life under peacetime conditions, which meant he didn't understand how things worked when plasma and explosives were flying around. He'd learn soon enough. The Hewer Administration had almost as little patience for remfies as Fromm did.

"In any case, I hope we can work together moving forward," Llewellyn went on. "I've also been made aware that several native vehicles were militarized without authorization. While I've been convinced they should not be decommissioned immediately" – he glanced briefly at the RSO – "I want you to make sure your men didn't embezzle any discretionary funds to build their toys, and if they did, I need those expenses noted. Under the circumstances, I suppose I must approve them after the fact, but any other such activities need to be run past the RSO and myself from now on. Is that understood?"

"Yes, sir."

If Fromm played his cards right, he might be able to reimburse Obregon and everyone who'd chipped in to equip Rover Force. Sometimes a Rat's devotion to bean-counting could be used for good instead of evil.

"Mr. Rockwell will keep a close eye on your behavior from now on. We have to present a united front. Stick to the chain of command."

"Yes, sir."

"Very good. You are dismissed."

Fromm saluted and left.

This assignment had started with a fight to the death, and he had a bad feeling it was only going to get worse.

Eight

Year 163 AFC, D Minus Eight

Heather McClintock needed answers, and she wasn't getting them.

People she'd come to rely on – never fully trust, of course, since they were all traitors – weren't responding to her attempts to contact them. Years of careful tradecraft, her own as well as her predecessor's, had been seemingly wasted. Her agents were either too scared to speak to her, or worse, had been discovered, maybe even turned, although in the latter case they should be eager to get in touch with her.

There was plenty of signals intelligence available – all phone and radio communications in Kirosha were an open book – but whoever was behind the current plot was cagey enough not to use such methods. She wished she could have planted bugs throughout the Palace complex, but one of the last actions of the current monarch's father had been to purchase a very expensive Wyrashat security suite. The alien anti-surveillance systems were good enough to handle the stuff her budget could afford: collecting intelligence in a primitive world of little strategic significance hadn't exactly been a priority for the Central Intelligence Agency, which also explained why a thirty-two year old field agent was in charge of the whole operation. This wasn't a prestige post, or even a career-enhancing one. Failure would kill her career just as dead as if she'd botched an operation against the Galactic Imperium, of course.

More importantly, under the current circumstances failure might literally kill *her*. It was time to be more proactive about getting answers.

Things had calmed down significantly in the two days since the incident, which made leaving the Enclave merely risky rather than insanely dangerous. The rioting and arson in the slums were over, for the time being at least. Even so, all AmCits were still being advised to remain in the Enclave. She wished she could heed that advice.

Heather and Locquar drove out in an unmarked private car, a pricey model that might belong to a mid-level functionary or a wealthy merchant. Her shawl and sunglasses hid most of her alien features well enough that a Kirosha peering through its tinted windows might not recognize her as a Star Devil. The driver was wearing a light armor vest with force field generators under his clothing. So was she. The city's peace might have been restored, but the realization of how quickly that peace could be shattered had sunk in.

A short while later, they waited for their quarry outside a gambling saloon, a discreet establishment in a seedy part of town, frequented by people who didn't want their vices to become public knowledge. They didn't have to wait long; Sub-Magistrate Preel Lood emerged from the building shortly before the end of his scheduled three-hour lunch and siesta break, giving himself some fifteen minutes to walk back to his office at the nearby House of Permission. Locquar started the car and drove until it was alongside the bureaucrat.

Heather rolled down her window. "Please allow me to drive you to work, Sub-Magistrate," she said pleasantly.

Preel froze mid-step, looking around as if searching for an escape.

"My driver will be happy to help you in, if you wish," she added. Locquar gave him a toothy grin from the driver's side. The violent reputation of the Sea Clans was well known, and Locquar's skin color and shaved ridge hair made his ethnicity obvious. The reluctant agent got in the car.

"That was the first wise thing you have done of late," Heather said as Preel looked at her with apprehension bordering in panic.

"A thousand pardons, most esteemed Starfarer," the sub-magistrate said. "My duties, you see, they have prevented me from being as receptive to your needs as…"

"Save it," McClintock cut him off, still speaking in flawless Kirosha but being rudely direct. "You took my money, Preel. You betrayed your office to pay for your gambling debts. In doing so, you went down a path you cannot change. You know what the penalty is for treason."

Preel blanched even further at the thought.

"I beg your forgiveness," he said. "I am yours to command."

"My forgiveness depends on what you have to tell me. What is happening in the capital? Why were rioters allowed to enter the city and attack Starfarers?"

Preel slumped in defeat and fessed up. "That was the doing of the Preserver faction. The City Prefect has joined them. Magistrate Eereen Leep is their new leader. The Prime Minister, who favored the Modernists, has resigned and been sent into exile Any civil servant with ties to the Devil-Lovers has been purged. Some have been imprisoned. That is why I dared not try to contact you. I feared for my life."

As he spoke, Preel kept casting glances in every direction, as if expecting the dreaded Royal Inspectors to appear out of thin air.

"How about the Army? The Merchant Guilds? The Crown?"

"I do not know. There are still elements in the Court that favor accommodation with the Star Dev… with the Starfarers, of course. Nobody knows which faction enjoys the favor of Her Supreme Majesty favors. Many Army officers, of the higher ranks are Modernists. The merchants as well, but…" Preel could not contain a sneer even in his frightened state. "Who cares what the merchants think? They are whores in fine clothing, woolly beasts to be sheared as needed."

Since First Contact, the merchant caste, long considered merely one notch above the peasantry, had begun to surge as a force to be reckoned with. They had led the way in adopting new technologies and their factories and trading posts were rapidly increasing Kirosha's wealth. To the bureaucratic, warrior and noble castes, they were still vermin to be exploited and otherwise ignored.

"Is there anything else you wish to report? I will be most vexed if I discover you were holding out on me."

"There is a rumor among the Learned," Preel said, using the traditional term for the scribe and bureaucrat caste. "A hooded figure has been seen speaking to high-ranking members of the Magistracy and the Courts. Some claim he is a foreigner, perhaps a Star Devil himself. I cannot say if those tales are empty gossip or truth to be recorded for eternity."

"I thank you, Sub-Magistrate."

They dropped off Preel a discrete distance away from the House of Permission and drove off.

"What do you think?" she asked Locquar. The driver had lived in Kirosha all his life; his family had been mercenaries and bodyguards in the capital for generations, although officially they remained foreigners and had to carry passports just as if they'd just arrived to the continent.

"My cousins are worried," he said. "They work for a number of merchant houses, and stood guard during the riots. They hear many things; their employers often forget guards have ears. I will call on them later today and see if they have anything to say."

"Thank you."

They drove past two dead drop sites, but nobody had left a message in them. After that, they returned to the Embassy; Locquar went off to visit his family and do his own information-gathering, and Heather sat down to generate a report about the meeting with her agent. She considered highlighting the rumor of a possible Starfarer agent was stirring trouble with the locals, but decided to hold off until she could verify it. The only polity that might benefit from upheaval in Jasper-Five was the Wyrashat Empire, and Kirosha's lanthanide deposits weren't exactly worth risking war with the USA. She was missing something, she was sure of it.

The rest of her day was spent reading the SIGINT take from her colleagues in the next office. It looked like both the Army and the Royal Guards were increasing readiness across the board: leaves had been cancelled, requisition orders for spare parts and equipment had shot up, and every general rank officer was in the field with the troops instead of hanging out in the capital rubbing elbows with the nobility, which was how the Kirosha top brass usually spent their time.

Just as she was about to go home for the day, Locquar came back. He did not look happy.

"All my cousins have lost their jobs," he reported.

"They were fired? Why?"

"The merchant houses have been told that no private armies of any kind are allowed within the capital. Their guards' permits to wield weapons will be cancelled by sundown tomorrow; we are required to turn them in or leave the city before then. Many of us have lived here all our lives. We hold property here, but now we have no employment, and soon no weapons. If the Final Blow Society goes hunting for foreigners, we will be among the first they will attack."

"How many people are we talking about?" Heather asked, thinking furiously. There was room in the Enclave – a lot of non-Starfarer foreigners had left as soon as the riots stopped – and she felt she owed Locquar.

"A hundred and thirty-three," he said. "Forty of them are Clan warriors."

That wasn't too bad. "You can bring them into the Enclave," she said. "At least until you can figure out a way to return to your homes."

Locquar blinked at her in gratitude. "I and all of mine will be in your debt. Ms. McClintock."

It would take some doing to convince the Embassy to help out, and more paperwork, but it would be worth it.

* * *

C.J. Carella

Timothy Brackenhurst only had three months left in his mission, and he still wasn't sure if he was happy to be going home or frustrated about leaving so much work undone.

The LDS mission on Jasper-Five had been established six years ago. It had begun as a purely humanitarian effort, with no attempts to proselytize, until it had become clear that the Kirosha Crown did not care if humans shared the Gospel: religion in the planet, or at least in the only continent humans had explored with any thoroughness, was a minor concern to most people. Their morality came from tradition, reinforced by draconian laws and a strict system of castes and customs where you knew the course your live would take from the moment of your birth, and where attempts to deviate from that course were met with penalties ranging from ostracism to death by torture, depending on the severity of the infraction. The Kirosha lived in a godless, merciless world, and when given the opportunity to show them a different way, the Latter Day Saints, the Star Baptists and the Catholic Church had all jumped at the chance.

During those six years, the LDS had accomplished a great deal. It ran a school, currently attended only by the lowest of the low, children of the Jersh Caste, whose assigned professions – fullers, garbage and manure collectors, morticians and fertilizer processors – rendered them unfit to associate with peasants, let alone any of the higher castes. Changes in technology had brought a measure of prosperity to some segments of the Jersh, but there were precious few ways for them to use their newfound wealth. Trying to educate their children was one of them, but until the arrival of the Starfarers it had been difficult and expensive. The mission's school had started by teaching Kirosha subjects – basic literacy, the planet's own mathematical system – which Timothy, who thought about becoming an engineer some day, had found rather elegant – and the same subjects that would be taught at a Kirosha academy. Just as Timothy's mission began, Starfarer sciences and history been added to the curriculum. It was too early to tell what effect of the new program would have, but Timothy felt confident it would be positive. One day, Kirosha – all of Jasper-Five – would venture forth into the stars, and he was sure that members of the Church, including many former pariahs, would lead the way.

The school had been so successful that members of the noble and merchant castes had inquired about hiring teachers as private tutors, or trying to set up a separate school for their own children. The mission president had politely declined, which Timothy

108

thought was a mistake, because now the upper castes of Kirosha society had been left to the tender mercies of the Catholics, particularly the Jesuits, who ran a much fancier school in the Palace Complex, or at least had done so until the recent troubles started.

"You seem rather pensive today," Timothy's companion, Jonah Ruiz, said as they finished their morning exercise routine. "Are you packing your trunks already? Thinking of home?"

For Timothy, home was back on Earth, in North California. Jonah was another Earthling, although his family lived in Sonora and he had no plans to go back there; the fifty-seventh state was still dominated by wilderness and haunted by the aftermath of First Contact. Jonah had been barely able to afford to pay for his mission, even with his family's help. He was planning on joining the Navy after he was finished here. Timothy envied his friend's certainty; he still had no idea what he would do in six months' time.

"Or is it the recent unpleasantness that is bothering you?" Jonah went on when Timothy stayed silent for a few seconds too long.

"It certainly doesn't help," Timothy said. He missed riding his bicycle into the capital; he'd been delighted to find out that bikes were commonplace in Kirosha, and riding down the crowded and colorful streets of the city had been an amazing experience. But no longer. The last time he'd been there, the usually amused stares of the locals had turned into angry or scared glances. Few Kirosha welcomed the sight of humans riding down the streets in their white shirts, black slacks, ties and helmets, not anymore.

Jonah's normally placid demeanor became glum. "I'm sorry, Tim. I shouldn't be kidding around when that kind of thing is going on."

"I hate to say it, but I'd expected things would have gotten much worse after the riots. I thought a new spate of murders would follow."

"Me too. Maybe the worst is over."

"I hope so. And in answer to your question, I was mostly concerned about leaving Kirosha when there is so much left to do."

"Ah. Well, we're doing the best we can."

"I'd wish we could help them deal with hunger and disease. They already know about the germ theory of disease, about proper sanitation, antibiotics, crop rotations. But the lower castes still live and labor under primitive conditions. Only the elites benefit from the new knowledge. It's not just unfair, it's stupid. Viruses and bacteria don't care about caste distinctions."

"They don't want to alter the Ka'at."

"Yes. The Way of All Things. A great excuse to let children die."

Jonah smiled sadly as they headed towards the showers. They'd had similar conversations before. "Change also brings disruption, Tim. This rebellion is a symptom of that disruption. And children have died because of it."

They continued the old argument over breakfast. "I just want to help them. Even if that means disrupting their precious Way."

"Back in Pre-Contact days, you would have been denounced as a cultural imperator, no, imperialist," Jonah said.

Timothy shrugged. History wasn't his forte. He knew that old America had been a land mired in decadence; that much had sunk in during school. Many viewed First Contact as the Lord's judgment over a lazy and unruly people who had turned their backs on Him. By contrast, the Church of Jesus Christ of Latter-Day Saints, long persecuted, hated and misunderstood even in the country of its birth, had prospered during the trials and tribulations America had endured. *We did travel and wade through much affliction in the wilderness*, as the Book of Nephi said. Much affliction, yes, but the faithful had survived, prospered and multiplied, so that they numbered one in six of the one and a half billion Americans in the universe, where once they'd comprised less than five percent. If that wasn't a sign that they were truly the elect, and that their ways deserved to spread across the galaxy, what was?

"I just want to help," he said.

"As do I, Tim. I just know it's not going to be easy. Many Kirosha dislike us merely because we don't look like them. Others are afraid we'll destroy their way of life, and rightfully so. It's no accident most of our converts are the Jersh, the people at the bottom, who have the most to gain with change. It's going to take time. Lifetimes, even now that we can all expect to live for centuries with proper medical care."

"Maybe I will stay, then, and spend two hundred years here, bringing the Gospel to this world."

The words surprised Timothy even as he uttered them. Maybe he had made a decision after all.

"Do you mean that?"

"I think so," Timothy said. "Something to think about. I already speak the language, with a little help from my portable device."

Like many Mormons, Timothy had chosen not to receive an implant, making do instead with a neck band that provided most of its functions, but could be removed when not needed, thus forgoing the temptation to use the device for more than writing letters home, checking the news and do the mission's work, which was all that was allowed while performing his two years' mission. It was hard, and yet another reason to look forward to its end, even if only to enter a different, more committed kind of service.

"Well, I hope you are happy wherever you end up," Jonah said. "For me, it's the Navy for at least twenty years, and then maybe the merchies after that, assuming I haven't gotten tired of doing the warp dance."

Timothy shuddered at the thought. His warp rating was Two, which meant he didn't need to have most of his brain turned off before going into warp, but he did not enjoy the experience one bit, not that anyone did. The thought of traveling between the stars on a regular basis had no appeal to him. Jonah was a WR-3 which meant he could be trusted to pilot a vessel in and out of that terrifying level of reality. He would do great in the Navy.

If Timothy chose to stay on Jasper-Five, he might never have to face warp space again. That alone made the idea worth considering.

* * *

About half of the bars in the Enclave were closed. That struck Russell as a very bad sign. In his experience, not being able to get booze meant the system was breaking down, or about to.

The watering hole he'd chosen for his meeting with Crow was still open, thankfully. All's Jake was owned and operated by an American, a miner who'd gotten hurt bad enough even nano-meds couldn't put him back together a hundred percent; the guy had taken his disability settlement and used it to open a bar catering to his former co-workers. He was doing better now than when he was operating a laser drill.

Come to think about it, Russell mused as he and Gonzo walked into the place, every bar that had shut down had been owned by Ruddies. And he couldn't see any of the regular ETs on staff, either. It was like the locals had decided that dealing with Americans was bad for your health, which might be nothing but the literal truth.

They made their way through the dark, crowded establishment

and ordered at the bar rather than rely on the single waiter, another human, working the room. Jake was tending bar his own self, his mechanical arm making a slight whirring noise that indicated it was overdue for a tune-up. Gonzo dropped twenty bucks for a shot of Earth whisky; Russell got himself a tall glass of fermented Jusha juice, just as much kick per ounce for one fifth the price.

Jake leaned over as he handed them their drinks. "Your friend is in the private room upstairs," he said.

"Thanks, dabrah." Russell had his imp add an extra fifty to the tab. It hurt his bottom line, but you had to tip the house to ensure nobody remembered who Russell and Gonzo had been meeting with.

They made their way up a rickety flight of stairs and entered the office.

"Two jarheads walk into a bar. There's got to be a punchline there," said the man sitting by the table.

Russell had been there once before, for a high-stakes poker game that had wiped out his savings. Back then there'd been seven people and the room had been full of smoke: tobacco, weed and Looka, a fragrant leaf the locals rolled into cigars and which got humans drunk and wired up at the same time. This time, the room was empty except for the 'trader' and a bodyguard, a Samoan so massive you could hang starship-grade force fields from his chest.

"Mister Crow," Russell said. Gonzo just nodded and grunted. "Sorry it took so long to set this up. We couldn't get leave until tonight."

"Understandable," Crow said. The trader/smuggler was a tough-looking, grizzled fellow, with an impressive collection of tattoos and scars showing wherever his skin wasn't covered up by a colorful Hawaiian-style shirt under a leather overcoat. His gray hair was cropped short, longer than a medium-reg, but not much. Russell didn't spot any motto tats on him, the kind of Marine symbols most boots got on their skins and soon lived to regret, and one of the easier ways to spot a former member of the Corps. If he had to guess, though, he figured Crow had spent some time in the gun club, and on the sharp end of things. He had too much of a hard case look to him to be a measly bubblehead, or a Person Other than a Grunt.

"But here we are now," Gonzo said, as unimpressed by Crow and his pet man-mountain as he was by anything else. Gonzo had maybe given two fucks, total, in his entire adult life, and he wasn't about to give a third.

"And you're wondering if I have the payment for the item,"

Crow said. "The answer, unfortunately, is no."

"And why is that?" Russell asked before Gonzo could open his mouth and turn the meeting into a bloodbath. He sent a quick STFU text to his partner in crime at the same time.

"We missed our window. The fucking uprising, you see. My ship couldn't wait for the natives to stop being revolting, and it had to leave before I could load the item. That means I won't be able to meet with the buyer in time, which means no sale, at least for a few weeks."

"That's disappointing," Russell said mildly. He'd figured on scoring fifty grand, personally, even after covering expenses and spreading the boodle among the four Marines responsible for liberating the damaged warp catapult. They were all out over a grand apiece already: bribing assorted bubbleheads to stow the catapult sections with the rest of Third Platoon's gear and shipping it along on three separate trips hadn't come cheap.

Nobody was going to be happy about this. Russell was especially not looking forward to breaking the news to Da Costa, who might be female but had undergone full muscle and bone replacement. She could bench-press Crow's Samoan bodyguard and had no sense of humor whatsoever.

Gonzo looked about ready to blow up, but he had enough sense to check with Russell first.

We kill him, right? Gonzo sent through his imp.

Belay that. Let's hear him out.

Out loud: "So what's the plan now?"

"Like I said, I can find a buyer and get your money within a few weeks. Or I can give you back the item. Maybe you can find a new buyer elsewhere."

Russell didn't like it one bit, but they had no choice. They'd counted on being deployed somewhere with actual space trade, where a buyer could be easily found, or back to New Parris, where worst case they could have sold the components piecemeal and still come out ahead. Instead, the Rats in charge had broken up the entire regiment and scattered it into platoon- or even squad-sized bits all over the fucking galaxy. Nobody in Jasper-Five was going to buy a warp catapult. The local primmies didn't even know how graviton-tech worked, let alone have any use for it.

"There's a Gack freighter that just came in from Grenada," Gonzaga said, trying to play it coy. "Mebbe they're in the market for a catapult."

Crow shrugged. "Yes, the *GACSS 1138*. The Pan-Asians would definitely be interested in the item. But they aren't exactly flush with hard currency, unless you don't mind getting paid with Sphere Credits."

"Fuck that," Gonzaga said. Russell agreed; the Gacks' money was constantly dropping in value versus both the US dollar and the Galactic Currency Unit.

"Besides, I'd be careful about doing business with the *1138*. They have a bad rep, even among the more flexible people in the trade. They'll deal with anybody."

Russell sighed. The Pan-Asians might be human, but they liked Americans about as much as the Lampreys did, and would be just as happy to butt-fuck anybody. Props to Gonzo for trying, but it'd been a weak hand. Besides, getting two tons of high-tech materials shipped back to their barracks under their current high-alert status wasn't difficult; it was plain impossible.

"We'll wait," he told Crow. "We'll wait for your ship to come back."

"I appreciate your patience."

They might as well be patient. Crow wouldn't just take the catapult and leave without paying; the man's word was good. The fuckers in the Asian ship didn't sound dependable at all; he didn't trust anybody who didn't even bother to name their ships.

He had a bad feeling about it, though.

Interlude:
The End of the Beginning

Risshah-Two, Year 35 AFC

King-Captain Grace-Under-Pressure missed holding court on the bridge of her ship, but she wouldn't have given up her current posting for anything, even a King-Admiralty. She was in the presence of history in the making, a moment that would be remembered until all Starfarer polities involved had achieved Transcendence or extinction.

"It is official, Mister President," Admiral Carruthers said. "We have met the enemy and they are ours."

The holotank at the center of the bridge of Second Fleet's flagship told the story. The last Risshah orbital fortress was slowly breaking apart as flames erupted from multiple breaches in its armored core. No more missiles or graviton beams emerged from the planet's surface, either; the Snakes' planetary defense modules had fallen silent or been destroyed.

The battle was over.

The mood in the command center of the battleship USS *Great Vengeance* was surprisingly sober. Perhaps it was due to the presence of the Americans' supreme leader, President Albert Hewer, who had chosen to accompany Second Fleet on its final campaign against the Risshah. It was unusual, to have a ruler be present during a battle, even one where the outcome was not in doubt. It made sense in this case, however, given the circumstances. A decision would soon have to be made regarding the fate of Risshah-Two, the Snake homeworld, and it should be made by the leader of the nation.

Grace had spent some time with the American President, since neither of them had any duties and little to do during the trek to Risshah. She had met him before, in the aftermath of First Contact. The man had changed a great deal during the intervening three and a half decades. The relentless quality Grace had noticed even during their first meeting had grown and become the man's defining characteristic. If it had been Hewer down on Risshah's surface, he would have fought to the end. There would have been no offers of surrender as long as he was alive.

"Thank you, Admiral," Hewer told Carruthers. "Are there any

115

strategic military facilities remaining on Risshah-Two?"

"There are seven planetary defense modules that still have energy signatures, sir. They are all damaged to some extent, and they have stopped firing."

"Destroy them all."

"Yes, sir."

Orders were given. Second Fleet had surrounded the Risshah homeworld; battlecruiser squadrons orbited every quadrant of the planet. Missiles and heavy beam weapons stabbed into the green planet below. Dots of fire appeared on the planetary display on the bridge, each marking the demise of one of the massive fortresses the Snakes' favored for ground defense. One by one, their energy signatures faded away.

Grace glanced around the bridge, once again grateful to have been selected to act as an observer during this phase of the war. One thing she noted was how young the crew was. Aboard most Starfarer vessels, the bridge complement of a flagship would be evenly divided between relatively young up-and-comers and career officers who had spent decades doing the same job and would remain at their posts for decades to come. Here, everyone belonged to the first category, except for Admiral Carruthers and a handful of senior officers.

Rejuvenation treatments had been made available by the Hrauwah as soon as they made contact with the US, but there had been complications, leading to the deaths of hundreds of thousands of aging humans seeking rejuvenation. The worst mortality rates had afflicted the political, financial and social leadership of the nation, with some very few exceptions, President Hewer among them. That might have been because the powerful and influential had been the first to get the treatments, and thus been exposed to the early, faulty process, but the Hrauwah King-Captain suspected politics rather than medical science had played a part in the demise of America's elites.

Whatever the causes, the USA was a nation of young people, and would remain so for a number of decades. The young were receptive to all manner of new things. Most people already seemed to accept President Hewer's reign as a matter of course. In Grace's opinion, that was a good thing. Her own King of Kings had ruled the Hrauwah wisely and well for several centuries. Continuity was a source of stability. She wished the President many years on his throne.

"All defense modules have been destroyed, sir."

"Are there any other military installations left?"

"Nothing capable of interfering with our operations, sir. But there are thirteen remaining army bases, three spaceports with potential military uses, and eight naval bases that…"

"Blast them. All of them. If it's got Snakes under arms, take it out."

"Yes, sir."

"Death by a thousand cuts, Al?"

The President turned towards Tyson Keller, his Chief of Staff. Grace didn't care much for the man, which was unusual. Hrauwah and humans felt an almost instinctual level of affection for each other, in most cases. There was a darkness within the advisor that triggered her fight-or-flight reflexes, however. The things the man had done to ensure the country stayed together might have had something to do with her feelings.

"See something you don't like, Ty?" Hewer said.

"I never get tired of watching Snakes die, Al. Like the great Mr. Jackson once said, 'I've had it with these motherfucking snakes on this motherfucking plane.' What I don't get is this drib-and-drab business. Are you going to give them a full dose of fire and brimstone or not? Nits make lice."

The President turned his gaze to the holotank, watching multiple planetary strikes show up on Risshah-Two's surface. Many of those bases were near population centers. Millions were dying. Millions more had died when the other defense modules had been taken out, and during the course of the battle. Space combat in orbit led to a great deal of collateral damage. At one point, a Risshah battlecruiser had crash-landed on top of a large city, immolating its entire population.

"I haven't made up my mind yet," Hewer said.

"The polls were pretty near unanimous."

"I know. If I pull this trigger, I do it in the name of every American left in the universe." Hewer looked around. "I know what I want to do. I just want to make sure it's the right thing to do."

The crew was clearly not comfortable with being within earshot of that conversation, but there were more than a few nods among them, and several mutters.

"Kill them all."

"Fuck 'em."

"Silence in the bridge," Carruthers ordered.

"We could make sure they could never leave orbit," Hewer said. "Set up space fortresses all around the planet, blast anything that looks like a space installation."

"And who's going to pay for that, Al? You aren't a liberal; you understand there is such a thing as opportunity costs. A space fortress here is a space fortress that isn't guarding one of our own planets. For what? So you can salve your conscience? We've already wiped out seven planets. Why hesitate at the eighth?"

The President of the United Stars of America hung his head. "You are right, Ty. I knew there was a reason I kept you around."

"I thought it was to make you look like a nice guy by comparison."

"That too." Hewer turned towards Admiral Carruthers. "I hereby authorize the destruction of every Risshah population center on this planet. For what we are about to do, may God forgive us."

For once, Carruthers didn't have any quotes handy. The admiral spoke a series of curt orders, authorizing the release of field-encasement thermal weapons and their use on Risshah-Two's fourteen billion inhabitants.

And thus did America join the community of Starfarers.

Nine

Year 163 AFC, D Minus Seven

RSO Rockwell wasn't happy.

"Three days before she deigned to meet with us," he muttered. "And not privately, but as part of a general audience."

"I agree; it doesn't bode well," Heather said as the Embassy car floated through the streets or Kirosha. The locals watched the grav-limo with almost religious awe; it was the only one of its kind on the planet. Neither the Vehelians nor Wyrashat had brought grav vehicles along, probably because their budgets didn't justify the expense. The power plants that anti-gravity engines required were out of range for most civilian applications. The Cadillac Phaeton they were taking to see the Queen had been gifted to the Embassy by the Llewellyn family, a naked display of wealth and patronage.

Heather doubted that any number of grav limos were going to keep the ambassador's ass in Jasper-Five, though. Not after the conflicting reports he and Captain Fromm had sent arrived to their respective destinations. No amount of influence would protect the ambassador from the fact he was ill-equipped to handle the current situation. She figured that Llewellyn would receive a terse note suggesting that he resign to 'spend more time with his family.'

It might take a while, though. The US freighter that had delivered Fromm to Jasper-Five had left the next day, carrying a set of reports that it would transmit to its the next port of call, where it would be picked up by other ships and retransmitted until it reached their intended recipients; that was how most communiques made their way between the stars. A very brief summary of the situation had also been sent via the Embassy's ENIGMA Machine; that was instantaneous, just not as useful as one would imagine.

The Entangled N-State-Particles Information Generating Modal Agent – blame the idiotic acronym on the device's primary developer, a physics weenie with a history fetish – could transmit information instantly across the galaxy by using quantum-entangled particles; changing one particle generated a change on the other, regardless of the distance between them. The effect had been known on Earth for decades before First Contact, but actually using it to transmit information had turned out to be tricky, even with Starfarer tech thrown into the mix. Keeping each particle pair entangled for a useful length of time required a great deal of energy and expensive equipment. As a result, transmitting one byte of information – a single letter or number – cost about ten thousand dollars, and each time you used an entangled particle in that way, you lost it. QE telegrams were shorter than their Morse Code predecessors. They also couldn't be used within five miles of an active graviton drive, so the systems could not be mounted in starships.

The embassy had fifteen kilobytes' worth of entangled particles in storage. It had used a bit under a hundred to deliver a terse status report:

LCLFRCSATCKUSCTS14AKIASITSTBRPTINBND

Translated, the QE-telegram read 'Local forces attacked US citizens. Fourteen Americans killed in action. Situation stable. Report inbound.' It wasn't much (and not worth three hundred thousand dollars, in Heather's opinion), just enough to let the State Department know to be on the lookout for a standard terabyte-long audiovisual report. Given interstellar traffic, the full report would have arrived to New Washington, Nebraska within forty-eight hours of the freighter's departure. Sometime yesterday, in other words. By the time the State Department made a decision, things might have changed dramatically on Jasper-Five.

Even worse, Heather wasn't sure the 'situation stable' claim was accurate. Yes, the rioters had dispersed without further violence after the convoy had made it to the Enclave; the Kirosha troops by the gates hadn't had to fire a single shot. Even the fires in the slums had abated. Several Final Blow Society leaders had been arrested, along with a thousand rank-and-file members, but thousands more were still camped all around the capital. The Court's unwillingness to clear them out worried her a great deal. The three-day wait before an audience was granted worried her more.

Heather had only managed to make contact with a couple more agents after her meeting with Sub-Magistrate Preel. The Seal-Bearer of the City Prefect confirmed that every outspoken member of the Modernist party in the city government had been fired or arrested. Her other agent, the servant of a Royal Guard Major, claimed that three Preserver-aligned colonels in the Guard had been quietly arrested and summarily executed. Heather had confirmed that none of those officers had been seen in public for a couple of days. A major power play was in progress between the two factions, and it seemed the Modernists still had a hold inside the Royal Guard. The Preservers had gotten a major black eye there, but they were still in the game and seemed to have cemented their hold on the bureaucracy. This audience would hopefully cast some light on the situation.

In any case, the freighter had also delivered a message to Lahiri, requesting fleet units for protection, and a QE telegram had let them know that a two-ship task unit would be on its way within the week. Once those ships were in Jasper, things would be handled gunboat-diplomacy style. At a minimum, the Kirosha would have to purge the Preservers if they wanted to keep the Kingdom in one piece. If they refused, it wouldn't go well for them.

Her attention turned toward more pressing concerns as the limo reached the low walls closing off the Palace District from the rest of the city. Heather had been there enough times to notice the number of Guardsmen on duty around the complex had increased at least twofold, maybe more. Even more surprising, several tanks and combat cars were conspicuously placed on both sides of the road, surrounded on three sides by stacked sandbags, their commanders visible through the turret's open hatches.

That's new. They're about ready to go to war. Only question is with whom.

Rockwell was looking at the display with a frown, clearly liking it as little as she did. On the opposite side of the passenger compartment, Ambassador Llewellyn and his wife were too busy whispering sweet nothings into each other's ears to notice anything. The current Mrs. Llewellyn – the third of that name – had been a fairly popular soap opera actress until she'd married up; she was fifty years his junior, still looked rather fetching, and from what little contact Heather had had with her, was as vapid as one would expect, besides being downright nasty whenever her wishes weren't promptly and wholly satisfied. Neither of them spared so much as a glance at the world outside. It must be nice to be so oblivious to reality, until reality decided to make its presence known.

The unsmiling soldiers let the limo through. A regular wheeled car flying the colors of the O-Vehel Commonwealth was right behind them, followed by a similar vehicle bearing the Wyrashat Emissary. Neither of the two Starfarers were happy, especially the Vehelians. Heather wondered if anybody in Kirosha understood the realities of their situation. Probably not. The Royal Court seemed to run largely on lies and illusions.

She looked back at the leader of the American delegation as he took a swig from a silver flask and offered it to his wife, who smiled and shook her head. The Kirosha were far from the only ones living in a dream world.

More Guardsmen were visible on the palace grounds. The feeling that she was wandering deep into enemy territory grew stronger. She wasn't armed – while Americans were exempt from the city ordinances forbidding firearms, that courtesy didn't extend to the Royal Palace – not that any portable weapon would change the outcome if the Kirosha decided to violate their guests' diplomatic immunity. Having her beamer handy would have made her feel a bit better nevertheless.

The limo glided gracefully towards the Great Pyramid; the massive structure gleamed in the early afternoon's light. The stepped pyramid was only used for ceremonial occasions, which meant the delegation wouldn't have to worry about climbing the ungodly number of stairs leading to the top. Instead, their vehicle headed towards an attached structure at the bottom, the smaller but much more hospitable Royal Palace.

Courtiers welcomed them as their car dropped them off at the entrance to the Lesser Courtroom, a small reception area reserved for more intimate audiences. Gorgeously-attired minor nobles of both sexes fawned upon the ambassador and his wife, and even spared a few bows and smiles for such nonentities as RSO Rockwell and herself.

While waiting for Her Supreme Majesty to show up, Heather spent some time exchanging inane pleasantries with some minor nobles. She noted that few members of the Magistracy were present. She'd expected a full set of Ministers to attend, but she only she spotted a few of them. The most prominent one was Eereen Leep, a roving functionary whose role was undefined but who wielded considerable influence, sort of a minister without portfolio. Eereen was avoiding most gathered notables and spending his time with the City Prefect, the only other bureaucrat with similar status.

Her musings were interrupted by the approach of the Wyrashat Information Officer.

"How lovely you to see you, Ms. McClintock," Breh said in English. The Wyrashat had four primary limbs and a pair of prehensile tails. Their necks were retractable and when fully extended could add as much as two feet to their height, and their skins were covered in small iridescent scales ranging in color from deep green to cobalt blue. Their heads looked vaguely crocodilian, except for their much-larger brain cases; their toothy, seemingly grinning expressions were downright intimidating.

"A pleasure as always, Officer Breh."

"May I have a word with you while we wait for Her Supreme Majesty to honor us with her presence?"

"Of course," Heather said.

American-Wyrashat relations had been relatively cordial. The Empire had only come into direct contact with the USA recently, after discovering a warp-valley that led to human space. Valleys, also known as 'ley lines' and 'dragon roads,' were regions of space-time where warp travel was greatly speeded up. Most space travel happened along those valleys, which made them the most important feature of galactic geography. Some nine years ago, a Wyrashat survey vessel had discovered one such valley, connecting an unimportant mining colony to Paulus, a white-dwarf planet-less system that had turned out to be endowed with no less than five ley lines connecting to several other worlds, including American-claimed Lahiri and Jasper. Having suddenly become neighbors, the two Starfarer nations were trying to develop a friendly relationship. Unlike other Class One sophonts, the Wyrashat were not brutally aggressive, so there was hope for peaceful coexistence there.

"It has come to our attention that the conflict between the Modernist and Preserve factions has reached a tipping point," Breh said. "The Preservers have taken control of the bureaucracy even as Modernist control over the Army has begun to waver."

The Wyrashat had better sources inside Kirosha than Heather's, apparently. "I see," she said. "I have heard similar things." A quid pro quo was expected, so she shared the news about the Royal Guard colonels' arrest and, more reluctantly, the rumor about a Starfarer visitor to the court.

"That is most interesting," Breh said, his half-lidded expression indicating concern. "If the rumors are true, that might mean this situation may involve far more than the fate of a minor mining concession."

"Who would stand to benefit from fomenting discord in Jasper-Five?"

"On the face of it, nobody. The Paulus warp-hub leads to Vehelian, Lahn Arkh and Hrauwah space, but to relative backwaters in each. That is changing, now that a trade route has opened up, but such things take time. Causing unrest here would only risk war with both America and Wyrashat. The most likely suspect, the Lahn Arkh, are vile but not insane; they would be foolish to start a conflict here."

"Agreed. All of this seems foolish, but if the rumors are true, someone believes otherwise."

Before the Wyrashat could reply, the Queen's imminent arrival was announced.

Music preceded her: gongs, cymbals, flutes and something like a hybrid between a harp and a violin played something unpleasant to Heather's ear, but which the locals seemed to enjoy. High Queen Virosha the Eighth was carried into the room on an elaborate palanquin made of wood, ivory and gold, borne by eight stout servants. The Kirosha in the room all squatted down to the ground and engaged in the ritual prostration their etiquette demanded. The Starfarers offered polite bows instead.

The supreme monarch of the continent and its three hundred million inhabitants was still relatively young, in her mid-thirties at most. Her vestments were light blue and gold, as elaborate as an Elizabethan court dress. Her skin was the lightest shade of pink, a mark of the Northern Kirosha, and her eyes a deep shade of purple. Neither her face nor her body language betrayed any emotion, as befitted someone raised in a court where revealing one's true feelings was considered a sign of weakness. Even so, Heather thought the monarch was tense; her movements seemed stiff, as if she was concentrating on retaining her composure a little too hard. The Queen sat down and quietly regarded the gathering. Silence filled the reception hall for several uncomfortable moments. Finally, she spoke.

"Shame."

The exact Kirosha word held many meanings. It was rarely used, and almost never by someone of importance. It was either a harsh accusation or an abject admission of guilt. Its very utterance in a public function was a major breach of protocol.

"Shame," she said again. Several courtiers gasped; the men pulled ornate fans from their coat pockets and hid their faces behind them and the women made motions of negation with their heads as their queen spoke on.

"For many years, our honored guests from beyond the stars have brought us gifts, wealth, new ways of doing things. And how do we repay them? Do we cherish them? Do we honor them, welcome them to our homes, offer them liquors and fine viands? No. We raise angry fists. We curse the names of their ancestors. We strike, burn, slay them.

"Shame."

Some of the noblemen were in tears at the sight of their monarch abasing herself in front of foreigners.

"We can never make full amends for the crimes some fools

committed in the name of Kirosha. Let this be a first step on the path to contrition."

Heather heard a strange sound coming from the rear of the audience chamber. Whimpers, getting closer, as if a group of sobbing children were joining the reception. She tried to peer past the gathered noblemen; she was taller than the average Kirosha, but their elaborate headdresses and coiffures made it difficult to get a look at whatever was coming into the audience hall. It wasn't until the closest courtiers saw what was being wheeled into the chamber and recoiled in surprise that she was finally able to see.

Grim-faced servants pushed six wheeled contraptions, flat wooden boards tilted at a sixty-degree angle. Four men and two women were attached to each board by nails driven into their wrists and forearms. They hung limply from their pierced limbs. Gags and tight straps around their necks made speech impossible; all they could do was keen softly, and most of them couldn't draw enough air into their lungs to do even that much.

Their legs had been severed above the knee, the stumps crudely tied off to avoid a quick death by blood loss. The weight of their unsupported upper bodies prevented the victims from taking full breaths, slowly asphyxiating them. Bright orange blood seeped through the stumps, running down the table and pooling into receptacles set at the bottom of the boards to keep the fluids from staining the marble floors.

Mrs. Llewellyn leaned forward and was noisily sick.

Her husband whooped.

That was the only way to describe the sound. Not quite a shriek or a howl. A whoop. It nearly startled Heather into laughter despite her own shock and revulsion. The ambassador and his wife held each other like terrified children. Not too far away, Deputy Norbert covered her mouth with her hand, suppressing a scream. Rockwell looked pale but kept his composure. Heather noted all of this, feeling vaguely disassociated from the reality of the situation. As long as she concentrated on analysis, she didn't have to deal with the mutilated victims being paraded in front of her.

"This is how we punish those who bring shame to our name," Virosha the Eighth said. "These are the people responsible for the attack on our honored guests. We offer you their deaths as a small token of respect."

As soon as the Queen uttered the word 'deaths' the attendants moved to the rear of the boards and started turning levers that tightened the straps around the prisoners' necks. Their whimpers turned to strangled gasps for breath as the straps strangled them, speeding up their demise.

It took a minute or two. It wasn't pretty.

The Llewellyns' near-hysterics were over, thanks to a quick infusion of sedatives via their nano-meds. The courtiers had watched their outburst with impassive expressions that did little to conceal their contempt. The ambassador held on to his wife and watched the executions quietly.

After the last of the prisoners died, the Queen nodded and the servants wheeled the six corpses away, leaving an acrid odor of blood and feces behind. Another set of servants sprayed a flower-scented mist to disguise the unseemly stench.

"Their heads will be delivered to your embassies, two to each of our guests. It is lucky there were six of them, or we would have to divide them up into smaller pieces."

The Wyrashat Emissary watched the proceedings impassively, only a slight widening of her nostrils betraying her displeasure. The new Vehelian Envoy went slightly pink around his ridges, bothered by the casual display of brutality but also hiding it well. Neither of them spoke.

Llewellyn did.

"This is barbaric," he blurted out in Kirosha.

Heather blinked.

Did he just say what I think he said?

"Barbaric!"

RSO Rockwell was using his imp to scream at the Ambassador privately; Heather could pick up the transmission although their security systems prevented her from eavesdropping. Llewellyn shook his head, dismissing whatever advice he got.

"How could you expose us to that... To that display?" he said, in English this time, but his words were rendered into Kirosha by a court translator almost as fast as an imp would have. "Civilized people don't do that kind of thing."

The man had snapped. Whether he was trying to compensate for his panicked reaction or had been overwhelmed by a mixture of adrenaline and the sedatives in his system, it didn't matter. He'd just publicly insulted the leader of an absolute monarchy.

Several courtiers began to move towards Llewellyn. None were armed, but they looked ready to tear the American apart with their bare hands. The Royal Guards on the edges of the chamber were just as ready to cut down the Star Devil and everybody around him. The ambassador spotted the advancing noblemen and he cringed from them, his anger replaced by a new wave of panic.

"Do something!" he shouted at Rockwell, as if expecting the

RSO to pull out a gun and start blasting away. Rockwell was looking around, trying to come up with a plan of action, and failing.

"No!" the Queen shouted, stopping everyone in their tracks.

"There will be no violence here," she continued. "Ambassador Llewellyn Javier, son of Ricardo. You respond to our kindness with insults. You are no longer welcome in this court. Take your servants and leave."

Llewellyn put an arm around his wife and all but ran for the exit. The courtiers reluctantly parted before him. The rest of the human delegation followed.

They rushed into the grav-limo and left. Heather let out a breath of relief.

"Sir..." Rockwell began to say.

Llewellyn started to sob uncontrollably.

* * *

No matter how many times he thought he'd hit rock bottom, Harry Routh always found it surprising how easy it was to dig himself a little deeper.

He'd already betrayed his country, his people, his very species. Committing an act of war against them was just another step down the road he'd chosen.

"We are finished, Great One."

Harry turned towards the speaker, a fat Ruddy clad in a Sub-Magistrate's robes of office. The alien tilted his head towards the workers who had been busily assembling the diverse components smuggled into Jasper-Five over the past several weeks. The last shipment had arrived on the *GACSS 1138*, where Harry was first mate. His years in the US Navy had earned him that position, despite the fact that the largely-Korean crew despised him. He didn't care if they liked him or not; they needed him too much to space him, although they saddled him all kinds of shit details, like this particular job. It wasn't just tedious and beneath him; if he was caught, the best he could hope for was a swift trial and execution in the US.

He looked at the devices that filled the factory floor. The previous three days' production had been taken and stored in a large warehouse after Harry had used his imp to inspect them. He did an inspection of the latest batch, knowing what the results would be. The Ruddies had done their best, but their best was shoddy by Starfarer standards, even though the components had been designed to be put together by primitives. His imp suggested failure rates in the thirty to forty percent range. Harry shrugged. He could hardly order the ETs to go back and reassemble their new toys, which would likely result in just as many defective pieces. Besides, as long as half of them worked as advertised, the Ruddies would be happy with the results. A fabber could have done the work of all fifty aliens, and done so faster and at higher tolerances, but smuggling a fabber and its operators into Kirosha would have been nearly impossible.

He'd earned every last cent of his blood money. There was only one thing left to do before he and the *1138* left this benighted planet and the fruit of his labors behind. By the time all the toys he'd helped put together were used, his ship would be light years away. That would be good, because by the time it was all over, there would be no living humans left on Jasper-Five.

"Take those outside," he ordered, pointing at the largest devices the Ruddies had built. There were only ten of them, each about twelve feet long and weighting almost a ton apiece. Their combined worth was about a hundred million Galactic Currency Units, enough to buy a corvette, and slightly under half the estimated Gross Planetary Product of Jasper-Five. The mercenary part of Harry had considered betraying his employers and stealing those components instead: the grav drives alone were thirty million GCUs, about a hundred million dollars, an amount of money he could barely comprehend.

You didn't betray the Lampreys and live to tell about it, though. The idle thought had never become more than that. Harry had been shown videos depicting the fate of those who'd taken the Lampreys' thirty pieces of silver and then tried to renege on their deals. He still had nightmares about what he'd seen.

Moving the black cylinders outside took two forklifts and the efforts of every Ruddy worker in the building. The stupid aliens dropped one of them halfway through the process. The massive weight rolled over one of the workers, crushing his legs. The ET screamed like a child in agony until the Sub-Magistrate gave a curt order and the screamer got smacked with a crowbar until his skull was crushed, which quieted him down right quick. Ruddies were nowhere near as bad as Lampreys, but they didn't exactly place a high value on life, either.

Harry could have engaged the devices' grav drives and had them float out into the yard, but he didn't trust his imp to maintain anything resembling precise control over them. One miscalculation and he might send them flying off at speeds that might actually damage the damn things. Better to have the Ruddies risk life and limb; dropping the cylinders wouldn't do anything. He didn't exactly place a high value on the Eets' lives, either.

Once they were lined up on the courtyard, he used his imp to activate the devices. The weapons lifted themselves off the ground, to the awe and delight of the gathered Ruddies. The ten cylinders flew up into the night sky, vanishing from sight in under a second. The workers cheered. They had finally struck a blow against the hated Star Devils.

You poor stupid bastards, Harry thought. All the Ruddies had managed to do was exchange one Star Devil for another. They wouldn't know that for a while, however. Might as well let them enjoy their ignorance.

He sent a message to the anonymous comm ID he'd been given by the captain of the *1138*. All he got back was a curt text acknowledging that the job was done. The Asian freighter would collect payment once they reached Primrose-Seven, the Wyrm warp-hub that, unknown to them, was being used as a staging ground for the Lampreys.

There was a good chance the butt-ugly ETs might decide to silence the crew of the *1138* instead of paying them off, of course. At this point, Harry wasn't sure he cared one way or another.

Ten

Year 163 AFC, D Minus Six

Shortly after breakfast, Jonah and Timothy joined several others at the mission's library for their customary two-hour Scripture study. They weren't the only ones using the facilities. A number of Kirosha students were there, taking advantage of the library's old-style books as well as the equally old-fashioned computers there. LDS tradition favored using traditional paper books for study; the Kirosha were not the only ones enamored with following the ways of their ancestors. In this case, tradition had helped the mission in reaching the Kirosha, whose own books were surprisingly similar to Earth's.

The Kirosha students wandered around the stacks or sat by one of the reading tables or computer desks in the common room. Timothy smiled when he spotted a youngster intently poring over a translation of *Tom Sawyer*. The book had been annotated to help make it more accessible to the local culture, but judging from his expression the kid was obviously struggling with it.

Timothy and his companion sat down with their copies of the Testaments. Mere minutes after they started, however, a commotion outside broke through the library's placid silence. People were crying out in pain and anguish. They were Kirosha: their high-pitched voices were unmistakable. He stood up and looked out of a window.

There were dozens of people just outside, filling the courtyard. Many were pupils at the school – he recognized several of them – but others were older and seemed to be their parents and relatives. There were wounded among them, their orange blood staining crude bandages or flowing from unattended cuts. What on Earth had happened to them?

He could hazard a guess, but he wanted to know for sure. Timothy was far from the only one who rushed out of the library, but he was one of the first to get to the door. Mission President Jensen had just arrived and was trying to find out what was happening, which was difficult with half a dozen Kirosha talking loudly at the same time.

"Brethren!" President Jensen shouted over the confused babble. "Brethren, please! One at a time. We will do what we can for you, but please, tell me what's happened to you."

An older man came forward, dressed in an expensively-stylized version of common laborer clothes. Timothy recognized him: Kroonha Veen, one of the wealthiest Jersh in the city, who owned several fertilizer plants that employed several hundred fellow caste members; he was the most prominent LDS convert on the planet. He was among the injured; dry blood was caked over his left temple, and the eye on that side was bruised and swollen. He waved the rest into silence, wincing at the pain the sudden move cost him, and turned to address President Jensen.

"Illustrious Mission President, brothers, sisters, we come here begging for protection!"

A familiar smell made Timothy look towards the city proper. The fires, which had disappeared in the last few days, had come back; he could see distant smoke rising once again, and this time he thought some of it was coming from inside the city rather than its suburbs.

"Of course, brother," President Jensen said. He was a solemn man whose tall, lanky frame and homely features reminded Timothy of a clean-shaven Abraham Lincoln, and the resemblance had never been so evident as it was at this moment. "Our doctors will be here soon. Can you tell me what happened?"

"The Final Blow Society," Kroonha said, confirming Timothy's suspicions. "They came at dawn, dozens of them, knocking down our doors, throwing us out of our homes and workshops, and setting them ablaze. They came for all converts, Catholics and Baptists as well as us. They knew who we were; each leader had a list of names. We were betrayed by our own neighbors. They watched us be expelled from our own homes, the miserable forni..." He checked himself and shrugged. "They will find little enough to rejoice about. An angry mob will not separate Christians from nonbelievers but will torment both. So will the fires they set. All Jersh will suffer."

The wounded man paused for a second, his eyes blinking in sorrow, his expression haunted by the disaster he'd just endured. "We have lost everything. We may yet lose our lives. At first, the guards at the gates to the Enclave would not let us through. We had to bribe them, give them what few valuables we managed to carry out of our homes. We..." He couldn't continue; his whole body shook as he sobbed, the sound so disturbingly like the crying of an inconsolable human child they made Timothy's eyes mist over.

Like every man and woman in the United Stars of America, Timothy had spent four years of his life in uniform, doing his obligatory military service. At that moment, he longed for the feel of the standard issue Mark I Infantry Weapon he'd trained with during Basic. There must be a reckoning for this.

Timothy shuddered and set aside angry thoughts. Revenge was not his concern now. He had to help these people, not avenge them.

There were over a hundred refugees around him, and he could see more coming.

Year 163 AFC, D Minus Three

"You don't look happy, sir," Gunny Obregon said when Fromm came back from the Embassy.

"You want the good news or the bad news first, Gunny?"

"Is there any good news?"

"Sort of. The RSO finally convinced the asshole to call for the cavalry. Priority QE message sent, reply received. The Fleet corvettes are moving up their scheduled visit; now they are due to arrive in sixteen hours. They'll drop off two more Marine platoons, so I'm finally getting a company. And if the Ruddy Queen doesn't agree to disarm all hostile elements in the city, the corvettes are going to turn that big-ass flattop pyramid of hers into a smoking crater. The Mickey Mouse bullshit is over."

"That *is* good news," Obregon said. "So what's the problem?"

"Llewellyn didn't wait for the corvettes to show up. He issued an ultimatum to the Queen as soon as he got confirmation the ships were on their way. The stupid asshole. It's like he never heard the definition of diplomacy."

"Haven't heard that one myself, sir."

"Diplomacy is the art of saying 'Nice doggy' while you look for a big rock. Llewellyn forgot to play nice while the big rock is underway. His excuse was, he wanted to forestall the Ruddies from doing anything; he figured if they knew the fleet was on its way they'd quiet down. But that knowledge gives them a window of opportunity, if they want to be unreasonable."

"You mean insane, sir. Nothing she does now is going to keep those corvettes from wrecking her little empire."

"I know that, and you know that, but so far the Ruddies have been acting like they don't know that. Maybe their culture makes it impossible to grin and take it, not after Llewellyn insulted their Queen. They haven't attacked us, but every Ruddy convert in the city's been herded into the Enclave. The ones they didn't murder outright, that is."

That was turning into a nightmare. Every fabber available had been put to work to provide shelter and supplies for the refugees, who had numbered in the thousands. Fromm had managed to keep his troops from joining in any relief operations: if an attack happened, he needed to be ready, not to have his platoon scattered all over doing humanitarian work.

And his gut told him an attack was likely. It didn't make sense, but that was how he felt.

"Everybody's as ready as we can be," Obregon said, correctly gauging Fromm's mood. It hadn't even been a week, but it had been a very intense few days, and he and his sergeant were getting a good feel for each other. Fromm had conducted a number of virtual field exercises, first with all the platoon NCOs, and later on with the entire unit. Along the way, he'd learned the strengths and weaknesses of the men and women under him.

Obregon himself was everything he could ask for, and possibly the best platoon sergeant he'd served with. He was a thinker and a doer who wasn't afraid to shoot down Fromm's ideas if he thought they were bad, and who could motivate the troops and kick their ass when he had to. Fromm couldn't have asked for a better second in command.

The rest of his NCOs were more of a mixed bag. Staff Sergeant Martin, leader of the mortar section, was conscientious but a bit of a plodder. As long as you gave him a concise set of orders he'd be fine; left to his own initiative he would follow the book, which wasn't bad most of the time. Sergeant Buford P. Jackson of the assault section was aggressive to a fault; during the simulated exercises he'd shown he would try achieve his objectives at any cost, which made him a good man to send out to fight if you needed something done, casualties be damned, and not so good for anything else. Sergeant Antonio Muller led the guns section with a bit more caution than Fromm would have preferred, but was otherwise a fine soldier.

The attached units were all right for the most part. Staff Sergeant Seamus Tanaka and a supply private ran were in charge of the platoon's armory, and had done a good job so far. His communications section consisted of four Navy spacers, commanded by Chief Petty Officer Lateesha Donnelly, a smart, detail-oriented woman who'd become Fromm's unofficial intelligence officer. Her mastery of the Kirosha language and skill at extracting information from the Ruddies' radio and telephone traffic had already proven invaluable. He even had a company's worth of corpsmen at his service, an abundance of riches he hoped he wouldn't need.

And then there was Staff Sergeant Amherst, Detachment

133

Commander of the Marine Security Guards. Technically, Fromm was the new Detachment Commander, adding yet another twist to the highly unorthodox posting, as that position was usually held by a staff NCO, not an officer. None of that would have mattered if Amherst wasn't an asshole, but he was an asshole. After going through his record, Fromm had realized the sergeant had gotten to his current position mostly by kissing copious amounts of ass. His combat record was minimal; he'd spent most of his time in the rear with the gear. Amherst's attempt to hinder the rescue attempt was probably enough to relieve him for cause, but Fromm needed every Marine he had, and the eight-man detachment represented two extra fire teams that might come in handy if the shit hit the fan. Fromm had kept Amherst at his post for the time being.

"At least the remfies let us dig in," Obregon said.

Fromm nodded. The beautiful flower beds around the embassy compound had been replaced by lines of entrenched positions, protected by rolls of smart concertina wire and portable area force fields. He peeked outside via his imp, and saw several hundred Kirosha, volunteers from the refugees now crowding the Enclave, digging a fallback set of trenches.

Embassy Row, the four-block square that contained the three Starfarer legations had clear fields of fire on all sides, being surrounded by parks that provided little cover for a good hundred yards in every direction, especially after the trees lining up the streets had been cut down and used for the trenches. Beyond the cleared area there were mostly residential buildings, no more than four stories tall, all the way to the Enclave walls, about six hundred yards away. A hundred yards of open ground was far from optimal – a running man could cross that distance in under twenty seconds – but it was better than nothing. Firing from fixed positions, his Marines could inflict gruesome casualties on anyone caught in the open.

The improvised fortifications were fine; the problem was he didn't have enough troops to fill them with. He could deploy a fire team for every two hundred feet of the perimeter, leaving him with one squad held back as a reserve. Even with modern weapons, that wouldn't be enough to hold off a determined assault if enough rioters were allowed into the Enclave. And if the Army or the Guard went on the attack, they were screwed. He needed more manpower, or even the high-tech defenses protecting Embassy Row wouldn't be enough.

The entire US compound could be surrounded by force fields that would withstand heavy artillery, but they were not perfect defenses. A good portion of Fromm's combat training revolved around understanding the limits of the seemingly-magic energy shields, which apparently no Starfaring race fully understood, having been handed the technology by older, long-gone species. On their default settings, the fields would intercept fast-moving objects – anything with a speed over sixty-three miles an hour – as well as most forms of energy beyond certain thresholds. They would do so either on one or both sides of the field; you could program them to allow outgoing fire to pass through unhindered. The invisible forces could be shaped in any number of configurations, from the body-hugging personal shields generated by Marine combat armor to gigantic domes like the ones the Snakes had used during First Contact, encasing cities so they could be burned to the ground without inflicting lasting damage to the environment.

On the other hand, objects and personnel moving below the speed threshold – a charging mob of sword-wielding fanatics or a tank moving below sixty mph, for example – could cross the field with impunity. You could increase shield densities to block out everything, but the energy costs increased geometrically. Force fields required a constant outflow of power; the amount of energy spent to successful deflect an attack was directly proportional to the energy in the attack. If not enough power was available, the field would experience a local failure, creating a temporary gap in the defenses. If enough force was applied to the shields, they would go off-line and require several seconds or even minutes to be restored.

All the Starfarer embassies had one or more gluon power plants, which manipulated the 'strong force' to generate energy in a variety of forms, including gravitons, photons and electrons. The US had two, each capable of supplying a pre-Contact city' every energy need. As long as one of those power plants was hooked to the force field generators, the compound was safe from anything less than a Ruddy multi-divisional artillery barrage. The Kirosha forces in and around the capital just didn't have enough tubes to batter down the shields beyond opening small localized breaches that would close up in a second or two.

Furthermore, as long as the Marines' swarm of micro-drones orbited the city and its environs, any attempts to move large numbers of troops towards the Enclave would be spotted long before they could be deployed, and his 100mm mortars would slaughter any enemy concentrations in short order. Even if the Ruddies launched a general attack with all available forces, he should be able to hold them off for a few hours, plenty of time for the corvettes to arrive and end this farce.

"Is there anything else we should be doing, sir?" Obregon asked.

"No. If we had more time, I'd look into getting more people into the trenches. The contractors and constables, maybe," Fromm said. "But there's no point now. We'll remain on high alert, though. I'll stop worrying when we've got friendlies in orbit."

"You and me both, sir. You and me both."

* * *

Lieutenant Commander Lisbeth Zhang of the *Feline*-class corvette *USS Wildcat* was enjoying her first independent command enormously, even if it was aboard an obsolete vessel that would have been phased out years ago if the Fleet wasn't still desperately short of hulls. If only those remfies in Congress hadn't seen fit to tighten the purse strings, she might be running a frigate by now. Like most men and women in uniform, Lisbeth voted for the Eagle Party with almost religious passion, but the last two elections had seen steady gains by the Federalists, who were growing in popularity among the wealthier planets, the ones who hadn't experienced war firsthand in decades and wanted to cut back on military expenditures.

Things were tight, she had to admit. Even after a century of growth, the USA still didn't have an industrial base big enough to produce both guns and butter in the required amounts. Most colonies didn't have modern power plants and had to make do with pre-Contact sources of energy; some didn't even have high-grade fabbers. The Navy itself was mostly teeth and not enough tail – the focus in the last several decades had been on warships, relying on civilian merchantmen to handle most of the logistics, and that was turning out to be unfeasible over the long term. All the expansion since First Contact had left America spread too thin.

But some of the idiots in Congress were talking about such idiocies as a 'consolidation and contraction period.' *Consolidation my ass*, Lisbeth pondered bitterly while she waited for the all clear from Lahiri's Port Authority. President Hewer should start putting traitors in work camps the way he had during the State of Emergency; the tree of liberty needed to have some deadwood pruned off.

Oh, well, politics weren't her concern. And she couldn't complain; even in this time of cutbacks, she'd still gotten her own ship in near-record time. Maxing out every eval since her cadet days helped; the medals she'd earned – the hard way – taking care of those pirates in New Berlin helped even more. And now she was leading a two-ship Task Unit, being senior to the captain of the *Bengal Tiger*. Admittedly, shocking and awing a dirt-bound primitive civilization was not the sort of thing that earned you commendations, or much attention unless you somehow fucked things up. But it was a command, and it would look great on her record when promotion time came around.

Promotions were downright glacial during peacetime, but peace wouldn't last much longer. Other than the Puppies and to a lesser degree the Ovals, the Wyrms and a couple others, every Eet out there hated humanity in general and America in particular. Their most common nickname for humans was 'Warp-Demons' and there was a near-religious element to their hatred that no amount of diplomacy could ever smooth over. Sooner or later, the Lampreys or the Vipers would pick a fight with the USA and the Navy would sail off and kick some alien ass.

"You are clear for departure, Task Unit Fifteen," a bored-sounding space traffic controller said, just as her imp launch status light flashed green. It was time to get this show on the road.

"Everything's ready, ma'am," her XO, said. Lieutenant Omar Givens was a great Executive Officer, always ready to back her up, or to give her his candid opinion in private. At first, Lisbeth had been horrified when she discovered her second in command was the grandson of none other than Admiral Sondra Givens, who'd been part of the Space Navy since there'd been a Space Navy. As it turned out, Omar had never taken advantage of his family connections, had earned his rank the old-fashioned way, and was an excellent officer; Lisbeth had no doubts he'd be commanding his own ship before too long, even if war didn't speed things up.

The two ships in Task Unit Fifteen – calling two corvettes a squadron would be pathetic – readied for warp transit. The two ships massed a combined five thousand tons total, making them among the lightest vessels in the Navy other than shuttles and gunboats. Fitting a platoon of marines each into their converted cargo holds had been a stretch, and she'd be glad when she was rid of them. The sad thing was the *Felines* would have been classified as frigates during Gal War One, back when every ET out there laughed at American ship designations, at least before warp shields and Marine boarding parties made them laugh out of the other side of their ugly faces. No self-respecting fleet used corvettes for anything other than custom inspections or anti-piracy patrols.

It's not the size of the ship in the fight, it's the size of the fight in the ship, she told herself, only half-believing her own words. The counter-quote to that slogan was *God is on the side with the higher tonnage.*

"Engage," she ordered.

Time to do the warp dance again. You never got used to it. Lisbeth had taken up paragliding as a hobby, had jumped from the top of Olympus Mons on still-terraforming Mars, and by the sixth or seventh time, the luster, wonder and fear of the act had worn off. Every time she went into warp, on the other hand, was as bad or worse as the last.

She didn't pray. Music was her coping mechanism. Her imp piped in a series of Warmetal songs right into her auditory nerves, and the warp-induced false sensory input faded away to tolerable levels. The harsh, pounding music, the brainchild of German immigrants of the first post-Contact decades, remained a popular art form a century and a half later. Warmetal would never die. At least among her generation; the current crop of children favored melancholy ballads about peace and love, when they weren't listening to Colonial Country. Pathetic.

Eight hours of warp transit was no picnic – it felt like a few days, or a week, depending on who you asked – but they made it, emerging into the Jasper Star System some three light-seconds away from its inhabited planet, the fifth rock from the local sun. Recovery took a few seconds, as the memories from warp transit faded away like a forgotten nightmare.

Warning sirens and red emergency lights greeted her before she snapped back into reality.

The Tactical Officer was able to shout one word: "Vampires!"

One of the cold realities of space warfare was that a warp emergence point could be detected the moment the ship entered warp space, hours or days before the ship came out the other end. That was the main reason entries into a hostile star system always happened far away from inhabited planets or installations; the rule of thumb was one light hour per hour of transit time, plus ten percent. Entry into peaceful systems happened at much closer ranges, of course.

The Lamprey stealth mines, assembled by Kirosha clock-makers and launched in the dark of night, had detected the warp emergence point eight hours before its appearance and flocked towards it, getting into position long before Task Unit Fifteen's emergence. Four of the ten mines engaged their drives, becoming anti-ship missiles, 'vampires' in Navy parlance. Each pair of weapons targeted a corvette. One of them malfunctioned and broke apart; the other three reached terminal velocity before the ships had fully recovered from warp transit. Their force fields were up, but their warp shields were not, and point-defense systems were useless at those ranges.

Lisbeth Zhang's world dissolved in flames as the *Wildcat* and *Bengal Tiger* broke apart under the ship-killing impacts.

* * *

"Jesus H. Christ," Fromm whispered as the priority message came through. He instinctively craned his head to look up at the sky, although daylight and distance made it impossible to see the disaster that had just transpired. No details were available, but the gist of it was bad enough: the Navy corvettes had been destroyed. Details could wait.

Down on the planet's surface, he had plenty of more immediate things to worry about.

"Get everyone ready, Gunny," he sent out, along with a copy of the message. The RSO was on the phone seconds afterwards.

"What's happening, Captain?"

"Sir, the micro-drones have spotted large numbers of armed irregulars moving from the suburbs and the city, headed towards the Enclave," Fromm reported, passing on the condensed information CPO Donnelly was collating and sending his way. "They started moving within minutes of the corvettes' destruction. I think that means…"

The live drone feed he was watching out of the corner of his eye went dead. It was replaced by another one, which went dead a moment later.

"What the fuck?" he screamed, forgetting the RSO was on the net.

"What is it, Captain?"

"Hold on," he said curtly while he raised Donnelly.

"They've got swatters," she said. "They've killed all the drones!"

Swatters fired wide beams of charged particles, more than powerful enough to instantly turn the unshielded drones into useless lumps of metal and plastic. Only Starfarer civilizations could build that sort of weapon.

They were blind.

139

* * *

"Move your asses!" Corporal Petrossian shouted at First Squad. "The Ruddies are coming!"

How many, and armed with what, nobody fucking knew. The fuckers had gotten anti-drone weapons. Which meant they could have anything.

Russell and his fire team got moving. At least they didn't have far to go, once they'd put on their armor over the bodysuits they'd slept in. The skipper had kept them in their assigned fighting positions all day and night, expecting the worst. Russell and everyone else had grumbled about having to sleep in the trenches, but it turned out the CO had known what the fuck he was talking about. Except the worst had turned to be even worse than anybody had expected.

Somebody was helping the fucking Ruddies. And that somebody had taken out two Navy ships. Russell tried not to think about that as he went to do his job.

Their doss was in the improvised bunkers behind the support trench. It was only three hundred feet from the first line, the one currently being manned by two of the three fire teams in Russell's squad. They joined them, jumping into the trenches after sending an imp-to-imp heads up to their buddies. You didn't want to surprise nervous Marines when they were cocked and loaded, not if you didn't want to eat a dollop or two of piping hot plasma.

The fire team spread out. They ended up twenty-five meters apart. The line of green icons looked awfully thin on the map display.

"Anything?" he asked Corporal Jeremiah 'Deacon' Watkins, who'd been at the trenches when the turd flew into the propeller blades.

"Nothing yet. A few Americans came in running. Couple Ruddies too, but they turned back when we fired warning shots."

"Yeah, no new Ruddies allowed," Russell said. He felt bad about any Christian Ruddies that got caught outside the compound, but most of them were already huddled inside their perimeter. Anybody outside could just as well be an infiltrator; he was plenty worried about the ones inside as it was.

"Hey, we got drones!" Gonzaga said.

And so they did. The bubblehead in charge of commo had launched a new flight of eyes in the sky. They would be taken down in a matter of seconds, assuming the Ruddies knew what they were doing with the swatters some Starfarer motherfucker had given them, but until then they'd be able to see what the fuck was going on. He watched as the vid feeds started dying one by one. Yeah, it was as bad as he expected.

A horde of Ruddies was pouring through the wide open gates of the Enclave, waving their pig-stickers, following leaders with their funny back-strapped banners.

"They ain't got nothing but swords," Nacle said.

"Wish that was true," Russell said. Yeah, most of the charging Eets were wielding hand weapons, but before the last video feed was erased he'd spotted a few of them with rocket launchers slung over their shoulders, and buddies carrying a few spare missiles on their backs. No rifles that he could see, but their RPGs were plenty bad enough. And if their Army butt-buddies had given them RPGs, they'd probably handed them some grenades, too. You could throw a grenade, or a satchel charge, right through a force field.

They had to get in close for that, though, and the mortar section was on the job.

He didn't notice the bombs flying overhead, but the multiple airbursts looked like a fireworks display as they rained death along every street leading towards Embassy Row.

"Cleared hot, motherfuckers," Russell growled. The closely-spaced buildings between the parklands around Embassy Row and the Enclave walls obscured the slaughter, but he knew what was happening in there, and he didn't feel bad at all about it. Any Ruddy out on the streets was heading this way to get a piece of Russell and his fellow 'muricans. They were going to learn that Marine scalps didn't come cheap. The rain of plasma and slashing ceramic fragments was the first of many lessons.

Some Ruddies started to make it through, though. There were only three hundred-mike-mikes in the section, and reloading them after they'd fired their wad took some time. The 0341s manning the guns were spacing their shots so at least one mortar was firing at any given time, but they just couldn't sweep the entire front with constant fire.

The first ET Russell saw came limping from around a corner. Russel used his scope to take a closer look and kept his finger off the trigger when he saw the poor bastard was trailing half his guts behind him. No sense wasting a bullet on the already-dead. The Ruddie took one more step and then went down face-first; he wouldn't be getting up.

The bunch that came on his heels were lively enough, though.

The ALS-43s and LML-10s engaged them first. The gunners fired three- and four-round bursts of 15mm anti-pers down the street, lashing the Ruddies with fragmentary rounds that didn't pack as much punch as mortar bombs but were plenty enough to send dozens of Ruddies to their final reward. The mini-grenades made little puffs of dark smoke as they went off slightly above head height, sending running figures tumbling. You could tell the wounded from the dead easily enough; the dead hit the ground flat, as if someone had dropped a chunk of meat on the ground. The wounded rolled and twisted around, grabbing at the spots where they'd been slashed or perforated. Either way, they stopped showing any interest in moving forward.

The Light Missile Launcher teams had been assigned to the streets outside the ALS-43s' fire lanes. They used high explosive rounds on the buildings closest to the cleared ground surrounding Embassy Row. Each HE missile had the power of a thousand pounds of TNT; the first salvo turned the buildings into rubble and lashed the Ruddies on the street with shockwave-propelled pieces of brick and masonry. Their second volley used plasma rounds, unleashing fireballs that enveloped everything within ten yards from the point of impact and set the Ruddies on fire at twice that distance.

"That's gonna leave a mark," Russell muttered. He wondered how many civvies had been in those buildings. Just about everyone had left for the protection of the Embassies or, if locals, had moved onto greener pastures, but there were always some poor bastards who didn't get the word, or hoped things would turn out for the best. They'd be telling their tale to Jesus just about now.

Ruddies stopped coming into sight; either they'd wised up or they were all dead. Mortars kept dropping on something for a few seconds, then stopped while a new flight of micro-drones went on another suicide run. Russell wondered how many they had in storage, and how quickly the fabbers could turn out more, along with more of everything else they would need. He hadn't fired a shot yet, but he didn't expect that would last.

He watched the video feed for as long as he could. They'd wasted a couple thousand Ruddies, and the rest had gotten cold feet and were milling around outside the kill zone while their leaders tried to raise their morale by yelling and using some metal whips on them. Fucking officers sucked in every planet. A string of mortar bombs burst overhead and turned the rally attempt into a slaughter.

Decisively Engaged

Just before the feed went out, Russell saw the massive forms of tanks coming into view.

Eleven

Year 163 AFC, D Minus Three

"Switch to Anti-Vehicle rounds, Martin," Fromm said as he managed the battle from one of the rear bunkers. Sending out anti-vehicle mortar rounds instead of frags and plasma would take the pressure off the Final Blow fanatics, but he didn't want the advancing tanks the drones had spotted to reach the lines. The AV rounds mounted cameras as part of their sensor systems, so sending them up would also provide him with more data without spending any more drones; they had only two dozen or so left, enough for four sorties before they ran out. A fabber was cranking them out at a rate of one every three minutes, but that wasn't enough to keep up, and the other matter-printers were busy making more ammo and other consumables. He could build bigger drones with integral force fields, but they would take ten times the time and materials to produce and would only survive for a minute or two before the swatters burned through their defenses. The game of drones was one of attrition, and fought at battalion or higher levels; he didn't have the resources to play it in the face of swatter tech.

Whoever had gifted the Ruddies with high-tech gear had picked the perfect weapon system. Swatters could even knock mortar rounds out; it took a few seconds to do so, which wouldn't affect the bombs at short and medium ranges, but he couldn't have them hovering in the air, which robbed him of many options. He shrugged. He'd play the hand he'd been dealt, as best he could.

The video feed from the seeker warheads wasn't as good as the drones': the viewpoint shifted too fast for the naked eye to follow, and it had to be processed by his imp. What he saw during the second or so it took the first three missiles to fly up, acquire a target and plunge toward them was good enough. A tank company was lumbering towards Embassy Row, twelve antiquated Mark IIs from the Army rather than the more sophisticated Dire Wolves from the Royal Guard. The three missiles broke up into fifteen sub-munitions, each one exploding five feet above their designated targets and sending a self-forged metal dart plunging through the turrets of the tanks. Fromm could imagine the carnage as the interior of each vehicle was filled with sublimated metal gases and bouncing solid fragments; at least it would be over before the crew knew what was happening. A series of explosions in the distance told the rest of the story. Scratch one tank company.

The brief respite in the mortar bombardment had allowed another Ruddy wave to get into range of the trench line. Once again, the ETs were slaughtered by the heavy weapons before any Marine riflemen had the chance to fire a single shot.

"Stop, you stupid motherfuckers," he muttered. "Stop making us kill you."

He couldn't call that slaughter a battle or anything resembling a fight. It had been a massacre, plain and simple, and its victims might as well have been holding flowers in their hands for all the good their weapons had done them. His imp estimated the aliens had suffered nearly three thousand casualties in a matter of minutes.

No more Ruddies came through. Off to the north, the Vehelian Embassy's defenders checked fire as well, their lasers falling silent for lack of targets. They'd done for about as half as many Ruddies as Fromm's men. The Wyrms hadn't had to fire a shot, being masked by the other two Starfarer compounds.

Some civilian was trying to reach him on his imp. He took advantage of the temporary lull to ID the caller. Hiroshi Delgado, from Black River Security; the commander/CEO of the largest military contractor on Jasper-Five.

"What can I do for you, Mr. Delgado?"

"I want to offer my support, Captain. I've got a platoon with me. You know our specs."

Fromm did. Nothing fancy: M5 carbines, their 5mm plasma rounds slightly less effective than an IW-3's, and likely firing a mixture of explosive rounds and inert bullets. Decent body armor but light personal force fields, which meant they'd take more casualties in a close-range firefight than his Marines. Their heavy weapons consisted of M-71 railguns; they'd be more than effective enough against the current enemy forces.

"All my boys are ready to roll," Delgado said. "They're all long-service vets, Navy or the Corps. Not a single Army fucker among them."

Fromm would have chuckled under different circumstances. The Army was the hind-tit service, most of its personnel stuck on Earth and a couple of the larger worlds. If the Air Force still existed, instead of having been folded back into the Army, it would be the only US military branch lower on the totem pole.

"I'll have to run it by the RSO, but I'll endorse the recommendation, Mr. Delgado."

"You won't regret this, Captain."

"Have your people ready. I'll send you orders when I have them."

Fromm called the RSO next. Rockwell looked rough, and something in his expression told Fromm something had gone down inside the embassy while his Marines were busy outside.

"I'm up to date on your status, Fromm. Got anything new to add?"

Fromm ran the military contractors' offer by him.

"Approved," Rockwell said. He made no mention of having to consult with the ambassador first.

"Uh, is there anything I should know, sir?"

"Oh, yes. Ambassador Llewellyn has resigned from his post, citing poor health. He suffered an accident in his office. Fell down. Repeatedly."

Rockwell scratched his nose, and Fromm noticed that the knuckles on his hand looked somewhat bruised.

"I see," Fromm said. Hell of a way to run a railroad, but he could read between the lines. Llewellyn had either punked out or broken down, and Rockwell had to take over. There would be plenty of fallout to follow, but Rockwell had to be alive to go to trial for assaulting an ambassador, and the best way to stay alive was to keep Llewellyn from making any more decisions.

He knew where Rockwell was coming from. Knew it intimately.

"Anything else, Captain?"

"No, sir."

"Carry on, then."

Interlude: Article 90

Astarte-Three, Year 163 AFC

Laser beams were invisible to the naked eye, but the sensors in Lieutenant Fromm's suit turned them into colorful lines of red light as they flashed towards his position. Wherever the crimson lines touched anything solid, they transmitted enough energy to shatter stone, melt metal or rip through flesh and bone.

The 'rebel base' First Battalion, 73rd Marines had attacked was supposed to comprise some four hundred effectives armed with small arms and a handful of heavy weapons. Instead, the Marines had stumbled into a *regiment* of heavily armed troops, including two dozen grav-tanks that had taken the Marines' LAVs by surprise and annihilated them in a brutal short-range firefight. Bravo Company had dismounted already; most of its personnel had survived the destruction of their vehicles, but they were now pinned down by the eight enemy tanks still left-standing and some two hundred or so laser-wielding infantrymen fighting alongside them. More enemy forces were massing behind them. What had started as a support operation for a US client had turned into a desperate battle.

"We're getting flanked, sir," Staff Sergeant Gruenwald said over the sound of multiple laser impacts.

Fromm consulted the grid map his imp projected into his eyes, along with the blue and red icons marking the position of friendly and enemy units, respectively. Bravo had made a stand at one end of a narrow gorge, the one place in the area where it could hold with some hope of not being overrun in short order. Even so, their line was thin and they'd been forced to screen the north side of the gorge – his left flank – with only a couple of fire teams. The Lampreys – it was Lampreys on the other side, he was sure of it – had found the weak spot and were making their main push there, trying to infiltrate enough laser troops to roll up the thin defensive line thwarting their advance.

His platoon was fully committed; he had no reserves left. Behind him, a couple thousand yards away, the rest of the battalion, or rather the survivors of the initial clash, was digging in and consolidating. Bravo Company needed to buy them time. Fromm selected a squad and sent it off to reinforce the left flank, knowing he was weakening the rest of the line too much to resist a determined assault. Third Platoon, entrenched behind the front line, was keeping the Lampreys busy with mortars and missile fire, but they were concentrating on the center of the line, leaving the forces facing the left flank free to maneuver.

His platoon was doing everything it could, but it needed more support. Fromm tried to raise Captain Chastain, and discovered Bravo Company's commander was not taking calls. "The fuck?" Fromm all but screamed, remembering at the last second to keep his cursing off the general channel.

"Take over, Gruenwald," he told his platoon sergeant. "I'm off to see the captain."

"Good luck, sir."

Neither Fromm nor Staff Sergeant Gruenwald had any confidence in Captain Terry Paget Chastain. On a data screen, the officer's stats looked great. Plenty of commendations, including a Silver Star for being the sole survivor from the Ushtun debacle, where an entire Marine company had been slaughtered by a tribe of headhunting ETs. After serving with the man for a couple of years, however, Fromm had eventually realized Chastain was a consummate and cunning coward, always contriving to be in the safest possible spot at any given time. In this case, he was well to the rear, behind the weapons platoon, on the reverse slope of a shallow hill, ostensibly to have a good view of the tactical situation. It might even be somewhat true. Imp systems, including sensors, were being jammed at random intervals by the enemy, yet another indication of how shockingly well-equipped they were. Eyeballs on higher ground couldn't be jammed. It also conveniently put the captain as far away from the fighting as one could be without deserting.

And now Fromm would have to leave his men behind to go talk to him face to face.

He crawled through the network of trenches – excavated by laying strips of 'digger' explosive charges on the ground – and dashed through a ten-yard span of open ground. A Lamprey scored a couple of hits on his back, and he felt the temperature inside the clamshell breastplate rise noticeably when some residual heat got through the force field and the armor beneath. Fromm dived for the next trench line; the rough landing hurt him worse than the laser hit.

"Watch it, domass!" a Marine growled when Fromm almost landed on top of him. "Sorry, sir," the man hastily added when his imp identified Fromm as an officer.

"My bad," Fromm said. "Carry on."

The Marine went back to reloading his ALS-43 while Fromm resumed his crawl towards the captain's position.

One more desperate run around the hill – a near-miss peppered him with shards of rock when it superheated a boulder and turned it into a good imitation of an artillery shell – and he was out of the way of direct fire, able to walk the rest of the way. He found the captain cowering at the bottom of a covered entrenchment, alone.

As it turned out, the reverse slope of the hill hadn't been as safe as Fromm and the captain had thought. The Lampreys had sent a guided missile towards it, and the duplex round had punched through the portable force field protecting the position had killed everyone on the hill except Chastain.

The captain had taken off his helmet and was applying a clotting agent to a scalp cut that that poured blood over his face an eyes. He looked at Fromm with a wide-eyed, terrified expression the gore only made more apparent. The man was panicking.

"What the hell are you doing here, Fromm?"

"I needed to talk to you, sir, and you weren't responding. I need you to shift fire to cover the left flank. We're in danger of being overrun."

"Forget the left flank. We're breaking contact and retreating."

"We can't break contact, sir. The Lampreys will slaughter us if we leave the trenches. And follow us and do the same to the rest of the battalion."

"I'm calling a fire mission to allow us to move. Warn everyone while I set it up; it's going to be danger close." The captain turned away and used his imp to call for artillery.

Fromm's map overlay showed him the coordinates the captain was sending out, and he realized Chastain was calling for fire right on top of the outer trench line. That wasn't 'danger close,' that was murdering half of Bravo Company so the other half could run away. Fromm couldn't believe the Regiment was going along with it, but he quickly realized that the Lampreys' jamming was making it difficult to see where the platoon was. They didn't know the storm of plasma, fragmentary-case and self-forging penetrators they were about to unleash would be hitting friend and foe alike.

"Sir, belay that fire mission!" Fromm shouted, using his imp to break into the channel and step on the captain's coordinate relay.

"Fuck you, Lieutenant! It's the only way!"

No time to argue. The hysteria in the captain's voice told Fromm only action would suffice. Before the company commander could reach the target acquisition officer again, Fromm punched him, his heavy gloves lending almost as much weight to the blow as a set of brass knuckles.

Chastain's head rocked back from impact. He looked at the lieutenant with disbelief, blood spurting from his broken nose. "You..."

Fromm hit him again. And again. Knocking someone out took work. He ended up slamming the captain's head into a piece of rock until he stopped struggling. At the end, Fromm was panting heavily, not so much from exertion as from the fear and rage driving him. He knew both officers' imps would be recording the entire thing, and that Article 90 of the UCMJ called for the death penalty for his actions. A court-martial was all he had to look forward to. But you had to be alive for one of those.

When it was over, he contacted the TAO. "This is Lieutenant Fromm. Captain Chastain is down. Sending you new set of coordinates. Belay the previous fire mission." Just in the nick of time.

Somewhere behind the lines, four Multiple-Launch Rocket System vehicles swung their launch boxes and sent a hundred and twenty supersonic missiles soaring into the air. They were all struck multiple times by air-defense lasers, but their force fields held long enough for them to reach their targets and detonate. A line of fireballs bloomed over the advancing Lampreys. Fromm watched a grav-tank's turret rising majestically into the air on top of one of the fireballs, its barrel twisted like a corkscrew by the detonation that had torn it from its main body.

Bravo Company could hold out a little longer now. Maybe long enough for the battalion to regroup.

Fromm might have lost his career and soon enough his life, but at least he hadn't allowed the asshole to kill his men.

* * *

"Sit down, Lieutenant."

Colonel Macwhirter's office was unusually Spartan, with few of the pictures and holographs that would comprise a typical 'I-love-me' wall. Most of the mementos Fromm could see marked some eventful moments in the colonel's life: a picture of a young Captain Macwhirter leading a warp assault on a pirated passenger starship; a holographic display of a battle in Vega-Eight, where Major Macwhirter had been wounded and nearly killed. And so on. Hardly any pictures of the officer paling it up with other VIPs.

Fromm sat down. Normally, meeting with the regiment commander would have been a nerve-wracking experience. At the moment, he was too numb to care. He'd spent the wait outside the colonel's office writing letters to the families of the dead. In the end, he hadn't saved his platoon. All of them had ended up as casualties; almost half had been killed.

"It appears that your implant's records were irretrievably lost when you were wounded. Same thing happened to Captain Chastain, strangely enough."

He couldn't think of anything to say to that, so he stayed silent.

"The Captain had an... interesting history, you might say," Macwhirter went on. "Some people thought he walked on water. Others had some reservations but nothing solid to base them on. The fact that he married the granddaughter of one of the wealthiest men on Earth didn't hurt, either. In any case, it's been decided that to look further into his demise will do nobody any good. Which leaves us with the question of what to do with you."

Remaining quiet seemed to be working, so he kept at it.

"For now, it means a promotion, *Captain* Fromm. Your actions saved most of the regiment, even if it cost you half of your platoon. Far better than anything that cowardly piece of shit would have managed, beyond saving his own sorry ass." The expression in Macwhirter's eyes told Fromm the officer had watched both imps' feeds before they were 'lost.'

The Colonel's eyes bore into Fromm's. "You're getting away with murder, Captain. Almost literally. The question is, what will you do now? Maybe you'll decide you're invincible, and fuck up until you get yourself and your command killed. What do you think you'll do with your free pass?"

"My duty, sir."

"Good answer. You better mean it. Now get the fuck out of my office. I need to think of a good place to put you."

Twelve

Year 163 AFC, D Minus Three

Timothy Brackenhurst winced when the heavy mortars fired off another volley.

He knew the carnage those weapons would inflict upon reaching their targets. He'd spent his obligatory service in an artillery unit with the Marine Auxiliaries, and seen firsthand just how destructive plasma and shrapnel bombs could be.

Part of him was horrified at the slaughter; the other part rejoiced, because those men the mortars were killing had come to the Enclave to kill, and they were now reaping what they'd sown.

They had decided to keep the refugees at the mission, which was inside the force field perimeter encompassing the embassy compound and the Caterpillar Building. That meant finding room for almost two thousand Kirosha in facilities meant to accommodate a tithe of that number. Classrooms had been converted to dormitories, furniture and bedding been salvaged from nearby abandoned houses, and they'd gathered and stored every bit of food they had been able to purchase, beg or 'borrow.' The swimming pool was now a covered water reservoir, just in case. While the embassy had their own well, its water supply would be strained by so many people.

President Jensen had held a meeting with the ambassador the day after the refugees' arrival, and it hadn't gone well. Timothy wasn't privy to the details, but the rumors made it sound like the ambassador would only provide aid for the humans in the mission, giving the Kirosha only whatever could be spared, if anything. The Catholic and Baptist missions had been similarly rebuffed; their facilities were too far from the embassy to be safe, so those missionaries and their charges had ended up setting up camp in the Caterpillar building, living off the charity of that corporation.

Now all of them huddled inside their makeshift homes, listening to the distant thunder of war and wondering when it would come nearer, and whether it would claim them.

"Oh my God!" Jonah Ruiz said suddenly, startling Timothy. His companion looked terrified.

"What happened?"

"They blew up two Navy ships."

"That's... How?"

"I don't know. Some say there's a stealthed Viper destroyer in-system, and that it ambushed our ships."

"That's ridiculous. If the Vipers were here, they would be bombing us from orbit already."

Jonah looked towards the sky, as if expecting city busters to start raining down at any second. "I hope you are right, Tim."

"I don't think we have to worry about a ship, but the Kirosha are getting Starfarer help," Timothy said. "My guess is space mines. Maybe they bribed a Wyrashat or Vehelian – or even a human – merchant to drop them off on their way out the system."

"Either way, that means war."

Timothy closed his eyes and took a deep breath. "Yes. War."

The last major conflict between America and other Starfarer civilization had ended a couple of years before Timothy was born. His father had been in the Navy then, and had helped battle the Vipers, who were distantly related to the Snakes; both came from Class One biospheres, carbon-based but very different from Class Two DNA-based species like humans, Hrauwah or Vehelians. So far, every ecosystem discovered by Starfarers was descended from one of four possible ancestors. The Baptists claimed it was certain proof of Intelligent Design, or even of the existence of God. Timothy tended to agree with their conclusion, but more as a matter of faith rather than reason; as an engineer, the level of proof needed for such extraordinary claims had not been met. Those four ancestral forms of life could have evolved independently somewhere, and simply overrun the galaxy before others could arise.

In any case, most Class One biospheres produced highly aggressive, antisocial species; there were exceptions, like the mercantile and service-oriented Biryam, a.k.a. the Butterflies, but not many. Four of the five wars humanity had fought in the century and a half since First Contact had been waged against Class One species. If Timothy had to guess, the most likely culprits were the Vipers or the Lampreys. The Wyrms would be a distant third possibility, although if that was the case, they could be attacked at any moment from their embassy. Something else to worry about.

Timothy's father didn't talk much about the war. His stories about his time in uniform had been mostly funny – misadventures while on leave, shipmates who always seemed to get in trouble, and other amusing anecdotes. Only once, while in a somber mood, he'd spoken about the destruction of the human colony of New

Houston – five million dead – and the thousand-fold revenge America had extracted from the Vipers.

"The universe is a harsh place, son," he'd said when he'd finished. "Harsher than the road to Deseret, and the Lord will test us sorely for centuries to come."

"Heavenly Father preserve us," Timothy muttered, much as he had that day.

The shooting had stopped, but he didn't notice until he'd uttered his prayer, and for a moment he wondered if his wishes had come true. "Thank thee for this day," he added.

Jonah nodded solemnly.

They looked out the window – or rather, peered out between the nailed boards that had replaced the glass, a precaution they'd completed the day before. This side of the main mission building overlooked the south side of the Enclave. They were on the third level, which allowed them to see the Enclave's wall – no longer a defense, since it was manned by Kirosha, although they hadn't used it as a firing platform yet – and beyond it billowing smoke rising from distant fires. The attackers had not restricted their violence to the Enclave, it seemed.

"They're probably burning out suspected Christian converts," Jonah said.

"Or simply destroying things for fun."

Jonah started saying something, but a sound Timothy couldn't identify at first silenced him. They leaned against the boarded window, trying to figure it out.

It was chanting. Kirosha voices, thousands of them, maybe tens of thousands, singing in unison. It was terrifying.

And the sound was getting closer. Coming from every direction.

"I think they're going to try again," Jonah said.

"And they might succeed." Timothy's heart was racing. He had to do something. The mission had no weapons; they had come to this world to help, not to do harm. But weapons could be found.

And he had the will to use them.

* * *

Heather's heart sank as she read the QE missive from the Department of State.

URGENT. SEVERAL US TRADE POSTS, EMBASSIES, CONSULATES UNDER ATTACK. ELEVEN ALREADY OVERRUN, 100% CASUALTIES. FLEET ELEMENTS

ENGAGED BY UNKNOWN ENEMY FORCES, PRESUMED TO BE LHAN ARKH AND NASSTAH. ALL FLEET FORCES IN LOCAL SPACE ENGAGED. HOLD UNTIL RELIEVED.

She looked at the steaming pile of a message one more time while the chanting of tens of thousands homicidal maniacs out in the city made the windows vibrate. HOLD UNTIL RELIEVED. Less than three thousand Americans and about half as many other Starfarers, in a Kingdom of three hundred million. And she'd thought Captain Fromm had been too paranoid when making his plans. She wanted to vomit.

RSO Rockwell looked at the senior members of the American delegation. Llewellyn wasn't there, of course; he was in his quarters, recovering from the fractured jaw he'd incurred during the incident that had led to his forced resignation.

"First things first," Rockwell said. "When he got the news about the corvettes, Llewellyn wanted to surrender the Embassy and all American civilian and military personnel to the Kingdom. Magistrate Eeren called him shortly after the incident and assured him we would be interned on a nearby island after being disarmed 'for our own protection.'"

"That's insane," Heather blurted out.

"I concur. We've all seen how the Kirosha treat their enemies." Imp footage of the royal reception and the ensuing executions had been made readily available to rest of the embassy. "I tried to convince Ambassador Llewellyn that accepting such an offer would lead only to our deaths, but he ignored my advice. I took matters into my own hands. If you want to arrest me and reinstate the ambassador, or take over from me, be my guest."

Nobody said anything.

"All this happened before that QE message arrived, not that it would have helped matters. We are at war, people, and the situation in Kirosha is part of that war. Human outposts across the galaxy have been targeted. It appears they are slaughtering every American they can find."

"Can we hold?" Deputy Chief of Mission Janice Norbert said. She was the most senior embassy staffer after Llewellyn. Heather didn't care much for her, but she was miles better than the former ambassador. Still, the older woman was clearly out of her depth. Nobody had attacked an American embassy in decades. US policy in those circumstances had been swift, disproportionate retribution. A thousand-to-one was the standard casualty exchange, and Norbert didn't strike Heather as being bloodthirsty enough for the job at hand.

"If we work together, we can," Rockwell replied, exuding confidence that Heather was certain was at least partially an act. "We'll need all Americans – all Starfarers – in the Enclave to cooperate. The security contractors on site have all volunteered already and Captain Fromm is already integrating them into his forces ASAP."

"We'll do whatever we can, too," said Gordon Melendez, Caterpillar's vice-president in charge of the Kirosha Distribution and Service Division. "I already had some of our earthmoving vehicles help build the entrenchments around the embassy and our own facilities. I've put together a list of employees with combat experience; they've all volunteered to assist in the defense of the Enclave."

Heather nodded. One could say a lot of things about the Obligatory Service Act, but it certainly made sure every able-bodied American knew which end of a gun to point towards the enemy. And most Caterpillar managers would have served more than the mandatory four-year term in the military; the company made it a point to hire people who went above and beyond the minimum. Those policies helped mitigate the hatred most people felt towards Rats in general. A Rat who'd had some sort of career in uniform was slightly less likely to be an asshole, or at least less likely to be a typical corporate asshole.

The Planetary Director of Caterpillar's local competitor, Star Mining Enterprises, also chimed in with pledges of support. Most of that corporation's heavy equipment was out in the field, but he offered everything he had in site, as well as the services of the small but well-equipped security forces he'd hired on. The local missionaries also volunteered their resources, which included a small but well-staffed clinic. Everyone seemed willing and able to do what they could. It was only a matter of figuring out how to organize things and coordinate with the Marine platoon.

They needed to get Fromm in on this, but he had to fight the current battle first. If he lost, none of their tentative preparations would matter.

* * *

"They're massing on all sides," CPO Donnelly said. She'd used the fabbers to add some stealth capabilities to the next batch of drones, but that only bought them a few extra seconds of life; the Swatters tracked on their grav-wave broadcasts and blasted them out of the sky shortly after they transmitted. Still, by having them record fifteen second clips and then sending them off, they'd been able to keep an eye on the Ruddy movements. "Looks like twenty thousand personnel, mostly armed with hand weapons, but at least a thousand have rocket launchers. They're coming from all points of the compass, sir. It's a general push."

"We'll push right back. Great job, Chief."

"Thank you, sir."

Fromm took a moment to assess the tactical picture. The Oval Embassy masked the northern side of his perimeter; the Wyrms did the same on the west. There hadn't been enough time to coordinate with the other Starfarers so far, other than a general sharing of information and assurances of mutual support. The aliens' own drones had also been swatted away, but an observation post on top of the Wyrm embassy could look all the way into the city proper, giving them some much-needed intelligence. CPO Donnelly had linked the ETs' data to the Marines' network, not bad considering none of the three Starfaring polities had worked closely with each other before.

It looked like the US compound would be getting hit hardest on the east and south, the east particularly so, since that side faced the Enclave's Main Gate, which was wide enough to accommodate hundreds of people at once. The southern gate was the smallest one; Fromm detailed one of the mortars to it; a regular dose of 100mm canned hell would slow down any attackers there. Fromm thought about thinning the line on the north side and use it to reinforce the east, but decided against it. He sent the Black River volunteers there instead.

That would have to do, until the Ruddies massing outside the walls decided to make their move. He could have kept up some harassing fire from the mortars, but he wanted to have them ready and fully loaded when things really got started. As it was, he'd burned through nearly a day's worth of mortar bombs and the fabbers had replaced maybe a quarter of it.

It looked like the Kirosha Army and Royal Guard were still staying out of the fight. Strange, given that he'd already blasted a tank company, but maybe the Crown was angling for some sort of plausible deniability in case the next in-system ship turned out to be American instead of Lhan Arkh. It didn't make much sense, but little about this situation did.

The Ruddies' singing increased in volume, if not in quality. They were working themselves into a proper berserk rage.

"Movement on all sides," CPO Donnelly reported.

The second round had begun.

* * *

"They ain't stopping for shit this time," Russell said. He had to turn up the volume on his imp to make himself heard through the hammer of the hundred-mike-mike explosions.

He could watch the feed from the Wyrm tower, thanks to the Navy NCO handling commo and intelligence, and the vid wasn't pretty. About two, three times as many Ruddies as last time were pouring in through the gate and heading towards them at a dead run, and their flag-men were doing a good job directing traffic and getting them moving through half a dozen different streets. The mortars – only two of them were covering that side – couldn't spread out their fire enough to stop them all.

"I got 'em," Gonzo said, opening up with the ALS-43 and filling his sector of fire with plasma and frag rounds. Further down the line, an LML turned a pack of Ruddies into crispy critters.

And they kept on coming. He had to hand it to the fuckers, they didn't quit. And they were in range. Russell leveled his IW-3a and sent a 15mm grenade their way. It wasn't as impressive as the mortars or the ALS-43, but the little frag sent a few Ruddies tumbling to the ground, and that was A-Okay. He tagged others with single shots, his imp painting one target after the next. It was as easy as could be; nobody was shooting back, at least not yet. His Iwo's plasma rounds blew the poor fuckers apart.

Some of them could shoot back, though. His imp tagged a Ruddy with a rocket launcher; the ET was trying to aim it but other bastards kept bumping into him before he could get it right. If he finally fired the rocket, anybody behind him would get barbequed by the back blast. He didn't get the chance, though.

"Nope," Russell said as he put a round through the rocketeer. The plasma jet speared right through the Ruddy – and into the two spare rockets in his backpack. The ensuing explosion swallowed up the charging aliens in a cloud of smoke and flames.

"Gotta love them sympathetic detonations," the Marine muttered as a couple Ruddies emerged from the smoke. One of them was on fire, the next one out was missing an arm. Putting them down was a mercy.

More of them kept coming.

Off to his left, a rocket corkscrewed towards the trench line, leaving a trail of white smoke behind. It hit the embassy's force field and blew up against it. One rocket wouldn't scratch the shield. Three or four might, if they hit close enough together.

Russell set aside his concerns and kept servicing targets. Stick to your fire sector; anybody who stepped into the kill box was a fair target. With his imp, he hardly could miss; technically you were expected to hit targets with ninety percent accuracy, but when it was for real and the fuckers were shooting back it was usually closer to sixty percent. With near zilch return fire, he was getting a much better score than that.

The Ruddies had come into the open at around a hundred yards; his rangefinder dutifully informed him he was dropping targets at under fifty yards now. The kill zone was littered with bodies, but more Ruddies were coming and getting much closer.

There was an explosion somewhere to his right, and it'd come from inside the perimeter.

"Grenades!" someone shouted.

Fuck. A tossed grenade would fly right through the area force field. Their personal fields would probably handle the blast and shrapnel, but that was a little too much like hard work for Russell's taste. He started turning his attention to the Ruddies who didn't have swords or spears, on the grounds they were most likely to be harboring grenades. His suspicion was confirmed by another sympathetic detonation that cleared his sector for several seconds.

More RPGs were coming into play, too; some Ruddies fired in groups, three, four at a time. The high-explosive warheads blew up harmlessly against the area force field; it looked like even a mass volley wasn't enough to punch through. None of the rocketeers lived to fire more than one round apiece. But the big-eyed bastards were getting closer. The fastest or luckiest ones lived to reach the coils of concertina wire stretched some ten feet off the edge of the force field. That's where their luck ran out: the razor edges of the wire cut or snagged their clothes and skin, and they died there, trying to hack through it with their swords or climb over it, which only got them a bit of extra suffering before they got shot.

Russell emptied his 15mm launcher over the concertina fence, filling his sector with dead and wounded ETs, but more Ruddies came behind the fallen and started to throw their own grenades. Others had Molotov* cocktails; they hunched down while they lit the wicks running into glass and ceramic containers filled with flammable liquid, then jumped up and flung them towards the trenches. Most of them got shot or fragged before they could finish, but not all.

Something slammed into him from behind. Grenade. His force field had stopped the fragments but enough kinetic force had seeped through to shake him. Russell cursed and went back to work. More bomb-throwers had arrived, and shooting them kept him too busy to stop the ones trying to jump over the wire. Some smart fuckers had two or three buddies grab them and fling them *over* the concertina barrier. Maybe not to smart, as two of the four who went over didn't clear the wire and got caught in the thick of it, but the other two made it. Russell shot them both, but some asshole on the other side of the wire nailed him with a Molotov cocktail while he was busy.

"Motherfuck!" He was on fire. His long-johns were fire-resistant, but he was still burning and more Ruddies were piling up into the wire and throwing shit his way. Another grenade went off inside the trench, close enough to stagger him while he beat at the flames with one hand and popped motherfuckers with the other. His clamshell armor's environmental controls sent a spray of cold gas all over him; the system was meant to deal with plasma penetration, but it worked fine on the jellied booze the fucker had splashed him with. He managed to scrap off most of the burning stuff with his free hand; he never stopped shooting.

A hundred-mike-mike dropped a bomb load across his fire sector; a line of puffs of smoke appeared above the wire, each marking a dose of slashing death.

Anti-pers fragments bounced off Russell's force field; that fire mission had been danger-fucking-close. He didn't mind the back-scratching, though, not when the Ruddies milling around the wire went down. Russell shot a couple that were still twitching. The fire on his suit was out; no harm done. His Iwo was almost empty; he reloaded, filled up on grenades, and went back to work.

Off to his left, Gonzaga mowed down hundreds of them. He'd switched to plasma grenades, and that and the mortar bombs finally got to the next wave of Ruddies. Or maybe it was the sight of all the dead bodies scattered in front of them. They hesitated near the middle of the open field, and many of them stopped cold, doing the worst thing you could do in a kill zone. You had to run when bullets were flying and there was no cover around. You ran, forward or back, or hit the ground and crawled, but you didn't stand still, not if you didn't want to go down and never get up.

The Ruddies didn't know better. They hesitated, and the Marines on the trenches sent another thousand of them to hell. That did the trick. The ETs ran back the way they came. Russell and his buddies shot them in the back, which some folk would have called unsporting, except this wasn't a game, and any Ruddy that lived today might come back tomorrow. They killed about as many of them on their way back as they had as they came forward, and the hundred-mike-mikes sent a few more anti-pers bombs their way as a parting gift.

"My God," Nacle said over the fire team channel after the shooting died. "Holy fucking shit. God."

"Leave God alone," Russel said as he changed magazines. "He's probably busy counting all the Ruddies we just sent to Hell."

"You..." The Mormon fell silent.

It was pretty bad, Russell had to admit. The stupid bastards had kept coming, even after seeing what the Marines had done to their buddies. These ETs might make good troops someday, if they could get them civilized enough to build their own starships and plasma guns. He figured that was why the US had been here, almost as much as for the fancy rocks they bought off the locals. The Rats in charge had tried to make allies out the Ruddies. Russell couldn't imagine the ETs would feel like being pals after the Marines had killed them by the cartload, but who knew? Stranger things had happened.

He lifted his helmet's faceplate. The smell was much worse without the filters, but the breeze felt good against his skin. Reaching into a pouch on his belt, he found a protein chew and popped it in his mouth, savoring the salty-meaty flavor as he closed the helmet again and turned his attention to the observation post's video feed.

The Ruddies were in full retreat all over. The Wyrms had filled their sector with bodies as well; their security guys had cut loose with flechette guns that fired thousands of hypervelocity ceramic darts, plus heavy weapons that included graviton cannons. The wounds those fuckers inflicted were downright gruesome; the Ruddies on that part of the battle looked like they'd been chewed up and spat out by an angry wolverine, or folded by some sort of industrial machine. The observation post couldn't see very far into the Ovals' sector but Russell knew how nasty their lasers could be; he didn't need visuals to picture thousands of dead Ruddies, either perforated and cooked from the inside out or cut in two by continuous beams. Ugly way to go.

"Then again, ain't ever found a pretty way to die," he said out loud.

"What was that, Russett?"

"Never mind, Gonzo. Just musin' 'bout nothin'."

* * *

"There are three hours of daylight left. We agree to cease fire until tomorrow morning. You can retrieve your dead until dusk, but you must move to the other side of the wall before it is too dark to tell a white thread from a black one," Deputy Chief of Mission Norbert said to the Kirosha Magistrate on the other end of the telephone line. He'd put the call on speaker, so everyone in the office could listen in.

"Agreed," Magistrate Eereen said. "I take it you still refuse to surrender and accept the protection of the High Queen."

"We must regretfully decline, yes."

"Very well. The Queen will make a statement over the radio waves tomorrow afternoon. I suggest you listen to it." The line went dead.

"Now what?" Heather wondered out loud.

"Nothing good, I'm sure," RSO Rockwell said. "In theory, the Queen could pretend the whole thing was a terrible mistake, the actions of a bunch of rebels, bandits and traitors or what have you, and try to set up a lasting cease fire. Considering there's a galaxy-wide shooting war going on, New Washington would probably be content bringing everyone home and leaving the Ruddies to rot until we can come back in force and exact reparations."

"That would make sense," Deputy Norbert said.

"Yes. But I doubt that's what the Queen has in mind."

"I agree," Captain Fromm said, sipping on a glass of fruit juice. "Today was just a probing attack. The Ruddies sacrificed thousands of their people just to get a feel for our capabilities."

"What do you think they learned, Captain?"

"Our effective engagement ranges, the volume of indirect fire we can deliver, and how much their swatters have degraded our surveillance capabilities. One thing they've figured out is that the walls surrounding the Enclave have to go; their gates are chokepoints and perfect targets for our mortars. They are beginning to knock down wall sections to create more entry points. They are learning fast. From what I've read about their military, they have a few capable generals in charge. That Seeu Teenu, for one."

"Yes," Heather said. "General Seeu was instrumental in modernizing the Royal Guards, mostly with equipment purchased or copied from the Western Federation, the most technically-advanced nation-state in Jasper-Five. His handling of the last rebellion in the south is worth studying."

"I did," Fromm said. "If he or one of his students is in charge, he'll put the knowledge he gained to good use. Meanwhile..." He paused for several seconds when an imp call interrupted him. "Sorry. Just was informed unarmed parties of Kirosha with wheeled wagons and trucks are beginning to collect the bodies of their fallen."

"Good." The last thing they needed was thousands of rotting corpses all around the legation buildings. Most local viruses and bacteria were utterly inoffensive to humans, but a couple weren't, and they had a couple of thousand Kirosha refugees crammed all around them to act as incubators for any disease those bodies might spread. Medical nanites could work wonders, but it made no sense to give them extra work.

"I have everyone on full alert, just in case."

"Of course."

"Moving on, we have the question of what to do about the spaceport," Fromm said, bringing up a problem nobody wanted to think about. The short answer to that question was: nothing.

"Is there anything we can do?" Rockwell asked. "I don't like the idea of over a hundred Americans being left out in the cold, but what *can* we do?"

"They are twenty-five miles away by the most direct route, which would take us right through the city, or forty-five miles if we leave via the south gate and take the old Post Road, which would keep a convoy out of range from the city fortifications. It's doable."

"I suppose. If you take most of your Marines out there, and at least half of the military contractors. Which would leave us pretty much helpless if they launch another mass attack, or worse, if they finally use their military against us."

"I have a few ideas about that, but let's set that aside. If we don't mount a rescue operation, how long can they last out there?"

Heather had the answer to that. "The port facilities have massive force fields, better than anything we've got here. They won't stop an infantry attack, but will keep artillery out. There are ninety-five Navy personnel and dependents there, including a thirty-man security department with combat armor and infantry weapons, plus another thirty-nine civilian workers. They have their own water supply, plus plenty of foodstuffs in their warehouses. Figure they can last as long as a month before running out, barring a mass attack."

"Which the Ruddies can launch whenever they feel like it," Fromm said. "They can move a couple Guard or Army battalions along with another ten thousand Final Blow fanatics and overrun the port in a couple of hours, if they don't mind the losses, and we've seen that they don't. Bringing the port's personnel here isn't just the right thing to do. They will strengthen our position here."

"Sure, and if we could empty those warehouses and bring back several tons of fabber feedstock, we'd be sitting pretty, too," Rockwell said. "Why not wish for a battlecruiser squadron while we're at it?"

"Like you said, the alternative is to let over a hundred Americans die, Mr. Rockwell."

"And if things go wrong, we risk the lives of over two thousand Americans here, Captain."

Alpha males must alpha around, Heather thought sourly. Out loud: "Gentlemen, let's try to work together. We've got the resources of a Marine platoon, three Starfarer legations, three humanitarian missions, two major corporations and a good half dozen smaller ones. Maybe we can figure out a plan of action that doesn't leave us defenseless."

The arguments and counterarguments went on for a while. By the time they decided to retire for the night, they had the glimmer of a plan but still too many unanswered questions.

What else can go wrong? Heather wondered before she went to bed.

The universe was happy to answer that question the next day.

Thirteen

Year 163 AFC, D Minus Two

Lieutenant Commander Lisbeth Zhang, formerly of the *USS Wildcat*, opened her eyes and found herself looking at an unfamiliar curved ceiling.

"What...?" she croaked. She was dehydrated and her whole body felt achy and feverish, all symptoms of a massive infusion of medical nanites to repair near-lethal levels of trauma. Whatever had happened had almost killed her.

She carefully looked around; it took her a moment to recognize the unfamiliar surroundings. She'd only spent any time inside an escape pod during Cadet training at Annapolis Novo. And a pod was where she was. Someone had strapped her onto a crash recliner inside a hollow cylinder some twelve feet long and five feet wide.

A corpse floated past her eyes, startling a gasp out of her. It was Lieutenant Givens. He'd bled out; the red stains on the walls and the droplets in the air told the story. Omar had dragged her unconscious carcass into the pod, launched it before the ship blew up, and managed to inject her with a nano-med booster before succumbing to his own injuries.

"Omar," she said reaching out and touching the cold skin on his cheek. "You'll be remembered for what you did," she promised him. "I'll see to that." He deserved a Navy Cross at least, the kind of award most recipients got posthumously.

Of course, first she needed to figure out a way to make it out of this floating coffin in one piece.

Lisbeth released herself from the chair and gently secured Omar Givens' body to it before getting down to work. The pod's emergency supplies included fifteen gallons of water and two weeks' worth of foodstuffs, among several other useful items. She downed a good sixty ounces of water and ate a couple of energy bars, allegedly apple- and chocolate-flavored, while her imp accessed the pod's systems. The overpriced systems – or so she'd thought of them until just now – provided life support, force fields strong enough to withstand atmospheric re-entry, and a rudimentary grav drive.

The pod also had a decent sensor suite, better than her imp's, and a comm system that would let her contact any friendly ships or facilities within ten light minutes of her location. The first thing she did was look for any other survivors. She spotted half a dozen pods floating within sensor range, mixed in with other fragments from the two ships. All had come from the *Wildcat*; the *Bengal Tiger* had been destroyed too quickly to allow anyone to escape.

As it turned out, the *Wildcat*'s crew hadn't fared any better. Two of the pods were empty. The rest contained only corpses. Only her pod had launched quickly enough to escape the shower of fast-moving debris from the shattered ships. Pieces of her vessel's hull had ripped through the other four escape pods, exposing the people inside to vacuum. Her own pod had taken a couple of hits, but the force fields had held. Sheer luck had kept her alive while the rest of her crew died.

Sole survivor. All the people in her command, caught by surprise and slaughtered. Her command. Her responsibility.

Stop making this about you, she told herself. *We're at war. Your duty is to reach friendly forces and rejoin the action. Even if you have to carry a rifle and play ground-pounder.*

Lisbeth raised the spaceport facility on Jasper-Five.

"I'm in an escape pod," she explained to the panicked-sounding space traffic controller after establishing her identity. "Do I have clearance to land?"

"We're surrounded by hostile Eets at the moment, ma'am," the Chief Warrant in charge told her after he joined the conversation. "Mostly armed with swords and the like, but the hostiles might have air defense artillery assets. We cannot guarantee a safe landing."

Lisbeth considered her options after Ground Control sent her the latest update of the situation beyond Jasper-Five, consisting mostly of the copy of a terse QE-telegram from the War Department. A coordinated attack against the US was underway, involving dozens of star systems. The chances any Fleet forces would be dispatched to Jasper-Five anytime soon were slim to none. This had been a quiet sector for decades; the corvette squadron which had dispatched her task unit consisted of four additional vessels, which would be needed to guard Lahiri until reinforcements arrived. The nearest other force not on a frontier picket was a flotilla on Third Deseret, a good twenty-five hours' warp transit away, and likely under attack or expecting an attack. She would run out of consumables long before any rescue force arrived. She could risk being murdered groundside or dying alone in space.

"I'm going to attempt a landing, Ground Control," she

announced.

"Aye, aye, ma'am. We'll ready the tractor grapples for you."

Getting to Jasper-Five while driving a pod was very much like in the training simulations. She strapped herself to a crash chair next to the one holding the body of her XO and used her imp to set the pod on course. Some four hours later, she plunged into the blue planet. The mini-ship was rated for atmospheric entry, but barely so; air friction surrounded the pod in a sheath of superheated air as it descended at high speeds and she turned all the power of its engines to slow her down enough for the spaceport's grapples to catch it. It was daytime, but her fiery reentry lit the pod like a plunging star, bright enough to be visible for miles and miles.

The pod started shuddering violently during its final approach. As it turned out, it hadn't escaped the *Wildcat*'s destruction unscathed after all, and its upper quadrant's force field failed. Pieces of fuselage peeled away, no longer protected from the laws of physics. Lisbeth tried to reduce its speed further, and the overstrained and, as it turned out, also-damaged graviton drive shut down.

"Too fast!" the ground controller shouted. "Veer off! Veer off!"

The world seemed to slow down as she set aside all emotions – mostly pure panic – and concentrated on the task at hand. She created a checklist in her mind and went over each entry. Use the emergency attitude thrusters to climb over the spaceport's force fields before the pod splattered against them. Restart the grav engine without engaging it, not until she could slow down enough to avoid another shutdown. The attitude thrusters were her only means of steering the ship until the engines came back online, and all they could really do was impart slight changes in course. She used them to aim the pod skywards, letting the planet's gravity reduce her velocity, and hoped the pod didn't come apart.

Her altered course took her over the city. Three sets of sensors painted her craft; her imp identified them as American, Wyrm and Oval systems. It appeared the alien embassies had air defense systems in place, which meant that her IFF transponder was the only thing keeping her from eating a laser or graviton burst. To add to her worries, more pod pieces broke off; nothing vital so far, but that couldn't last; most of the pod was made of important or essential systems.

Nothing she could do about either problem, so she concentrated on her flying. The pod left the big city behind; she found herself soaring over dark countryside with only a few scattered pinpricks of light indicating the presence of fire or electricity down below. Out in the distance, a smaller town's lights flickered weakly. A few moments later, she left the land mass entirely; she was over the ocean, and if she couldn't fly back she was going to have to swim home.

Gritting her teeth, she engaged the graviton engine once again. Another emergency shutdown might result in catastrophic damage which would leave her with nothing but momentum and the attitude thrusters, neither of which would keep the aircraft aloft for very long. She idly wondered what the local sea life would make of her.

The engine caught on; the pod started vibrating violently, but she was in control again, instead of trying to steer a missile. Her imp sent her the result of the system's diagnostics: the news wasn't great. She had maybe two, three minutes before the engine gave up the ghost. That might be enough to get her back to the spaceport. Might. There were cracks in the outer fuselage; the pod might fall to pieces before the drive died.

"Here goes nothing," she said to herself as she changed course and headed back the way she'd come.

* * *

"Figgered I had to share this," the smuggler said.

Fromm looked at the neatly-stacked crates that filled the basement of the warehouse. A hidden basement, shielded from a possible custom inspection by a rather fancy stealth system. One of the crates was open, revealing its contents.

"Ruddy designs," he said, picking up one of the assault rifles from the crate and hefting it. It looked just like a Royal Armory's CR-11: .29 caliber, 20-round magazine, able to fire single shots and 3-round bursts. It was the cutting edge of Kirosha's small arms technology. Unlike normal CR-11s, though, this model had an integral electronic scope, a pistol grip, and a folding wire stock. "But improved."

"Yessir," the smuggler said. "We added a decent rangefinder with a lowlight and laser-targeting scope; figger they'll increase accuracy a good fifty, sixty percent. We was gonna sell 'em to the Ruddies in exchange for gold and other heavies, plus silk and some organics."

"I see." Technically, it wasn't illegal. The current trade treaty forbid the sale of modern weapons to the locals, but these weren't modern, technically speaking; even the electronic sights weren't state of the art, although they were easily fifty years ahead of Kirosha's technology. The rifles had been fabricated in some US planet for little more than the cost in materials and fabber time, brought in hidden with other cargo, and stored in the sub-warehouse until a buyer could be found. It'd all been done covertly to avoid the risk that some officious bastard in the diplomatic service would object to the sale of weapons to the natives and scuttle the whole operation. Or possibly because Crow had been toying with the idea of selling them to Kirosha's enemies instead.

"How come you haven't sold them already?" he asked the free trader.

Howard Crow's personal files identified him as an independent trader, co-owner and licensed operator of a small freighter, the five-thousand ton *Alan Dean Foster*. The starship was currently in transit to Lahiri; its cargo allegedly consisted of ingots of assorted metals plus a variety of luxury Kirosha goods: artwork, several tons of a local variety of silk with several potential uses, and a number of 'medicinal' organic compounds, including a variety of intoxicants and narcotics. The FDA, like most non-military government agencies, was chronically underfunded and understaffed, so new drugs could be sold with impunity for decades before being declared controlled substances, if they ever were.

The same files claimed he'd only served his obligatory four years in the service, and that his record was perfectly clean. Fromm suspected those files were as trustworthy as a politician's promise. It was hard to cheat the system, but not impossible. At the moment, however, he was only interested in the smuggler's weapon cache. He wasn't a cop and had much bigger fish to fry.

"I had a deal all set up, but the Ruddy bigwig who agreed to buy the fuck'n guns got the chop last week," Crow explained. "He was too chummy with us Starfarers, mebbe, or pissed off the wrong VIP. Whofuck knows?"

"How many?"

"Two thousand rifles. Million rounds, full metal jacket .29 caliber. Better'n what the locals make."

"Good." His platoon only had a couple dozen or so spare IW-3 rifles. The fabbers could make more, but doing so would eat up on their feedstock supplies, and they needed those to replace all the ammo they'd spent stopping the attack. While the antiquated rifles were nowhere near as effective as Starfarer weapons, they were infinitely better than nothing. "I'll take them."

"Hoped you'd said that," Mr. Crow said.

"I e-mailed you a War Department voucher. Verify that you got it."

Crow took a second to read it and smiled, revealing several gleaming gold and grav-transistor teeth. "Looks good. Figger I can pay this year's taxes with it."

"Thank you, Mr. Crow," Fromm said. "I'll send a work detail to come pick up the guns."

The smuggler hesitated for a moment before speaking again. "Ah... there's one more thing, ser."

Fromm had a feeling that the smuggler's semi-illiterate speech patterns were as genuine as his official files. "What is it?"

"Gots a piece of military gear you might find useful. And since I figger yer boys are gonna toss the place anyways and find it, might's well tell ye."

"Smart of you."

Fromm followed him to the other side of the warehouse, where several large containers were piled up. Crow was right; his Marines would have gone over those boxes sooner or later. And when he opened the nearest one he understood the smuggler's reluctance. The round white surface and the circuit-board ridges were unmistakable.

"Those are components of a warp catapult's launch pad."

"Yessuh. Figger I kin let you have it for cost."

"Figure I won't charge you for holding stolen goods and just take it instead. And I won't even ask you which of my Marines sold it to you."

"I was holding it on consignment. They ain't gonna be happy 'bout not getting' paid."

"Feel free to pass this on: I don't give a fuck who they are, but if they make any sort of stink, I'll start giving a fuck."

Crow smiled. "Gotcha."

There were a good half-dozen problem children in the platoon; any or even all of them could have been involved in taking the device and trying to sell it in the black market. If nothing else, its components could be ground down into fabber feedstock, but if the catapult could be made whole again, that opened up a number of possibilities. He'd detail Staff Sergeant Tanaka to it, and maybe some of the civilian engineers, some of whom might have worked with warp engines.

As Fromm left the warehouse, he reminded himself to order the work detail to check the rest of the building for any usable cargo; the place was near the three legation buildings, in an area that hadn't been under fire during the last attack, but it was outside the force field perimeter, which meant it would be lost sooner or later. If necessary, he'd write another voucher for Mr. Crow.

He sat down on the rear of the grav-limo, which had become his command vehicle, and headed back to base. A call came through just as he arrived.

"A survivor from Task Unit Fifteen is attempting to land, sir," CPO Donnelly said.

"Only one?" *Feline*-class corvettes had eighty-nine crewmembers apiece, and the task unit had been ferrying two platoons of marines besides. One survivor out of almost three hundred was better than he'd expected, but not by a hell of a lot.

"Yes, sir. The captain of the *Wildcat*."

"That's one lucky bastard," Fromm said, calling up the skipper's files as he walked to his office. LC Lisbeth Zhang. On the young side for the rank, but she had a decent record, until now. The Navy wasn't going to feel kindly disposed to someone who'd gotten two ships blasted under her. It wasn't even her fault, considering the threat board had been clear when she emerged into Jasper, but somebody had to be held accountable, and it wouldn't be the flag-rank assholes who'd allowed the Lampreys to launch a mass attack on America without anybody being the wiser. Heads would roll; he could only hope some of them deserved it.

All above his pay grade, of course. He sat down and went back to work on his plan to rescue the spaceport's personnel. It mostly depended on the fifty or so Caterpillar and Star Mining volunteers currently working on a new fleet of technicals. He'd have preferred to launch the operation tonight, before the Ruddies could get their shit together, but Rockwell still wasn't convinced. The poor bastards on the port would have to fend for themselves for at least another day.

"Sir, the escape pod has entered the atmosphere."

He watched the spectacular reentry through his imp. The ship started coming apart in midair, veered off course, and flew over Kirosha like a rogue comet before making a wide turn to head back towards the spaceport. She almost made it there.

"She's calling in a mayday, sir. Losing engines once again." A brief pause. "She's gone down, sir."

Fromm lowered his head. Nothing he could do, but it really sucked, surviving the attack on her ship only to die on an alien world a few hours later.

"She made it, sir! Survived the landing, and will attempt to reach the spaceport on foot. Looks like she's ten miles away."

He considered launching the rescue mission right then and there for a moment, but the vehicles weren't ready and the RSO wouldn't go for it.

"Hope you've kept current on your E&E procedures, Commander," he said to himself, hating the situation, hating the idea of a fellow officer out in the wild with no hope of rescue.

Hope she saves a round for herself, just in case, he thought.

Being captured by the Kirosha would be a hard way to go.

* * *

Any landing you could walk away from didn't count as a crash in her book, although most people looking at the deep smoking furrow that the pod had carved in a fallow field would likely disagree.

Lisbeth Zhang hadn't died. She only wished she had.

When the graviton drive failed for the second and last time, she'd had just enough time to use the attitude thrusters for a desperate attempt to nose up the tiny craft. About half of the pod had been torn loose, luckily the half she hadn't been sitting on, and the force fields on the bottom quadrant had held just long enough. She hit the ground at a shallow angle rather than head on, and the force fields shunted off just enough of the impact's kinetic energy to keep the craft more or less in one piece. The shield hadn't protected her from massive whiplash when the pod came to a rather sudden stop. The impact had nearly snapped her spine and made her pass out for a couple of minutes.

She woke up feeling as if she'd been beaten to within an inch of her life. It took everything she had to crawl out of the crash chair, grab a first-aid kit and give herself a couple of shots: an extra dose of nano-meds to repair the damage, and a hit of Walking Dead, a mixed cocktail of painkillers and stimulants designed to keep you going even if you had one foot in the grave. As soon as the WD shot took effect, she stuffed herself with protein and energy bars; the meds' metabolic costs were huge. Even chowing down on six, seven thousand calories wouldn't keep her from crashing into a near-coma as soon as the Walking Dead wore off. Additional doses would only postpone the inevitable for a few minutes, at the cost of an even nastier crash. She figured she had thirty, forty minutes before she had to lay down. Not a lot of time to E&E.

Evade and Escape. That was the name of the game. Every Eet within a hundred miles would have seen her fiery final descent.

Anybody nearby only had to head towards the flaming spot the pod had created to find her, and given that the locals were intent on killing every American they could find, she definitely didn't want to be taking a nap when they arrived. She had to move as far away as possible and find a hiding spot.

Luckily, escape pods were outfitted with the expectation that their passengers might land behind enemy lines. The first thing Lisbeth did was replace her standard uniform with a stealth bodysuit; the escape pod carried two of those. The smart nanofiber outfit stretched to fit her body, and included a full head covering that turned her into a featureless figure. The suit was skin-tight except for two bulges at her waist for the batteries that powered the suits' systems and a leg holster that would fit a standard issue beamer. The outfit could change colors to match its surroundings and use a photon field to blur her outline, making her effectively invisible at most ranges, especially when standing still. The nanite fibers it was made of would protect her from most weather extremes while also obscuring her IR signature and preventing any body particles from leaking into the environment, making her impossible to track by scent or most enhanced vision systems. Her main problem would be leaving footprints behind, and if she moved slowly enough, the suit could project a static stream that would sweep after her, erasing her tracks. Against gravity-wave sensor systems, a stealth suit would only reduce the range of detection; when dealing with low-tech alien civilizations, however, it was pretty much a cloak of invisibility.

The stealth suit's only drawback was that all those features consumed too much energy to accommodate such necessities as force fields. The energy packs would only last for twenty-four hours of constant use, after which the bodysuit would revert to its natural grayish-green color. Hopefully she'd be somewhere safe before then.

She quickly grabbed all the supplies she could scavenge. Lisbeth stuck a standard issue beamer in the suit's integral holster. She hadn't fired one of those since Basic, but with her imp doing her aiming for her, she didn't need to rate Expert to hit a target most of the time. She grabbed a backpack with similar stealth capabilities and filled it with food, water, medical nanites and four spare energy packs which could be used for the bodysuit or the pistol.

By the time she'd outfitted herself, exhaustion had begun to creep over her. That thirty-minute estimate might have been a tad optimistic.

Time to go. She followed the path of wreckage and disturbed soil the pod had left on the field, where her footprints would be harder to identify without taking the time to sweep after herself. There was a stream nearby; she thanked her lucky stars as she waded into it and walked through the water. She stayed in the stream for as long as she could; it wasn't deep, and the current wasn't too strong, but it was a slog nonetheless. Five minutes into her hike, she sent a self-destruct signal to the pod. She felt bad about consigning Omar' body to the flames, but she couldn't leave the pod and its contents to the natives. When this was over, she would do her best to recover the XO's ashes and send them to his family.

Each step was harder than the last. Her suit's smart-fibers were waterproof and their environmental controls warmed her lower extremities, but her feet were going numb nonetheless. She had to find shelter.

A wooded hill to her left beckoned to her. Lisbeth left the stream and headed there, trying not to leave too many telltale signs of her passage, but she could barely keep her eyes open so she probably messed that up. She'd messed everything up. Her career was as good as over. Her first ship command, lost with all hands. She was a failure.

Lisbeth shook her head, trying to clear it of evil thoughts. Depression was a sign the Walking Dead was wearing off. A mental command accessed her music playlist and piped it directly into her eardrums. The harsh melodies of Flaming Totenkopf got her heartbeat up and helped her walk the rest of the way to the tree line.

The local tree trunks looked like a collection of stacked rings, with two or three trunks linked together at their base and thick leaves sprouting all along their length. No branches, and she didn't think she could climb very high anyway. She squeezed herself between one the largest trio of trunks and drifted off to sleep while Flaming Totenkopf screamed in her ears about the Children of Winter, come to wash the world in blood.

Fourteen

Year 163 AFC, D Minus One

"General Jusha attempted to mobilize his men, but my troops had surrounded his encampment. He tried to fight nonetheless, but his own men slew him, to avoid being massacred. Jusha did not know his men, and he did not know his foes. Thus, he was doomed before he began," Grand Marshall Seeu Teenu concluded. Behind him, a scribe faithfully stored his words in a newfangled magnetic-strip sound recorder, so they may be later transcribed for posterity. "My officers are all capable men, and have performed well."

The newly-appointed supreme commander of all the armies of Kirosha sounded rather proud of-himself, Magistrate Eereen Leep thought ungraciously. For all his overly-fulsome self-regard, the notorious general had his uses; he had swiftly and bloodlessly captured all Modernist leaders in the Army, and gained the fealty of the rest of the officer corps. The progressives who wanted to deal with the Star Devils were all dead or languishing in the dungeons beneath the Great Pyramid. And the Queen had finally thrown her support behind Eereen's faction. The American Devil's insults had been the mite that collapsed the roof, as the saying went.

The only spot of trouble had occurred the day before, when a bright object had overflown the capital at incredible speeds, sparking panic among the populace. Eeren himself had been briefly horrified, thinking the Star Devils had returned to exact vengeance. Fortunately, their ally had explained the small craft had been a piece of the larger vessels his gifts had helped destroy, and calm had been restored. Eeren had dispatched some troops to hunt for the craft and its pilot, to use as trophies, and turned his mind towards more important matters. Everything was finally coming together.

"We thank you for your service, Grand Marshall," Eereen said. "Jusha and the renegade Prince Nooan were the last leaders among the Devil-Lovers." He turned toward the throne in the center of the room, squatting down in front of its occupant. "Your Supreme Majesty, all the Kingdom's men and cannon are now yours to command."

"They were always ours to command," High Queen Virosha the Eighth said. "Ka'at has been restored, all things returned to their proper station." She paused dramatically. "Except for one."

"Your wisdom in discerning Truth is unparalleled," Eeren said with a deep bow, his obsequious demeanor hiding a surge of panic. Whenever the Queen saw fit to correct you, there was a small but very real chance you would be dragged outside and executed. All members of the court had to learn to anticipate and fulfill the Queen's desires or risk death and worse. That too was Ka'at, the Way. "The Star Devils still pollute our land."

"Since the time of our father, High King Pirosha, Fifth of that name, it has been so. Our ways have been tainted by strangers from beyond the sky. We were patient, but when their ambassador insulted us under our own roof, our patience was exhausted. It is time to make our displeasure known." She turned towards the military commander. "What say you, Grand Marshall Seeu Teenu? Is victory at hand?"

"In war, certainty is attainable if enough knowledge is available. I have studied the enemy, and learned much from our honored ally."

The 'honored ally' was not present; the Star Devil's appearance was too noxious to be tolerated at court, and he was so unwittingly rude he would likely have offered enough offense to merit death, regardless of the consequences.

"Some questions are not easily answered, however," Seeu continued. "Their weapons are superior to ours, much like the armored knights, musketeers and artillerymen of the Tee-Kir Dynasty were superior to the tribesmen of the north. And yet, in time, the tribesmen prevailed, and eventually overwhelmed the house of Tee-Kir."

Eeren glanced fearfully at the Queen; the history lesson could well strike a nerve, since the current dynasty descended from said tribesmen, who had conquered Kirosha and become the new ruling class some two centuries and a half ago. The monarch gave no sign of taking offence, however, and instead continued to listen intently as Seeu spoke.

"There are many factors in our favor. The morale of our army is excellent. We were striving to build the most powerful force on the planet when the Star Devils arrived, and we have improved our tanks, artillery and tactics ever since. Even though the Devils will not sell us weapons, they often unwittingly allowed us to learn much from their history books and technical manuals. The Kingdom is as strong as it has ever been.

"Time is also on our side; eventually their supplies will grow low. Whether they run out of bullets or food, the end result will be the same. However, there is no need to wait that long, nor indeed is it desirable. Sieges are wasteful and lengthy, and no kingdom ever benefited from a protracted conflict. Instead, we shall seek a quick decision, in a matter of days.

"Tonight, we will set a trap for them and possibly slay some of their best warriors, should they venture forth beyond their lair, as I expect they will. Once war is officially declared, we will attempt a stratagem against them, striking at their weakness rather than their strength."

"And will you use the Final Blow Society for this?" Eeren asked. His faction controlled the peasant militias, and they had taken severe losses already. There were still tens of thousands inside the capital, and more were coming, but the supply of foolish, fanatical peasants willing to blunt cannon fire by smothering it with their corpses was not endless.

"The martial societies will comprise the bulk of the attacking force, but they will not be alone. From studying the Americans, I have learned that they love children, even Kirosha children, more than they love their own lives. Their missionaries cherish youngsters above all other thing, bringing them food and toys, caring for even the whelps of the lowest castes."

"That means the Devils are weak," Eeren said. Children had few uses until they were old enough to work, and more were always born than were needed, especially after the Star Devils brought medical knowledge that insured few died at birth or in their early years. Yes, parents should feel fondness for their young; that was part of Ka'at. But to put them above all other things was a violation of the Way, and a breach of common sense. You could replace children, so long as your people and culture survived.

"We will exploit that weakness," the Grand Marshall said. "If that does not work, we use the Guard and the Army in earnest. And that *will* work. I simply prefer to spare our best tools until they are truly needed."

Eeren, who had some inkling how much treasure had been spent in training and outfitting the modern forces gathering at the capital, wholly shared that sentiment, even if it meant his warrior-peasants would suffer. Come to think of it, now that Kirosha's other factions had been neutralized, the martial societies' usefulness was nearly at an end. Might as well send the best and bravest among them to their deaths, lest they decide to turn their virtues against the Crown.

The Queen nodded. "Then we give you our blessing. You have

our supreme confidence, Grand Marshall Seeu Teenu."

* * *

"Switch production to solid rounds," Fromm told Staff Sergeant Tanaka. The supply sergeant and armorer was the unofficial logistic officer of the American Defense Force, as Fromm had labelled the collection of irregulars, militia and auxiliaries that were now under his command. He'd gone from running half a company to an oversized regiment. While he'd often thought he could do a better job than most colonels he'd met, Fromm hadn't expected to get the chance to prove so, not at this point of his career.

"Explosive bullets are overpowered against unarmored personnel and they consume too many resources" he explained. "I'll instruct the troops to save the plasma bullets for when vehicles come into range."

"Yes, sir," Tanaka replied.

Solid steel-copper bullets with pre-fragmented casings wouldn't have the stopping power of standard issue Marine ammo, but the 4mm rounds would break apart upon hitting flesh, inflicting nasty wounds. More importantly, producing them would use a tiny fraction of the fabber feedstock plasma rounds did, since their components could be easily be made from locally-available materials. That would also allow the fabricators to build another hundred IW-3 rifles for an auxiliary company. He needed to think about logistics, organization and grand strategy, and hope he'd have enough time to think of everything before he had to face a new onslaught.

Luckily for him, the Ruddies seemed to be taking the day off. No attacks before or after reveille, which had given him time to meet with the auxiliary commanders and get things organized. Intercepted radio chatter indicated the enemy was conducting some housecleaning within their ranks. The chaos of the previous days had been due to the maneuvering of rival factions within the Army, the Guard and the militant societies. It looked like whoever had come on top was making sure all dissenters were taken care of. In a way, it reminded him of the first years after First Contact, when former Defense Secretary and newly-appointed President Hewer had unified the country by means fair and foul. You could read between the lines of even the most rosy-colored accounts of that time period, and it hadn't been pretty. That process had taken some years on Earth; Fromm suspected the Ruddies would take care of things much more quickly, since they were apparently just executing faction leaders by the carload. Meanwhile, he'd take advantage of the unofficial lull for as long as it lasted.

Turning hundreds of volunteers into semi-coherent units hadn't been quite as hard as he'd feared. As it turned out, there were some fifty NCOs, half a dozen former lieutenants, two captains, and a major among the civilian volunteers, although the latter had been with the Army Corps of Engineers and suggested he'd be more useful helping fortify the area than getting back in uniform. All the other officers and NCOs had been reactivated at their former grade, with Fromm retaining command by virtue of being the only infantry officer.

He'd put the six lieutenants in charge of oversized companies of two hundred men each, drawing from the civilian volunteers with the most combat experience, and had the captains divide those companies into two battalions with three companies each. Each company would have an IW-3 platoon; the rest would be armed with the assault rifles Mr. Crow had turned over, and they wouldn't have any organic heavy weapons, which made their effective firepower a fraction of what his Marines had. Thankfully all the volunteers had neural implants or portable equivalents, making command-and-control relatively easy, especially with CPO Donnelly's communication team helping organize things. The hundred or so contractors he left as they were; each unit was used to working together, so it was best to let them operate on their own, under his overall command. The Black River group had its own transport, six-wheeled hydrogen-cell American-made ATVs. They had light force fields and railgun mounts. They would act as mobile reserves, ready to bolster any hard-pressed section. Fromm spread the other mercenary units along the perimeter as a ready reaction force.

The Ovals and Wyrms had joined in without reservations. The alien consulates were on their own and their survival was dependent on cooperating with each other. Each legation had brought along about a company's worth of combat effectives; there were another hundred or so low-ranking diplomats, spacers and merchants who'd been impressed into service, but that was about it. On the other hand, the weapons of the three hundred alien volunteers were state-of-the-art stuff, as good as what his Marines fielded. Fromm detailed one of his new battalions to man the trenches protecting the two alien embassies, with the second one evenly split between the human and ET buildings. The aliens themselves he spread out as impromptu heavy weapon units, along with two thirds of his Marines. That should provide plenty of firepower to the entire line of defense.

That left the matter of the Ruddy refugees inside the compound. A few people had demanded they be thrown out, but the missionaries had made it categorically clear they would not stand for that, and Fromm and Rockwell had backed them up. The Kirosha were so caste-conscious that he couldn't imagine infiltrators posing as the despised Jersh under any circumstances. The local refugees would make the most loyal kind of allies: people who literally had nowhere else to go.

Unfortunately, except for Locquar's gang – about sixty or seventy mercenaries – the Kirosha allies didn't have any kind of military training, or any experience with firearms. The entire Jersh caste was forbidden from owning weapons of any kind, with even knives restricted to certain lengths and hefts. A couple of Mormon missionaries with military experience had volunteered to raise a company out of the most promising refugees; Fromm had given them two hundred rifles and plenty of ammo for practice. The rest of the Kirosha converts were already helping; all able-bodied males and females were busy digging more entrenchments and contributing their labor wherever necessary.

All he needed now was time. Everybody was working as hard as they could, and thanks to the Caterpillar earthmoving vehicles and the Ruddy pick-and-shovel volunteers, all the backup trench lines would be finished before nightfall. If the Ruddies gave him that long, the Starfarers' position would be much stronger.

Whether or not it would be strong enough remained to be seen.

Fromm didn't have many illusions about the effectiveness of the makeshift formations being put together. A fighting unit was more than troops and equipment; it took training, hard work and time to forge it into a reliable force, not to mention effective leadership. As a newly-minted captain, he knew he lacked the experience for proper large unit management. Beneath the outward confidence and optimism he had to project at all times lurked creeping doubts that he wasn't up for the job.

But there was nobody else. Rockwell was ex-Navy; he would help a great deal with the staff work required to manage the improvised army, but he couldn't offer much in the way of tactical advice. McClintock was Intelligence; Fromm would trust her with a gun at his side, or leading a squad or even a platoon, but she was more useful working with Donnelly to process information. And the last senior Embassy staffer, Norbert, was useless, a draftee who'd spent most of her time in uniform working for the Judge

Advocate General, a lawyer by trade. Useless. At least she was staying out of the way. Llewellyn was also keeping out of sight, after being warned that he'd be drafted to help dig trenches if he showed his face in public or otherwise attracted attention to himself.

The captain wasn't afraid of responsibility, only of failure. The last time he'd been faced with an impossible situation, he'd done what he thought was right.

He could only hope he'd be able to do so again.

* * *

"Bring us the Speaking Wand."

A servant approached the Queen, bearing the gold-plated microphone which would carry her words over the airwaves, to be heard in every home and public establishment with a radio receiver. The monarch waited patiently while another servant counted down to the time of the speech; when the servant raised a red flag to show she was on the air, she began to speak in a carefully modulated voice.

"We are Kirosha. We are the Throne, the Will of the Land, the Voice of the People. Today, we call upon the Devils from the stars to make amends for their crimes. Today, we demand the unconditional surrender of every outlander in the City and Kingdom of Kirosha. We are prepared to be merciful. Only those guilty of murdering our loyal citizens will be punished. All others shall be spared, and sent into exile in the Hanpeer Islands until such time as they can be delivered to the darkness from whence they came.

"If the Devils refuse to surrender, then all Kirosha must raise their hands against them. Slay them without mercy. Plunder the graves of their ancestors and dig up their bones. Crush the skulls of their children beneath your feet. There will be no mercy. Any Kirosha who betrays Ka'at by worshipping the Devils and their false gods will be punished so that death will be seen as an act of supreme mercy.

"To the Devils, we say this: you have until the hour of noon tomorrow to surrender. When that hour is past, there will be no mercy.

"That is all. We now return you to your regular programming."

* * *

Heather McClintock turned the station off just as what passed for Kirosha martial music filled the airwaves after the Queen's speech was over.

"Well, that is that."

"I take it that surrender is not an option," Deputy Norbert said, not for the first time.

"At the very least, every one of my Marines, and very likely all the senior diplomatic staff, including yourself, will be among those 'punished' for their crimes," Captain Fromm said. "I think we all know what that means."

Norbert shuddered and shook her head, remembering the scene at the Royal Court. "Not an option."

"Neither the Wyrashat or Vehelians will surrender, either," Heather said. "The loss of face incurred by giving up to non-Starfaring primitives is unacceptable to either culture."

"Very well. No surrender," Rockwell said. "Moving on. Captain?"

"This ultimatum narrows our window of opportunity to rescue the spaceport personnel, not to mention Lieutenant Commander Zhang," Fromm said. "If the rescue mission's going to happen at all, it has to be tonight. Tomorrow at noon they will attack every Starfaring facility they can reach."

"Are you sure your plan will work?"

"The Kirosha don't normally fight at night; their night vision is worse than a human's, probably because they have that huge moon turning night into day half the time, and we've never sold them any low-light or night vision equipment. Tonight that planet-moon – the Eye of God is what they call it – is 'closed,' so it'll be as dark as it gets. We've been monitoring their radio traffic, so we have a good idea where their modern forces are. If we move fast, we can drive a flying column through their lines before they can react."

"Flying column?" Norbert asked. "Do we have any aircraft?"

"It's a technical term for a mobile force," Fromm explained while everyone else tried not to roll their eyes at the Deputy. "It would consist of ground vehicles only. As to your question, there are three flight-capable vehicles under our control, corporate-owned atmospheric shuttlecraft, heavy and slow-moving. The Kirosha have aircraft of their own, roughly equivalent to early twentieth century models; a squadron was shot down by the Vehelian delegation when it attempted an overflight of the Enclave, so they're keeping their planes on the ground for now.

While the local air defense artillery and aircraft would probably be ineffective against the shuttles, we don't know if the enemy has been given high-tech anti-air assets, so I'm not risking them for the time being."

"I see," Norbert said.

"The plan is to push through any screening forces, reach the spaceport, evacuate its personnel and destroy anything they might use against us. We definitely don't want them to seize the shield generators, power plant and heavy equipment there."

"Could they use any of it, even if they captured the facilities intact?" Rockwell asked.

"Normally, probably not, but they've got to have Starfarer advisors stashed somewhere. They provided the mines that destroyed the corvettes, not to mention the Swatters. We can't afford to take the chance. The correlation of forces is adverse enough as it is."

"And you are sure they won't attempt a night attack once they know you've sortied?"

"Nothing is certain, but I doubt they will, and they will suffer badly if they do. Their ability to coordinate will be degraded, while every implanted human can see perfectly well at night. And we will keep most of the Marines and heavy weapons in place."

Rockwell nodded. "Very well. You may proceed, with one condition. You cannot lead the sortie. We can't afford to lose you."

Fromm looked like he wanted to argue, but finally shrugged. "All right. Obregon can handle the mission as well or better than I could." He didn't sound happy about sending his people out without him. Captain Devil Dog was a leads-from-the-front type. Very strong, very brave, very handsome, and very... well, not very stupid, not really. More like focused on the job at hand, to the exclusion of everything else, including his survival.

You'll never make it to flag rank with that attitude, buddy, Heather thought.

"Anything else? No? Then this meeting's over," Rockwell said.

Heather stayed behind. "I've been monitoring Kirosha radio traffic," she reported. "All of my agents are dead, executed for treason. Along with every trader, government official or nobility member who favored accommodation with the US. It's a clean sweep for the Preserver faction."

Rockwell frowned. "They clearly don't expect the Fleet to come back, ever."

"Which suggests they expect the Lhan Arkh or Nasstah to

show up at some point."

"If that happens, we might as well kiss our collective ass goodbye," the RSO said. "The Lampreys and Vipers don't treat their prisoners much better than the Kirosha. When they bother taking any. And there's more bad news, I'm afraid."

"What do you mean?"

"I got an eyes-only QE telegram just before the meeting," the RSO explained. "I needed to talk about it with someone, and I know you can keep your mouth shut. Besides the Lampreys, possible hostiles now include the Vipers – and the Imperium."

"Jesus." The Lampreys and Vipers were no surprise; the US had fought three wars against them, one against the former and two against the latter. The Galactic Imperium, on the other hand, had held a long and relatively peaceful relationship with America. It was the only Starfarer polity that was a true consortium of multiple species. And it was also the largest and most powerful civilization in the known galaxy. "How certain are we of this?"

"Not certain at all. 'Tentatively-identified Imperium vessels have fired upon Fleet assets' is how the telegram put it. If it's true, it's a disaster. We can handle the Toothsome Twosome, together or separately, even after all the rearming they've both been doing. We could probably hold our own against the Imperium, one on one. Against all three? After all the cutbacks? I don't see it, unless we get the Puppies and Wyrms on our side."

"We're going to lose entire worlds," Heather said.

"We've already lost over a dozen trading posts and a minor colony. The massacres are a matter of policy. The aim is to kill all Americans – all humans – they can get their hands on. The Pan-Asians' holdings are being targeted, too."

"We can count on them, at least," Heather said.

"Yeah, for what it's worth. The GACS has been improving its Navy, but it can only field about one tenth as many ships as we can, and most of them are obsolete models that we and the Puppies sold them. We'll probably have to use more assets to protect their colonies than anything they bring to the table."

"Maybe we should have helped them more along the way."

Rockwell shrugged. "Maybe. They weren't exactly good friends to the US. The Sino-Russian alliance actually launched nukes at us, back in the day."

"Which our Puppy-given tech blasted clean out of the sky."

"Yeah, but after that, not exterminating them was the best you could hope for."

Heather could have argued the point, but decided it wouldn't be good for her career. She didn't want a 'politically unreliable' mark on her record.

Of course, given the news, none of that might matter for long. Whoever was behind this didn't want concessions or surrender.

They wanted humanity gone.

* * *

Lisbeth Zhang's first day on Kirosha was nobody's idea of fun.

She woke up with a start shortly after dawn, still wedged between the three alien tree trunks, sore and ravenous. A few gulps of water and several protein chews and energy bars later, she felt somewhat better, but still not quite up to snuff. The nanites had fixed the injuries she'd sustained during her all-expense-paid trip to colorful Jasper-Five, but at the cost of leaving her wrung out. A few extra hours of sleep and another five or six thousand calories would fix that; the calories she could get, but sleep would have to wait.

After using her imp to triangulate her position, she looked at a detailed map of the area. She was about fifteen klicks from the spaceport as the crow flew. There was a major road connecting the port with the capital city not too far away from her position, and several minor ones sneaking throughout the area and connecting several farming villages. If she paralleled the main road she could make it to the spaceport before nightfall, give or take a few hours.

Her imp linked up with the Navy's net. She'd uploaded a brief report before going to sleep last night, but she wanted to talk to somebody.

"What's your status, Commander?" the CPO on the other end asked.

"In a word, FUBAR," Lisbeth said. She explained further and let them know her plans.

"Be advised that there are irregular forces around the spaceport," the comm tech told her.

"I'll be sneaky. Anything else?"

"Be careful, and best of luck, ma'am."

"Thank you."

Lisbeth started walking. She skirted a farming village that she had no doubt terrorized when she landed; the locals must have been too scared to come out of their homes to check on the wreckage, which was fortunate for everyone concerned.

The long walk was largely uneventful. In fact, SERE training had been tougher than this, although she hadn't been in a pod crash beforehand, so it kind of evened out. She was still tired, and the long trek around the edges of populated areas didn't help. A couple of times, she heard the distant roaring of vehicles. Lots of vehicles. Enemy patrols? Troop movements, and if so, in which direction? She considered walking closer to the road to find out, but decided against it. The stealth suit was great, but the Jasperians' unknown benefactor had given them space mines and other toys; they might be able to detect her presence if she ventured too close. Best to play it safe.

She would live to regret her decision.

Fifteen

Year 163 AFC, D Minus One

Timothy was hard at work when President Jensen called him.

He put down the entrenching tool with a sigh of relief when his portable device announced the call. There weren't enough shovels to go around, and the Marines had kindly lent out their digging equipment. "Here ya go, civvie," a weasely-looking jarhead had told Timothy. "Same e-tool the Corps' been using since long before First Contact." The short collapsible shovel wasn't as good as a regular one, and the unfamiliar stoop labor had taken its toll on him. He stretched his back while he answered.

"We're trying to organize an armed group of Kirosha volunteers," President Jensen explained. "Would you and Jonah consider helping train them? Brother Thalman was a staff sergeant in the Marine Corps; he will assume command."

Timothy glanced at Jonah, who was linked into the call. His companion nodded enthusiastically. Neither of them would complain about their current duties, but teaching Kirosha how to shoot sounded better than digging, and since they hadn't tried to shirk their duties but been asked to switch jobs, they wouldn't even have to feel guilty about it.

"We would be glad to, President Jensen."

Soon enough, Jonah and Timothy stood by the side of Elder Michael Thalman. The missionary was an older man, who with his wife had devoted his life to missionary work after retiring from the military. He did not look happy to be holding a weapon in his hands yet again; Timothy supposed Elder Thalman had thought that part of his life was over and done with.

None can guess what plans Heavenly Father has for you, Timothy thought.

"Very well. As of now, you two are sergeants," Elder Thalman said. "You will each command a company of a hundred men. Yes, that means you should be officers, but you plain aren't; you're not even qualified to be NCOs, but we've got to use what we have." He tilted his head to the Kirosha that milled around on the mission's soccer field. which they'd taken over as a training ground.

There were two distinct groups of them, standing apart from each other. The larger contingent were Jersh, the refugees the

Enclave had taken in. The others were not Kirosha but a different variant of the species; their skin was several shades darker, and their clothes and demeanor were different; they favored leather leggings and vests with chain mail patches sawn over their upper torso and shoulders. They also looked tough and confident; Timothy could tell their very presence intimidated the Kirosha. One of them stood out by virtue of the American-style business suit he wore.

"The fellows in the leather outfits are Clansmen from the islands south of Kirosha," Thalman explained. "They served as bodyguards and hired guns, and the Embassy foisted them on us. I'm keeping them together as an independent unit, under the command of Locquar, the man in the suit. I don't want to stir things up by putting them with the others, so you won't have to worry about them.

"The ones you'll be dealing with have never held a weapon, except for a couple of criminal types who're likely to be more trouble than they're worth. We need to teach them how to shoot, mainly. If they get deployed at all, it will be inside entrenchments. Fighting from fixed positions is about the easiest combat job there is. As long as they don't run the moment someone starts shooting at them, that is. Remember what you were taught during Basic, try to pass it on, and hopefully we will not disgrace ourselves. Got it?"

Jonah and Timothy nodded, soberly aware of their responsibilities. *There are no bad regiments, only bad officers.* Timothy remembered reading that line, but not where and when. Whatever Elder Thalman had said, he was an officer now. The realization felt like a lump of ice-cold stone in his guts.

The two of them helped the former sergeant organize his new charges into a regular, evenly-spaced block. They went through some very basic drill moves. No gun training, not on the first day. First they had to get them used to obeying commands, to moving as units, to feel like a group rather than a random clump of individuals. And that was going to take longer than a day, or even a week. They tried to jump-start the process by grouping together people from the same family, profession or neighborhood. That took advantage of any pre-existing camaraderie, although that had its own risks regarding discipline.

Timothy watched the Kirosha volunteers as they dutifully followed every order he and the other two humans gave them. They had grown up being told they were good for nothing other than collecting filth and engaging in the most noxious trades. The common Kirosha epithet for the Jersh was 'stinkers;' a more accurate translation of the word was 'shit-smelling scum.' Timothy tried to picture himself in their shoes and found it difficult. In North California, Mormons were thirty percent of the population; they weren't outsiders, and while there were plenty of disagreements between them and their non-LDS neighbors, nobody hated each other. Well, not much, he ruefully corrected himself, remembering a number of schoolyard brawls. He'd even gotten detention a couple of times, which took a lot, since school policy was usually to let the kids work things out by themselves except in cases of extreme bullying and violence. Still, he couldn't really understand what it meant to live in a society that utterly despised you.

They had to harbor a lot of anger, he thought, studying their expressions as they did the whole left, right, about-face routines. He'd gotten somewhat good at reading Kirosha expressions, the way their wide eyes would shift dramatically in size when surprised, shocked, or angry, and the blinking that was complex enough to serve as a coded language of its own. A half-lidded, narrow stare was a sign of rage. He didn't see much of that there, or, surprisingly, the wide-eyed, raised-eyebrow look of fear. Their faces looked mostly resigned, which in retrospect wasn't all that surprising. Kirosha culture encouraged fatalism. Things were what they were; it was all part of Ka'at, and you accepted them or you set yourself up for disappointment or worse.

They were also converts who had learned that there was a loving God and that they were all His children, and that good works and faith meant more than the caste system or the old ways of their ancestors. But they still expected their fate was sealed. They had been condemned by their betters, and that meant their deaths were inevitable.

And yet, they were there, learning how to fight. Timothy wasn't sure how that combination of resolve and pessimism would affect their behavior in combat.

He wondered how he would do when lasers – well, bullets here – started filling the air. He had never experienced combat outside the admittedly-realistic simulations he'd endured during Basic. Like many of his generation, he'd lived without the fear of imminent war long enough to think maybe he would be spared. Circumstances had proven him wrong.

"Moorrah! It's left-right! Do I have to color-code your feet?" he growled at a recruit, trying to hide his doubts in the work at hand.

* * *

"This shit ain't fair," Gonzaga groused while he did one more weapons check. "We already went out and kicked Ruddy ass. And now we gotta do it again?"

"Gonzo, you forgot the prize you get for kicking ass," Russell said wearily. Gonzo was okay, but whenever his sense of right and wrong got engaged, the little guy liked to bitch up a storm.

"What prize?"

"More asses to kick, that's what. Skipper figures we won't fuck up too badly, so off we go."

"Wasn't no skipper. It was Obregon, that's who. He figgers if we're out there we ain't getting in no trouble over here."

"Not much trouble to get into, now that we're under siege," Russell observed as he did his own unnecessary weapons check. He was just as nervous as Gonzo, just keeping it under wraps better. The last rescue operation had been a cinch. They'd been up against a bunch of poorly armed Eets, and the round trip had been a couple miles all told. Now they were going to have to drive forty-five miles to the spaceport and the same distance back. Even if the Ruddies were asleep at the switch the first half of the trip, they sure as fuck were going to do something about them on the way back.

"It don't matter none," he said, as much to himself as to his partner in crime.

"At least it's not just First Squad this time," Nacle said. He didn't look all that worried. It wasn't that the kid was stupid; in some ways he had more going on upstairs than either Russell or Gonzo. Nacle knew he could get killed; he'd been in enough dances to have lost any teenager belief in his own immortality. The bastard just didn't worry about it all that much. If he caught a bullet or got his throat slit open, he was sure his Heavenly Papa would be waiting for him on the other side, complete with a welcoming committee of all his friends and relatives and a marching band. Lucky bastard.

If there was a God, He wouldn't be so happy to see good ole Russell; if he ended up anywhere, he figured it'd be a lot hotter and less pleasant than whatever awaited Nacle, who'd only gotten his dick wet that one time in Lahiri and then cried himself to sleep for a week afterward.

"Russet?"

Russell snapped out of his daze. "What'd I miss, Gonzo?"

"I said, what do you think about the rest of the team?"

"Oh, them." He glanced to the other groups getting ready in the assembly area, a warehouse they'd picked up because its rolling doors and empty space were big enough to fit all the vehicles and personnel comprising Task Force Able. There were three distinct groups in the hangar. Russell nodded towards the Americans in the black outfits. "The mercs are all right. Most of them used to be in the Corps."

And some of them had been POGs when they'd been in uniform, and were trying to make up for it by carrying guns and acting like a pack of badasses. He noticed a lot of motto tattoos on some of them, which could mean they'd been overeager boots before reality had knocked some sense into them, or they were wannabe operators who'd been 6800s or some other useless MOS. Russell kept his thoughts to himself; no sense making Gonzo feel worse.

"How about the ETs?" Nacle asked. "Don't know if it's a good idea, working with ETs. Even if they say they're on our side."

The aliens in question were a pack of Ovals, their big bald heads looking like they were about to hatch something big and nasty. There were about a dozen of them, and they were loaded for bear, their body armor studded with enough force field generators to protect a tank, each of them packing a heavy laser, two disposable rocket launchers, and half a dozen grenades, plus a couple personal weapons: heavy pistols, knives and, in one case, a big-ass axe. Ovals didn't fuck around.

"They're okay, Nacle."

The ignorant shithead wasn't dumb, but he'd grown up in New Deseret, and aliens just didn't visit New Deseret. No reason to; all the planet produced was assorted foodstuffs and ultra-orthodox Mormons, the kind that really wanted to stick to the old ways and thought the Presidency and Apostles on Old Earth were a bunch of radical near-heretics. Over in New Deseret, they thought aliens didn't have souls. They certainly wouldn't send their people to do missionary work among non-humans. To each their own, Russell supposed. As long as they paid their taxes and did their Obligatory Service, the feds basically left them alone. You could get away with a lot, as long as you paid your taxes and did your part to defend the country. There was even a People's Star of Chippewa, full-fledged commies who paid their taxes, did their military service and tried to run their planet the way they liked it. People kept leaving Chippewa, though; that was the other thing the Feds cared about: you couldn't keep people on a planet if they didn't want to stay. Voting with their feet, they called it, the only form of democracy that always worked as advertised.

"The Ovals are good guys," Russell went on. "Almost as nice as the Puppies, and who doesn't like the Puppies?"

"I don't know about them hound dogs, Russet," Nacle said. "They kinda abandoned us a couple times."

"Yeah. There is that. In the end, everyone looks after their own first. But the Ovals over there, they ain't got nowhere to run. We're rescuing their people, too. If they want to survive, they got to play ball, fair and square."

"I suppose."

"Worry about the fuckin' Ruddies," Gonzo said. "They're the ones who're gonna skin your pale ass while you're still alive, if they catch you. You hear me, choirboy?"

"I hear you, Gonzo."

Russell ignored the byplay and finished his checkup. His Iwo was as ready as it could be; he spent a few seconds patting all the pouches on his suit. Plenty of grenade clips, extra mags, combat knife, spare water bottles, couple rat packs in case he got the munchies, and other sundries. Good to go. He had over a hundred and fifty pounds of equipment on him, but his suit's exoskeleton carried most of that, and they'd be driving both ways. Despite all that, he had a bad feeling about the mission.

Overconfidence. That's what worried him. So far the Ruddies had obligingly attacked piecemeal, with next to no weapons at all, coming in dumb. That couldn't last forever. They'd probably killed most of the stupid Ruddies in the last couple engagements. Sooner or later, one of the smart ones was going to take over. Maybe not tonight or tomorrow, but the ETs had time. The Navy wasn't coming for weeks, if ever.

Obregon walked past him. The Gunnery Sergeant didn't look worried, but Russell knew that was an act. The Gunny's demeanor helped calm him down, though. Whatever happened, Obregon wouldn't take it lying down. He'd adapt, overcome and kick ass. That didn't mean they couldn't get killed, but they'd get killed getting shit done.

"All right, people," the Task Force leader said, his words relayed via their imps, and also translated for the ET contingent. "Do one last gear check and mount up. We're rolling in five."

Instead of looking at his stuff yet one more time, Russell studied the rest of Task Force Able. His fire team would be in the original Rover Three, the up-gunned truck they'd used during their first combat mission in Ruddy-land. In this case, the cargo space was empty; they'd fill it with spaceport personnel and anything else they could fit in. Fabber stock would be on the top of the list; you could feed dirt to a fabber, but only if you wanted to make simple tools and didn't mind the wait while the gizmo separated useful materials from the rest of the crap. The fancy stuff required lots of special ingredients. The only thing keeping the aliens off their backs was massive firepower, and they'd need all the ammo they could make. Word was they'd start issuing non-explosive Iwo rounds to save on feedstock.

Not for this mission, though. Only the best stuff would do, when you sent a short platoon to do the job of a regiment.

Five of the other eight vehicles belonged to the Black River mercs. Six wheelers, three-man crew plus a borrowed Marine manning a ALS-43 on a pintle mount on top. The cars also mounted a railgun with a short traverse on the hood, in case the driver or whoever was riding shotgun got bored. The 3mm rounds the railgun fired wouldn't penetrate shields or heavy armor, but would do a number on hordes of ETs wearing silk bathrobes or field khakis. They had shield generators on the front, sides and back, giving them as much protection as the technicals Obregon had cobbled together, and their six-wheeled drive was much better than any local vehicles. Russell wished he was on one of them; his truck had some off-road capabilities, but 'some' was usually a way of saying 'not enough.' If they had to go cross-country at any point of the trip, Rover Three wasn't going to make it home.

The Ovals were on two ground-effect hovercraft. The squat turtle-shaped vehicles were currently resting on their metal skirts. When activated, eight fans would blow enough air to lift and propel them over just about any terrain. Hovercraft were lousy platforms for anything with a recoil, but the ETs used lasers, so that wasn't an issue. The hovers were converted cargo haulers, with brand-new shield generators and three heavy laser mounts. They'd provide Task Force Able with a lot of firepower and cargo space, since each of them could fit ten tons of personnel or materiel in its hold. Rover Three sucked shit by comparison.

Obregon would lead the task force from his brand-new command car, which had started out as the ambassador's overpriced grav-limo before being requisitioned and refitted. Its overpowered gluon power plant provided enough juice for a full set of field generators, giving it as much protection as a tank; they'd outfitted it with one of their 100mm mortars and two graviton cannon the Wyrm embassy had generously donated to the rescue effort, which gave it as much firepower as anything on this planet. That bastard could chew its way through a Ruddy tank battalion; its existence was the only reason Russell didn't feel even more anxious about the trip.

They were bringing out their A-game. Russell figured they could ride roughshod over anything smaller than a brigade equivalent, and outrun and outmaneuver anything else.

He still worried.

* * *

"These things are magical," Colonel Neen Reeu said, not for the first time, as he watched over the dispositions of the 103rd Kirosha Artillery Regiment, the pride of the First Army. He knew that his three anti-tank batteries, twenty-four tubes in total, were hidden in the hills overlooking the only road leading to the spaceport. He still couldn't see them, despite being on an observation post above them, and despite the fact he was using a pair of Starfarer binoculars on multi-spectrum mode.

When he'd been told his regiment was getting a shipment of blankets from their Star Devil benefactor, he'd scoffed. But these were very special blankets.

"The material not only blends with the background, making anything under it invisible, it will also defeat the advanced sensor systems the Americans use," Captain Jeenu said, his enthusiasm making him sound younger than his twenty-nine years. Jeenu was a member of the Modernist faction and a technology enthusiast. Only Colonel Neen's patronage had saved his young aide-de-camp from being purged in the last few days. Praising otherworldly technology was not safe anymore.

"Yes, the Star Devils like their little tricks, but in the end, good planning and courage will carry the day," the colonel said, his narrowing eyes wordlessly warning his aide. The captain nodded in understanding.

"It has been done as you instructed, Colonel. We made sure of it. All radios were disabled. All orders were delivered via non-electronic means."

The regiment's commander tilted his head in acknowledgement. The original order had come from Grand Marshall Seeu. The Star Devils could listen in on radio communications; it was only natural, since it was they who had provided the technology to the Kingdom. But their ability to overhear their enemies' orders had made the aliens complacent. For centuries, Kirosha armies had maneuvered and communicated through a complex system of flags, semaphores and heliographs, as well as runners and written instructions. The old ways had not been forgotten, and the regiment had been moved into position without broadcasting a single message. His troops now lay in ambush, hidden by the stealth blankets their Lhan Arkh ally had provided.

The aliens' vehicles would be protected by their invisible shields, but Neen's troops had been issued new shells for his 93mm pieces to deal with them. Each gun had five enhanced two-stage explosive shells, and twenty sabot-discarding tungsten armor-piercers. The duplex rounds used Starfarer technology designed to punch through their vaunted force fields. A direct hit had a thirty percent chance of penetrating the best protection the devils were likely to have, a chance that grew with successive shots. The tungsten rounds were less effective: their chance of penetration was a mere fifteen percent, but there were more of them.

Occupy a strong position on a path the enemy must follow. That was one of the Grand Marshall's many aphorisms. Colonel Neen had a small-print copy of the latest edition of *The Book of Martial Sayings* tucked in his tunic's front pocket.

Sometime tonight, the Americans and their running dogs would come, and his regiment would be waiting for them.

* * *

Task Force Able raced towards the South Gate under cover of night.

Gunnery Sergeant Obregon kept his attention on a map projection with all the players marked with bright-colored icons. Friendlies in blue, hostiles in red, civvies in light purple that would turn red at a moment's notice. He knew that those icons didn't tell the whole story: without their drones, his imp was limited to using all the information gathered by the task force soldiers and the sensors in their suits and vehicles. They were bound to miss things, and any one of those things might pop up and bite them in the ass. But you used what you got, and if that wasn't enough they carved your name and dates of birth and death in the massive Marine Memorial Wall in New Parris.

The status icons of the flying column's vehicles were all nominal, as well they should be, mere seconds after kickoff, but Obregon had seen the Dark God Murphy in action, and he wouldn't have been surprised if one of the vehicles broke down without warning right out of the gate. None did. Not yet.

The South Gate was smaller and narrower than the main one to the west. It didn't see much traffic, as it led towards largely uninhabited marshes and a non-navigable branch of the Keelu River, the main waterway of the region. It also led towards a modern road, however, which made it good enough for their needs. More importantly, it wasn't guarded by heavy forces.

As soon as Obregon's command car turned a corner and entered the broad street leading towards the gate, about a hundred yards away, he sent a signal and the two mortars left in the embassy compound fired a single round each.

"Brace for impact," he relayed to the column as it continued its advance.

The two guided bombs hit the gate a fraction of a second later. Their thermobaric warheads sprayed a thin mist of highly volatile chemicals and ignited them in another fraction of a second.

Night turned into hellish day.

The fireball that engulfed the gate, walls and battlements consumed every living thing in a hundred-foot radius. The same volume was also exposed to over ten pounds per square inch of pressure. The wood-and-metal gate and stone walls, never meant to resist such forces, shattered into a million pieces. Fragments peppered the command car's frontal force field as it led the way towards the smoking remains of the wall.

"Police the gap," Obregon told Hendrickson. The driver increased the density of the force field and turned it into an invisible bulldozer spade, pushing aside any debris that might impede the wheeled vehicles of the task force. Only a gluon power plant had the juice to pull that kind of trick, and only briefly. The lead vehicle went past the Enclave wall at a steady thirty miles an hour, clearing a path for the rest of the column. Nobody fired or otherwise reacted to their passage. Anybody who had survived the apocalyptic explosion was either too stunned to do anything or had better sense than attracting the attackers' attention. Smart of them, Obregon thought. Nobody in the task force was willing or able to take prisoners. Anybody who got in their way was dead.

"Guess this means we're officially at war," Hendrickson said as they headed towards the highway.

"We shoulda sent them a note or something," Obregon said.

"They probably got the idea."

"Yeah." Question was, what would the Ruddies do about the sortie? What *could* they do? Captain Fromm thought the answer was 'not much.' Most of their mobile forces were arrayed around the capital and the palace, all the way on the other side of the Enclave; the rest were scattered around; they wouldn't be able to react before the task force reached the spaceport. The trip back would be a different kettle of fish, of course.

All in all, though, Obregon was happy to be on the move. Sitting in one spot and waiting for the bastards on the other side to do something didn't feel right. The Corps taught you to seize the initiative and make the bastards react to your actions, not the other way around.

"Spaceport command, this is Able Force actual," he sent out. "We're on our way. ETA forty, that is four-oh, minutes. Pack up your shit, we're coming to get you."

Flickering flames illuminated the ruins they left behind.

Sixteen

Year 163 AFC, D Minus One

Captain Fromm paid a visit to the communications center for lack of anything better to do.

Given the existence of neural implants and gravity-wave communications that could run unimpeded through a planet's core and had a range measured in light-seconds, a communications room seemed unnecessary. Human beings tended to work better in groups, however, and trying to run everything through one's imps ran the risk of information overload. Having some of the data on display somewhere other than one's field of vision could be helpful.

The room in question was filled with vid screens and was barely large enough to accommodate four Navy techs, their equipment and a coffee maker that clearly was in constant use. Fromm returned the techs' salutes and poured himself a cup, choosing the local brew over imported coffee. The latter was more expensive, and the dark purple-brown tea made with Kirosha's Ibee leaves had about three times the caffeine content and a rich, vaguely spicy flavor he'd come to enjoy. He idly wondered if Mister Crow was selling the stuff off-world while he went over the comm-techs' work.

The Kirosha were reacting to the attack on the South Gate, and they displayed none of the chaos of the previous days, which showed their recent housecleaning had paid off. The Guard units were readying for combat, but their posture was largely defensive and designed to prevent another breakout, especially one aimed at the nearby Royal Palace complex or the capital proper. Spotlights along the walls of the Enclave came on and illuminated the area as vehicles roared to life and sleepy soldiers formed up in front of their barracks, weapons ready. Fromm kept an eye on the visual display while he watched CPO Donnelly at work.

Lateesha Donnelly had been born in New Detroit and joined the Navy as part of her obligatory service during her junior year in high school. Her shaved head was covered with bright metal studs that starkly contrasted against her brown skin; each stud was a high-power implant with enormous processing capabilities. Very few humans could handle so many computer links, but the chief petty officer was one of them. With those enhancements, Donnelly could run an entire starship by herself, or use pseudo-AI subroutines to handle the communication services of a small city. She was clearly overqualified for a support posting on the back end of nowhere. Her official records hinted at some issues that had led to her current assignment, but Fromm decided not to delve any further into them. Whatever had brought her to Jasper-Five was turning out to be a godsend under the current circumstances.

"The spaceport crews are all ready to go, sir" she reported after flashing him a brief, shy smile. "Two buses are filled with personnel. They've loaded six cargo trucks with supplies, including all the fabricator feedstock in storage and the smallest fabber on site. The other two were too heavy for transport. They have extra supplies boxed and on forklifts, ready to be loaded onto the task force vehicles."

Fromm nodded gratefully. With those supplies they would have enough consumables to endure a six-month siege. Throw in the extra trained personnel, and their chances would improve dramatically.

"They have set up explosive charges around the remaining fabbers, the force field generators and all other heavy equipment," Donnelly added. "There were no demolition-trained personnel on-site, however, and the volunteers in charge followed implant-provided instructions. They request that somebody from Task Force Able check their work."

"I'll let Gunny Obregon know."

Imps could theoretically guide people through complex tasks, but in practice it was too easy to screw things up. The two Marines in Obregon's command car were 0351s: assaultmen, trained in demolitions as well as in shooting missiles. They would make sure the explosive charges worked as advertised.

"Elements from the Kirosha First Army are on the move," Donnelly went on. "They aim to block the road leading to the South Gate. Their estimated response time is two hours. My personal estimate is closer to three."

"They should be back before then. And we can hammer any nearby troop concentrations with our mortars. I think we're golden."

"I concur, sir." The young woman's eyes lost focus for several seconds while she communed with the computer banks inside her head. "I only have one concern; there seem to be some Kirosha Army units whose radio chatter doesn't match our sensor data. An infantry battalion and an artillery regiment. They are supposed to be marshalling outside the Palace, but there aren't enough warm bodies in their bivouacs to match their unit sizes."

"Pity we can't send drones out to take a closer look," Fromm said. Donnelly could massage a great deal of data even from long-distance sensor readings, but she couldn't expect to catch everything. "Maybe those units took losses during the recent purges and their current numbers aren't up to administrative strength."

"That could explain it, sir. I'd feel better if I knew for sure."

"You're doing great, Chief. No perfection this side of Heaven."

"Yes, sir."

"Keep me posted."

He left them to it.

The waiting was the hardest part of the job, he mused as he walked towards the command post in the rearmost bunker of the triple line of trenches. All the defensive works were more or less complete, thanks to the efforts of human and Kirosha work crews. The Ruddy converts had worked their asses off. The prospect of death by torture had made them focus their efforts like nothing else would have. Hopefully that meant that the volunteers the Mormons were training would stand their ground if he put them on the line. That could wait at least a week, unless things became so desperate he'd have to put every warm body he could find inside the trenches.

It probably will never come to that, he told himself. All they had to do was hold for a couple of weeks. The fleet would send a relief force by then, if not before. *You keep telling yourself that.*

Sergeant Amherst was on watch at the command post. "Everything's quiet so far, sir," the NCO said. He'd shaped up rather nicely and was clearly trying to unfuck himself after his first-day screw-up. "The Ruddies are sticking to the walls so far. Looks like they're worried we'll be coming after their sector next."

"That concerns me," Fromm said. "They've got to know we don't have the numbers to mount an assault. The sortie to the south was easy enough, but they know what our objective is, and all our available routes. That gives them plenty of options."

"They can't react in time, sir. And our tech will handle anything they can throw in our way."

"You're probably right," Fromm admitted.

Otherwise, he might have sent thirty men to their deaths and condemned another hundred to the same fate.

* * *

Nights in Jasper-Five were either very dark or very light, depending on the position of the second planet of the binary system. When Jasper-Four – what the locals called Nuuri-osh, the Eye of God – was fully visible in the sky, its reflective surface provided enough illumination to read a book. When it wasn't, the night was much darker than on Earth; chemicals in the upper atmosphere made most stars invisible to the naked eye, plunging the night side into pitch darkness. *When the Eye of God is closed, all are blind*; the Kirosha saying was particularly apt that night. The rescue operation would have the full cover of darkness.

All of which suited Russell just fine. Their suit sensors made fighting in total darkness no more difficult than at high noon. Everything looked clear as day, in full color; intellectually he knew the colors were computer-generated approximations, but they looked real enough, and that was all that mattered. He could see well enough to tell that the bouncing figure that ran across the road was some sort of possum-deer thing and not a Ruddy with a rocket launcher and murder in his heart, which meant he didn't waste a round on the critter as it barely avoided getting run over by his truck.

"Fucking wannabe roadkill," Gonzo said as they drove past the lucky beastie.

"They don't know any better," Nacle said. "Not their fault."

"Not our fault if we squish 'em, either."

"Guess not."

They were all a bit on edge, mainly because things had gone off without a hitch so far, and luck that good never lasted. Russell and the rest of the team would have felt better if something had gone wrong. Nothing big, a minor mechanical glitch, an accidental discharge that scared the shit out of them without doing any harm, or even a bunch of Ruddies stumbling into them. Nothing had happened, though, and Russell's superstitious side felt like they were building up a reservoir of bad luck that might come crashing on them at the worst possible time.

"Launching drones," Obregon announced over the imps. They'd gone far enough away from the capital to risk the little buggers. The Ruddies couldn't have too many Swatters, and they were likely to be around the Enclave, not out in the boonies. The bubbleheads at the spaceport had eyes on several concentrations of Ruddies around them, and it wouldn't hurt to get a closer look.

"All right, we have several campfires. About two thousand fighters split into two main groups, and another few hundred in small bunches. One of them is right on top of the highway, behind barricades. No heavy weapons in sight."

Russell looked through the drones' beady little eyes. Yep, it was more assholes in their black bathrobes. Armed with their traditional pig stickers, plus a few rifles and RPGs. And they were up and about, which meant they were expecting company.

"ETA five minutes. Shit, they're moving. Looks like they're mounting a general attack on the spaceport."

"Hostiles inbound!" the Chief Warrant in charge of the spaceport announced; Russell could hear the sound of blaster fire in the background. "You jarheads better hurry up!"

"Fucking Ruddies," Russell said.

"Think they'll overrun the port before we get there?" Nacle asked.

"Nah. Ten to one odds ain't enough," Gonzo said. "All they gonna do is get caught between a rock and a hard place when we show up."

"Yeah. Should be a piece of cake. So tell me why I'm worried."

"You just ain't happy unless something's wrong, Russet. Piss poor attitude to have, if you ask me."

"Nobody asked you, G. Keep your eyes on your sector. We're about to be knee-deep in sword-swinging motherfuckers, just like in those Conan the Barbarian movies you like so much."

"By Crom, you're right." Gonzo said; he jacked a round into his ALS-43. "This is gonna be fun."

Conversation drifted off after that, as they got ready for the upcoming fight. Russell watched drone videos showing a wave of attackers rushing towards the fenced enclosure. The landing platform of the spaceport was a good sixty feet higher than the surrounding area, and the only way up was through a winding path around it, making it a fortress of sorts even without the line of defenders on shooting at the black-bathrobe maniacs below. Over a hundred Ruddies went down before they even made it to the fences. The electrified fences. Another dozen Ruddies started convulsing and spouting smoke as lethal currents ran through their bodies. The ones behind them paused and got picked off. That didn't last, though; some of the attackers had satchel charges and rockets and they started taking the fence apart.

The barricades were up ahead. Several rockets flew out and splattered onto the shields of the lead vehicles without doing any damage. About the only problem the task force had was that the road was only wide enough for four vehicles abreast, limiting the firepower they could bring to bear. Not that it mattered. A barrage of plasma and laser fire turned the barricade into a bonfire and its defenders into scattered pieces of charred flesh.

"What'd I say, Russet?" Gonzo crowed. "Fun."

Before Russell could reply, an eruption of light and smoke engulfed the merc combat car in front of them; the smaller vehicle tumbled end over end as it was flipped up by the explosion. Spotlights came to life on both sides of the road, spearing Task Force Able with bright halogen beams as flares rose into the sky and dispelled the night. An instant later, a massive impact on the side of Russell's truck sent them veering off course.

Gonzo was wrong.

None of what happened was fun at all.

* * *

Lisbeth Zhang stumbled into the hell that was ground combat.

E&E was as much of a pain as she remembered, with the added bonus that failure wouldn't result in a permanent down check on her record but a chance to get acquainted with the locals' hospitality and sexual customs. There were parties of armed men wandering the countryside, either looking for her or heading towards the militia encampments surrounding the spaceport, and even with her stealth suit she'd had too many close calls for comfort. She was utterly invisible to anybody beyond fifty feet; closer than that, she had to stay still; any movement would catch someone's eye. At ten feet, someone who was paying close attention would spot her even if she didn't move.

A couple of times, enemy patrols came to within a few feet of her position. It'd been a miracle they hadn't seen her. A miracle, and the fact that the Jasperians had been busy chatting with each other and smoking some noxious tobacco equivalent to notice little old her.

Her estimated time of arrival had been dead wrong. Night had fallen while she was still three klicks away. Nightfall had been a boon; the locals were effectively blind and were mostly congregating around campfires, which further ruined their night vision. She covered the last leg of her journey much faster than she had before.

Which meant she was just outside the spaceport when the shit hit the fan.

After following a game trail for a good hundred yards, she emerged from the woods onto the cleared ground surrounding the fenced perimeter. Finally! Now all she had to do was let people know she was there.

A screeching chorus of alien voices to her left froze her before she could call the spaceport. She hid behind a tree as a horde of armed Eets rushed toward the fences, waving swords and screaming in high-pitched voices that would have sounded funny under any other circumstances. They were struck by a storm of fire from the spaceport's landing platform. A storm of fire that was too close to Lisbeth's position. Shit on a shingle.

She ran back the way she came as not-too-distant impacts tore through trees and brushes. *Screw this ground-pounder shit!* She had to put some decent terrain features between her and that firefight, or her unshielded hide would end up eating a plasma blast or a bullet. There were some hills a quarter of a klick back; she'd hole up behind them and try to catch the relief column on their way back.

As soon as she reached a ridge, she discovered there was no safety there, as several gun positions came to life before their eyes. Camo sheets were flung aside: sophisticated, IR-signature-obfuscating camo sheets, better than what the Marines used. The large artillery pieces and crews the sheets had been hiding scrambled into action and began engaging somebody down range, using flares and spotlights to turn night into day. Their target wasn't the spaceport, which was protected by heavy force fields. They were attacking the relief force down the road.

Lisbeth cursed herself. The vehicles she'd heard earlier that day must have been part of this. She could have warned the rescue force if she hadn't been too chickenshit to take a gander.

Nothing she could do about that, but there might be something she could do about the current situation. She placed her imp feed on a priority channel so the relief force could see the gun emplacements she'd spotted. That might help, but not enough. If the locals took out the flying column, everybody in the spaceport was doomed. She had to do something.

Surviving the destruction of her ship made the last twenty-four hours nothing more than borrowed time. If she had to follow her dead crew, she might as well do something useful beforehand. Lisbeth crept toward the gun positions. The depressed barrels indicated they were direct-fire weapons; from the frantic calls she was hearing from the humans on the other end, they were effective enough.

She dialed her beamer's power to its maximum level, which would deplete its battery after five shots. Better make them count.

There were ammo limbers behind each truck, designed to be towed by a vehicle, each containing a couple dozen rounds. She found a firing position two hundred yards away, used her imp to find a proper aiming point, and took a shot.

A glowing red circle marked the spot where the metal surface of the artillery ammo container had sublimated away. Nothing else happened. Maybe she'd missed the explosive propellant in the cannon rounds. Maybe...

Light overwhelmed her sensors before something hot and huge slapped her even from across two football fields. Lisbeth ducked behind cover as debris rained all around her.

Scratch one artillery piece. Time to find another.

They weren't too far apart, and not exactly inconspicuous, not now that their camo nets weren't hiding them. This time she knew better than to hang around and watch the results of her shots. She was on the move before another explosion consumed the firing position. Two down; how many more to go?

As many as she could hit before they ran her down. She hoped she was making a difference.

She hoped it would be enough.

* * *

The first sign Obregon had that things had turned to shit was a flare going off in the sky, followed by a HEAT round missing his command car by a couple of feet and going off on the other side of the road. Spotlights stabbed down towards the task force and more explosions went off between the moving vehicles.

"Motherfuckers!" Hendrickson roared as he spun the vehicle towards the source of the threat. The closest gun emplacement was on a hill, a thousand meters out. The artillery crew snap-shot a second time four seconds after the initial volley, and the grav car shuddered under a direct hit. The shields held, though, and then it was the Marines' turn.

Da Costa was the designated gunner; she sent a long double burst of graviton beams uphill, walking the shots towards the source of the attack. The pulses of twisted space-time chewed through dirt and rocks until they hit something that went boom. The hill vanished in an expanding cloud of fire and smoke.

Obregon barely noticed the destruction of the gun; he was too busy trying to figure out what the fuck was going on. Chief Donnelly sent him a brief sit-rep which he downloaded straight into his memory. The drones had been swatted just after the ambush was sprung, and they hadn't detected anything beforehand. The Navy puke who'd crash-landed out in the wild had spotted several artillery emplacements, and the observation post in the spaceport identified several more. Over twenty guns, a fucking anti-tank *regiment* was all around them, and those 93mm fuckers packed enough punch to flip a truck over even if they didn't get through its shields.

"All elements, engage enemy artillery! Take them out!"

The order was unnecessary, of course; everyone was doing just that, except for a mercenary crew who tried to rabbit and took a no-deflection shot up the ass for its troubles. The HEAT round went right through the rear force field of the combat car and turned it into a flying fireball. Another car had been overturned by a hit; a follow-up shot finished it off. Fuck.

The two Oval hovercraft maneuvered wildly, evading several shots, and brought their lasers to bear; they took two guns under fire and exploded them in a couple of seconds; after that, they dashed towards the hills, pumping coherent light into anything that moved. Da Costa dropped mortar bombs on two more; they were anti-pers but the frag charges shredded the gunners and silenced the guns. Somewhere behind Obregon's car, a long ALS-43 burst from Rover Three scored another kill. The Navy chick took out three guns with nothing more than a hand beamer and sheer guts.

That left a good dozen guns still around, still belching fire every five or six seconds. Most of them missed, although a glancing shot sent his grav car veering off course. There were some direct hits; a merc combat car's frontal shield failed in a shower of sparks as an armor-piercer bounced off it; the vehicle was fine but its force field was off-line. On the other side of the road, a lucky or very skilled team lined their gun perfectly and sent a long-rod penetrator into the unshielded underside of an Oval hovercraft just as it crested a hill. The metal dart punched through the car, destroying one of its fans, and turned one of its crew into a splash of liquefied flesh and bone as it flew out the other side; the vehicle crashed a moment later. The driver and a gunner survived the shot and the crash, but they were both badly hurt. Icons on Obregon's display flashed yellow or went purple and black as they became casualties or fatalities. Ruddy infantry leaped from their own concealed positions and opened up with small arms and rockets.

How the *fuck* they had managed to sneak a force this size into place, Obregon couldn't begin to guess. The Navy officer had mentioned camo nets; that still didn't answer how they'd moved this many troops without anybody twigging to it. Of course, none of that mattered. All that mattered now was wiping out the ETs as soon as possible. The battle turned into a mad scrimmage as the remaining vehicles of Task Force Able fought back. Merc railguns dropped infantrymen back into their ditches and smashed spotlights. The Marines raked hilltops with their ALS-43, silencing a few more guns. It wasn't going to be enough.

"Take us up," he told Hendrickson.

"You sure?"

"Take us the fuck up."

Only way. His was the only vehicle with all-around shield coverage and enough energy output to take multiple shots and survive. The car rose up, spewing mortar bombs and death rays all around as it engaged multiple targets at once. He left Da Costa in charge of the mortar and took over the grav cannon, noting the Navy chick on the ground had taken out a fourth gun; she ought to transfer to the Corps.

He and Da Costa rained death on the Ruddies while Hendricks ducked and weaved, moving too fast to be hit by anything firing over metal sights except by blind luck. A lucky point-blank shot did just that, but the sabot-discarding armor-piercer bounced off the limo's heavy shields. The Ruddies' technology just wasn't up to the job.

Unfortunately, the Kirosha's benefactor had provided them with ten state of the art Flying Fang surface-to-air missiles. Four had been deployed alongside the ambush force. Three had been destroyed before they could be used, struck by mortar bombs or bursts of autofire. The last missile team targeted the grav car and opened fire. A moment later, a 15mm grenade incinerated the weapon and its gunners, but the damage was already done.

The self-guided duplex warhead went off near the driver's side. A graviton charge blasted a hole in the force field; the secondary shaped charge sent a jet of plasma into the car. Superheated gas tore Hendricks apart, knocked Da Costa unconscious and burned through both of Obregon's legs at the calf. It also cracked the containment field of the luxury vehicle's gluon power plant.

Obregon blinked back into consciousness; he'd been out only for a second before his nano-meds killed the pain and sent a rush of stimulants into his bloodstream. His imp took over the car's controls just before it crashed into a hillside. A quick glance at the status display showed him he was a dead man walking; the car was going to blow up. Only thing left to decide was how he checked out.

Two anti-tank guns were still firing. He had just enough time to steer the dying vehicle towards a point between them.

Mama said there'd be days like this, he thought just before the power plant's containment field broke.

* * *

Gluon plants aren't designed to explode, unlike the similar gluon-quark mixtures found in naval missile ordnance. When the subatomic force particles are let out into the wild, however, they react rather energetically with normal matter. The ensuing release was powerful enough to erase the last two anti-tank cannon from existence, turn the nearest hill into a shallow bowl, and consume the wounded Vehelians and their crashed hovercraft, all while producing a most impressive light show. Russell wished he was in a better position to appreciate the sight. On another planet, watching it on a vid screen while sipping whisky, maybe.

"Gunny's bought it," Gonzo said.

"I know." That was tough. Obregon had been a hardass, but also a good guy. Losing him was a stone cold bitch.

"Who the fuck's in charge now?" Gonzo said on the command channel.

"I am," a female voice responded.

"The fuck?"

"I'm Lieutenant Commander Lisbeth Zhang, that's who the fuck this is. I'm assuming command of this Charlie-Foxtrot under direct orders from Captain Fromm. All operational squadrons, beg pardon, Task Force elements, converge on my position and carry on. The ambush force has been destroyed, but we've still got a thousand Ruddies to clean up and more hostile forces likely to be on their way. Move it, people!"

"Fuck me," Gonzo said after making sure he was only talking to his buddies in the fire team.

Nacle didn't say anything as he carefully backed the truck out of the ditch he'd driven into during the brutal firefight. There were still Ruddies milling about and taking potshots at them, but railgun fire from the mercs' surviving combat cars were keeping their heads down for the most part. Gonzo turned a dozen ETs into charred hamburger with his ALS-43. Russell dropped a string of grenades into a nearby foxhole. After that, enemy fire became fairly sporadic.

"Guess we're in the Navy now," Gonzo said.

"Check the imp feeds, dabrah. She took out four of them guns by herself. She's got *guevos* enough to be a Devil Dog."

"Hope she's got brains as well as balls, or we'll be seeing Gunny in Hell soon enough."

Seventeen

Year 163 AFC, D Minus One

Colonel Neen watched unbelievingly as the survivors of the ambush moved on. The speed with which the Star Devils had reacted had been dizzying, sickening. Their weapons and training were superb; they had broken the teeth of his carefully-coordinated ambush, and while their losses had been terrible – half of their vehicles were down – enough of them had survived to carry on their mission, which was more than could be said for Neen's force. All his tubes had been destroyed; he doubted one in five of his regiment still lived. The worst part was, he'd lost his regiment without accomplishing his objective.

"Sir?" Captain Jeenu said. "What are your orders?"

The regiment commander shuddered and forced himself back into a semblance of self-control. He still had his duty.

"Have the men rally here. Use lamp signals to reach any surviving warrior militias you can find. We will attempt to stop them on their way back. Gather as many rocket-propelled grenades as you can; they're the only hand weapon with a chance to get through their energy shields. There are a few mines somewhere. Find them and plant them on the road; the enemy can detect them from too far away to be effective, but they'll have to slow down to clear them, and that's when we'll attack. Maybe we'll slow them down enough for a real blocking force to move into position."

"Yes, sir."

Gone were his certainty and enthusiasm. All Colonel Neen expected was to die heroically, hopefully after inflicting some small harm on the Star Devils.

"Grand Marshall Seeu, give me back my regiment," he whispered into the night.

* * *

"I hate ground-pounder crap," Lisbeth muttered under her breath as she clambered aboard a six-wheeled vehicle with clearly improvised force field attachments and a gun mount somebody had slapped onto its hull with space tape and baling wire. The personnel inside weren't even Marines, except for the ALS-43 gunner. All the others were mercenaries. It just kept getting better and better.

"Let's roll," she said, checking the status of the force she'd taken over. The jarhead captain hadn't sounded happy about her strongly-worded suggestion she assume command of the operation, but his only option would have been to appoint a corporal for the job, and there was a good chance the mercs or the Ovals would balk at following his orders.

Task Force Able was down to five vehicles out of an original nine. Sixteen dead out of thirty personnel. The losses in firepower were even worse, proportionally: seventy, eighty percent at least. It was like assuming command of the *Titanic* just after it hit that big chunk of ice. Her next assignment would probably be the control room of a gluon reactor a second before it went critical. The temptation to curl up somewhere and sob uncontrollably was rather strong, but you couldn't do that after they put gold oak leaves on your collar. There was no crying in the Navy.

Her imp fed her the things she needed to know: vehicle speeds and survivability ratings, weapon specs, the last known enemy dispositions. There were over a thousand aliens still storming the spaceport, with as many as twenty rocket launchers among them. Best way to proceed was to mow down all the sierras – no, tangos – in sight.

"Task Force Able; fire at will."

They drove past the destroyed fences and up the winding road, shooting at everything that moved. She took control over a hood-mounted railgun and sent short bursts of supersonic metal disks into running forms, watched men fall or have limbs torn off. A rocket-propelled grenade sailed over her vehicle. A moment later a laser washed over the missile team and detonated their extra ordnance: the explosion rocked her vehicle and flattened another dozen warriors. The six-wheeler bounced up and down as it ran over bodies, dead or still twitching.

Ground-pounder crap. In her world, war meant blips vanishing from the tactical holotank display, or watching your friends and colleagues consumed by fire for a few seconds before either order was restored or swift oblivion ended everyone's suffering. Here, the slaughter just went on and on.

They reached the summit of the spaceport, where a rough barricade of cargo containers barred the way and a scattering of corpses showed the high-water mark of the attack. A magnetic crane moved forward and made an opening for the task force.

"Are you ready to get the hell out of here?"

"Yes, ma'am," Chief Warrant Corrigan said. "Only thing,

about the demo charges…"

"What about them?"

"We were hoping some of your Marines could make sure they were properly emplaced."

Lisbeth checked on her remaining Marines. There'd been twelve of them, three in the command car, six spread out among the merc vehicles, and three on a truck. Six were gone and none of the survivors were trained in demolitions. Nobody else knew any more about setting up explosives than the spacers who'd gotten stuck with the job. Demo charges were fairly idiot proof, though.

"Got nobody demo-qualified, Mister Corrigan. Just pile some more explosive ordnance around the targets and hope for the best."

"Aye, aye, ma'am."

"We roll out in ten minutes."

It took more like fifteen minutes. She used the sensors mounted on the spaceport's air traffic control center to watch their surroundings while the evacuation got under way. The Jasperians weren't using radios to communicate; instead, they were flashing lights at each other, their patterns reminding her of the Morse Code she'd read about in history class. It looked like the locals were trying to set up a blocking force. It was going to be a race between two one-legged runners; nobody was at their best, but, as an old jarhead boyfriend had once quoted to her, winning meant 'getting there firstest with the mostest.' Only one way to find out got to be firstest.

The evacuation column finally got moving. Six cargo trucks and four buses were added to the convoy, along with three personal cars. The buses and one of the trucks had been fitted with makeshift force fields, but all the other vehicles were unprotected. If they ran into any determined opposition, they were going to take losses.

No choice. Anybody left behind would end up tortured to death. They'd have to take their chances.

"Time to go."

* * *

"Another bunch of dumbasses," Gonzaga said; he fired a burst towards a group of hostiles who'd made the mistake of thinking darkness and a copse of trees would conceal them. The plasma charges turned both trees and men into burning chunks of organic matter.

"Not many of 'em left," Russell replied. Most Ruddies had

been caught between the spaceport and Task Force Able and gotten chewed up. Some ETs were scattered among the surrounding woods, but only a few seemed to have any fight left in them. Russell spotted half a dozen aliens trying to run away; he fired a single 15mm grenade at them just to keep them running. Two Ruddies went down; the rest picked up the pace. "That's right, bitches! Keep going!" he called after them.

"You'd think the Ruddies would get tired of getting killed," Nacle said from the driver's seat.

"Just 'cause they look a bit like us don't mean they think like us." That went for humans too, or even fellow Americans, Russell knew. He kept that bit to himself, though; no need to confuse Nacle.

The drive back to the big city was going to suck. Russell was sure of it.

"We've got mines up ahead," the Navy LC in charge said a minute later. "Vehelian-One, clear them. Stay sharp, people!"

The Oval hovercraft darted ahead, using lasers to blow up the explosives. They were working fast, but the convoy had to slow down, just like the Ruddies had intended.

Dozens of hostiles appeared as f by magic and volley-fired rocket launchers from both sides of the road. The bastards were using camo netting, same as in the previous ambush. Russell's truck staggered under a hit but kept on rolling, same as all the vehicles with force fields. That left four trucks and two cars protected by nothing more than luck.

Two of them took multiple hits in their cargo trailers; the RPGs made holes in them and likely fucked up anything fragile inside but otherwise had no effect. One truck was blasted right in the nose, destroying its hydrogen cell engine and sending it jackknifing off the road. The last one was struck in the driver's compartment, killing everyone inside; the out-of-control truck sideswiped a combat car, moving too slowly to be stopped by its force field. Truck and car were smashed together and turned into an immobile mass of twisted metal that blocked half of the road.

The Ruddies' success didn't save them. They'd unmasked their positions, all within a hundred yards of Task Force Able, and they were mowed down in short order; their camo nets burned along with their corpses. The damage was already done, thought.

"Rover Three!" the Navy chick called out. "Pick up survivors from Truck Three and Car Six and burn the wreckage! Car Four, look for survivors on Truck Four. Cars Two and Three, cover the perimeter. Vehelian-One, scout ahead. We're moving in five!"

Five minutes was probably four minutes too long, but leaving people behind wasn't the American way. Russell and Gonzo unassed and rushed to the crashed vehicles. The cargo truck driver and the three people who'd been sharing the cab with him were all goners, and one of the mercs in Car Six had broken his neck. The two survivors helped them drag the bodies out, load them up on Rover Three, and drop some thermal grenades on the wreck to make sure the Ruddies didn't get anything out of the ambush but a long KIA list. They could hear the stutter of railguns and the screech of lasers not too far away; the ETs were still around, even after the massive losses they'd suffered. Humans, and just about every other Eet they'd encountered would have packed up and gone home by now. The Corps ought to set up a recruiting station in this planet.

Squeezing the two live mercs and the dead bodies into the back of the already-crowded truck took some doing, but they were done and ready before the five minutes were up. The diminished convoy got moving, leaving three more of their number behind.

It was turning into a hell of a long night.

* * *

Colonel Neen watched the enemy drive on and wondered about the futility of it all.

Considering the numbers and firepower involved, his second ambush had been even more successful than the last. Armed only with hand weapons, his men had destroyed three enemy vehicles and damaged at least two more. The camouflage blankets had once again proved their worth, but they had all been destroyed alongside the last remnants of his regiment. Years of training and careful nurturing had vanished in the space of a few minutes. He could not even contemplate starting over; it would feel like raising a child to replace the one you lost, all the while knowing he was doomed to die as well.

Other elements from First Army were assembling further down the road, but they didn't have any means to hide from the enemy's sensors, and in Neen's opinion would lack the necessary strength to achieve much. They might destroy one or two more unprotected cargo vehicles, and maybe damage the rest, but would take gruesome losses in return. If Neen were in command, he would order them back, to conserve their strength for another time.

He wasn't in a position to issue any orders, of course. He was an officer without a unit, and he expected to be arrested as soon as he reported back to headquarters. Failure of this magnitude was a capital offence.

There was another option. His headquarters company was personally loyal to him; he'd carefully weeded out any informants or doubters among them. He could probably glean another fifty or a hundred men from among the survivors of his regiment, and they could take their motor transport, which had largely survived unscathed, and flee. The southwest still seethed with rebellion; its population refused to accept the descendants of Northern barbarians as the true rulers of the land. He could join their forces and spend his remaining days as a skulking bandit in the hills.

Neen dipped his head in negation. He had sworn an oath to the Crown. Even if his superiors had failed him and his regiment, he would not betray that oath. He would assemble his surviving men and march back to the capital to accept whatever punishment he deserved.

* * *

Fromm watched the scene unfold from multiple points of view.

A third truck broke down and had to be destroyed and abandoned. Fromm listened in as his Marines cursed at the truck driver for fucking things up.

"That's the last of the fucking fabber powder," one of them said as he turned the irreplaceable cargo into useless slag with a brace plasma grenade. They were only able to move a handful of the fifty-kilo blocks into their already-overloaded vehicles before destroying the rest.

The KIA list was raised by one: an injured mercenary died of his wounds as the convoy moved on. Six black icons flashed on the roster list on the bottom left quadrant of his field of vision. Obregon, Da Costa, Hendrickson, Bauer, Martinez, Findley. His people. Another dozen dead from the rest of the force he'd sent out into the night. He set all that aside and concentrated on the job at hand, jumping back and forth between personal sensor feeds, the view from the Wyrm observation post, and the short-lived drone videos.

"Looks like three, four companies total, from two different regiments," he said after assessing the size of the last Kirosha force standing between Task Force Able and safety. "Still not using radios much – smart of them – but we got enough drones up there to spot them before they got swatted down. Assuming they don't have more camo-nets available."

"I don't think so," the intelligence operative said. "They would have used them for the first ambush if they had more."

"Maybe. If we have to make assumptions, we assume the worst. They could have spared enough for another infantry force like the one at the second ambush."

"It's possible, yes."

"This time they are in range of our two remaining mortars. We don't need to spot them to kill 'em all. I'm going to cover both flanks of the convoy with two full spreads." That would use up half of their bomb supply and would take forty-eight fabber-hours to replace, but he wasn't taking any chances.

He'd screwed up enough times tonight.

* * *

"Here we go," Commander Zhang muttered. Out loud: "Fire at will."

Vehelian-One engaged the enemy barricade a klick away, laser bursts punching through the piled-up cars and the soldiers behind them. The Kirosha had brought in a couple of anti-tank guns, but only a couple, and the Oval hovercraft engaged them at long range and tore them apart before they could get a shot off. The rest of Task Force Able followed suit; anything with a human-sized heat signature was targeted and taken under fire. 100mm mortars lashed both sides of the road, targeting manned Kirosha positions and any possibly concealed ones. Many of the bombs struck nothing but dirt and trees – there were no more camo nets for Kirosha to hide under – but that was small consolation for the Kirosha who were in the area of effect. Five hundred soldiers were obliterated in the span of three seconds. The Ruddy blocking was obliterated without inflicting a single casualty on the task force.

"Check fire, check fire," Lisbeth ordered; her force had achieved a rare result in military operations, a total wipeout. According to all sensors, not a single Kirosha had survived; the only heat signatures left were those of burning vehicles and rapidly-cooling corpses. "Cars Three and Four, clear the road."

Task Force Able made it home without further incident.

* * *

"The last of the enemy forces have entered the Enclave, sir."

Grand Marshall Seeu accepted the report without comment. Magister Eeren Leep found the military genius' calm demeanor annoying. Yes, all high-caste Kirosha were taught since early childhood to guard their private emotions, but there were subtle, polite ways of conveying one's feelings on any matter of importance. The Grand Marshall acted as if the loss of an elite Army regiment and the mauling of two others was of no import at all.

"It appears the ambush was not as successful as one might have hoped," Eeren said, a calculated insult.

"The ambush had three objectives of descending importance," Seeu replied, speaking as he would address a group of eager new students at the Academy of Arms. "First, it must inflict as much damage on the enemy as possible, to weaken them for the battles to come. Secondly, it was intended to force them to hurry when abandoning their port, to prevent them from destroying valuable assets. Third and last, it provided us with more information about their weapons and tactics. All objectives were achieved."

"You say it is so, therefore it must be so," Eeren said, letting a hint of doubt creep into his carefully-worded statement. "To a less well-informed observer, it would appear otherwise."

"Ignorance is a grave burden, but a cure is easily available," the Grand Marshall said in a mild tone. "Half of the force that left the Enclave was destroyed, including one of their three heavy artillery pieces. More importantly, our benefactor has examined the spaceport. He believes much can be salvaged from the wreckage there. The demolition charges the Star Devils left behind were not as effective as they thought. Furthermore, our honored ally was nearby and he managed to defuse several of them, saving many things that we shall put to good use."

"That is good news." Eeren would have to sound optimistic when he made his personal report to Her Supreme Majesty. He had hoped to cast some aspersions on the character of the Grand Marshall, just enough to warrant some minor loss of favor, but given the results of the ambush, it would probably be best to be as positive as possible. If the Queen found herself unhappy with the war against the Star Devils, she might remember that Eeren Leep had been prominent among those pushing for it. Court games were complex and often deadly. Best to back the Grand Marshall for the time being.

"Tomorrow, we strike the first blow of the real war," Seeu Teenu said.

"May it be short and victorious."

* * *

Heather McClintock knocked on the door.

"Come in."

The small apartment was on the second level of the Marines' building, and it had a private staircase that allowed visitors to access it without going through the barracks proper on the ground floor. She'd never been there before; Lieutenant Murdock and she had run in very different circles, back when the platoon's assignment to Jasper-Five had been an annoyance and budgetary problem rather than the difference between life and death. Things had changed a great deal.

Captain Fromm was stretched on a couch in the studio apartment; a bottle of Kirosha clear liquor was on the coffee table next to him, about a third of its contents already gone. There were no glasses in sight. The officer watched her in silence as she walked in.

"May I?" she said, gesturing toward the bottle. Fromm nodded and she took a swig. The stuff was made from the fermented fronds of a coastal tree; it had a slightly briny taste and kicked like a mule. The burning liquid warmed her insides as she sat down on a wicker chair facing the couch.

In an emergency, the nano-meds in Fromm's system would purge any alcohol in his bloodstream and administer counteragents to bring him back to sobriety in a matter of seconds. Drinking during ongoing military operations was still against regulations, and a terrible idea in any case.

"I'm sorry about Obregon," she said.

"You don't know how sorry you are. Not yet. Whoever I promote to replace him isn't going to be half as good as he was. And I got him killed."

"The spaceport had to be evacuated. You saved over a hundred lives."

"And lost a tenth of my command doing it. Decimated. Worse than decimated. Six out of fifty-six. I underestimated the enemy. I sent insufficient forces to do the job." He reached for the bottle and put a dent on its contents. "I'm doing a bang-up job so far. I'm going to lose the platoon. Just like the last one."

Heather had looked up Fromm's actions at Astarte-Three. His platoon had been hit hard; twenty-three KIA, everyone else WIA. The losses had been necessary to fulfill the company's objective – to hold off an enemy advance that might have resulted in the destruction of an entire Marine regiment – but Fromm had taken them personally. This incident had hit too close to home.

"You're what we got, Fromm. You know your duty. Getting drunk and wallowing isn't going to accomplish anything."

He shrugged. "I needed to take a few hours off. Found Murdock's stash hidden in a compartment inside a wall, and figured getting wasted wouldn't hurt and might help."

"Did it help?"

"Not much."

"I thought I might help," Heather said.

"By talking? Or were you planning on fucking me better?"

"A little of both, I suppose. Figured getting us laid couldn't hurt."

We both could use this, she thought. Something besides killing and fearing death. Or failure, which was worse.

His expression changed into something that wasn't quite a smile.

"Sure, why not?"

"Just what every girl wants to hear," she said, unbuttoning her blouse.

Afterwards, they lay together in bed, tired and relaxed.

"We lost most of the feedstock from the spaceport," Fromm said, still unable to let go of the thousand worries of the job. "One heavy-duty fabber made it, though. It's just a matter of using what we've got. Improvise, gear down. We're not fighting Spacefarers with graviton technology. We've got enough food for three weeks without rationing. All we have to do is hold out until the fleet shows up. We can do this."

He was still talking to himself and figuring out solutions to the problems at hand when she drifted off to sleep.

Eighteen

Year 163 AFC, D-Day

Despite all the fighting of the previous days, the official commencement of hostilities between the Kingdom of Kirosha, the United Stars of America, the Wyrashat Empire and the O-Vehel Commonwealth happened at noon the day after the rescue of the spaceport's personnel. Once again, the High Queen of Kirosha went on the air.

"Despite the treachery of the outsiders from beyond the sky, we have waited for a response to our demands until the appointed time. The Star Devils remain silent. Therefore, war is declared against all foreigners polluting our soil. They may be slain out of hand by any subject of the kingdom, and their property will be assigned to their slayers as a reward. The Star Devils brought their fate upon themselves. There shall be no mercy."

Fromm listened to the radio address from the command bunker, paying only partial attention to the Queen's words while he went through yet another logistics report. Despite the losses of the previous night, the defenses around the legation buildings were stronger than ever. The volunteer units were in place, except for the Kirosha and the Navy personnel, who would take at least a week of training before he felt confident enough to put them in the line. On the other hand, the enemy had numbers and initiative.

His imp chimed a priority message. The Ruddies were on the move. A flight of drones took off to get a better view of the situation. Fromm grunted when he saw what the enemy was doing.

"They aren't swatting the drones near the walls," CPO Donnelly said. "They want us to see this."

"Those bastards," Fromm said. "Those fucking bastards."

It was another mass attack, over twenty thousand strong in the first wave alone. About half of the Kirosha pouring into the Enclave were Final Blow Society warriors.

The other half were children, eight or nine-year-olds.

The drone videos made it clear. Kirosha children of that age were not only smaller in stature, their heads were noticeably oversized for their bodies, and their legs were shorter than an adult's, making them look more like running babies than children. They were carrying short spears and singing as they marched at a trot in blocks of ten or twenty, led by adult leaders. Whenever their pace faltered, their handlers berated them or used leather straps to whip them forward.

Kirosha Army regulars were following the first wave, infantry formations. They would rush the embassies when the child soldiers had reached the trench line.

"You fucking bastards," Fromm repeated. In a few minutes, his people were going to have to make a dreadful choice, unless he could think of something.

There were over two hundred human and a thousand Kirosha children inside the compound. Kill ten thousand of theirs to save twelve hundred of his? Let them swarm your trenches so their soldiers could follow with rifles, rocket launchers and satchel charges?

A though occurred to him. He called the Oval Centurion.

A few seconds after the call a hundred dazzler munitions soared out of the Vehelian legation and detonated over the Kirosha version of the Children's Crusade. The paralyzing lights burst over blocks of marching troops; everyone collapsed mid-step. He'd asked the Ovals to spend their entire stock of the area weapons, but it'd been worth it. The attack had been stopped in its tracks.

There were fatalities among the children, of course. According to his imp, at least one percent; some whose nervous systems failed under the flashing lights, others who broke their necks or cracked their skulls when they fell, and those buried under masses of limp bodies, suffocating to death before they could wake up. A hundred out of ten thousand, minimum. Likely more. Hopefully enough to convince the other side that if the same trick was tried a second time, he wouldn't hesitate to do what was necessary.

"Contact the Kirosha commander. Tell him we will allow them to remove the children. Next time, however, we will not answer for the consequences."

"Yes, sir," CPO Donnelly said. She hesitated for a second before continuing: "Thank you, sir."

Fromm shrugged. "As you were."

He left the bunker.

* * *

"Tell the Americans we will do as we are asked, and offer a twenty-four-hour cessation of hostilities," Grand Marshall Seeu said over the telephone before turning to his civilian counterpart.

"You will not send more children?" Magistrate Eereen asked.

Seeu dipped his head. "There is no point. The American,

Fromm, has sent us a clear message. He will slaughter our children if he has to. Dozens of them died when they were knocked unconscious. He does not wish their deaths in his conscience, but he will do what he must. They may love all children, but they love their own more, as any species with a will to survive must. I underestimated his resolve."

"What are we to do next?"

"The time for stratagems is over. When maneuvering is no longer possible and one stands on deadly ground, fighting is the only course left. A siege might prevail in the end, but to keep so many troops in the capital for very long raises the risk of rebellion or invasion elsewhere. Her Supreme Majesty shares my dislike for sieges in any case. As soon as the armistice is over, we will assault in earnest. We have a few gifts from our benefactor that we have yet to use."

"One hopes for swift and devastating success," Eereen said. Inwardly, he was elated at the result. If Seeu had won with his army of children, his fame would have reached legendary levels. Now it would come down to a campaign of hard blows, as each side bled the other and found out who ran out of blood first. Victory would be costly, and Seeu would find it hard to wrangle much prestige from it.

Eventually, the aliens would be gone, the Grand Marshall would be remembered as a respectable but not extraordinary general, and Ka'at would flow on as it should.

The new Star Devils had promised they would never send missionaries to Kirosha, or build schools or hospitals. In fact, their hideous emissary had promised no Lhan Arkh would set foot on Kirosha for as long as the Kingdom stood. An odd turn of phrase, but good enough for Eereen.

Year 163 AFC, D Plus Two

Admin work was traditionally looked down upon by most naval officers, despite its importance, and Lieutenant Commander Lisbeth Zhang was no exception. All branches in the military had been run by fighters ever since First Contact. She had to go through reams of virtual paperwork to handle her new – not to mention unofficial and highly unorthodox – posting, and she didn't like it one bit. One had to learn to handle bean-counting, but few officers on a command path found it enjoyable.

Not that I'm likely to be assuming any sort of command after this is over, she thought. For the time being, however, circumstances had left her in charge of about half as many personnel as when she had led her doomed Task Unit, even if there were no ships involved in her current command. She now was in charge of eighty-seven spacers, eleven petty officers and six warrant officers, and it was her job to manage, feed, care for and, if necessary, send them to their deaths with guns in their hands. More ground-pounder crap, in other words.

Lisbeth went over the stats of the ad-hoc unit she might command in combat. A hundred spacers had been organized into a company, divided into three platoons, all done Marine-style; on shipboard the crew would be broken up into divisions and watches, but here they were using ground-pounder rules. The rest of her administrative force was broken down into standard divisions. The whole thing smacked of desperate improvisation, but when you gave spacers rifles and put them in trenches, things were well and truly desperate.

Luckily the jarhead-in-chief wasn't throwing her people into the line right away. Her people would have some time to run simulations and learn their new roles, guided by the spaceport's security crew, who would serve as cadre. For now, all she had to worry about was doing paperwork and getting everyone as ready as possible before the enemy tried something else.

They'd had two days of peace and quiet after the child-soldier attack. More Ruddy units were assembling around the capital. The current estimate was that an entire field army was in place, and more units were being added to the mix, not to mention tens of thousands of spear-chuckers, although those had only managed to get killed in job lots, which made them of rather questionable military value. Still, there were enough Ruddies to bury the Enclave with their bodies.

Lisbeth didn't have any illusions about how long it would take before a relief force arrived. It'd be weeks, at least, before any fleet assets could be spared to go to the rescue of a couple thousand humans in a remote planet. And that was if the US didn't lose the next round of the war.

News were coming in dribs and drabs. Quantum Entanglement communications worked like that; if you went into too much detail you risked using up your supply of entangled particles and falling completely out of the loop. What had gotten through was nasty, though: millions of Americans in dozens of outposts across the galaxy were confirmed dead. The only enemy force that was taking prisoners was the Galactic Imperium, which had interned some two million humans after formally declaring war. The others were in a 'kill them all' rampage.

Two can play that game, she thought coldly.

She looked up from her status reports when her imp sent out a warning. The enemy was on the move again. Moments later, a series of explosions echoed loudly overhead, followed by a rumbling sound she'd never heard before but was able to recognize. Artillery.

The Kirosha armed forces had finally committed to the attack.

* * *

"For what we're about to receive, may the Lord make us truly thankful," Russell muttered as the first explosions echoed in the distance.

Nacle was looking a bit green. It was the kid's first time under heavy artillery.

"Don't sweat it, Nacle. This is primmie artillery. The shields will hold."

At least, Russell thought they would hold. He asked his imp how many guns were dropping shells on the compound. Seven heavy artillery brigades were in the game: according to the imp, those were all the modern guns the Ruddies had in the continent, over a decade's worth of purchases and production. Each brigade had twelve 133mm howitzers, ten 111mm mortars, and fifteen 93mm triple-purpose cannon. Which made it a grand total of two hundred and fifty-nine guns dropping ordnance on them. Then there were another hundred 60mm fast-firing pieces from the towers around the Enclave, adding their own weight of metal to the mix. The force fields could handle that. They'd shut off all nonessential systems so the power plants inside the embassies could keep pouring juice into the shields. They should hold.

The noise and smoke the shells produced when they went off two hundred feet over their position were impressive as hell, though. Best show of the week so far, even though the noise was a bit much even with their helmet baffles working hard to protect their eardrums.

His fire team was spread out as before, twenty-five yards apart, but now there were more troops in between them: civilian volunteers armed with Ruddy rifles. They were okay, for POGs, but Russell mostly ignored them.

"How long before they run out of shells?" Gonzo asked through the fire team channel.

"Damfino. They've had a good while to prepare. Weeks, at least. Maybe never."

224

"Great."

The steady pounding went on for several minutes, until a massive single detonation stood out from the rest. Dozens of shells had hit the force field at the same time.

"Time-on-target," he muttered. It took some decent firing control to have several artillery pieces hit a spot all at once, especially with the primmie equipment the Ruddies used.

"Oh, no!" Nacle shouted.

Russell tapped into the Mormon's sensor feed and watched smoke pouring from the top of the Wyrm embassy behind them and to their right. The observation tower on the roof was teetering like a drunken bubblehead. A moment later, it went down.

"Holy fuck." Either the time-on-target volley had been powerful enough to get through the fields, or some of those shells had high-tech anti-shield warheads.

"They got through the shields, Russet," Nacle said.

"They sure as fuck did. Means we're not gonna just sit it out. Means we're probably fucked."

Another massive explosion shook the air above them, and something went boom behind the lines. That had been a single shell. The Ruddies had shield-breaching charges, then. Not too many, or there'd be a lot more explosions going off inside the perimeter, but any was too many as far as he was concerned.

"May the Lord make us truly fucking grateful," Russell said. Nacle grunted at the blasphemy but didn't say anything.

"The enemy is moving forward," headquarters announced. "Armor and infantry."

"They're serious this time. Look sharp, people. Ruddy's come to dance, and he wants to lead."

"Fuck that," Gonzo said, readying the ALS-43. "Kill! *Teufel Hunden!*"

You knew things had gone to shit when Gonzo started shouting classic jarhead mottos.

The Ruddies picked up the tempo, dropping a continuous barrage of shells, with the occasional round punching through the force fields and doing who the fuck knew behind the lines. If one of those bad boys hit his spot, he was done, but you couldn't worry about that shit.

Explosions going off among the houses ahead told him some of the Ruddy shells were falling short and hitting their own guys. Friendly fire wasn't fucking friendly at all.

"Where're the fucking mortars?" Gonzo growled. There were supposed to be six of them in play now, although four were

225

simpler designs with much lower range, rate of fire and accuracy. The fabbers weren't up to the task of making proper auto-loading pieces.

"Worry about your fucking job, Gonzo," Russell said. He figured the mortars were hitting back at the enemy cannon-cockers, or working the gates to the Enclave, although that wasn't as effective now that the Ruddies had knocked down big sections of wall to let their troops pour in.

And pouring in they were. Russell looked through his sights and spotted enemies moving between the still-standing buildings, heading towards the clear ground around Embassy Row. Mostly Ruddies on foot, spear-chuckers mixed in with regular troops. He dropped a full load of 15mm grenades on them, the overhead bursts knocking ETs down by the half dozen. The rest dived for cover.

A line of explosions hit the force field maybe a hundred feet aboveground. Ruddy tanks and self-propelled artillery firing over the infantry. A section of force field flickered, and some shells went through. Russell figured that out when the ground under him shook hard enough to stagger him. Smoke rose from somewhere to his left, and he heard screams even through the constant roar of artillery. He checked the status lights of his fire team. Everyone was green.

Gonzo called for medics. "Three civvies got pulped by that round," he said. "Went off behind the porta-shields. Motherfuckers."

"Keep killin' Ruddies; only way to make 'em quit," Russell said.

"Roger that."

Russell didn't get a chance to reply. Sound and darkness washed over him like a monster wave.

He blinked and found himself staring at a smoke-filled sky. He was on the bottom of the trench and his back and neck hurt like a mother. It felt like Crow's oversized Samoan bodyguard had slammed him against a wall.

Another shell had made it past the force fields and hit the trench line. The porta-shield had stopped most of the explosion, but enough of the blast had gotten through to knock him off his feet. His imp let him know he'd been out for fifteen seconds or so. Several volunteers were also down. No fatalities he could see, just people knocked silly by the shockwave.

Russell went back to his firing position, shrugging off his aching back and neck. Everything would hurt a lot worse if the

Ruddies got into the trenches.

And they were getting close. A few made it to the wire, but didn't live long enough to throw grenades. More were coming, though. A tank – an ugly boxy thing on tracks with an over-and-under double cannon on a turret – poked out around the remains of a building, three hundred yards away. Russell let it have a burst of 4mm plasma rounds, nailing a line of bright spots on its front glacis. The turret started to swing in his direction but stopped before firing a shot. Smoke poured out from the tank as it ground to a halt. One of the plasma jets that punched through its armor must have found something to ignite. Nobody tried to come out; he figured the Ruddies inside had gotten broiled too quickly to escape.

Russell emptied his Iwo on a handful of grunts and grabbed a new mag, loaded with solids this time; all of the targets he could see were on two legs, and if another tank showed up, he'd send it a 20mm care package. 4mm pre-fragmented bullets didn't tear people to pieces like plasma rounds, but they were good enough for government work.

More artillery landed right above and in front of the trench line, but nothing got through. A moment later a burst of 100mm bomblets cleared Russell's sector. The mortars had finally switched targets. The Ruddies retreated back to the ruins. They'd be back, but not for a while. Maybe not until tomorrow or the day after.

Russell had an itch under his chin, but damned if he was going to raise his faceplate to scratch it. Artillery bursts were still going off and it would just be his luck if another leaker hit the trenches while his face was exposed.

This was beginning to feel like hard work.

Nineteen

Year 163 AFC, D Plus Two

The US Embassy building took a hit from a duplex round, blasting a third-floor office into a burning ruin. Luckily, all noncombatants had been evacuated to a force-field protected sub-basement. Fromm wished Heather was down there where it was safe, but she was sitting right next to him in the command bunker, helping with the comm section and wearing the uniform and tabs of a Petty Officer First Class, her old rank in the service. Which put her in his chain of command, which made what they'd been doing a possible Article 134 violation, but that wasn't important now.

"They only seem to have a few advanced shells, thank Whoever," Heather said.

"They aren't supposed to have any," Fromm replied, suppressing the urge to snarl at her. The high-tech surprises the Ruddies were dropping on them were taking their toll on everyone. "Any luck tracking the guns firing them?"

"Working on it." Somewhat later: "There is a dedicated brigade doing time on target barrages to take advantage of the duplex rounds; they've fired about ten high-tech rounds so far. They are six miles away; got their coordinates."

Only their remaining 100mm automatic mortars could range that far. "Let them have it," he ordered Staff Sergeant Martin.

The high-tech mortars stopped hitting the infantry rushing the trenches and switched targets, leaving their previous job to the improvised replacements the fabbers had cobbled up. Those mortars had a rate of fire of sixteen rounds per minute, instead of five rounds per *second*; they were better than nothing, though.

"Took another hit on the northern sector."

Fromm's display showed him the damage. A duplex round had gone off right over the trench line, cracking the force field open for a couple of seconds, more than long enough for a heavy shell to get through and blow half a dozen men to kingdom come. Black River mercs; the poor bastards had been taking it in the chin ever since hostilities began. Corpsmen and Ruddy volunteers rushed forward to retrieve the wounded and the dead. The survivors picked themselves up and lashed the enemy with railgun fire. Behind them, a graviton cannon turned a Kirosha tank into a

228

twisted mass of metal.

A squad from the Second Volunteers moved forward to relieve the mercs. They wore light armor vests and helmets, the best the one fabber they had dedicated to the job could produce and worse than what the mercs wore. If the Ruddies got close enough to use small arms, it was going to be rough on them.

"We got drone visuals on the mortar strike," Donnelly reported a few minutes later. "Patching them through."

Fromm saw the burning remnants of several artillery batteries. The Ruddies had dug in and done a fairly decent job of it, but that wasn't enough to deter the mortars' plasma charges. The destruction they'd wreaked on both guns and their trained artillerymen had been devastating.

That had to be an elite unit, to be entrusted with Starfarer shells. Hopefully their replacements won't be anywhere near as good.

He could feel a measure of sympathy for fellow professionals doing their jobs, but his main concern was for his people, who wouldn't have to suffer under the hammer of those guns anymore.

The Ruddy general attack ceased; the enemy stopped feeding more brave boys into the meat grinder awaiting them. Soon, they'd be offering another armistice to bring back their dead. Although the Ruddies weren't very religious, they had very strict funeral rituals, and would spend a great deal of effort retrieving the corpses of their fallen. That worked out just fine for the Starfarers. Any break from the fighting worked in their favor.

His own dead and wounded were a tiny fraction of the enemy's losses, but the totals were beginning to climb up. This had become a war of attrition, and while the Ruddies did not have an inexhaustible supply of trained men and relatively modern equipment, the Americans and their allies would likely run out of both before the enemy did.

We've got to seize the initiative. His training was focused on battles of maneuver. Sitting in a spot and letting the enemy dictate when and where to fight ran against every instinct in his body. He was working on a couple of plans to change the equation, but they would take time.

It all came down to time.

Year 163 AFC, D Plus Twelve

"Stand by for rotation."

Timothy yawned and stretched his back. After a few days in the front lines, he'd discovered that war, or at least the kind of war they were fighting, was boring as heck, except for the times when it was plain disgusting and the briefer but memorable times where it became horrifying. His platoon was due to be relieved so it could get some time off to rest and refit. They'd earned it.

They'd spent five days in or near the trenches, and had fought off two attacks. Timothy's first taste of combat had consisted mainly of shooting at tiny figures in the distance while checking on his men to make sure they didn't run or do something stupid, like forgetting to reload. Neither attack had lasted very long; the enemy had fired a few rockets at their position, which the force fields had stopped, and retreated.

The residential buildings beyond the defensive perimeter and the fortified walls around the Enclave had been turned into rubble. Where dozens of buildings and houses once stood, only the outlines of walls and basements remained, surrounded by churned earth and dug-in fortifications. The curtain walls that had been part of the skyline around the mini-city were gone, destroyed by mortar fire or the Kirosha themselves when they discovered they were slowing down their troop movements. The enemy had turned some of the ruins into entrenched positions, allowing them to slowly move their troops forward without taking unbearable losses. The Marine mortars and the Starfarer heavy weapons still worked a fearful slaughter wherever they struck, but the Starfarers didn't have enough firepower to constantly sweep the enemy lines.

Timothy glanced at the no man's land and then looked back, towards the troops that would be relieving his platoon. It was the Cops and Robbers, a company made up of the uniformed constables who had kept order in the Enclave – and several dozen former residents of the Enclave jail. He didn't know who'd had the brilliant idea of mixing policemen and convicts together, but by all accounts they were performing about as well as all the other improvised units in the Enclave. Most of the prisoners hadn't been hardened felons anyway, but rather miners and machinery operators guilty of being a bit too rowdy while out on the town. They now had the chance to be as belligerent as they wanted.

"Pack it up, guys, we're going home," Timothy told his men before greeting Precinct Captain Patel. The officer was wearing riot gear in lieu of battle armor; he lifted his helmet's transparent visor and smiled.

"It's another lovely day, isn't it?" Captain Patel said. "Anything I should know?"

"The Kirosha haven't done much. They tried to move a few light artillery pieces closer, but the Marine mortars took them out.

Other than that, it's the usual."

'The usual' consisted of sporadic artillery barrages and rocket volleys. Sometimes the artillery would include a shield-piercer, and if you were unlucky, your section of the trench would be in its path. Those special munitions had cost the defenders about a dozen people over the last ten days; ordinary artillery, which sometimes managed to blast through the shields on their own, had wounded or killed about twice as many.

Patel nodded. "Nothing we can't handle, then."

"Best of luck."

Timothy led his platoon out of the trench and they marched to the armory to turn over their guns, and then to the mission, where they stood at attention while he addressed them.

"You've done well. You have two days of liberty. When it is over, I expect you to be here at six in the morning. You are dismissed."

The Kirosha cheered like children at recess and then broke apart, becoming individuals or groups of friends once again. They would be back, two days from now, Timothy knew. They wouldn't dream of deserting their posts, not when they were standing between their families and certain death. Not to mention everyone knew everyone, and a coward would get no sympathy from his friends and neighbors. Timothy wondered how many of his men were more afraid of shaming themselves in front of their fellows than of the enemy.

He searched for Jonah; his portable device informed him that his companion was on duty on the northern side of the perimeter. Timothy sighed. President Jensen had exempted them from their missionary duties for the duration of the emergency, but it still felt strange, being apart from his companion after a year and a half of hardly ever being out of sight from one another.

Several artillery shells burst overhead. He ignored them as he walked to his room.

Year 163 AFC, D Plus Twenty

"They've got a fabber," Heather McClintock said. "A salvaged one from the spaceport is my guess."

Peter – even after weeks spending their nights together, she found it hard not to think of him as just Fromm – sat up in the bed.

"You probably should have brought that up during the intelligence briefing this morning."

He had one arm around her, something Heather usually didn't care for, but which in this case she found rather comforting. She leaned against him, her fingers idly tracing one of the many scars on his chest. Nano-meds did wonders, but hastily-repaired tissue always left marks behind.

"It just came to me. About two minutes after I came, as a matter of fact," she added with a mischievous grin.

Peter smiled back at her. "So you were working while we were, um, in *flagrante delicto*? That kind of devotion to duty deserves a commendation. And probably a spanking."

"Promises, promises. It was mostly my imp doing the work. I had it running figures and collating data. Lots of data. Like using sound recordings from all the Kirosha artillery barrages to determine just how many duplex rounds they've used so far."

As she spoke, a sudden spate of Kirosha-made thunder broke out somewhere in the night. The enemy was keeping up a steady stream of harassing fire, twenty-four seven. You got used to it after a while. At least, Heather had. A few embassy staffers had to sedate themselves into unconsciousness to get any sleep. Word was that ex-ambassador Llewellyn was relying on massive quantities of alcohol to achieve the same effect. He was not the only one.

Peter looked up for a second at the sound of the explosions, probably gauging how close they'd been, before leaning forward and kissing the top of her head. When it was just the two of them, he could be tender, gentle. A completely different man than the cold, detached leader who had overseen the deaths of tens of thousands already, and would likely help kill many more. They set business aside for a while more.

Only for a while, though.

"So how does the data support your fabber theory?" he asked her as they cuddled together and got ready to sleep. For some reason, talking shop just after making love made her feel at home.

"They've been using a standard anti-shield warhead. Nothing fancy, a plasma sub-munition designed to fit any number of artillery shells in the 80-150mm range. The standard explosive detonates and triggers a breaching graviton charge, weakening or piercing the force field, and then the secondary charge unleashes a plasma jet. The second discharge is about sixty millimeters wide and five hundred meters long."

"Nasty stuff. If they'd used them at the ambush, they would have wiped out Task Force Able, instead of just killing half of it."

"The thing is, they *did* use them at the ambush. I reviewed those records as well. About fifty shells. Most of them missed. Several of the rest malfunctioned; about half of the ones that scored a hit."

"That's a damn high failure rate."

"My guess is, the components were put together by hand. Even with modular designs, the locals didn't have the tools to ensure the proper tolerances. The saboteur in charge couldn't exactly run detailed quality control checks, either."

"So the only reason we didn't lose everybody at the spaceport was lousy quality control?"

"Call it luck. No matter how good you are, if it turns bad you're screwed."

He nodded. "I know. It's fucking frustrating."

"You telling me? I'm a control freak. The very idea makes me break out in hives."

"Let me check. I don't feel any hives here. What about under here?" His hands roamed beneath the covers.

She laughed. "No groping during intelligence briefings, please."

"Sorry. Continue."

"Their quality control remained lousy for their heavy artillery. Data crunching indicates they've fired about three hundred augmented shells at us; a fragment of a percent of the total, which is a whopping twenty *thousand* shells a day, give or take."

"Jesus. I hadn't bothered to check the totals."

"Could be worse. A truly sustained rate of fire would be more like a hundred thousand shells a day."

"I knew they've been stockpiling ordnance for a while, but they can't keep that up. Can they?"

"They have several munition factories working nonstop, plus they're buying more stuff from other countries, trading some of the electronics they've been getting from us. We're not quite dealing with the entire industrialized might of the planet, but certainly a goodly percentage of it. It's going to bankrupt Kirosha – probably already has – but I guess they're hoping their Lhan Arkh allies will bail them out."

"That's the kind of stuff that keeps me awake at night."

"Anyways, of those three hundred high-tech shells, about a hundred and twenty malfunctioned; their sound signature is distinct enough even when they fizzle, so we were able to pick them out. Things changed three days ago. The number of duplex rounds dropped considerably – about a dozen per day, down from twenty, thirty per day – but their reliability went up."

"To what?"

"A hundred percent, just about."

C.J. Carella

"And that's how you know they've got a fabber."

"Only way their warheads could have gotten so good all of a sudden. They've used up the hand-made ones and are switching to the good stuff."

"So they got a fabber. That means they need a team of operators."

Heather nodded. Fabbers could crank out ordinary items automatically, but high tech devices weren't just produced; they were *created*. A sapient being had to link with the machine and *think* certain components into existence, including the gravitonic circuitry that was the backbone of Starfarer civilization. The whole thing smacked of magic, although pre-Contact scientists had seen glimmers of it in such things as the 'observer effect.' High-tech industry couldn't be fully automated; instead, you needed a significant percentage of your population working in the industrial sector. The fabbers in the Enclave needed the efforts of over two hundred people, split over three shifts, cranking out advanced munitions, nano-meds and other vital items.

"Without imps, training Kirosha operators to use a fabber, even for a specific component like a duplex warhead, is going to take at least two, three weeks. Say eighteen days, which coincides with the new shells beginning to show up."

"Which means they started production a few days ago," he said.

"That'd be my guess."

"We didn't leave any feedstock behind, so their fabber's only got whatever was in its storage bins at the time."

"Yes. That's the only bit of good news."

"So assuming it was fully loaded, at worst it could produce what, another two hundred warheads? Two hundred and fifty?"

"Worst case, two hundred and sixty-five," she said. "That was a pretty good guess."

"I've learned more about fabbers than I ever wanted to. I can recite production rates by heart, without using my imp. Maybe I'll switch my MOS to 0401 after this is over and become a Logistics officer. Counting beans and bullets has got to be easier than spending them."

"Yeah, I bet that's just where you'll end up."

Fromm chuckled before getting back to business. "Let's bottom-line this." He paused for a second while he queried his imp. "Even two hundred and fifty shells aren't enough to take us out, not if they keep wasting them on long-range artillery with a CEP measured in hundreds of meters. Almost half their rounds

234

end up landing somewhere outside our force field perimeter."

"And they should know that."

"Which means...?"

"They could be stockpiling them for a big assault. Or they might have switched production to something worse than shield-piercing ammunition."

"Either way, it's going to be bad."

She nodded.

"And if they salvaged a fabber from the spaceport, it might not be only thing they got."

Year 163 AFC, D Plus Twenty-three

A battery of anti-tank guns fired at the same time and at the same target, a cargo truck three hundred yards away.

The four shells detonated against an invisible barrier before they struck their target. When the explosions dissipated, the truck stood unharmed.

"We have stolen their magic!" he shouted triumphantly before the echoes of the guns had faded away.

"Not magic," Grand Marshall Seeu said, his impassive demeanor unchanged despite the joy he must be feeling. "Technology, no different than gunpowder or the internal combustion engine, except in the fine details."

"You are of course correct, Grand Marshall," the magistrate admitted.

They turned towards their honored ally, who politely lowered his hood even further to spare them the discomfort of looking at his stomach-turning features.

"You have done us a great service, Most Esteemed Guest," Eereen said.

"It was easy enough," the alien said. "I was able to disarm some of the explosive charges the enemy left behind. Putting together a power supply took some work, but the fabber did most of that, once we had enough operators to use it. You now have an area force field generator that is somewhat smaller, but otherwise as good as the ones protecting the enemy's buildings. It will create a protective sphere with a radius of a hundred meters, protecting all inside from high-velocity, high-energy impacts. The generator is portable but heavy. You should be able to mount it on a vehicle of some sort."

"How long will the shield last? It is powered by... what? Electricity? Diesel?"

"Something like that. Its power source will last for several days of combat operations, based on the firepower available to the enemy. Their weapons will be able to open temporary breaches, however; your men will take losses, although they will be a fraction of what they would suffer otherwise. I recommend you warn them beforehand."

"My men will do their duty. But what if the enemy hits the generator, or its power source?" the Grand Marshall asked.

"They are protected by a smaller force field. The chances that any weapon they have will be able to breach both fields at the same time is negligible."

"Very well. Using this weapon wisely will take some thought. For one, we must shift the use of the special piercing munitions from heavy artillery to tank and mobile gun rounds. Our indirect artillery is too inaccurate; we are squandering those precious shells without inflicting decisive damage on the enemy. I understand today's heavy usage is necessary." A general attack had been launched to help disguise their test, which their ally claimed could be detected unless the special artillery shells were used to confuse the enemy sensors. "But after today, we must cease their use and save them for a decisive attack."

"That is not a bad idea," the alien said, which was high praise for him.

"We will prepare as heavy a blow as possible. When we are ready, we will strike with every ounce of our strength."

Out in the distance, cannon roared.

"Unless our spoiling attack carries the day, of course," the Grand Marshall said. "We did allocate fifty enhanced rounds to it, after all."

He did not sound terribly hopeful. Eereen could not blame him.

* * *

"They just don't learn," Russell muttered as he took down a Ruddy right on the edge of the area force field. He'd been the last survivor of yet another ET wave attack. Spear carriers, mostly, but with enough rocket teams mixed in to make things interesting, not to mention a lot of heavy artillery liberally sprinkled with duplex rounds. It was getting downright interesting.

The Ruddies always tried to hit the lines with an ongoing mass of attackers, but the mortars had thinned out the ones coming behind the latest wave and more of the little bastards were taking cover instead of running forward, resulting in lulls in the attacks. Maybe they were learning. The really brave bastards were probably dead by now.

Something went off somewhere behind the line. Something big.

"Whetef?" Gonzo shouted over the roaring explosion.

Russell tapped into the sensors and saw a massive fireball rising next to the Oval Embassy. His breath caught in his throat when the flames twisted into a funnel-cloud shape that was sucked down, out of sight. A moment later, a second flash-and-bang shook the ground beneath him with earthquake force. The visual feed wavered for a second; when he could see through the sensors again, there was a big hole in the ground where much of the ET compound had stood. Only a gluon reaction could produce that sort of effect.

"Fuck. They hit a power plant. Half the Oval embassy's gone."

"So's their force field," Gonzaga said. "We're gonna get flanked."

"Worry about this sector, shithead," Russell growled. More Ruddies were coming, as if the explosion had been some sort of signal instead of a colossal dose of bad luck. "The skipper'll let us know if we need to pull back."

He fired short bursts at the charging figures. All solids; they'd stopped issuing Iwo plasma rounds for a couple of days, and he missed their stopping power. Some Ruddies got hit two or three times and kept coming, dead on their feet but lasting long enough to throw grenades or fire rockets.

Gonzaga swept the front with a series of short bursts, and his plasma grenades stopped the charge cold, or rather, hot. Bits of cooked Ruddy were the only things that came out of the inferno the team gunner created. All along the line, the civvie volunteers kept up a steady fire with their low-tech Ruddy guns. The attackers were dropping like flies, but they kept moving forward; the sight of dozens of shells going off inside Embassy Row were drawing them in.

Russell reloaded and hoped like hell their flank didn't get turned.

* * *

"Steady! Steady now, hold your fire and let our people through!" Elder Thalman shouted, his voice hoarse from all the yelling. The Kirosha volunteers didn't have implants or comm devices like Timothy's, so every order had to be spoken out loud. Timothy hadn't paid much attention to history class, but he was sure this was primitive even in pre-Contact days, like something out of one of the World Wars, when Napoleon and Hitler had slugged it out in the Crimea, or something like that. He'd have to Woogle it when he had time.

Not now, though. He watched as the survivors from the first trench line streamed through the dug-in communication trenches between the lines. Elder Thalman was right; no sense risking hitting their own people. The enemy was still out of sight, slowed by concertina wire and a series of Claymore mines; the directional explosives detonated all along the outer trench and tore apart the first Kirosha to reach the fortifications. More would soon follow, however. The only good news was that the enemy had stopped shelling their position now that their infantry had reached the trenches. Now all they had to worry about was being shot or stabbed.

We're all going to die.

Despair is a sin. Perhaps he and the rest of his company would die, but if the line didn't hold, the Kirosha would murder everyone. He looked around; his people, men and women both, looked determined enough. Scared, yes, but also angry.

Shapes began to emerge from the smoke. "Fire!"

Timothy followed his own order, feeling the now-familiar kick of the Kirosha rifle against his shoulder as he shot. His portable device painted targets for him, and he blazed away at them, smoke and chaos making it hard to tell if he hit anybody. Men stumbled and fell as they climbed out of the first trench line. The ones who attempted to follow the fleeing defenders through the communication tunnels found they'd been collapsed or filled with anti-personnel mines that made that route more dangerous than clambering out into the open.

Two Vehelian heavy lasers swept the killing ground, and dozens, hundreds of Kirosha were sliced into two or more pieces, some of which continued to flail about. Timothy fought off a surge of nausea and kept firing until his gun was empty. He reached for his bandolier, discovered that he'd already used a spare magazine despite having no memory of it, reached for the next one, and reloaded. By the time he was ready, the enemy was much closer. A few of them had rifles and were shooting back. Someone grunted in disbelief before beginning to wail in agony; the sound was loud even compared to the staccato cracks of gunfire. The screaming went on and on, the sound driving shivers of terror down Timothy's spine.

Please shut up. Shut up and die, Timothy thought as he shot a

Kirosha in the gut just before the alien could throw a grenade into the trench. He ducked down just before the explosive went off, sending dirt and debris raining down on everyone. A few moments later, the screaming ceased; Timothy felt grateful and terribly guilty at the same time.

"Die, sibling-fornicators!" one of Timothy's soldiers shouted as he fired three-round bursts as quickly as he could pull the trigger, mostly spraying bullets up into the air. A thrown axe came out of nowhere; it split the young Kirosha's skull open and sent his limp body sliding down onto the ground. The enemy was at the wire, twenty yards away, those few who hadn't been cut down by lasers, explosives or bullets. Timothy rose up and shot at them, noticing a series of explosions over the first trench line. The Marine mortars, he thought, their fire cutting off the lead attackers from reinforcements. A few moments later, more men joined his volunteers in the trenches: men and women in Navy uniforms and body armor, wielding Iwo rifles and at least two ALS-43s. The Kirosha facing them were slaughtered.

"Come on!" a woman with a Lieutenant Commander rank icon shouted through her implants. "The force field is back! Retake that trench!"

The spacers followed her. An implant command from the officer flattened the concertina wire blocking their way, leaving only the corpses of the enemy as an obstacle. And enemy fire. A rocket-propelled grenade struck a Navy man; his shields held but his body was flung back and he hit the rear edge of the trench with bone-crushing force. He didn't get back up.

"Forward!" Timothy ordered his own people, and scrambled out into the open. All the Kirosha volunteers still on their feet followed his lead, screeching in a mix or terror and fury, and for a moment Timothy felt himself transported to a higher state of being, part of an entity made of multiple individuals with a single, overwhelming purpose.

A moment later he was back in a world of impossibly loud noises and revolting smells and sights, but he kept going, pausing only to fire three times into the body of a Kirosha who'd reared up and stabbed a spacer in the leg. The warrior jerked around as the bullets punched through him and finally fell still. Timothy exhaled as he took aim and shot him one final time in the head.

"Thank you, brah," the spacer said as he struggled to stand up. Timothy helped him up, and the Navy guy felt the spot where the spear had hit him. "Didn't go through the fabric, but man, am I going to feel it in the morning."

"Glad you're okay," Timothy said, and kept going. Several of his people had gotten ahead of him already, and his place was in front of them.

There wasn't a lot of fighting left by the time he got there. Most of the Kirosha at the first trench line had been massacred by mortar fire, as had any vehicles that had tried to follow them. More indirect fire swept the area ahead; it looked as if all the mortars in the compound were concentrating their fire there.

Timothy jumped into the trench. He landed on a torn up corpse; there were too many bodies to do otherwise. He stepped on the yielding, disgusting surface as he reached a firing position. Some distance off to his right, he spied Jonah; his companion's left arm was wrapped in blood-sodden bandages: grenade fragments, perhaps. He looked pale, sickly and much younger than normal, like a child playing soldier in a much too-realistic game.

He waved at him. Jonah spotted him and waved back. A second later, his expression went suddenly slack; blood and brains exploded out of the side of his head and Timothy's companion collapsed limply onto the corpse-strewn trench.

Timothy's scream of anguish was lost amidst the thunder of war.

Twenty

Year 163 AFC, D Plus Twenty-three

"Are you sure?"

Spacer Apprentice Heinrich Gutierrez nodded resolutely, not the least bit intimidated by being braced by two superiors at the same time.

"You can check the tape, ma'am. That space-time distortion is a shield activation. A big shield. Lasted at least forty-five seconds."

Chief Donnelly wasn't ready to buy the sensor tech's theory. "Could be bouncers off our shields. Those duplex rounds generate all kinds of gravity emanations, and we're under constant bombardment. Not to mention the Wyrashat grav-cannon; those mess up sensor readings like nobody's business." She tapped on the screen where a graph displayed variations in local space-time. "We got hit with a couple dozen special munitions at the time of your 'blip.' Followed by the Vehelian's power plant going off." That event wasn't a spike in the graph but rather a long curve that filled the next several minutes. "Between the enemy artillery and the gluon plant blowing up, it's hard to tell what was happening at the time."

"Which is suspicious in itself," Heather said. "That barrage was unusually heavy; they've been stingy with their duplex rounds lately. That kind of maneuver is just what I'd do if I was trying to conceal a force field test."

"Expensive *maskirovka*," Donnelly replied, using the traditional Russian term for military deception. "They launched a general attack at the same time and suffered massive losses."

"We did too. That distraction almost finished us off."

The O-Vehel embassy had been partially destroyed; only the building's heavy field compartmentalization had kept any of it standing after a lucky duplex round had destroyed one of its two gluon power plants and temporarily knocked out the area shielding for that section of the line. They'd almost lost the war right then and there, and all the forces in that sector had taken over ten percent casualties.

"Which is why..." Donnelly started to say before she froze in mid-sentence and slumped in her seat. "I'm sorry. I just realized I'm trying to think of reasons why it isn't true because I don't *want* it to be true. I'm sorry."

"I get it. I don't want it to be true, either." Heather turned to the Spacer Apprentice. "Good job, Spacer Ortiz. Carry on."

"Thank you, ma'am."

Heather went to share the bad news with Captain Fromm. She couldn't afford to think of him as Peter at the moment.

She found him in his apartment, where he'd had his first full night's sleep in three days. After the brutal battle, both sides had agreed to a twenty-four hour (well, twenty-five-point-three hours, a Jasper-Five day and night) armistice to allow for the removal of the dead and some much-needed wound-licking. The Enclave's two clinics, the Marine's BAS and a hastily-built field hospital were full of wounded personnel, and the fabbers couldn't produce nano-meds fast enough, not without the risk of running out of bullets and other indispensable consumables. The fabber operators were working non-stop; some of them had become casualties from overstrain, and they still couldn't meet the needs of the Enclave. Not that it mattered; they were running low on feedstock as well. A couple more battles like the last one, and they'd be reduced to using low-tech weapons.

Fromm had used the armistice to catch up on his sleep. There were still plenty of emergencies, but none of them required his attention. Until now.

Her imp woke him up; he invited her in and indulged in a brief hug and kiss before getting down to business.

"The Kirosha have tested an area force field," she said. Fromm listened quietly while she outlined the findings of Spacer Ortiz.

"The spaceport. They didn't set the demo charges right, and their pet Lamprey was able to salvage a field generator along with that fabber," he said when she was done.

"Maybe they did everything right. A field agent's imp can hack into military systems. If the Lamprey was close enough, he could have disarmed some or all of the charges. I'm guessing it was only a few of the charges, since the Kirosha don't have access to the three fabbers and four area force fields we left behind. Not that assigning blame is an issue at this point."

"You're right, it isn't. The only important thing is the result. We are fucked. With an area force field, they can march tanks and artillery right into our lines and overwhelm us. If I were them, I'd launch a general attack like the one we just survived while they deploy an assault force behind the shield. We won't be able to concentrate on it without risking a Ruddy breakthrough somewhere else. And once they're through the trenches in numbers, it's all over but the screaming."

He closed his eyes as he worked it all out. "We could fall back into the embassy buildings and hunker down behind their shields, as long as we don't mind abandoning half the civilians and all the refugees, since there just isn't enough room for them. And that will only buy us a couple more days, maybe less, before they storm each building in turn and finish us off."

"Unless?"

"What makes you think there's an 'unless' in this situation?"

"I can think of a couple things, and I'm not a jarhead. I figure you can come up with something better."

"We can try deploying mines, but we'd need days to produce them, and I doubt we have that long. Or we can use the cargo shuttles to launch an airmobile raid, except we know the enemy has anti-air assets; that's how they killed Gunny Obregon. Which leaves us with the warp catapult."

"Is it ready?" Heather asked. There'd been arguments about using precious resources to rebuild the catapult, but Fromm had made a passionate argument for having the ability to strike back rather than just surrender the initiative to the enemy.

"It took a while, what with everything else taking precedence, but it's about ready," he said. "Sort of. I was thinking of using it to raid the Palace, take the Queen hostage, maybe, or just whack the crazy bitch and hope whoever is next in line is more reasonable. Except we can't aim the fucking thing worth a damn; the thieves only took the platform, not the attached sensor suite. Without it, we would need a beacon of some sort, like the energy signature of a power plant."

"Like the one maintaining their field generator."

"Yes. It should work, but it's not going to be easy. The warp aperture is unstable. Anybody we send through is going to be exposed to warp turbulence. They estimate we'll take as many as ten, fifteen percent casualties just from going in."

"Rockwell's contacting the other embassies. Maybe they can help with your tech problems. And help outfit the task force, too. This has to be a multi-species effort. You might even call it the International Warp Catapult Project."

"Sounds like a typical State Department boondoggle."

"Not everything has to be a hundred percent American, you know."

"I suppose. It feels weird, counting on ETs."

"This is a case of hanging together versus hanging separately."

"Guess it can't hurt to have them take a look."

"Good. Of course, even if the warp drop goes swimmingly, the task force will have to fight its way back to us."

"It's a one-way trip, Heather. A force on foot, armed only with what we can carry on our backs, facing hundred-to-one odds, and that's just counting the units directly in contact..." He shook his head. "Accomplishing the objective will be hard enough. After that, we'll be cut-off and surrounded. At seventh and last, the Ruddies can dogpile us and stomp us to death. We aren't coming back."

"And all that 'we' shit means you want to lead the way."

"I'm not sending my men on a suicide mission while I sit on my ass. Fuck that."

"You're thinking like a Lieutenant. Like a *Second* Lieutenant. Not thinking at all, in other words."

Fromm shrugged. "If we do this, I'm leading the operation. That's final."

Heather raised her hands in surrender and turned away from him. "Okay, sir, Captain Fromm, sir. I won't get in your way. And I'll talk Rockwell into going along. But first you've got to promise me something."

"What's that?"

"Stop treating this as a suicide mission. Suicide is for losers. Promise me you'll do everything in your power to come back."

Their eyes met.

"I promise."

Year 163 AFC, D Plus Twenty-Five

"... and sometimes the bear eats you," Russell said, turning his cards over. "Four kings, dabrahs."

Gonzo dropped his hand in disgust as Russell scooped the chips. His imp recorded the transaction; his account was nicely in the black. Not as much as it would have been if he'd just banked a quarter of his pay like he was encouraged to do, but saving money just wasn't as much fun as winning it off other people.

It'd been a quiet few days since the general attack that almost made it through the wire. The Ruddies were probably resting and refitting, getting ready for an even bigger push. And if they had a working area force field, it'd be up to Russell and his fellow devil dogs to save the day.

"It don't matter nohow," Private First Class Dubicki said, sounding gloomier than he had any right to be, having folded as soon as the second king had shown up on the table. "We're all gon' get kilt."

"Stow that bullshit, Doobie," Gonzo told him. "That's loser talk. If we get killed, we'll do it smiling and singing *The Battle Hymn of the Republic* or somesuch. Nacle will be lead tenor or whatever the fuck you call it, won't ya, Nacle?"

Nacle looked up from a corner in the common room, where he'd been composing an email while the rest of the guys did fun stuff. "Been telling you since I met you, Gonzo. I can't sing worth spit."

"Can't drink. Can't fuck. Can't swear. Can't sing. The fuck you good for?"

"I can shoot," the Mormon said; his glare made it clear who he had in mind for a target.

"Take it down a notch, willya?" Russell said. Everyone was worked up. Doobie had a point; the mission briefing they'd gotten sounded a bit too much like suicide. And it was all Russell's fault. If he hadn't stolen the fucking catapult, there would be no mission.

He got a private imp message from Gonzo a second later. *You sure Crow won't sell us out?*

If he was going to, he would have already, Russell sent back.

That catapult had been nothing but trouble. They'd gotten screwed just about every way possible. Well, no arrests or court-martials, granted; the skipper wasn't looking to jam anybody up. But they were out a ton of cash, and were probably going to get killed to boot.

Life in the fleet sucked ass sometimes.

* * *

The cell was deep beneath the Great Pyramid, carved into the foundations of the sacred building. It was cold and damp, and stank of offal and despair. Despite all that, Colonel Neen – the former Colonel Neen – counted himself lucky. The torturers hadn't started in on him yet. Every once in a while, he could hear the screams of far less fortunate prisoners. Political dissidents, disgraced government officials, courtiers who had given offense to the Crown or to someone high-ranked enough to have them thrown in this most august of prisons, they all were dragged down into the dark knowing they would never again see the sun or the gentle glow of the Eye of God. All they had to look forward to was the release of death, a gift that their jailors would sadistically deny them until the last possible moment.

How long had he sat alone in the darkness, his only company the biting and stinging vermin that shared the cell with him? Neen

245

had no idea. Besides the screams from his fellow captives, the low rumble of artillery was the only other constant of his current existence; the war against the Star Devils was still going on. Neen suspected that his fellow officers were not having any more success than he had. Probably much less; he had managed to inflict some damage on the enemy, and he knew that assaulting fixed positions defended with alien technology would lead to massive losses for far lesser results. How many regiments, how many entire divisions had been thrown away so far? How many lives been lost, against a foe who had not done any harm to the Kingdom until Kirosha chose to turn trading partners into deadly enemies?

His cell door opened, casting enough light into the cell to temporarily blind him. Neen wasn't hungry, so it couldn't be meal time; he was usually starving by the time someone remembered to bring him some thin cereal mash and a jug of stale water. An unscheduled visit could mean several things, none of them pleasant.

"Leave us," a familiar voice said. The cell was plunged back into darkness a moment later as the guards shut in Grand Marshall Seeu with his former protégé.

"What brings you here, Teenu?" Neen said as rudely as he knew how, deliberately using the Grand Marshall's personal name and omitting his titles. "Come to inspect my new quarters? If the war against the Star Devils lasts much longer, you may find yourself partaking in similar accommodations."

"It was not my decision to send you here," Seeu said.

"It does not matter. I am here. I wish I had died along with the rest of my regiment. Alongside my dead boys."

"To be a commander is to love one's army. To be a commander is to willingly kill that which he loves."

"Yes, I am familiar with your wise words, Teenu. I've read your book plenty of times. Do you have a spare copy you could leave with me? It is too dark to read in here, but I could use its pages to wipe my arse."

"You are angry."

"My men are dead. Are you going to bring them back? Are you going to give me back my guns, my troops? I suspect you are not. So say your piece and leave me be."

"In two days, we attack the Star Devils, using some of their own devices against them. This will be the decisive moment. If we fail, we will not have the resources to attack again. We will be reduced to mounting a long siege and waiting for our new allies to arrive and finish off the Star Devils. Which they will do, for a price. Our esteemed ally made it clear that if we cannot win by ourselves, our current agreement will be modified accordingly. We will once again be reduced to servitude, dependent on our new masters to protect us."

"You knew it was madness to go to war with the Americans," Neen said, feeling exhilarated for the first time in years. To be free to speak his mind at last was a heady experience. "Even if we kill every Star Devil on the planet, our fate is wholly contingent on whose ships will next appear over our skies. If it is the Americans, we are doomed. If it is the Lahn Arkh, we will bow our heads to them, and from everything we've learned, they are unlikely to be a better choice."

"All you say is true," Seeu admitted. "I have given orders to capture alive as many Americans as we can, if we win. If need be, we can use them as hostages should their fleet be the one to appear next."

"We promised the Lahn Arkh we would kill all Americans on the planet."

"What is one more broken promise? They can be disposed of easily enough if the Lahn Arkh arrive."

"What a weak reed we are, to bend this way or that, as the wind blows," the former colonel said.

"We *are* weak, Neen. I have played this game as well as I could, just as you did. You executed the ambush perfectly. It is not your fault that the enemy was strong enough to break free and turn on you. Sometimes the game is lost before it begins."

To hear himself exonerated brought warmth to Neen's entrails even after all the dishonor and indignities heaped upon him. He began to regret his harsh words.

"You honor me, Grand Marshall. Here you stand, discussing strategy with a former soldier, now a condemned captive. I am curious as to your reasons for doing this."

"I note with gladness that you have remembered some of your manners, Neen. I am here to make you an offer. I will make similar offers to several other prisoners. One must plan for defeat as well as victory. If I win the day, I swear to you, I will use whatever influence I earn from my triumph to have you released and restored to your offices."

That was more than Neen had ever dreamed of. A smell ember of hope began to burn in his liver.

"And if I lose, I will need your help," Seeu went on. "Your help, and that of the others, for we will face desperate times, and the Kingdom's survival will require desperate measures."

"Whatever happens, the old Kirosha will be gone," Neen said; he was beginning to understand what the Grand Marshall had in mind. "You do realize that, I hope."

"Change is fraught with danger. It is sometimes necessary. Even Ka'at is not immutable."

Neen should have felt elated at the prospect of escape and possible revenge. Instead, he was suffused with sadness and a quiet sense of purpose. He squatted down, hands held in a sign of obedience.

"Lead me, Grand Marshall."

* * *

"It's a kludge, all right," Sergeant Seamus Tanaka said as Fromm walked around the end product of weeks of frantic work, not to mention the expenditure of precious materiel and fabber time.

A normal warp catapult looked like a flat circular surface, dull gray in color, surrounded by a rim of brass and gold gravitonic circuitry, with a gluon power plant underneath. The Marine thieves had carefully sectioned off the launching pad, along with the circuitry rims; the power plant had been destroyed or proved to be too massive to transport and conceal. Tanaka, several engineers from Caterpillar, two Wyrm Savants and a retired Oval warp-drive designer had busted their asses to reassemble the pad, hook the rebuilt device to a Wyrm power plant, and graft an Oval computer to the whole thing to coordinate the wildly fluctuating energies involved in creating two warp points on a planetary surface.

The improvised power plant and computer clashed horribly with the catapult's human design. The whole thing looked as if a not-particularly-smart child had taken three toys from different manufacturers and welded them together. But the simulations said it would work, and the Oval computer would hold things together much better than a human model, turning the possible ten percent loss rate into a much-less-suicidal half of one-percent. Given that the pad would only be able to launch twenty-five people in total, there was a good chance nobody would die in transit.

The survival chances of twenty-five infantrymen suddenly dropped in the middle of a Kirosha multi-regimental evolution was another thing altogether.

They would be the best-equipped twenty-five soldiers possible, at least. Their Starfarer allies had contributed weapons and equipment. The force would have to be one hundred percent human, of course, being the only species able to endure warp space with only the protection of a pressurized suit. At least a third of the personnel of a Marine combat unit had to be warp-drop rated, even now that warp drops were almost as rare as paratroop operations back in pre-Contact days. All his warp-capable men were going on what promised to be a forlorn hope.

"It ain't pretty, but it'll work," Tanaka said.

"I'll bet my life on it, Sergeant."

The important thing was, it was finished, and not a moment too soon. All indications were that the Ruddies were massing for another general assault. They would attack soon. Another couple of days, tops. The Ruddies had brought another army into the capital, and they were gleaning the best units from them and assembling the biggest assault force yet. They might win the day even without a force field.

A QE telegram had announced that a combined American and Wyrm fleet was meeting a Lamprey force at the Paulus star system, twenty warp-hours from Lahiri — and seventeen hours from Jasper. Whoever won that fight would be in position to send ships to the system and decide who lived and who died. If it was the Lampreys, nothing Fromm did would matter, but if things went the other way, all they had to do was stay alive a little longer.

Just a little longer. They'd fought off an entire country for almost four weeks already. Food was running out. Water was strictly rationed, even with a set of recyclers converting waste into potable water twenty-for seven. If it hadn't rained for the better part of a week, they would have been screwed. Their feedstock and common material stockpiles were almost gone, too. Even if they won the upcoming battle, they might not be able to fight a second one.

He couldn't let the big picture overwhelm him. He had to face each crisis in turn.

One step at a time.

Twenty-One

Year 163 AFC, D Plus Twenty-Seven

Heather McClintock checked her IW-3 one more time. It'd been a while, but some things stayed with you.

"We're not that short of riflemen," Lieutenant Commander Zhang said one more time. "You've been doing a lot of good work in Intelligence."

"For the next twenty-four to forty-eight hours, there's no need for spook work. The Kirosha are going to come knocking today or tomorrow, and we've got to keep them out until the jarheads give them a good warp-borne butt-fucking."

"Crude, Petty Officer, but accurate," the younger woman – and her superior officer – said with a grin. "Have I mentioned how much I hate ground-pounder crap?"

"Once or twice, I think."

Heather had come to like the Navy officer. She suspected that Zhang's confidence had bordered on arrogance before the loss of her ships had shaken her certainties to the core, but if so, the experience had proved salutary. The LC had helped unify the naval personnel in the compound; leading the charge that drove the Kirosha back from a breach in the lines had cemented her reputation, and her administrative skills had played a major role in keeping things going. Fromm trusted Zhang enough to leave her in command when – or if – he went forth to lead the warp assault on the Kirosha force field.

Maybe it wouldn't be necessary. Heather had played with all available sensors, calibrating them so even a twinge of space-time distortion would be instantly picked up, and nothing had shown up since the first alleged force field test. She held on to the hope that Spacer Ortiz had been wrong after all, or that the force field generator had been too damaged to function after that one try. She hoped for the best and prepared for the worst.

"Let's go," she told her platoon: except for four security crewmen, they were cooks, clerks and techs, none of whom had held a rifle since Basic, long before ending up stranded on picturesque Jasper-Five, home of a hundred thousand murderous maniacs with swords, tanks and rocket launchers, oh my. The platoon's former officer had broken his neck tripping and falling into a trench, hitting the hard-packed dirt with just enough force to kill without triggering his personal force field. You could die in the stupidest ways. Heather hoped that her own run-in with the Grim Reaper would be somewhat more dignified, maybe a heroic last stand ending in a fusillade of lead, cutting short what might have been a long and fruitful career as an intelligence officer.

Not that it matters, when it's over and the monitor lines go flat. Humans could live for centuries – so far there were a few dozen double centenarians running around – but in the end everybody went, gently or hard.

Heather set aside the morbid thoughts and led her troops towards the trenches.

Year 163 AFC, D Plus Twenty-Eight

"Force Field activation detected. 3.5 km, coordinates attached."

"This is it, people," the skipper called out through the command channel.

"You heard the man. Time to dance," Russell said as everyone geared up. They hadn't been in the trenches for days, but precious little of that time had been spent on R&R. Instead, they'd had to familiarize themselves with the gear their ET friends had provided for their raid, and made sure all the new toys worked properly. Their armor had extra force field mounts and power packs, enough to make them damn hard – but not impossible – to kill. Most of the grunts had switched their Iwos for heavy lasers. After playing with the unfamiliar weapons for a bit, they'd had to admit the ET gear had better penetration and stopping power than their customary 4mm plasma rounds. Much lighter, too, which allowed them to carry even more stuff. In addition to the lasers, they were packing as many self-propelled grenades as they could fit, a couple of pistols apiece, and anything they could think of, including entrenching tools, just in case they needed to send somebody to Jesus up-close and personal. Those little shovels worked really well as battle-axes. Russell had personally used them on a couple people: one ET and one bubblehead asshole that nobody would miss.

Of course, if it came down to hand-to-hand, they were certainly fucked. Then again, they were very likely fucked any way you looked at it.

The four squads – two from the assault section, and two from Russell's guns section – were assembled and ready to go; each squad was short a guy, casualties or just left behind to help bolster the line. Twenty-four enlisted and Captain Fromm commanding.

The rest of Third Platoon would keep things together while they went out and took care of business. Their orders had been drafted a couple days ago, and they'd run several exercises in different simulated areas, since they didn't know where the Ruddies would deploy their force field until it happened.

Well, they knew now. Russell's imp displayed a column of tanks and self-propelled tracked artillery moving forward, dismounted infantry marching in blocks between the vehicles, all under the umbrella of the force field. Tens of thousands other ETs were advancing in all the other sectors as well, guys with spears walking next to tanks and riflemen. Some of the uniforms looked different from the Guard and Army units he'd seen. New units, probably. He wondered how far they'd had to march or drive just to get killed here.

It looked like the biggest attack yet, maybe big enough to get through with or without the force field.

Nacle was praying as they waited for their turn on the catapult. Russell wished he could join in.

The catapult was a smallish model, allowing fifteen or so people to step into its circle at a time. They would be going out in two waves. They couldn't land on top of the generator; warp holes and gluon power plants couldn't coexist in close proximity to each other. They would aim at the location of the power plant, and would emerge between fifty and a hundred feet from its location; each group would land some fifty feet apart. It didn't matter what was at the landing point, since the warp aperture would suck anything in range just before dropping the Marines in, which would be bad news for the poor bastards on the spot.

Captain Fromm and two squads went out first. The skipper was loaded for bear himself, with a heavy grav cannon they'd borrowed from the Wyrms, its power pack strapped to his back; the assault squads were likewise equipped. The captain shouldn't be running around doing sergeant's or lieutenant's work, but Russell figured Fromm had decided to play hero. Russell didn't like heroes: in his experience, heroes were born when someone had fucked up.

The warp catapult activated.

Russell had watched dozens of jumps, but they never got old. Something that wasn't light or smoke but something between the two belched up, filling the platform and swallowing the people on the platform. A moment later it was gone, along with its passengers.

"Second wave, step in!"

They walked onto the platform and arranged themselves in a circle, outer rank kneeling down, the troops behind them standing up, weapons ready. It was going to be a hot drop.

Transition.

You didn't see warp space, not really. Your brain just made shit up to compensate for the fact you were in a place where light and sound either didn't exist or didn't work the way they did in the real world. The only thing that interacted with that place was the brain. Everybody was affected in their own way. For Russell, it was like being in a dark room until a spotlight started revealing people from his past. It was never someone pleasant, none of the call girls he remembered fondly, or the drinking buddies he'd partied with. Nope. It was always people he'd rather never see again.

Some sanctimonious bastards said warp space was Hell, and every time you dipped your toes in Hell you were asking the Devil to come claim your soul.

The first person Russell had killed dropped by for a visit. Some kid from the projects in the Zoo, as Kepler-Three's New Chicago was not-so-affectionately known. He didn't even know the kid's name, just that he and his friends weren't from the neighborhood, which made them the enemy. The dead kid's throat was still slit open just the way it'd been after Russell and his straight razor had finished the job. The living corpse grinned at the Marine, and blood ran down his mouth, staining his teeth.

Russell ignored him. There'd been plenty more after that, some while working for Uncle Sam, others while on personal business. The next ghost belonged to a pimp in Saint Martin's star base; that fucker had thought a drunken horny Marine would be easy prey and had ended up out an airlock for his troubles. The dead pimp looked angry. Russell couldn't blame him: he'd had a mean streak when he was young, and he'd taken his time before sending the bastard on his way.

The ghosts gave way to daydreams. He watched several close calls turn out differently. The kid in the Zoo gouged Russell's eyes out; the pimp cracked his skull and sent his dead body out the airlock. Those weren't so bad; the daydreams were lies, and lies had no power over him.

This was a short jump; it only felt like five, six minutes of Hell.

Russell blinked, seeing light again. There were Ruddy bodies and equipment scattered all around them. Warp holes made a mess of their arrival point. There were also live Eets in his sights: a platoon of tank-grenadiers in open-topped half-tracks, the soldiers inside beginning to turn around in response to the explosive arrival of the Warp Marines.

Sucked to be them. Russell set his laser on continuous beam and drew a diagonal line with it. Men and weapons were bisected and fell apart as the laser cut through two half-tracks and found their fuel tanks. He rocked on his feet as a some of explosion's force got through his shields; pieces of metal, wood and charred bone rained all around him. Gonzo and Nacle were firing as well, reaping their share of ETs. The neatly-ordered army dissolved into chaos as survivors scattered away from the murderous bastards that had materialized in their midst.

Russell's imp painted an objective for him: a burned-out building which would provide some cover. He directed his fire team there. They had to keep the Ruddies behind them busy while the Captain and his crew hunted for the field generator.

They moved while engaging any targets that got in their way. A Ruddy tank came into view. Its turret was trying to bear on them, but Gonzo's laser butt-fucked it before it could, the energy pulses punching through the thin rear armor and setting shit on fire. The turret stopped swinging, and the tank commander and gunner scrambled out of the smoke-filled interior. Nacle cut them down before they got very far.

Russell thought he recognized the street they were in, but he wasn't sure. Mortar shells and raging fires had completely rearranged the landscape. All the houses had been gutted; their objective could have been a residential building, a coffee house or a whorehouse; now it was just a few bits of wall that could be used for cover and concealment. They ran towards it. A Ruddy rifle squad took them under fire, but another Marine team took care of them. Russell got hit a couple of times; he only knew that because his imp reported the impacts; his new shields soaked up bullets like so many raindrops.

They set up behind a knee-high wall section that gave them a good field of fire; the guys with the grav guns started picking off vehicles while the others threw grenades. The smart bomblets took flight towards the targets their imps had highlighted, blowing up as soon as they reached their optimal blast distance. Plasma and ceramic fragments tore into packed Ruddy formations.

It was a slaughter, murder pure and simple. In short, it was what a properly planned and executed combat mission should be.

Russell knew the good times wouldn't last. The Ruddies would pull their heads out of their asses and rake them with heavy weapons until something gave. The only question was whether it would happen before the raid could fulfill its objective.

Hopefully the skipper knew what he was doing.

* * *

"There's the force field," Timothy said to himself. He saw a trio of mortar rounds blow up against the curved surface before the mortar team switched their focus towards targets it could affect. The force field was moving towards his section of the trench. Lucky him.

Nothing we have here can punch through the field, except maybe the heavy lasers. The feeling that the assault rifle in his hand could do nothing to stem the tide was bad. The creeping certainty that all the death and destruction of the past weeks had been for nothing was much worse. The memory of Jonah's sudden death hit him again. *He was a good man, a brave man, and in the end none of it mattered.* His companion was with Heavenly Father now, but the knowledge did not bring him as much comfort as it should.

The enemy came into view, tanks and infantry, soldiers marching confidently between the tracked vehicles. Timothy's platoon opened fire; even from three hundred yards away, he could see spots where their bullets sparkled off, creating little points of light as the force field shed the impacts without any noticeable effect. Behind and above him, the Vehelian lasers struck. A pulse burst did nothing; a continuous beam made the field fluoresce brightly, followed a moment later by a breach: three Kirosha soldiers were pierced by the beam and fell, clutching at the bloodless wounds where the light beam had left a tiny through-and-through hole and cooked them from the inside. That was all the laser achieved before it ran out of power. The force field closed up once again.

The Kirosha returned fire at two hundred yards, able for the first time to unleash their full fury without enduring terrible casualties. Tank cannon roared, along with rifle, machinegun, rocket and lesser artillery volleys. The area force field protecting Timothy's trench became visible as it contained the flames and smoke of multiple explosions and bullet impacts.

And failed, when three duplex cannon rounds struck in rapid succession. Jets of plasma burst through the shields and struck the line.

One of Timothy's men had been peering over the lip of the trench and its own portable force field. His head vanished in flash of superheated tissue and bone. Something sharp stabbed Timothy's right biceps. He looked down and saw blood running down his sleeve; a piece of the dead man had torn into him. The pain was nothing compared to the sight of the headless body and the three severely wounded men next to the corpse. They had borne the brunt of the explosion as their fellow was turned into a bomb.

"Corpsman!" Timothy shouted. A group of younger Kirosha came running through the connecting trench and hauled the bodies away. As they did, a few of the men cast glances at the zigzagging trench leading towards the rear and safety.

"Nobody run!" he yelled at them. "There is nowhere to run!"

They held, for now. But the tanks were getting closer, and more blasts were getting through; the enemy had saved all their special shells for this moment. Most of the plasma jets struck nothing but empty air, or buried themselves into the ground in front of the trench line, but others hit just right, sending sandbags and pieces of bodies flying in the air. One of the Vehelian lasers blew up a tank, then another. But there were at least six or seven more just in the first wave, and reinforcements were coming.

Timothy kept firing. "Pour it on!" he shouted. "Send out enough bullets and some will get through!"

It was a lie, a cruel lie, but if he kept them shooting they might not run. His men screeched in defiance and followed his lead, and he felt a burst of savage pride coursing through him.

They would make their stand, come what may.

* * *

The Wyrm portable cannon delivered bursts of unstable space-time at a cyclic rate of three hundred pulses per minute. Whatever they touched was hit with enormous kinetic force, and worse, was twisted from the inside out. Unarmored Kirosha were torn apart, or turned into grotesque meat sculptures, some of which lived on for several seconds. Vehicles broke apart and exploded. Fromm and the other gunners in the two squads turned a city block into a hellish nightmare of burning hulks and mutilated corpses.

The field generator was somewhere up ahead, and a good portion of a Royal Guard tank regiment stood in their way.

"Forward!"

Two undersized squads, thirteen men, stood up and walked down the street in a line formation. Against a foe equipped with modern weapons, the order would have been nothing but suicide.

With their enhanced shields, and facing an opponent armed with primitive slug-throwers, it was merely insanely risky.

The men followed him, firing from the hip, spraying grav beams, coherent light and plasma with inhuman accuracy as they walked forward. At first, the enemy was too stunned by the surprise attack to react, and they were packed too tightly to maneuver. They had concentrated within the shelter of the force field, planning to deploy once they got close enough to the trench line to take it under fire. That doomed them. Tanks and personnel carriers melted and blew apart. Men were mowed down by the dozen before they understood what was happening. The elite of the Kirosha armed forces, lavishly trained and equipped, melted under the withering firestorm.

Thirteen men, even as heavily armed as they were, could not keep that volume of fire for long, however. As power packs and magazines ran dry and had to be replaced, their onslaught lessened in intensity. Different weapon types had varying sustained-fire times, so the shooting never stopped, but more and more Kirosha down the line lived long enough to realize a pack of killers was behind them, and reacted accordingly. More enemy troops engaged them from the flanks, where only a single Marine faced them.

Bullets lashed at the two squads as they kept walking in the open. Even heavy machinegun rounds bounced off their personal shields, although the kinetic bleed-through of multiple rounds started to push them back. They leaned forward, as if against a heavy rain, and kept advancing, kept pouring it on. One of their LML troopers sent three area-effect rockets down range and immolated a dozen vehicles, scattering blazing debris everywhere.

A Kirosha tank round fired from further back struck the assaultman a moment later.

It was pure bad luck; Ruddy tanks didn't have the accuracy to reliably hit a human-sized target even under ideal conditions, let alone shooting through the firestorm between them and the advancing Marines. For Private Second Class Lawrence Calvert, it was the worst kind of luck. The high-explosive anti-tank round detonated against his enhanced shields, punched through them and the body armor underneath, and turned him into scattered gobbets of flesh and bone. His remaining missiles hadn't been armed, so they merely became pieces of flying metal that peppered the Marines on either side instead of exploding, which saved the squad from instant destruction. The line's advance faltered nonetheless, men going down on one knee while they shot back, in a futile attempt to make themselves a smaller target.

"Keep moving!" Fromm shouted into the command channel. "March or die! Home is that way!"

The survivors stood up and followed him forward, trading no-deflection shots with the Kirosha, who stood and fought with desperate courage Fromm could appreciate. An anti-tank rocket sent a Marine flying back. A heavy machinegun hammered at another one until his shields failed; the follow-up bursts blew dime-sized holes through both sides of his clamshell armor. Icons went black or purple. Thirteen became ten, became eight.

His imp finally gave him the target he'd been seeking. The generator and its power plant had been mounted on a tank chassis. The vehicle had kept moving as Fromm's troops emerged from warp, and was now a hundred and fifty feet ahead of him. Behind him and his remaining seven men, the other two squads in the task force were slowly falling back while engaging the Kirosha at their rear.

Several rocket-propelled grenades and tank rounds emerged from the smoke and flames as Fromm designated the target for his platoon. One more icon turned black, but everyone still on their feet cut loose with everything they had.

The generator had its own shield. It stood up against the stream of plasma and missile fire for several seconds before finally failing. Long enough more incoming to lash back at the few Marines still on their feet.

The ground rose up beneath Fromm's feet as fire and sound enveloped him.

Darkness.

* * *

Russell and his team were further back, playing leapfrog with the ET formations coming up from the rear while the skipper and his crew tried to blow up the field generator. It'd been going pretty well, all things considered. Most Ruddies were too far back to hit them without having to go through their own force field, and the ones who made it past the field's perimeter were coming in dribs and drabs, easy meat for the two squads as they fired from cover and retreated the slow and steady way.

The mad bastards with the skipper stood up and walked down the street like this was some sort of sim-drama about the Old West. Even for devil dogs, that was on the crazy side of macho. It worked, though. Russell knew it worked because of the hellacious blast that reached out and touched his fire team, nearly overloading their shields, and letting enough momentum through to knock them all down.

It was a big one. Multi-tons of TNT big. Russell glanced back and saw a mushroom cloud rising up. Not a very big one as those things went, granted, but still.

"The fuck?" Gonzo shouted.

"Power plant done blow up, is my guess."

"Good. Time to go home."

Easier said than done, of course. With the force field gone, the mortars could provide covering fire, though. Even better, the Ruddies seemed to take the loss of their shield and the Guard regiment inside pretty badly. They sure as hell weren't pushing as hard as they had been a moment before. The two squads were even able to sling several casualties over their shoulders as they retreated back to the lines. All the Marines near the blast were down, several of them missing limbs; the force fields gave you the most protection to the torso and head, the bits you needed to stay alive long enough for med-techs to regrow the other bits. In other words, all five survivors they found were basket cases, except for the skipper, who'd only lost two legs at the knees and half of one arm. Russell ended up carrying him on his back as they evaded and escaped toward Embassy Row.

It was no picnic. Plenty of Ruddies were still alive on their flanks and rear. The task force survivors took fire from three directions as they made their way toward the crater where the field generator and its juice box had gone up. The bullets still felt like raindrops when they hit Russell's shields, but it was a fucking downpour now. A couple rockets flew past him as he ran, and he almost dropped the skipper so he could move faster. Almost. Too many of his buds were around to get away with that kind of Bravo-Foxtrot shit.

He dived into the crater and let the captain drop so he could lean out and return fire. His laser gun was kicking ass: he used a sustained beam to slice-and-dice a tank and a platoon of grunts huddling behind it. The turret slid off from the main body before the whole thing brewed up, and the Ruddies further back actually turned tail and ran when they saw what happened to their buddies. Russell sent a couple grenades their way to keep them running. That left him with three; hopefully he wouldn't need more than that.

The mortars dropped a hefty dose of hellfire all around them, and it was danger-close time; some of it was landing a bit too near the crater for comfort. Corporal Petrossian, the highest-ranking grunt still standing, managed to raise Staff Sergeant Martin and got him to shift the barrage away from their position. The good news was that the Ruddies between them and Embassy Row had been mostly wiped out by the power plant explosion, and the few survivors hadn't lasted much long after that. It looked like they might actually live through this.

They poured it on. Every Ruddy tank in range ate laser burst or an AP missile. Russel burned off the last of the laser's power packs and switched to his pistols, pew-pewing ETs with 3mm plasma bullets that didn't have an Iwo's punch but were still plenty good enough to maim and kill. The hundred-mike-mikes walked their fire back and forth all over the area, and the relentless sweeping-broom explosions did the trick. The Ruddies broke under the steady pounding. They didn't retreat or even run; they routed, many of them throwing down their weapons as they fled.

"Guess they're learning," Gonzo said.

"Learning what?"

"That fucking with the Corps ain't ever a good idea."

Twenty-Two

Year 163 AFC, D Plus Twenty-Nine

Rockwell handled the negotiations while Heather and Deputy Norbert listened through their imps.

"Yes, Grand Marshall," Rockwell said, agreeing to yet another armistice so the Kirosha could bring back their dead. There were plenty of those. The attack had been pressed to the hilt, and losses had been brutal on both sides. Every makeshift unit defending the legation buildings had taken severe loses.

A soldier jumped into the trench; Heather barely deflected his bayonet thrust with her Iwo and countered with a kick to the balls and a brutal blow with the gun's butt that broke the alien's jaw and spun him to the ground, where a point-blank burst finished him off. A volley of plasma rounds washed over the lip of the trench, obliterating the last attackers, and she rushed back to the top to shoot at their retreating backs...

She shook her head, vanishing the day-old memories, knowing they would come back in nightmares and flashbacks. It'd been bad, at the end; her sector had been nearly overrun until the massive explosion marking the destruction of their force field broke the Kirosha's spirit once and for all.

Their losses had been the worst yet. They included Locquar and many of his clansmen. The warriors had stood their ground even after their trench line was hit by multiple duplex rounds. The line had held, but Locquar hadn't lived through the brutal fight.

I will see to your family, she promised her dead driver. If they survived this, all the clansmen would be taken care of. She would make sure of it.

It had been bad, almost as bad as what Peter Fromm and his men had endured. Fifteen Marines had come back, seven of them as mutilated near-corpses. Two of those had died despite the medics' best efforts, leaving a total of thirteen lucky survivors.

Peter was still in a coma, but was expected to recover, even though his missing limbs couldn't be regrown until he was taken to a proper medical facility. The local clinics and field hospitals no longer had the supplies for that kind of procedure; just keeping the wounded alive was challenging enough.

"Forty-eight hours will be fine," Rockwell went on. He had demanded to speak directly with the Grand Marshall, and after some wrangling he had gotten his way. "After that period is over, we will resume our attack on the Kingdom," Rockwell said.

"I do not understand. You will attack us?"

"Now that our warp catapult is fully operational, we will start launching raids behind your lines. Starting with the palace and the Great Pyramid. I suggest you use the armistice to evacuate civilians and perhaps remove any irreplaceable works of art in those facilities. We intend to demolish both buildings and kill everyone found inside them."

"I do not believe you have the capability to conduct such an assault."

"You might want to ask your newfound allies about our capabilities. Humans are known throughout the galaxy as the Demons from Warp-Space. I prefer that term to 'Star Devils,' to be honest. It took some time to build the device, but now we have the capability to strike anywhere in the Kingdom. Destroying the Palace Complex will be a largely symbolic gesture, of course. Of more importance will be the follow-up attacks on your logistical installations, both around your capital and on other fronts."

"I do not believe you."

"You may believe we are serious when we strike, say, the Southern Provinces, which if I recall are still poorly pacified. Or when we put your factories and grain silos to the torch. We have cut our rations by a quarter, to ensure we may endure a year's siege. It is only fair that your subjects also know the joys of scarcity. How many targets lie within our reach, Grand Marshall? More than you can protect, I wager."

"You think to win by fear what you cannot through the strength of your arms."

"Perhaps. You will discover the truth after the armistice is over. Or we can talk about peace instead."

"I can only discuss lesser arrangements like the one we just agreed upon. I cannot even accept your surrender, merely present it to Her Supreme Majesty for her approval."

"Then I suggest you present our promises to her. Let her know that we will embrace death rather than the dishonor of surrender. Let her know that even if your allies appear in this star system, they will not be able to spare your kingdom from our vengeance, for we will spend every last ounce of our strength making sure nothing remains of Kirosha except for a charred carcass to be picked clean by its many enemies. Tell her those things, Grand Marshall, or she will learn of them in a more direct fashion."

"I believe this palaver is over," Seeu Teenu said. The

connection went dead.

"Think I laid it on too thick?" Rockwell asked the room.

"I think if we're going to win this through words, those were the right ones," Heather said.

"Big if," Deputy Norbert said. "If it comes down to it, could we carry out those threats? Any of them?"

"According to Sergeant Tanaka and his gang of experts, the catapult is good for two, maybe three more drops. They would have a maximum range of fifty miles or so, and they would be nearly random, even with the Wyrm targeting system. We can't foment rebellion down south. We can send a couple of teams out to raise hell within a couple days' walk of the Enclave. They'd be certain suicide missions, of course. Nobody is going to walk fifty miles back here. Or back from the Great Pyramid, for that matter."

"Not necessarily," LC Zhang said. "We have enough stealth suits to outfit a squad. We could drop in, plant some bombs and sneak out. That might be enough to convince them we mean business."

"Risky," Rockwell said. "Stealth suits don't have force fields, and no exoskeletons. The squad wouldn't survive any sort of firefight."

"I never said it was a good plan, Mr. Rockwell. Just a slightly less suicidal one"

"True. And it is doable," Rockwell said. "Do you think you could scare up enough volunteers?"

"You can count me in," Heather said.

"I think every warp-rated marine would step up. They aren't happy about what the Ruddies did to their skipper."

"Very well. Draft a plan, Commander. Hopefully we won't have to put it into effect."

Heather nodded in agreement. Taking the initiative was better than waiting for the rat bastards on the other side to come up with something. Even if it meant going on a one-way trip.

It's the least I can do. Peter did. He even managed to come back, most of him at least.

If she had to go, Heather hoped he'd wake up soon, so she could say goodbye before leaving.

* * *

"They are lying," the Lamprey said. His hunched posture seemed furtive, but that was the way the Star Devil always looked. The creature was too different for Magistrate Eereen to discern his true feelings.

"You were wrong before," Grand Marshall Seeu said, in the same tones he would use to pass a death sentence. "You never warned us the Star Devils could appear behind our lines much like your ships jump through the void between the stars. They slaughtered one of our most elite units. Two dozen destroyed three thousand of our best soldiers, and they managed to fight their way back to the Enclave. Another ten thousand died in the general attack, including. We don't have enough troops to endure these losses. We have squandered our best forces, for negligible results.'

"They shouldn't have a warp catapult. Such things are used only at the battalion level. A mere platoon could never be expected…"

Seeu cut him off with curt hand gesture. "And yet they did. If they could use it once, they can do so again."

"If they could send more than twenty or thirty troops at once, they would have. And they transported them less than a mile away. Any further, and they would be trapped far behind your lines. They would never make it back."

"And how much damage would they inflict, before we ran them down? I cannot send regiments to stand watch over every possible target. There aren't enough troops to face an enemy that can appear anywhere, at any time. How do your people fight such foes?"

"There are ways to prevent warp emergences from taking place," the Lamprey said.

"Can you provide them for us?"

"No."

"That is not an answer to gladden my heart," the Grand Marshall said. "Very well. I will present my recommendations to the Queen tomorrow. I must take my leave of you. There is much work to be done." With those blunt words, the military commander left the room.

Magister Eereen took his leave himself, having no desire to spend any more time in the company of the alien. He did not get any rest that night, however. Worry made it impossible to sleep. The losses incurred in the last attack had been beyond atrocious. Half the Royal Guards had been killed or wounded since the war began. First Army was no more, its survivors a collection of broken battalions fit only for garrison duty. More units were arriving, but they were filled with barely-trained conscripts. Most of the incoming infantry regiments were equipped with bolt-action rifles and a handful of water-cooled machineguns; they would be only marginally more useful than the sword-wielding peasant militias, which had themselves taken devastating losses in the ill-fated attacks.

The Kingdom had bankrupted itself fighting the war, and all it had accomplished was the destruction of its modern forces.

Seeu would not survive the Queen's displeasure. After the Grand Marshall was gone, the only likely course of action would be to conduct a siege and starve out the Star Devils. But what if they could indeed send their troops across vast distances in the blink of an eye? The Kingdom was already reeling; it would not take much more before a general revolt destroyed the very fabric of the realm. All this death and destruction – and over what? Fear of the change the outsiders were bringing to the Kingdom? Looking back on his own actions, Eereen faced the realization that he might have caused irreparable damage to the very traditions and culture he had been trying to protect.

He did not sleep at all that night.

The next morning, the weary magistrate abased himself in front of the Queen, along with the assembled courtiers. No military officers were present other than the Grand Marshall and the captain of the Royal Guard detachment, a gaunt officer Eereen did not recognize. After the failures of the past weeks, the sight of military uniforms had become displeasing to Her Supreme Majesty.

"What say you, Seeu Teenu?" the Queen spoke after the courtly rituals had been followed. The omission of the soldier's title did not go unnoticed, and the courtiers nearer the Grand Marshall subtly moved away from him, lest his disgrace prove to be contagious.

"I say that continuing the war against the Foreigner's Enclave is no longer an advisable course of action – if it ever was."

Courtiers gasped and fanned themselves in shock at the insult to the Queen.

"You dare question our decision?"

Eereen had never seen the Queen look so angry. Seeu would likely be nailed to a table and bled to death right in front of the court.

"If defeat in battle is certain, then one must not fight, even if the Queen wishes otherwise," Seeu Teenu said.

"The only certain thing is your death, for defying your Queen!"

"I think not."

The Guardsmen in the Audience Room leveled their rifles – towards the throne and the assembled courtiers.

"What is the meaning of this?"

"I anticipated this moment, and replaced the Guards with my men. Perhaps you would have done better had you paid enough attention to your servants to recognize their faces. You might have realized that the new captain of the guard is Colonel Neen, formerly of First Army and a true servant of Kirosha."

The Queen gasped, clearly at a loss for words. Eereen looked around for a way out, and saw more Guards – or rather, more Army men in Guard uniforms – enter the audience chamber, blocking all exits. False Guard Captain Neen blinked pure hatred towards the Queen and the assembled courtiers and magistrates before him. His men looked equally resolute.

The Marshall had been truly busy last night.

Eeren's legs grew rubbery, and he swayed on his feet. He refused to believe his fortune could collapse so swiftly and completely. He had put thousands to death with a stroke of a pen and without giving the matter a second thought. That he might one day share their fate had never seriously occurred to him, not with the visceral understanding that overwhelmed him at this moment.

"If a ruler would lead her people to slaughter and defeat, that ruler must fall. That too is Ka'at," Seeu Teenu told the Queen before turning to his men and making a curt gesture.

Twenty rifles went off in unison.

Year 163 AFC, D Plus Thirty-Three

Fromm opened his eyes.

Heather was sitting next to his bed; she smiled at him.

"Awake at last," she said. "Took you long enough."

"How long?"

"About five days. Five eventful days."

"I could query my imp, but I have a headache and I really don't want to check my messages yet. Will you brief me on what I missed?"

"Straight to business, eh? I can appreciate that. We have an extended cease-fire in place. There's been a major political realignment in the Kingdom. The Queen's dead, and her only surviving son – the other three all suffered unfortunate accidents on the same day Her Supreme Majesty died – has been designated as the Heir Apparent, under the regency of former High Marshall Seeu Teenu. The Regent has repudiated the Queen's decision to attack the Enclave, and claims she fell prey to bad advice from the Preserver faction and their 'pet monster from beyond the stars.' He shipped us the head of said monster, inside a gift-wrapped box, by the way. A sign of good will, he said. It was indeed a Lamprey. Hard to tell what killed him, with just the head to autopsy, but my guess is he was hacked apart with assorted chopping implements."

"Couldn't have happened to a nicer guy."

"They've restored water service and food deliveries to the Enclave. They even sent us the fabber they salvaged and its remaining feedstock. It's not much, but it helped us care for the wounded."

"Seeu is a wily bastard. I'm never going to forget or forgive what he did, sending children off to die, but I have to respect the son of a bitch," Fromm said. "Although he must be hoping like hell that the next ship that shows up is one of ours."

"Yeah. He really burned that bridge when he beheaded the Lamprey secret agent. Then again, the Marshall has been studying Starfarer history, and he realizes now that the Lhan Arkh wouldn't make good allies. He claims he never wanted war, but was just following orders."

"I think I've heard that line before," he said. "Maybe one day he'll get to recite it in front of a firing squad."

"We'll see. Not sure what we'll do with him, not that anybody is asking for my opinion. Above my pay grade. Oh, forgot to add: we got a QE-telegram about the battle at the Paulus System."

"Way to bury the fucking lead! What happened?"

Heather made a 'V' sign with her fingers.

Fromm grinned.

Year 163 AFC, D Plus Thirty-Seven

"Are you sure about this?" President Jensen asked Timothy for the third and hopefully last time.

"Yes, Elder. I will not abandon these people."

He glanced up at the sky, where the American transport ship tasked with evacuating all Starfarers on Jasper-Five floated in low planetary orbit. A flotilla had arrived after the combined American and Wyrashat fleets had defeated the Lamprey's attack. It had been a tough battle from all accounts, but this corner of the galaxy had been secured.

"The State Department has made it clear that anyone who stays behind does so at their own risk," Elder Jensen said. "I feel terrible about leaving myself, but I have to see to the welfare of everyone in the mission."

"I understand. But they need me, the Jersh Caste. Five thousand of them at least, possibly twice that number. They can't stay here, and the US won't take them in. They need me."

"And I will do what I can to help," the mission president promised. He already had done a great deal. The refugees would be ferried to a distant island chain that had never been inhabited. Several fabbers would be left with them, along with metric tons of Kirosha weapons and equipment. There, they would be safe to learn, build and seek their own destiny.

Timothy knew it would get lonely, being the only human there. But after the war was over, other missionaries would come. Until then, he would be happy building and helping his fellow Saints, only fighting if absolutely necessary.

It would be a good life.

* * *

Lisbeth Zhang enjoyed her final dinner on Jasper-Five in the company of Heather McClintock, who no longer wore a Navy uniform now that her spookier skills were back in demand. Heather's gyrene boyfriend was too busy doing paperwork to join them.

"It'll be nice to go home again, back in CONUS," Lisbeth said after savoring the local version of wine, which didn't half bad and lit a warm fire inside her. "Even if I'm headed towards a demotion or even a court-martial."

"I somehow doubt it. The demotion and court-martial bits, that is. Everyone involved here is putting a good word in for you. Peter's letter has you all but walking on water."

"Ground-pounder shit. Out in the black, where it counts, I got my ships blown up."

"We'll see," Heather said after taking a sip of her drink. "My guess is, we are going to need every trained officer we have."

"I hope you're right."

Things went quiet for a bit while they considered the situation. Lisbeth had a better appreciation than most people of how bad things were. There weren't enough hulls to cover every possible front in the coming war, and building new ones would take time. The Lampreys had seized several major warp nodes, giving them the initiative. They were going to take losses, a lot more than they already had.

All we have done is awaken a sleeping giant and fill him with a terrible resolve.

An enemy had said that about the US, many decades before First Contact. Things were different now, however. Filled with resolve the US might be, but if it was a giant, it was surrounded by other, taller giants.

"Cheer up," Heather said. "It's not that bad."

"It kind of is, but fretting about it won't help. Where do you think you'll end up, oh, alleged State Department hack?"

"Heh. I'm hoping I get a crack at the Galactic Imperium, myself."

"Better you than me. Their ships are massive; I wouldn't want to trade broadsides with their battlecruisers, even if they gave me a battleship. Forget about their capital ships."

"On the other hand, they are the most decent of the bunch. And they are a federation of different species. Which means there are a bunch of fracture points to exploit, if one is crafty and cunning."

"Not my kind of thing. I'm into fields of fire and sensor sweeps and blasting the enemy into floating debris."

"It's going to take all kinds of things to win the war."

If we can, Lisbeth left unsaid.

* * *

Shipboard again. The old regiment was being put together at New Parris. Russell would be glad to see some of the old bastards from his battalion. Some more than others, of course, but even the assholes would be better company than any fucking ETs. When lasers and gravitons were flying, the only people you could count on were your fellow Marines.

He'd also be happy to see the whores at New Parris. He hadn't spent any more time with Ruddy women even after the ceasefire. He'd killed too many locals to ever feel safe among their kind; most of those whores must have lost a brother or cousin or father in the fighting, and you never knew if one of them might decide slicing off a Marine's balls would do for payback.

Might as well make the most of his time on Leatherneck Planet, because they wouldn't stay there for long. This war was going to be a whooper. No less than four ET gangs were involved, making it one of the biggest shindigs in recent galactic history. To Russell, war was a time for opportunity. Lots of fighting, which he didn't mind, and plenty of angles to play; a smart and enterprising fellow stood to build up a nice nest egg. Well, he might if he didn't blow it on whores and booze, but most of the time he figured they were worth it.

He looked at the people around the table: Gonzo, Doobie and three spacers who'd joined in the game. The spacers had a lot of money burning holes in their pockets, and they couldn't bluff for shit.

This was going to be fun.

* * *

Fromm watched Jasper-Five receding into the dark as the transport headed towards its optimal warp jump coordinates. Heather was in the transport as well. The Powers that Be had arranged for a week's leave in Lahiri for both of them. Fromm suspected former RSO Rockwell had been behind that unusually-kind gesture. They would make the most of it.

After that, they would be going their separate ways. Once his leave was over, he would head to New Parris to meet up with Charlie Company, his new command. Third Platoon would be waiting for him there as well; he reminded himself not to treat it as his personal unit. It was time to stop thinking like a lieutenant.

Heather would be going to Earth. Same war, different assignments. They'd made no promises to each other. It was the smart thing to do. They lived in a universe full of broken promises.

Jasper-Five disappeared from view. Fromm idly wondered what Regent Seeu would do with his new kingdom. The US had let him keep his job, at least for now. The bastard would probably surprise everyone.

Not his problem, though. America had its own problems. The biggest war it had ever fought was at hand. Twelve million citizens had died; his desperate battle at Jasper-Five had been a tiny victory, one of a handful outposts that hadn't been overrun and slaughtered during the month-long period that history would refer to as the Days of Infamy. America, the Asian Co-Prosperity Sphere and the Wyrashat Empire faced the Lampreys, Vipers and Galactic Imperium, three of the oldest and wealthiest polities in known space. The odds weren't good.

Fromm shrugged. They couldn't be worse than they'd been in Kirosha.

The ghosts of the dead awaited for him in warp space.

Dramatis Personae

Brackenhurst, Timothy: Civilian missionary, Latter-Day Saints.

Carruthers, Anthony: Captain/Admiral, US Navy

Crow, Howard: Owner/operators of the civilian freighter *Alan Dean Foster*.

Donnelly, Lateesha: Chief Petty Officer, US Navy

Edison, Russell ('Russet'): Lance Corporal, US Warp Marine Corps

Eereen Leep: Magistrate-Without-Portfolio, Kingdom of Kirosha

Fromm, Peter: Captain, US Warp Marine Corps

Givens, Sondra: Commander, US Navy

Gonzaga, Raymond ("Gonzo'): Private First Class, US Warp Marine Corps

Grace-Under-Pressure: King-Captain, Hrauwah War Fleet

Hamblin, Hiram ('Nacle'): Private First Class, US Warp Marine Corps

Hewer, Albert P.: President, United Stars of America

Keller, Tyson: Chief of Staff, United Stars of America

Llewellyn, Javier: Ambassador, US State Department

McClintock, Heather T.: Deputy Charge D'Affaires, CIA covert operative.

Neen Reu: Colonel, Kingdom of Kirosha Army

Norbert, Janice: Deputy Chief of Mission, US State Department

C.J. Carella

Obregon, Miguel: Gunnery Sergeant, US Warp Marine Corps

Rockwell, Mario: Regional Security Officer, US State Department

Ruiz, Jonah: Civilian missionary, Latter-Day Saints.

Seeu Teenu: Grand Marshall, Kingdom of Kirosha.

Virosha the Eighth: High Queen, Kingdom of Kirosha

Zhang, Lisbeth: Lieutenant Commander, US Navy

GLOSSARY

AFC: After First Contact. The new US calendar has Year Zero beginning on the day the Risshah bombed the Earth, killing some four billion people.

Blaster: Slang magnetically-propelled slug-throwers that usually fire plasma-explosive bullets. Also see Infantry Weapon Mk 3.

Biosphere Classes: The four known forms of life in the galaxy, which appear to descend from four primordial biology groupings that somehow spread throughout known space. Class One. Two and Three Biospheres are carbon-based but each has a distinct biochemical makeup that make them incompatible with each other. Class Four entities are silicon-based and can only survive under environments other classes find uninhabitable.

Bloomie: Thermal-pulse weapon of mass destruction, which generates a distinctive force field-contained 'blooming onion' shape that persists for several hours. Designed to minimize damage to the ecosystem, it generates heat without producing radiation or other effects, and the force fields radiate most of the heat beyond the planet's atmosphere after reducing everything within the area of effect to molten slag.

Bubblehead: slang for Navy spacers, from the shape of the 'astronaut' helmets issued during the early years after First Contact.

Dabrah: Pal, friend. Short for 'dudebro.'

Domass: Stupid, idiot. Contraction of the words 'dumb' and 'ass.'

ET: Extraterrestrial, common vernacular for aliens.

Eet, Eets: Slang version of ET; both terms are used interchangeably.

Full Goldie/Goldilocks Planet: A world with conditions nearly identical to Earth's (95% or higher on all major categories, including oxygen/nitrogen mix, gravity, and average temperatures).

Gacks: Slang and derogatory term for the Greater Asia Co-Prosperity Sphere.

Galactic Imperium: The largest known Starfarer polity, and the only one comprising several member species of roughly equal power.

Greater Asia Co-Prosperity Sphere (GACS): A federation comprising China, India, Russia and an assortment of Asian countries and former Soviet Republics. Other than the United Stars, it's the only human polity with a presence beyond the Solar System. Commonly referred to as the Pan-Asians or the Gacks.

Hrauwah: Starfaring species and early US ally. Pseudo-canines with arboreal adaptations, the Hrauwah are social obligate carnivores vaguely resembling a cross between a dog and raccoon. Also see Puppies.

Imp(s): Short for 'implant,' a catchall term for the numerous bionic systems most humans use for communications, first-aid, protection and entertainment. Imp services include: full biomedical monitors, virtual reality displays, mapping and location apps, targeting and sensory arrays, among many others.

Infantry Weapon, Mark Three (IW-3): The standard issue personal arm of the Marine Corps, a dual-barreled grenade launcher and assault rifle, firing 4mm explosive plasma rounds and 15mm airmobile ordnance grenades.

Iwo: Slang for standard-issue Infantry Weapons.

Kirosha: A continent-spanning kingdom on the planet Jasper-Five; the same term is also used to refer to the inhabitants of the kingdom and its capital city.

Lampreys: Slang term for the Lhan Arkh species.

Lhan Arkh/Lhan Arkh Congress: Class One Starfarer species, commonly known as the Lampreys due to their funnel-shaped, tooth-ringed mouths. The Lhan Arkh Congress, a sort of communist oligarchy, is one of the largest polities in the known galaxy.

Obligatory Service Term: A four-year military conscription system all US citizens must participate in. Eligibility starts at age sixteen; one must be enrolled before age twenty. Failure to comply is punishable by a four-year prison term and loss of citizenship status. In addition to basic military training, OST conscripts receive basic education equivalent to the last two years of high school and/or vocational training.

Nasstah/Nasstah Union: Class One Starfarer species, bearing some morphological and cultural similarities to the Rishtah (a.k.a. Snakes). Their largest polity, the Nasstah Union is openly hostile towards America and humanity in general. Commonly known as the Vipers.

Ovals: Slang term for the Vehelian species.

Puppies: Common term for the Hrauwah species, due to their resemblance to short-haired humanoid canines.

Rat: A derisive term for corporate employees, bureaucrats and city dwellers of all stripes, originating from a popular song from the First Century AFC.

Remfie: Civilian, especially those with little understanding or appreciation of the military. Less-commonly, military personnel operating far behind the lines who show same. Origin: REMF, Rear Echelon Motherfucker.

Risshah/Risshah Nest Collective: A Class One species brought into Starfarer society as a client of the Lhan Arkh Congress. The Nest Collective was largely destroyed in war with the USA, although a few million members survive under Lhan Arkh patronage.

Snakes: Derogatory term for the Risshah.

Textic/Textic-American English: Written form of modern English, notable for the use of shortened words, anagrams and other minimalist techniques to maximize meaning with the minimum number of letters, numbers and characters possible. The spoken version can be found mostly among the lower classes in human cities or enclaves.

United Stars of America: A nation comprising the former United States, Canada and portions of Mexico on Earth, as well as several dozen star systems around the galaxy.

Vehelians/O-Vehel Commonwealth: Class Two Starfarer species that has a mostly commercial relationship with the USA.

Vipers: Slang term for the Nasstah species.

Warp Rating: A living being's ability to endure entering warp space, ranging from 1 – can only endure warp travel while sedated or unconscious, to 4 – can enter warp in a sealed suit and survive. Less than ten percent of most Starfarer species (the average is closer to five percent) are warp-rated. Humans, for reasons not yet understood, are an extraordinary exception, with fifty percent of their population rated at level 1 or higher.

Wheteff: Curse. Abbreviation of 'What the fuck?' or 'WTF' in Textic-American English.

Wyrms: Slang term for members of the Wyrashat species.

Wyrashat Empire: A Starfarer polity dominated by the Class One species of the same name.

C.J. Carella

.

Made in the
USA
Lexington, KY